JAMES
DUNBAR
MOLE CREEK

For all those who lose when politicians play games.

JAMES DUNBAR

MOLE CREEK

echo
PUBLISHING

echo
PUBLISHING

An imprint of Bonnier Books UK
Level 45, World Square,
680 George Street
Sydney NSW 2000
www.echopublishing.com.au

Bonnier Books UK
4th Floor, Victoria House,
Bloomsbury Square
London WC1B 4DA
www.bonnierbooks.co.uk

Echo Publishing acknowledges the traditional custodians of Country throughout Australia. We recognise their continuing connection to land, sea and waters. We pay our respects to Elders past and present.

This is a work of fiction. Names, characters, businesses, places, events, locales and incidents are either the products of the author's imagination or used in a fictitious manner. Any resemblance to actual persons, living or dead, or actual events is purely coincidental.

First published 2023

Printed and bound in Australia by Griffin Press

The paper this book is printed on is certified against the Forest Stewardship Council® Standards. Griffin Press holds chain of custody certification SCS-COC-001185. FSC® promotes environmentally responsible, socially beneficial and economically viable management of the world's forests.

MIX
Paper | Supporting responsible forestry
FSC
www.fsc.org FSC® C018684

Editor: Abigail Nathan, Bothersome Words
Page design and typesetting by Shaun Jury
Cover designer: Debra Billson
Cover images: West Wall in Walls of Jerusalem National Park, Tasmania, by Viktor Posnov / Alamy Stock Photo; Background of dark clouds, by gyn 9037 / Shutterstock

NATIONAL
LIBRARY
OF AUSTRALIA

A catalogue entry for this book is available from the National Library of Australia

ISBN: 9781760687977 (paperback)
ISBN: 9781760687984 (ebook)

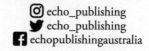

echo_publishing
echo_publishing
echopublishingaustralia

ABOUT THE AUTHOR

James Dunbar is a journalist, television scriptwriter, travel writer, university lecturer and website editor. *Mole Creek* is his first venture into the serious crime thriller and espionage genre. Published as Jimmy Thomson, he is also the author of two crime 'caper' novels and two true-crime memoirs, as well as several books about Australian army engineers (sappers) during the Vietnam War.

SOUL ALLEY, SAIGON, 1969

The movement of the bed as the girl rolled off the skinny mattress was almost imperceptible, but the motion and the rusty squeak of tired bedsprings was enough to wake the young officer from his fetid sleep.

Sensing he was somewhere he shouldn't be, he defied the hammering inside his head and opened his eyes. The room seemed to be swimming in shades of brown and grey, muted tones, but for a determined strand of pale sunlight that had squeezed itself through a crack in a weather-warped wooden shutter.

The girl searched for her clothes, tiny fingers lightly lifting scraps of cloth and lace from the floor. Their eyes briefly met. Focus. There was no smile. They always smiled, but this time there was just a look of ... what? Sorrow? Pity? Contempt? As she dressed unselfconsciously in front of him, he realised that she was young. Fuck! How young? They all looked young, the local girls, but she ... Holy Jesus Fuck!

'Honey,' he said, as he reached for her wrist, but she turned and tripped away, nimbly, balletically, and left him clutching at air – a dance she'd clearly performed many times before. Light poured through the door, acid in his eyes, when she opened it to leave. The skinny Vietnamese man who entered cast a shadow as narrow as a clock hand.

'Wake up!' he said, shaking him by the shoulder. 'You wake up now!'

'I'm awake,' the tall white man said, sitting up, a movement that seemed to make his brain clunk against his skull and his throat rise to the root of his tongue. He felt rather than looked for his shirt and pants. Fuck. His wallet. His side-arm. Fuck! His side-arm? Everything else was there except his pistol and chunks of memory, gaps in his recollection of the previous evening as he zipped and buckled himself into sweat-damp clothes, lifting the mattress, throwing aside the sheets, checking his pockets one more time.

'Come,' the local commanded. 'Bad men here.'

'Ain't that the truth,' said the blond soldier, catching a glimpse of himself in a mirror stained brown by lost patches of silvering. The imperfect reflection permitted him to see that he looked as rough as he felt. Splinters of memory seemed to seep out of the glass as he hopelessly patted down the mattress, knowing it had no secrets to reveal. Someone's demob party. Officers mess. *Let's hit the city.* More drinks at the Rex and the Caravelle, then a Black voice says, *'Soul Alley'.*

Soul Alley, a couple of miles from Tan Son Nhut airport, and a no-go area for white men – at least those on their own. Good ol' boys with no Black comrades to watch their backs ended up in doorways and gutters, bruised and bleeding, still breathing if they were lucky. A couple of streets and their connecting veins of twisting lanes housed cafes, bars and brothels populated by the disaffected, the pushers and grifters, many of them deserters, trained and armed by a country that they now declined to serve. Run by local pimps and mama-sans, the military police wouldn't venture there because it would all turn to several shades of shit very quickly. Even the press corps, who would go anywhere for a drink, steered clear. And as for cameras? Vision of white American on Black American gun battles would not play well on TV back home. At least, that was before the American Army realised it was becoming too much of a magnet for young Black men for whom having an arm shot full of heroin was better than having a body shot through with bullets.

'What goes on here?' the newly arrived recruit had asked his escort, a gym-toned Black sergeant from Baltimore.

'Anything you want, my brother,' the sergeant had said, passing him a fat, fully lit joint, as they squeezed behind a rickety wooden table in a bar where an ancient jukebox seemed to be stuck between Marvin Gaye and The Doors.

Now, hours later – maybe days for all he knew – he was being herded, pushed, nudged, pulled and enticed down a series of twisting laneways, some of which he was sure he'd been along just minutes before. Who were the bad men he was running away from? What bad men? How bad were they? For fuck's sake, he was a soldier. A trained killer. Why was he running away?

A soldier with one sleeve rolled above the elbow looked him up and down balefully then closed his eyes as a local girl, dressed only in panties and tank top, pressed the plunger of a syringe to release the essence of sweet freedom into his vein.

Abruptly, they stopped at a slatted green door set into a wall just where the laneway took a dramatic twist to the right. The local guy rapped on it twice, then once.

'Come,' said a loud but reedy male voice, demanding authority rather than projecting it.

'Go in. He your friend. He help you,' the escort said as he opened the gate.

The blond man stepped inside to find a skinny white man in his late thirties, sweating his way out of a dark suit fashioned from material thinner than a doss house bedsheet, sitting at a grey metal desk, scribbling on a notepad. The soldier tried to guess the man's nationality from his appearance, but his rodent features gave nothing away.

However, the red ring around his neck, etched by the remnants of cheap detergent in his collar being dissolved by sweat, suggested he hadn't been in Saigon long enough to find a good laundry. It also suggested he wore a tie to work every day, as he did now.

Was he American, British, French? Did it matter? The young soldier didn't need a friend. He just needed to get the fuck out of there. He turned to leave just as the man in the suit looked up, opened a drawer, and pulled out a gun. His gun.

'Are you looking for this, Lieutenant?'

The soldier tentatively reached for the weapon and the man behind the desk gestured for him to take it.

'Thank you for joining us,' he said, flicking through a clutter of monochrome eight-by-tens on his desk. 'It seems we have so much to talk about.'

His heavy Eastern European accent sent a chill through the soldier, who was instantly transfixed by the shuffle of blurred images slipping and sliding under the stranger's bony fingers. A trickle of memories is turning into a flood.

***

Fifty years later, two men sit at right angles to each other in an extravagantly upholstered booth in the Romeo and Juliet restaurant in the Reverie hotel in Saigon, now known as Ho Chi Minh City – though mostly to loyal Communist Party members, civil servants and tourists. The restaurant's Italianate décor might be considered extravagant in any other context but here it provides subtle relief from the overly opulent red and gold, black lacquer, and white marble of the reception areas, designed to make rich Chinese visitors feel they have Arrived.

The men are speaking Russian, which would not normally have caught the attention of passers-by. Russian oil men are extracting black gold from the Eastern (formerly South China) Sea and have replaced American and Australian soldiers in the girly bars and beaches of the former R&R haven of Vung Tau, two hours to the south. However, a young Vietnamese waiter pauses as he passes the table.

'Can we help you?' the older man asks, still speaking Russian.

The waiter smiles. 'Just practising my Russian,' he replies haltingly in that language. 'I'm studying it, but I don't have chance to speak or hear it too often. Everyone speaks English.'

'Good luck with that,' the younger Russian says with a warm smile. 'Now, if you don't mind ...'

The waiter takes the hint and scurries off.

'I cannot over-impress you with the importance of this mission,' the older of the two men says in a voice that barely rises above a whisper. 'This is a fifty-year project that's about to come to fruition. Decades of careful nurturing mean we are about to achieve something beyond anything our predecessors would ever have dared to dream.'

'Don't worry, comrade,' the younger man says, then slips into a convincing Australian accent. 'She'll be right.'

The older man looks at him and shakes his head. 'Your great-uncle recommended you for this. I hope he hasn't allowed family loyalty to cloud his judgement.'

'My great-uncle proposed me for this because he knows I am the best man for the job, comrade,' the younger man says, having reverted to Russian.

'Comrade, again? A word from my past, not yours.'

'My present and future, perhaps.'

'Perhaps. But remember, our leader is watching. He is taking a personal interest in this project. Failure is not an outcome that you will easily survive.'

Later that night, the Russian-language-student waiter is retrieving his scooter from a sidewalk parking area, three blocks away, where dozens of motorbikes are slotted together like two-wheeled sardines. He feels something slightly sticky inside his riding mitts but there's nothing to be seen when he checks his hands.

It's about twenty minutes later, when he is in the midst of a shoal of homeward-bound commuters, that he starts to feel dizzy. Five minutes after that, he falls off the scooter, submerged by the pile-up he causes. He dies that night, apparently from his injuries. It's the next day before the passing nurse who held his hand while they waited for an ambulance also succumbs. Panicked medics, fearful of a pandemic, test for viruses but find nothing. They never think to look for Novichok, the deadliest nerve agent known to man.

***

Seven thousand kilometres away, just outside the tiny Tasmanian village of Mole Creek, legendary but long-retired cop Pete McAuslan is dealing with an unfamiliar feeling of indecision, having reached a conclusion to which he's not sure he wants to lead anyone else. He is staring at his laptop, his hands hovering over the keyboard, a two-fingered hunt-and-peck typist frozen by the terrifying power of words to take an idea, a fear, a theory, or an accusation and propel it across time and space – ephemeral as clouds yet as destructive as the wind. Surely, accusing someone of betrayal, someone you once loved, is just another betrayal? Doesn't the simple act of typing a name convict and condemn that person, regardless of whether or not they are guilty? In these days of social media and conspiracy theories, he thinks, it does. All it takes is an accusation and the court of public witchfinders will ignore honours and achievements, and sentence reputations to a lingering death.

He types a name then hits the backspace key as if he's tapping out a call for help in Morse code, the name disappearing from his screen, letter by letter. Outside the cabin, trees sway and rustle in the breeze. Darkness has rolled down from the hill in front of the brick-and-timber holiday home, enveloping everything in a starless night. Starless and bible-black. He pours himself a generous measure of Laphroaig from the litre bottle that had seemed bottomless when he opened it but looks sadly inadequate barely a day later.

'Is it you?' he says. 'Are you making me weak and afraid?'

He looks at the empty space on the screen, the flashing cursor, and a name occurs to him that makes him smile as he leans into the keyboard once more. But doubt floods in again. What if this falls into the wrong hands – or the right ones? What's to be gained by even allowing this to exist? Hasn't a crime committed half a century ago been eroded if not expunged by the waves of guilt that he knows the perpetrator will have felt over the years? Delete the whole damn thing and let it lie. Someday karma may allow someone else to do the same for his crimes of the heart and misdemeanours of the flesh.

A timber creaks outside on the deck. Was that the wind or a careless footfall? Stray wildlife in search of edible garbage?

He types laboriously into the gap between words previously occupied by the real name, then allows his finger to dally again over the backspace key. Pete takes another smoky, burning sip of his whisky and considers the page of bullet points on his screen. This isn't writing, not like Xander would do. It's not a narrative, it's a list, but it tells a story he wishes now he'd never uncovered.

Search and replace. Search and replace. Search and destroy.

There's a movement at the window. Or was it just the reflection of his reach for the bottle? Viewed through its flawed lens, Pete imagines he sees the door handle turning slowly and thinks he may have had enough whisky for one night.

A harbinger blast of cold air lifts the corner of a two-day-old newspaper and, through dimmed, distorting eyes, he sees the familiar features of someone who shouldn't be there – if for no other reason than she's been dead for more than fifty years.

CHAPTER 1

Xander McAuslan realises he's done it again – walked into trouble from which he should have been running. To be fair, he's been threatened. A hollow-eyed scumbag with misspelled inspirational tattoos on his neck and bad prison tatts on the backs of his hands and forearms, has sidled up to him at the bar in his local, the Terminus Hotel. The man, otherwise distinguished by fading, spiky orange hair, simply stands, looking. His face is a vacant lot awaiting renovation, his eyes darkened by some long-forgotten pain, or whatever he took to help him forget it. His skin is damp parchment stretched over a jumble of loosely connected bones. His ripped and faded clothes might have cost a fortune in a fashion store, were they not bearing a patina of grime. Eventually Xander turns, his head tilt asking the unspoken question: 'Are you looking at me?'

'Trackie says to shut the fuck up or you're a dead man,' Ginger Man says.

'Oh, does he now?' Xander replies in a tone of confected mild surprise.

'There's already a contract out to give you a kicking. And I'm first in the queue to collect.'

'Hey, don't let fear hold you back,' Xander says, as if he were encouraging this not-very threatening presence to try hang-gliding or abseiling. 'I'd hate to deprive you of an earner.'

Ginger Man's furrowed brow tells Xander his response has

found its mark. Bravado and bullshit are being replaced by confusion and concern. How come this little bloke in his smart chinos and office shirt isn't shitting himself? What does he know? What does he have in his trendy computer bag? What Ginger Man couldn't possibly appreciate is that Xander could dismantle him like a badly constructed Lego robot. But Xander does know this and it shows in his eyes.

'Just don't start anything in here,' Xander says. 'I don't want to get barred ... again.'

'You're a fucking dead man,' Ginger splutters as he turns away, witty banter clearly not his forte.

'Not yet, obviously,' Xander replies and looks at his watch. 'But I'll be out in about half an hour if you can wait.'

'Fucking dead man,' Ginger shouts from the door, briefly silencing the hubbub of chatter in the bar as he exits.

The Terminus, known affectionately to its denizens as the Terminal, is a fine old pub that's been spared the worst excesses of beer-barn modernisation or faux speakeasy décor inflicted on some of its contemporaries elsewhere in the city. Its clientele has, however, been minimally upgraded over the years from commercial travellers and railway workers to computer geeks and journalists, many from the nearby outpost of Rupert Murdoch's media empire.

But there are still a few old codgers around who've seen more fights than Don King and know instinctively when to shuffle to the side and protect their drinks. To them, Ginger Man's outburst is no more alarming than a passing police siren; someone else's problem. That's one of the reasons Xander likes the Terminus. That, and its proximity to his flat and Sydney's not-particularly-grand Central Station.

'You all right, Xander?' Sam the barperson asks. 'Never seen him before. I'll take great pleasure in bouncing him down the street if he comes back.'

'No worries, Sam,' Xander replies. 'Could I possibly have another schooner of your finest summer ale?'

'You're too cool for your own good,' Sam says, shaking her head. She is stunning: six foot two without her stilettos, and perfectly formed. She doesn't so much look too big as make everyone around her look Lilliputian.

Chugging his beer like a late arrival for the six o'clock swill, Xander briefly considers his dilemma. He has received a credible threat, albeit via someone who is a barely credible source, and he knows why. On the other hand, Trackie Vella knows what Xander's capable of, and if he wanted to frighten him he'd send an emissary who was more dangerous than a badly drawn matchstick man. Xander is curious but unfazed. At the very least, if he were to go missing he knows enough cops who would start tugging Trackie Vella's chain. Or he could decide to lay low for a while. Or he could call his ex-cop grandad, Pete, for advice.

A couple of hours later, riding the clunky lift to his apartment in Surry Hills, Xander takes stock. The scuffed fake-timber interior of the lift looks as worn as he feels and the eight floors take an age, which gives him plenty of time to consider the evening's events. The source of the threat in the pub, Trackie Vella, is a former minor-league thug who's transformed himself into dubious respectability as a developer of cheap and cheerless apartment blocks. His nickname stems from the fact that, before he graduated to Armani, he wore nothing but tracksuits. Xander is writing a story about how the supposedly reformed enforcer hasn't quite left his past behind him. Vella's PR flacks will deal with any fall-out from the story – at least the parts Xander's written so far – so it is unlikely to do his legit business any harm. But his standing as a serious businessman and his reputation as a once-ruthless gangster are in direct conflict and Xander has squeezed a story from the cracks in between.

It was Pete who'd first suggested Vella may not be as squeaky clean as he purported to be, a thought that reminds Xander of an email he received earlier that day.

> Xander, I'm at Mole Creek. I've started writing my story, yeah, I know, like you've been telling me for ages. Anyway, I've hit a roadblock. There's part of it that I've never told anyone, and I need to talk to you about it first. It goes back to Vietnam. Can you get down here, maybe this weekend? It's something we need to do face to face.
> Pete.

Distracted by a mixture of curiosity and concern about what Pete could want to tell him that he'd never told him before, and wondering if it's even worth calling him this late in the day, Xander is putting away his phone as he slides his key into his apartment door lock. It meets no resistance as he turns it. Strange. Did he forget to lock his door when he left? Unlikely. His building isn't exactly Fort Knox; anybody who can get into the block can get to any floor, especially anyone with basic lock-picking or tailgating skills. Alcohol, that wonder drug that allows us to ignore our experience and instincts, encourages him to enter.

'Hullo?' he says tentatively, and silently scolds himself. Anyone who might be in the flat is unlikely to exchange friendly greetings.

The light goes off. Befuddled, Xander is wondering how to react when a tall figure darts out of his second bedroom – the one he uses as an office – grabs him by the shoulders, flips him around so he is facing the wall, then slams him against it.

'Don't fucking move or I *will* kill you,' a man with a distinct but unlocatable European accent breathes in the ear that isn't pressed against the wall.

'Okay,' Xander says defiantly, if surrender can ever be defiant. 'What do you want?

'I want you to shut the fuck up,' the man says again. 'Then

I want you to count to 100 before you do anything stupid like calling the cops.'

'Or what?'

'Or I'll kill you!'

'But you won't be here, so how are you going to do that?' Xander says. 'Remote control?' The booze was clearly mixing well with the adrenaline from this encounter.

'Okay,' says the man, 'then there's this.'

With that, Xander's assailant punches him three times hard in the lower back, just where his liver sits – or sat, before it was moved several centimetres into his torso. The second and third punches aren't necessary. Xander is already on the verge of a physical shut-down after the first blow.

As he lies on the floor, squirming and silently screaming with the pain, the intruder grabs Xander's right hand and presses his thumb against something, then there are bright flashes. One. Two. Is it lightning? Or his brain overloading? Or is this fucker taking souvenir pictures with his phone? Xander watches as the tall, thin man in black trackpants, ski mask, unbranded hoodie and cheap anonymous trainers exits into the explosion of light from the lift lobby.

Xander has often wondered about the efficacy of the semi-mythical liver punch. Now he understands. Delivered by someone who knows what they are doing, it doesn't kill you, it just makes you wish you were dead.

***

Morning sneaks under the blind in Xander's bedroom and knees him in the lower back. It had taken him an hour to find a position that allowed him to sleep, and another to work through all the things he could and should have done to his assailant, rather than being a smartarse inviting greater punishment. Reverse headbutt to the face, elbow to the gut or groin, and leg-breaking stamp-kick to the thigh above the knee was the final combination he settled on before drifting off, his mental martial artistry having served little purpose except to pump his adrenaline and push sleep farther away. The French have a phrase, *l'esprit de l'escalier,* for those arguments you've lost but continue in your head long after the verbal jousting has ended. Xander wonders if there's also a spirit on the stairs for physical fights that you continue in your head after you recover from the blow that knocked you out.

He thinks guiltily about his daily routine of Wing Chun kata. That is, it was 'daily' until a year ago when he'd used work pressure and his soon-to-be former girlfriend's demands for sex in the morning as excuses to phase out the exercises he had performed every day since he was eight years old. Almost twenty-five years of effort and commitment erased by the combined powers of lust and lethargy. Will getting himself ready for another attack make a difference to the outcome? Perhaps. Will it hurt a lot just to move? Definitely. He promises himself that he will start again tomorrow, gets up and switches on the coffee machine on his way to the bathroom.

He thinks about chucking a sickie from work but concludes he'd feel cheated because he really is sick. Okay, not sick, but certainly feeling pain and concern about the rust-coloured urine in his toilet bowl. He'll drop in and tell them he's working on a story; in reality he plans to spend the morning calling around his criminal and cop connections, wondering who they might suspect of having broken into his apartment, assaulted him and, on the face of it, stolen only his phone. He fires up his PC to access his backup contact files – or tries to. The lights are on, but nothing is whirring or beeping. At first, he scrabbles around his desk for one of the myriad emergency reboot memory sticks he keeps for just such disasters, only to discover they are gone too. All of them. Every little half-scrap of useless information and incomplete story he's ever punched into his keyboard is missing, presumably taken by his assailant from the previous night. Yet the room seems untouched, although some of the piles of books, files and newspapers seem more organised than when he'd left them. His intruder had clearly been looking for something but wanted to leave no immediately obvious trace of his search.

The processor box sits precisely where it has for months but Xander doesn't need to call computer experts to confirm his suspicions that the hard drive is missing. When his PC fails to respond to the combination of keyboard clicks and curses that usually brings it back to life, he opens the back of the black metal box and there is a hole where the hard drive should be. Obviously, the intruder has taken all his electronic records, and maybe some printed material too, and then he's carefully fitted the cover back on. But who? And why? Okay, had he not disturbed the intruder, theoretically it might have been days before he'd realised he'd been robbed. The man in black was not to know that the first thing Xander usually did whenever he came home was to check the news feeds on his PC. He's glad he'd gone straight to the Terminus from the office, leaving his laptop locked in his desk. At least the thief didn't get that.

It's time to go old school. Call after call, laboriously dialled numbers from his rarely used paper contacts book on his equally neglected landline; nobody has heard anything, although a couple of would-be comedians from both sides of the law say they'll reward the culprit handsomely if he's ever caught. Pete is uncontactable, but that's nothing new between his suspiciously frequent forgetting to charge his phone and occasional unannounced and unexplained trips away. Finally, reluctantly, he calls suspect number one, Trackie Vella.

'Hey, McAuslan, I hear you had a visitor last night.'

'Bad news travels fast,' Xander replies. 'Just to let you know, all my files are backed up in the cloud and at work.'

'I'm happy for you,' Vella says. 'Or I would be, if I gave a flying fuck.'

'To be honest, Trackie, I don't really think it was you. The job was too professional. Clean. Tidy. Obsessive even. The hard drive was surgically removed. I might not have even noticed if I hadn't walked in on the guy.'

'Fair call,' Vella says. 'My boys? They take the whole computer, smash things up, maybe shit on the floor. We don't do sneaky. Next time, I'll show you.'

'Thanks, Trackie. That's very reassuring.'

'Hey, Sandra,' Vella says, employing the nickname that he and no one else used for Xander. 'Was there anything about me on those files?'

Xander says nothing.

'If there's shit about me and it gets into the wrong hands, it won't be your computer that goes missing, capiche?'

Vella hangs up and Xander looks at the phone, briefly impressed at the way psychopaths can always make other people's problems about them. He calls Marnie Hernandez, a friendly police detective, and once upon a time more than that. Having established that he is alive and not critically injured, she finds it all highly amusing.

'I've told you a dozen times that place isn't secure,' she says. 'Could have been a sneak thief, seeing what he could get.'

'He knew what he was looking for.'

'Which was?'

'Computer files. He took them all. And before you ask, if I knew which ones he wanted, I'd be halfway to knowing who it was, or at least who he was working for,' Xander says. 'He was a pro. Surgical gloves, ski mask, unlabelled shoes and clothes, and a ruthless efficiency when it comes to violence and stripping computers.'

'Efficiency and above average computer skills?' she says. 'Wasn't one of us, then.'

She is only half-joking. Xander isn't the flavour of the month with certain sections of the forces of law and order, ever since his exposure of suspiciously over-zealous prosecutions in the child sex offences squad had – they said – led to one officer's reluctant retirement. There are no grey areas in that dark territory. That aside, there were plenty of reasons for some cops to be pissed off with Xander, but nothing that would normally lead to a home invasion, extreme violence and data theft.

'I think he took pictures of me when I was down,' Xander says.

'Pictures?'

'On his phone. Or maybe even mine. He took that and I saw two flashes.'

'Well, if he was taking selfies and posts them on Instagram, we'll have him pretty soon.'

'Very fucking funny,' Xander says.

'Maybe he was proving to whoever hired him that he's done the job,' she says.

'Yeah, that's what I thought. But wouldn't the computer files be enough?'

'Who'd want to see your computer files?'

'Trackie Vella. I'm working up a series on him.'

'Does he know that?'

'Yeah.'

'How can you be sure he knows?' she says.

'Mostly because I told him,' Xander replies.

'You're doing it again, aren't you?' she says after a brief pause, her tone changing to weary concern.

'Doing what?'

'Looking for trouble when you don't need to,' she says. 'Putting yourself in danger. I thought you were seeing a psychologist or therapist or something.'

'I was. I did.'

'And? What did he say?'

'She, actually,' Xander says, thinking 'one point for the unreconstructed men'. 'She said I was trying to relive the violent death of my father and create a more positive outcome.'

'Sounds plausible,' Marnie says.

When Xander was about eight years old his policeman father had been killed when a woman he'd been trying to protect from her knife-wielding partner picked up the dropped blade and stabbed him. It was a kind of fucked-up Stockholm syndrome, Xander thought now, where the victims of long-term maltreatment were so desperate to reconcile with their abusers that they would join forces against their rescuers. He didn't blame the woman – she was a victim too – but the unfairness of it burned in him, even twenty-six years later.

'So?' Marnie asks.

'So what?'

'What are you doing about it?' Marnie says. 'This David and Goliath act of yours is a fucking addiction and it's going to get you killed. You are thirty-five fucking years old.'

'Thirty-four,' Xander protested.

'Whatever! Why don't you do something safer, like heroin?'

'What do you have to do to be a victim around here?' Xander says. 'I didn't have any choice in the attack in my flat. The guy came out of nowhere.'

Marnie sighs. 'Look, I know this is boring, but if you want us to follow up on this, you need to come down to the station and give us a statement.'

'Yeah, I'll think about it,' Xander says, adding his farewells and a half-hearted invitation for a drink at some unspecified time that they both know will never arrive, and hangs up.

As he walks down to a mobile phone shop in Chinatown, his lower back and side jarring with every second step, he wonders about this 'addiction', as Marnie called it; the thing that makes him step up when he knows he should walk away. Is prising a drunk, maybe drugged, young woman from the clutches of two guys she clearly doesn't know, any crazier than jumping out of a plane hoping your parachute won't fail? Is getting between three muscle-car-driving hoons and a delivery guy they've knocked off his bike any more foolish or risky than hang-gliding or rock climbing?

They offer the same rush – fear, adrenaline and the life-affirming satisfaction of survival – although, to be fair, the incident with the delivery rider had resulted in a visit to A&E. Choose your addiction. At least he isn't one of those cowards who sneaks up behind people and punches them in the head. No, he is the innocent by-stander who doesn't stand by, tackles the assailant and sits on his back till the cops arrive. Fear, adrenaline, survival. Not looking for trouble but happy to find it, enjoying the fact that he is a lot more capable of handling himself in a scrap than he appears. Loving it when bullies discover that, when push comes to shove, you ought to be careful in your choice of who to push.

But then there are the others. The people who push and shove for a living. Those who relish every opportunity to test themselves in physical confrontation but have the sense and restraint to pick their times and their targets. Like the guy who introduced him to this world of hurt the previous night. Xander resigns himself to a psychically, physically, and financially painful day of phone buying, sim card registering, hard drive purchasing and software downloading. Somewhere in the midst of this digital nightmare he should buy a new lock for his front door, hope he has the requisite tools to install it, and check into the office to retrieve his laptop, which contains all the passwords he's going to need to rebuild his home-office connections. And he needs to call Pete to find out what was behind his cryptic message, now gone in his stolen phone.

Later, hoping to be unnoticed by colleagues who might ask why he's walking like a constipated octogenarian, Xander smuggles himself into the office in the middle of a surge of coffee-runners. He is retrieving his laptop from his desk when he looks up to see a senior police officer being directed to the editor's office. The tall man in full uniform glances at him as he strides past, holds the look for a second too long, then quickly looks away. The clear signs of recognition and unease have Xander's alarm bells ringing 'twos and blues' like a cop car that's already too late. He suppresses the guilty urge to make a run for it before he is questioned about a crime that he might have committed but can't remember.

Is the break-in and assault the reason for the visit? Has Marnie passed on their conversation, and they've discovered something significant he hadn't thought of? A connection to a bigger crime, perhaps? It surely can't be a touchy-feely follow-up call. It's really not that big a deal in the general scheme of things, and neither is Xander, for that matter. Knockabout crime reporter gets assaulted and robbed? Hardly 'man bites dog' or even 'influencer gets proper job'. I must be in serious shit this time, he assumes instead.

Maybe it's about the next instalment of the Trackie Vella story that's been bounced by the newspaper's lawyers so many times that the words are falling off the pages. If it is ever published it will reveal that several former 'persons of interest' in the criminal game, having been edged aside by younger players with access to vast quantities of methamphetamines, have apparently gone legit, moving into property development – mostly of small apartment blocks of highly dubious quality, if you could call that 'legit'.

But while some of the skill sets are similar – deception and intimidation being useful – the methods employed can differ. Established property developers use amoral lawyers to scare their disgruntled clients. Semi-reformed crims tend to employ more directly interpersonal techniques, often involving baseball bats. Xander has been digging into the collapse, possibly deliberate, of an apartment-block project where the developers' two-dollar company evaporated and the apartment purchasers were left with a half-built building and no money to complete it.

As the first parts of the story were printed, more information had emerged from emboldened victims who might otherwise have stayed quiet. To Xander's delight and concern, some celebrities and even a couple of senior cops and media figures had been revealed as co-investors when the companies had gone into receivership, owing millions. Is that why the officer is here – to stop the story from ever making the light of day? Even so, a chief superintendent?

He looks across the half-empty newsroom to the fish-tank editor's office, where he can see the silhouette of the tall man in dark blue looming over the boss's desk. In between Xander and the office lie ranks of abandoned desks and chairs, like gun emplacements after a humiliating retreat. Pins in the partitions show where family pictures and signed celebrity shots once hung. Only out-of-date pizza takeaway menus remain. The moveable feast has moved on. The paper is clearly long overdue another contraction to a smaller office to save space and rent and allow the survivors of the latest cull to huddle together for the illusion of protection and co-dependence.

Xander chides himself for imagining that the police visit has anything to do with him. Paranoia? Guilt that he might have carelessly trodden on the wrong toes to get another headline?

'It's not always about you,' Pete would say. 'In fact, it hardly ever is.'

Movement in the editor's office catches his eye. The blinds are being drawn. Then his desk phone rings, a flashing light next to the button for the editor. Maybe it is about him after all. He looks around the room for some clue in the faces of his colleagues, but there's nothing. Journalists are always the last to know.

*****

Xander walks in a half-trance back to his desk to collect his jacket, new phone, and laptop. It really wasn't about him so much as it was about his grandad. It was a sign of the respect and esteem in which Pete is ... was ... held, that they sent a chief super in full dress to break the news that the old ex-cop had taken the same exit door as so many others. 'Ate his gun,' Xander hears a too-loud whisper from another cubicle. So soon? He assumes someone had spotted the uniform, called a contact at police HQ and got the news at the same time Xander was receiving it. The rumour mill may take a while to get going, but once it cranks up it runs fast and has no respect for reputations or personal feelings.

Standing at his desk, Xander stares at a blank computer screen, looking at his reflection, which seems just as empty and lifeless, as if he too is no longer computing. The screen turns every reflection monochrome but he knows exactly who he's looking at. Reddish brown hair and grey-green eyes – he could not look more Anglo-Celtic if he wore a tartan bowler hat. His slightly pinched features, however, mean no observant bookie would take bets against his name beginning with O', Mac or Mc, as it does. Shorter than average at 165 centimetres, or five-six in old money, Xander is not a striking physical presence. Neither too tall nor short, wide nor thin, he has the ability to move through crowds without anyone recalling having seen him, a great talent in his chosen profession where the overheard remark is often the key that unlocks doors that would otherwise have remained firmly closed.

Xander wishes his brain was in sleep mode, like the computer ... if only. Suicide is not Pete, no way. The big man simply wouldn't have. Not after all the shit he's been through in his life. All the crap he's survived. But then, Xander knows the power of denial better than most. He's seen it so many times in those left behind, when he's had to ask the dumbest question of a disbelieving civilian who's just been told that the kid whose face is the screensaver on their phone, or the sibling they'd just spoken to an hour ago, or the lover that had left them still damp from their encounter, wouldn't be coming home: How do you feel?

Denial isn't just a river in Egypt, goes the joke. No, it's a fucking tsunami of remorse and regret, an impotent scrabble-grab for a last chance to put things right that should never have been wrong. What had he missed in his last conversation with Pete? What signs that should have been obvious, did he completely overlook? Christ, what kind of a journalist was he, to not see this coming? What kind of a grandson?

Pete had travelled to Mole Creek, the village in Tasmania where they had a weekender cottage and had gone trout fishing many, many times. Only on this occasion Pete went alone and for a couple of months, rather than a weekend. He'd told Xander he'd gone to write his memoirs, a book Xander was sure would be an eminently saleable recounting of forty years of tracking down and jailing a variety of villains.

'Keep it under your hat,' he'd told Xander. 'There's a lot of people who wouldn't want any of this to come out ... on both sides.' Was that the roadblock he'd referred to in his email? Had he tugged at an unfortunate thread? Had word got out that the old cop was about to reveal too many secrets, so he'd been silenced permanently? But then, he did say it was something to do with his time in Vietnam.

Xander realises he is grasping at some slender and slippery straws.

It's too late to get a flight to Tasmania, so he leaves work and goes into a faux-Irish bar where some of his police contacts drink beer, wine and whiskey and morph – or is it Murph? – into their version of the Boston and New York cops they've seen on TV. Xander just wants to get numb, comfortably or otherwise, but the manly hugs, shoulder squeezes and teary kisses are speedbumps on the road to oblivion. In any case, the unaccustomed weight of the door lock in his bag reminds him he has some DIY to attend to. Clutching his laptop tightly under his arm, as if it were the very source of his power and reason for his existence – which it is – he ghosts out without a word of farewell and makes his way to a nearby bottle shop intending to buy Pete's favourite single malt, hoping to make as big a hole in it as he can before catching a plane in the morning.

The ever-smiling, bearded and turbaned Mr Singh looms over the counter at Xander, unaware of his grief or he would already have wrapped him in the sofa of his chest. Instead, he scans the label on the whisky and nods. 'Excellent choice.'

'I thought your lot were supposed to be against alcohol?' Xander replies, as he passes his credit card over the reader.

'My lot? Bottle-shop franchisees? That wouldn't make much sense, now, would it?'

'Sikhs,' Xander says with a roll of his eyes.

'Only drinking it,' Mr Singh says. 'The scriptures of my particular branch do not forbid the selling.'

'What *do* your particular scriptures forbid?' Xander asks, genuinely curious.

Mr Singh's splendid eyebrows meet as he considers this. 'Not a lot,' he finally replies. 'Sati – throwing widows on the funeral pyres of their husbands is frowned upon. And hard to organise at your local crematorium.'

'Lucky widows,' Xander replies.

'And we are discouraged from eating meat that has been prepared as part of a religious ceremony. Like halal or kosher.'

'Hang on,' Xander says. 'You *can't* eat halal or kosher food?'

'No loss,' Mr Singh says. 'We get their bacon … provided the pig is not scared before it is slaughtered. Why the sudden interest in my religion?'

'I was thinking maybe it's time I had one,' Xander lies.

'Sikhism is great,' Mr Singh says with a grin. 'I think it is the only religion that forbids celibacy.'

'Awesome ...'

'But your lot have an excellent choice of religions,' he says with a grin. 'More varieties of Christianity than Heinz soup. And Judaism if you want to go old school.'

'My lot?' Xander replies. 'You mean journalists?'

'Touché, Xander,' Mr Singh says, as he puts a twist in the neck of the paper bag concealing the whisky.

Xander smiles to himself as he walks to the station, thinking Pete will love the line about committing *sati* at the local crematorium. And for the first time that day, he tastes salt in the corner of his mouth as tears roll down his cheeks.

CHAPTER 2

It was early spring, towards the end of February or beginning of March, 1970. Lieutenant Pete McAuslan had lost track. It was easy to do. There were two seasons in Vietnam: very hot and mostly dry, and mostly hot and very wet. Spring was a transition between wet and dry. In Juicy Lucy's, the bar in Vung Tau he had made his unofficial office, Pete was oblivious to the tinny music spilling from a cream-coloured Bakelite speaker that was attached unconvincingly to the rattan canopy. It swayed in the intermittent breeze from an ailing ceiling fan that had survived a battle with a flying bar stool and refused to die, despite having one bent blade. Johnny Cash was singing about a boy who'd been given a girl's name, getting louder and quieter as the speaker tilted and swung. Next up, the Archies would be serenading sugar and then Neil Diamond would insist the good times never felt so good. Pete knew this without listening because he had heard this playlist a hundred times before, probably more. Almost certainly more, courtesy of an eight-track tape player but only one tape that had been bequeathed to the bar by a departing Australian sapper. Thus the music in Juicy Lucy's was stuck forever in 1969 and, sadly, little of it was the good stuff. That said, in a few minutes the Stones would rip out 'Brown Sugar' from a parallel universe that allowed some of the best rock music ever recorded to co-exist with much of the blandest, most banal pop ever fabricated.

27

The world was like that, Pete thought, as Keith Richards' opening chords chugged out, ripping through the technical limitations of whatever speakers they were played through, wherever they might be. Parallel universes where Australians and Americans killed and were killed in proxy wars on an endless loop on what seemed like a living eight-track cassette, finishing but never ending, occasionally pausing to let you hope it might be over, before starting again. Meanwhile, somewhere across the oceans, people watched bad TV and listened to awful music, safe in their homes. Is that the freedom we're risking our lives for? Pete thought. Bubblegum pop music? Still, it was better than the American Forces Radio pumped out by the other bars. The trade-off between more current music and morale-boosting propaganda, interspersed with reminders to get your commander's John Hancock on a travel form if you were taking your furlough overseas, soon became a deal with the devil. There wasn't enough of the good stuff to mitigate the bad.

Pete waved his coffee cup at the owner, Lucy. Except her name wasn't Lucy. She was named after the bar, rather than the other way round. Her real name was Trang Minh – she pronounced it Ming – and she was a young widow, left behind when her husband was dragooned into the South Vietnamese Army and didn't come home. Or he was a Communist, arrested and executed in one of the frequent raids by army and police. Or he was alive and fighting on the other side of the war. Vung Tau was a city that thrived on rumours, hints and allegations. Lucy never spoke about what had happened to her husband and no one ever asked.

Pete liked Juicy Lucy's because, despite its name, it was neither a clip joint nor a brothel. Lucy allowed working girls from next door into the bar, provided they weren't working. They could chat to each other and flirt with the soldiers, but the first signs of any transactions and the girls and their potential customers would be ushered out into the chaos and heat of the Vung Tau street.

Pete got here as often as he could, escaping the stiflingly efficient office life of the Australian Logistical Support Group, of which he was nominally a member, and the Australian Military Police – technically the Provost Marshal – to whom he'd been recently attached. Their HQ was the last in a line of hastily constructed offices, with the Quan Cahn (the Vietnamese MPs) and the Vung Tau City cops on one end, the American Military Police front and centre, and the Australians stuck at the far end, despite nominally having control over the region. To be fair, the American MPs were a large fighting force as well as law enforcement, and this was very much their war, so they had earned their pride of place.

ALSG were based in Vung Tau because it was the main naval access point to the rest of Phuoc Thuy province, the Aussie Army's patch. The Provos were based in Vung Tau because that's where Australian soldiers went for R&R, and that's where there was the frequent need to deal with mood swings that ranged from the homicidal to the suicidal in the time it took to consume a couple of beers. Combat soldiers hated the MPs and a lot of MPs hated their jobs. Another duty of the MPs was to accompany and protect visiting dignitaries from Vung Tau to the Australian army base at Nui Dat.

Pete was floating between Logistics, the Provos and Army Intelligence because, having been a cop in civilian life, he was useful to all of them but didn't quite fit in with any of them. For his part, he exploited their lack of direct control over him by always being 'needed' at one of the other two units, especially when he was given shit jobs like providing support for the small ships sailing up the river to Ba Ria and beyond, or – worst of all – manning shore patrols to sweep up the violent drunks and their victims spat out by this booze-fuelled town on the southern coast.

Meanwhile, to his immense frustration, the one piece of real policing he'd been asked to do – find a deserter who had allegedly killed a superior officer in a hand-grenade attack – was being thwarted by their American allies. He couldn't operate in American territory without their permission and that simply wasn't forthcoming. Communications were either not answered or rebuffed with a 'leave it with us'.

He had few friends in uniform and no desire to spend his downtime in the drinking dens and fleshpots of Vung Tau. Instead, he did the rounds of his various HQs then parked himself in Lucy's, drinking the coffee from the café's ancient Elektra machine. This hissing and gurgling brass monster, all gleaming spouts, pipes and taps overseen by an angry bronze eagle on its dome, dominated the small café. A French former diplomat turned restaurateur, visiting the café for old times' sake, had showed Lucy how to use it properly and clean it when she was done. Otherwise, it had lately been kept in working order by an Australian sapper who went by the unlikely name of Lorenzo. Perhaps it was his Italian nickname that gave him an affinity for the coffee maker.

Lucy's also had a telephone that worked, so between caffeine and communication, Pete had everything he needed and let the world come to him when his skills were required. Lucy placed a steaming cup of coffee on his table. Her coffee was okay, and at least it wasn't the painfully slow-drip mixture of Vietnamese coffee and condensed milk that locals preferred. Even worse was the egg and sugar concoction they used when sweetened tinned milk was in short supply.

'This is your third, Petey. You'll be bouncing off the walls,' she said, almost scolding. She was small – although not for a Vietnamese woman – but neither slight nor stocky. Her round face and pert nose suggested she might have Chinese antecedents a couple of generations back – Hell, the country had been part of China many times in the past thousand years. The occasional flash of anger in Lucy's eyes was something else. That anger would flare when newcomers failed to accept her advice that, no, this wasn't a girly bar and, no, she didn't do blow jobs for 10 bucks a pop, nor did she provide the services of girls who did.

Juicy Lucy's had been a coffee house called Je Suis Ici – hence, Juicy – back in the days when Vung Tau was a beach retreat for the French from the winter heat of Saigon. In summer they'd headed up to the mountains around Da Lat. The bentwood chairs and chipped Formica tabletops hinted at its more elegant past but also betrayed how long it had been since the café had been filled with the chatter of traders and diplomats – or more often, their wives.

Even so, it was tidier and less makeshift than some of the other bars around, where sex was as high on the menu as cold beer, and almost as cheap. But Juicy Lucy's was haunted by its past. The dust-scoured and cracked green paint on the walls carried outlines of missing pictures, ghosts of images now condemned to unreliable memory. The Eiffel Tower, General De Gaulle, the Arc De Triomphe, even Napoleon, all consigned to a dusty corner of a shed out the back that Pete had stumbled into after a wrong turn en route to the head. Now there was a wonkily hung aerial shot of a half-built Sydney Opera House and Harbour Bridge, a framed portrait of the British Queen, and a nondescript football team that, to the untrained eye, had too many players in it. The pop-art colours on a tattered poster for the movie *They're A Weird Mob* seemed to fade while Pete looked at it, as if his eyes were wearing it out. The decorations had been left by soldiers in transit, returning home or heading off to the front lines towards their grim destiny. It was unmistakably an Australian bar.

Shade fell into the room as a tall figure propped in the doorway, taking a second or two to allow his eyes to adjust to the gloom he had created. He carried the threat of a Wild West gunfighter entering a saloon, ready to settle a score. Pete's eyes followed him as he strode purposefully to the bar.

'Haven't seen you for long time,' Lucy said with a wicked

31

smile, suggesting she intended the double entendre. 'What will it be, Donnie?'

'Just a Coke, Lucy,' the tall man replied in an American accent that could have been from either side of the Mason-Dixon line. 'So cold it hurts.'

'Well, if it isn't Major Jumping Jack,' Pete said to his back.

'Goddam, it's you, Pete!' Donnie Carrick said. 'I thought you were a drug dealer or a pimp in that Hawaiian disaster you're wearing.'

'Day off. And a bit humid for jungle greens,' Pete said, looking down at the thin cotton, printed with palm trees and hula dancers, sweat-stuck to his chest.

'Go on, why the Jumping Jack crack?' Donnie asked.

Pete looked up, guessed the American was smiling but he was back-lit by the sunlight streaming in from the door so he couldn't see his expression.

'I was there for the dust-off, after that thing in the Long Hais,' Pete mumbled after a long moment's silence.

'Oh.'

'Yeah, oh! There's a special place in Hell for whoever invented the Jumping Jack mine.' Pete took another sip of his coffee. 'One charge to pop it up to waist height then the other main one spreads sideways to cut you and everyone around you in half. What kind of civilisation creates a weapon like that?'

'They're supposed to be a deterrent,' Donnie said, softly. 'They're not meant to be a booby trap.'

'Tell that to Charlie,' Pete said. 'We planted 22,000 of the fucking things, just north of here. It's like a free armoury for the VC. They dig them up and bury them somewhere else for us to find the hard way.'

Donnie took a long pull at his Coke. Pete stared at his coffee as he felt the sweat from the nape of his neck and shoulder blades form a river that streamed down his spine and pooled in the small of his back.

'They're calling it Black Saturday in the papers back home,' Pete said, to no one in particular. 'Eleven dead and fifty-nine wounded without a fucking shot being fired.'

'Every day's a black day for someone in this war,' Donnie said. 'May I?' he added, tapping the back of the other chair at Pete's table.

'I have neither the energy nor the rank to stop you,' Pete replied, gesturing vaguely at the empty seat. Donnie sat and Pete looked up at his new companion, then leaned forward. 'You know more of our men are being killed by your landmines than by Vietcong bullets?' Pete said.

'They're your landmines now,' Donnie said. 'We didn't tell you to build a minefield then leave it unguarded. That's tactics 101.'

'ARVN were supposed to guard it,' Pete said, pronouncing it Arvin – Army of the Republic of Vietnam, or the South, for simplicity's sake.

'Well, there's your problem,' Donnie replied with a snort.

'There's some good blokes in ARVN,' Pete replied, not buying into the widely held disdain of their allies.

'No doubt. No doubt,' Donnie replied. 'But there are also more than a few VC. Actually, that's partly why I'm here.' He leaned back and his chair hit the bar, which shifted slightly under his weight, being a painted plywood addition to the original service counter.

'Do tell,' Pete said with a sigh, feigning a lack of interest.

'Well, you know they're planning to lock Vung Tau down?'

'Yeah, I heard. Got a memo somewhere. Half-read it but it was so boring I fell asleep. What does "lockdown" mean, exactly?'

'It means that in a couple of weeks only Australian and New Zealand troops will be allowed to walk around in civvies. We have to be in uniform. The American R&R facilities will be closed, all the MPs are being moved into Saigon or Long Binh. Only the guys on the docks will stay.'

'Good. Should mean fewer brawls, for a start,' Pete said.

'Oh, come on,' Donnie replied. 'You guys could start a fight in an empty room.'

'All right, so why are they doing this? Vung Tau, for all its flaws, operates pretty well as an open city.'

'Yeah, well, some people think it's a little too open. I think "Casablanca on the South China Sea" was the phrase one of the brass in Long Binh used.'

Long Binh was the major US Army base a couple of hours north and just east of Saigon. It was, effectively, a small city populated almost entirely by heavily armed Americans.

'The word is that, with the program of Vietnamisation, the opportunity for espionage has increased exponentially ...'

'Man, you do love your syllables,' Pete said. 'But tell me, how could there possibly be more spies than there are now? I mean, it's like half the army and more of the civilians are VC, whether they want to be or not.'

'Yeah, well, Major Tang has got a bee in his bonnet.'

'Major Tang? That prancing martinet ...'

'Yeah, I know you're not a fan of our ARVN liaison. But he wants to clean up the city before the shutters come down and he's not getting any push-back from his superiors.'

'Okay, but why would I care?' Pete said. 'I'm not a spy.'

'He calls you the Quiet Australian,' Donnie said. 'He says you sit here in this bar gossiping about missions and plans.'

'That's bullshit,' Pete said. 'And he knows it. And even if it were true, it wouldn't make me a spy.'

'Not you,' Donnie said, and nodded pointedly to where Lucy was wiping the countertop. 'Be warned, Tang is determined to take a few scalps before the bad guys are driven deeper underground.'

CHAPTER 3

The cabin in Mole Creek is exactly as Xander remembers it. He stops and listens to the illusion of silence. Some birds are singing, others are responding with caws and croaks. Ravens and butcher birds, he guesses, though he doesn't know for sure. Wildlife isn't his thing. Maybe he should get an app for identifying birdsong, like that one you use in bars to identify the familiar tune that you can't name that's playing on the sound system. He'd be very surprised if there wasn't already one for birds, now that he's considered it; computer innovation seems to occur at the speed of thought.

The sound of a car engine. Xander slowly looks out of the cabin window then back inside again, scrabbling on a side table for the plastic wraparound shades he bought off a wire rack in the gas station when he topped up on caffeine and water. They do the job, dimming the otherwise welcome rays of sun that now seem to be trying to cauterise his retina while amplifying the whisky hangover that punished him every metre of the short flight from Sydney and the slightly more time-consuming, over-the-limit drive to the cottage.

With light now filtered to a less-piercing yellow, his gaze follows the caramel-coloured dirt track that meanders down from the cabin through close-cropped grass to a barred metal gate at one end of an 'airlock' exit. The three-metre-high fence adds to the impression that this is a high-security compound, designed to keep bad people out or even worse ones in. But it's neither. This is an alpaca farm and the fence is there to dissuade the animals from wandering in front of crew-cab utes driven at crazy, country speeds – saving their lives until they are ready to fulfil their destinies as wool-growers and nature's shepherds.

A huge, glaring-white 4WD is coming up the track slowly, edging animals into a spreading circle like it has an invisible force field around it. The blue-and-white chequered stripe and the roof-rig of lights are a giveaway. This must be the cop who was supposed to meet him at the airport, Xander assumes. It's okay. He knows the way here.

He watches as the 4WD pulls up and a tall, angular woman in a dark-blue pant suit unfolds herself from the passenger door. She leans in and takes a smart brown leather briefcase from the rear seat then looks at Xander through the cabin window, with a half-nod and a half-smile. Half-communication already. Xander walks out and meets her on the timber deck. He notes the almost ethereal lack of pigment in her face relieved by a smattering of fading freckles across her elevated cheekbones and the bridge of her chiselled nose. Young Sissy Spacek meets Tilda Swinton, right down to the eyes looking at you and through you at the same time. She is slightly taller than him and, he's guessing, a little overweight, judging by the way the buttonholes on her crisp blue blouse tug at their fastenings. She hasn't said a word but he can tell she carries that air of intelligence, confidence and superior knowledge that terrifies him in women and irritates him in men. Her light brown hair is scraped back into an authoritarian bun. Her smile may be professionally friendly but her look is otherwise all business.

'Senior Constable Althea Burgess,' the woman says, holding out her hand for Xander to shake. 'You must be Alexander.'

'Xander,' he replies, stressing the Z sound at the beginning of his name and invoking a slightly puzzled frown from her.

'Xander?' she says with a curious smile. 'Is that Scandinavian?'

'Scottish,' he replies reluctantly, unwilling to engage on any level of banter.

'Of course,' she says. 'McAuslan. Burgess is too, from way back.'

Xander responds with a shrug and her smile fades.

'You weren't at the airport,' she says.

'I was,' Xander replies. 'That's generally where aeroplanes land. There was no one to meet me.'

'I was ... tied up,' Althea says. 'Something else. A fatal. Kid on a quad-bike. But I was late – and I apologise. However, you should have waited.'

'Not big on waiting,' Xander says. 'Anyway, we're both here now. You're the lead detective on this?'

'Family liaison,' she says, then hesitates. 'There are no detectives on this. I'm in my civvies because some people find it less confronting,' she says, gesturing to her clothes.

'Are you *that* short-handed?'

'There are no detectives because there's no investigation,' she says. 'As far as I know, suicide is no longer a crime, even in Tasmania.'

Xander frowns and shakes his head in exasperation. 'You've decided it was suicide. Just like that?'

'No signs of a struggle, no signs of forced entry ... and there was this –' she unclips her briefcase and hands him a transparent document sleeve. Xander can see through the scuffed cover that it's a print-out of an email to someone called David Danzig, who is apparently the station commander in Launceston. For all intents and purposes, it's a suicide note.

Dear David,

Sorry I won't be able to make lunch – I reckon I would forget anyway, the way my memory is going. Anyway, I got a bad cancer test result, so I reckon it's time I was on my way to the great cop shop in the sky while I still have some dignity and honor left. Tell Alexander I'm sorry. Send a coroner's van to Mole Creek, Crabbity Farm cottage just off the main road past the pub. I don't want to stink the place up.

Pete.

'It was sent from your grandad's phone, night before last, round about the time the farmer heard the shot.' She gestures with her head towards a farmhouse half a kilometre away, halfway up a hill. 'He didn't call it in. Between dealing with foxes and rabbits, late-night gunshots aren't that unusual around here.'

Pete and Xander jointly owned the cottage. Originally it was going to be an investment holiday home for rent but increasingly Pete had been staying there, not least because it was a place he could go where no one could find him, regardless of their reasons for doing so. Pete and Xander leased the land around it to the neighbouring farmer.

'Chief Inspector Danzig was at a dinner with the mayor when the message arrived,' Althea says. 'By the time the troops got here it was way too late.'

'Pete didn't write that email,' Xander says, shaking his head.

'It came from his phone,' Althea replies. 'And the phone is locked.'

'Pete hardly ever used his phone to send emails, he never called me Alexander and he would never have spelled honour without a U.'

'But Alexander *is* your name,' she says, irritated. 'And do you really think he'd worry about spelling when he's about to take his own life?'

'You obviously never met him,' Xander says. 'Also, he hated typing on phones – big fingers on small keys – and I could never get him to try voice input.'

'Never heard of auto-correction?' Althea replies.

'He hated that, too.'

'The phone is locked. It would need a password or thumbprint, so he wasn't *that* much of a Luddite,' she says, triumph and irritation competing for the tone of her voice.

'Thumbprint. It amused him greatly that the technology he once used to catch crims was now a way to activate his phone,' Xander says, half-smiling at the memory. He looks again at the email, and the finality of the note, or what it signified, becomes a sick feeling in his stomach. Xander walks back into the cabin. As soon as his eyes adjust to the gloom, he surveys it again, looking for discrepancies, things that are where they shouldn't be, and aren't where they should. The way Pete would have. He's only distracting himself from dark thoughts and he knows it.

Althea lifts the corner of a glossy pamphlet, one corner of which is discoloured, leaving a lighter triangle in a deep burgundy stain on the table. The pamphlet is called 'Living with Prostate Cancer'.

'That looks like a reason to me,' Althea says.

'I'm sure it does,' Xander mumbles. 'To you.'

'Maybe your grandad was dealing with cancer the best way he knew,' Althea says. 'There's no need to be mad at him.'

Xander looks at her, biting back the smartarse replies lurking behind his deliberately blank expression.

'This looks like a suicide, cut and dried,' she continues. 'I'm sorry and I know it's hard to take but we don't have the resources to explore ... um ... unlikely scenarios.'

'You been doing this family liaison thing for long?' he says.

She shrugs. 'Why do you ask?'

'Because you really suck at it.'

'Thanks for the review,' she says, mostly for her own benefit. 'Put it on TripAdvisor.'

'Maybe, if someone else was involved, they wanted it to look like suicide,' Xander says over her. 'Does that sound unlikely?'

'You're a journalist, aren't you?' she says, trying to make it sound less of an accusation but achieving the opposite effect. 'Is that why you came here first, rather than visiting his ... your grandfather?'

'What does that have to do with anything?' Xander says. 'I'm not here for a story. I'm doing what Pete would have done. Visiting the scene of the crime before the trail gets cold.'

'There is no crime and there is no trail,' she says. 'But, okay, tell me, did your grandfather have any enemies? If so, you should let us know.' Her voice is laden with patronising exasperation.

'He was a cop for more than forty years,' Xander says. 'What do you reckon?'

'And why was he here?' she says.

'He was writing a book,' Xander says, immediately recalling the stuff he was beating himself up for not registering at the time. 'His memoirs. Something like that.'

He picks up an empty one-litre Laphroaig bottle and studies the label. There's another one, untouched, on the table beside it.

'Oh, yeah, the lab said his blood alcohol level was off the scale,' she says. 'That's pretty common in these cases. And he told you he was coming here to write a book?'

'Yeah,' Xander says, distantly. 'But he didn't tell me he was taking a trip overseas.'

Althea looks puzzled.

'Litre bottles of single malt. You only see them at duty free.'

'Goodness, you are quite the amateur sleuth,' she says, pacing her words so that 'amateur' can bury itself in his thoughts. 'We'll need you to identify the body,' she says after a moment, softening her tone with what he assumes is a well-practised pitch at sincerity. 'Just procedure.'

'Of course,' he says. He makes for the door then stops and looks back at the desk.

'Where's his laptop?' he says.

Althea follows his line of sight into the room. 'No laptop,' she says, and can't help herself. 'Kind of puts the kibosh on the book theory.'

Xander points at a cable snaking out from a wall socket and ending impotently at an unattached charging plug, and another cable leading to a small printer.

'There was a laptop here at one point,' Xander says, pulling his jacket from the back of a chair. 'Maybe you've got a murder-robbery on your hands.'

'Or a sticky-fingered local or ambo, more likely,' she says. 'Or cop. Or funeral director.'

'What did he use?'

It takes her a moment to make the connection. 'There was an old Browning automatic in his hand. Unregistered, from what we can tell. I'm guessing we'll find a bullet from it when we do the autopsy.'

'It's his,' Xander confirms. 'Army issue. A souvenir from Vietnam. Surprised he brought it here. Must have come on the ferry. Less screening. Maybe he knew he was in danger.'

'Or maybe he had already decided what he was going to do.' Althea sighs and shakes her head, frustrated but sympathetic. Xander can see she wants to say that the only danger to Pete was from himself. He walks outside and she follows him to their vehicles.

'I can call some cleaners, if you want,' she says. 'Specialists in this kind of thing.'

'What? Destroying evidence?'

They stare at each other for a moment, both simmering with different shades of the same anger.

'I need you to come to the mortuary,' Althea says again, some softness having returned to her voice. 'Better if it's a close relative.'

'Sure.' Xander nods.

'You staying here?'

'I've found somewhere in Launceston,' he says. 'I thought this might be off-limits. And I'll need to make arrangements.'

'Phone,' she says, holding out her hand. He passes his newly acquired mobile to her, knowing the routine, and she types in a number, presses send and a trill rings out from somewhere deep inside her jacket.

'Text me when you get back to town,' she says, handing back his phone. 'I'll fix up a time.'

'Don't put yourself out,' Xander says. 'It is only a suicide.'

'I'm sorry you feel so little about your grandfather's death,' she says. 'I'll organise the cleaners. They're very reasonable.'

Later, driving down to the main road, Xander tries to ward off another bout of *l'esprit de l'escalier* and focuses for distraction on the missing laptop. There could be a logical reason why it wasn't there – he'll do a round of repair shops in Launceston in the morning just in case the laptop wasn't working and Pete had taken it in for repairs. And, hey, if Pete wanted to go, it was his choice. He must have had a good reason and his greatest fear would have been being a burden on anyone else. And if his laptop *was* being repaired, yeah, he would have used his phone to send a message as a last resort. A very last resort.

Xander's hangover headache has almost gone, leaving a thirst that could dry beach towels. He pulls into Mole Creek's very last-century petrol station and parks in a customer spot, having barely used a tenth of the hire car's petrol and requiring no top-up, especially not at country prices. A large black SUV pulls in two spaces along from him but the driver doesn't get out.

Xander reaches the cold drinks cabinet inside the shop when he realises he's left his wallet in the car. When he exits to the forecourt, the clatter of the gas station screen door alerts a tall, thin man in a padded hiking jacket and black wool beanie who is peering into the rear of the hire car.

'Can I help you?' Xander asks.

'Roomy at the back, is she, mate?' the man replies in a thick Australian accent, turning away to look into the car again.

'I've got no idea. I only picked it up at the airport this morning,' Xander replies. 'Why do you ask?'

'Thinking of tradin' down,' the man says gesturing at the SUV. 'This tank is a bitch to park in the city.' He points at the boot. 'Mind if I have a look?'

'Sure,' Xander replies. He presses the door release on his car key fob and the tailgate swings up to reveal a recently valeted boot, empty but for his duffel bag.

'Ah, so it's manual,' the man says with his head inside the boot. 'The tailgate. Mine, you just kind of wave your foot underneath the rear bumper and it opens. Handy for when you've got a shitload of shopping. How about the front end? Plenty of leg room?'

'Wouldn't know, wouldn't care,' Xander says, estimating the SUV driver to be at least six-foot tall. 'Have a look.'

He's about to open the passenger door when they both become aware of the insistent rumble of a motorbike pulled up alongside them. Xander sees from its tank decal that it's a Triumph. Its low-slung, faux-Harley profile suggests it's the America model, favoured by those who can't afford a Hog or, like him, not overendowed in the height department. Seeing a motorbike here is no great surprise. As it snakes through foothills, the tree-lined road from Mole Creek to Launceston is a motorcyclist's dream, twisting and turning for a few kilometres, then opening up to fast straights before returning to its intermittent meandering. This is about the tenth motorbike Xander has seen today. It's being ridden by a slight figure, even shorter than him, clad in black, wearing the kind of helmet with a one-way visor that would trigger alarms in most banks.

'Sorry, mate. I'm holding you up,' the man says, staring at the motorbike rider as if he's trying to penetrate the dark glass visor but

43

only seeing a reflection of his own thin smile. 'Thanks. Enjoy your visit.' And with that, he turns away and walks back to his vehicle.

As Xander digs his wallet out of his laptop bag, which is tucked in the seat well on the passenger's side, he hears the SUV reverse out of the parking spot and drive off. He turns around to look but the smoked glass windscreen and dark interior render the driver all but invisible. The motorcyclist lingers a moment longer but then also takes off in the direction of Launceston. By the time it dawns on Xander that neither the SUV driver nor the motorcyclist had bought anything at the gas station, they are both long gone.

Xander buys two Diet Pepsis and chalks down his concern over the incident to a combination of his own paranoia and Tasmanian idiosyncrasy. After all, the hotel up the road is a shrine to the Tasmanian tiger, the long extinct marsupial dog-like creature that the hostess of the pub claims she saw once. That claim has led to the pub's unique décor and theme, right down to its quirky menu. In the past, Xander and Pete have been as close to regulars as occasional visitors can be. He contemplates dropping in for a hair of the thylacine but dismisses it quickly. Despite his overnight excesses, he might just about pass a breath test now, but only just, and another drink would put him back in licence-loss territory.

And he needs a clear head. There was something about that encounter with the other driver and the kid on the motorbike that was both strange and familiar.

'Enjoy your visit?' the man had said. How did he know Xander wasn't local? Maybe it was his remark about the hire car from the airport. Yeah, that would have been it. Drinking deeply from a plastic bottle of cola, he gets in the car, fires up the engine, switches on the radio and the familiar nasal croak of Bob Dylan taunts him with 'Ballad of a Thin Man'.

'There's definitely something going on and I really don't know what it is,' Xander says to his reflection in the windscreen as he slips the car into reverse.

CHAPTER 4

Xander is exhausted but now is not the time to weaken. The mortuary in Launceston's main hospital has a smell that's familiar but he knows he'll never get used to it; sterility and morbidity combined. But he's seen enough dead bodies to have acquired a little guilt – the end of their stories are usually the beginnings of his. The ambulance got there within hours of Pete's death, and now, stretched out on the gurney, he looks like he's sleeping peacefully, the shadow of a smile on his lips, although his skin is paler than normal and there's a small hole in his temple, a singed halo around it. Xander squeezes Pete's arm over the thin white sheet, and kisses him on the forehead, sensing the chill for the first time. A tear escapes but he traps it with his cuff and draws his grief back inside with one deep sigh. 'Take a spoonful of cement and harden the fuck up,' he hears Pete whisper, but there's no customary punch in the shoulder to follow.

Xander wonders if his reluctance to accept the suicide theory is misplaced loyalty. Or maybe it comes from a sense of his own regret. Could have called him more often. Could have visited. The fishing trips used to be a highlight of their relationship but lately they'd become compensation for a lack of real connection. Maybe if he'd responded to that email and said he was coming for the weekend ...

Reluctant to leave Pete alone, Xander sits on a scratched steel-framed folding plastic chair. Memories slide towards him like waves fading on an empty beach. Death arrives in so many different guises. His father's signalled by serious men in smart uniforms at Pete and Nanna Kate's door. Hushed voices and a barely suppressed howl, Pete's face, grey and tear-stained – the only time Xander can recall seeing him cry. Nanna Kate folding his half-grown, uncomprehending body to hers and hugging tightly like she was using him to suppress her own sobs.

Then the emptiness that followed, the realisation that his father, his hero, wasn't coming home. And being told that Pete and Kate really, really wanted him to stay with them, and choosing to believe it rather than the uglier side of that truth, that his mother and her new husband really, really didn't want an additional mouth to feed.

'Bye, mate,' Xander says, gently touching Pete for the last time, dragging his thoughts back. He looks up into the professionally sympathetic eyes of Althea Burgess. He'd forgotten she was even there.

'You okay?' she asks.

'The entry wound on the side of Pete's head has a burn mark around it, indicating the weapon was held close to his temple, as you'd expect in a suicide,' he says, slipping into crime reporter mode.

'No shit, Sherlock,' she replies, then thinks. 'Sorry, that was uncalled for. It's just ...'

'At least Pete didn't actually "eat his gun". Thank God,' Xander says, ignoring the jibe. 'Were his hands tested for gunshot?'

'Of course,' she replies, her tone reassuring rather than rebuking. 'Initial forensic reports revealed gunshot residue on his right hand and sleeve, again, as you'd expect from a suicide.'

'But then there was the missing laptop.'

She nods. 'Yeah, strange,' she says, almost dreamily, then she too slips into business mode. 'I asked the farmer if he maybe took it for safe-keeping. That was a "no". Resounding.'

'A weird thing happened on my way back from Mole Creek,' Xander says. 'I stopped at the gas station –'

Althea looks at her watch in alarm. 'Oh shit, I forgot to say. The area commander wants to see you. Like *now*!'

'Okay, why?'

'Just to pay his respects.'

Xander nods. Ten minutes later, he is trying to sit up in his seat in the station commander's office, but weariness, shock, sorrow, dehydration, and an ailing air-con unit's inability to deal with global warming are getting the better of him.

'I'm truly sorry for your loss,' Chief Inspector David Danzig says.

Truly sorry, rather than fake sorry, Xander thinks, but says, 'Thank you.'

Even sitting down Danzig looks tall; he's a fit, handsome-looking man. In his late forties, Xander guesses, with a mop of black hair that would have pleased Hugh Grant. Half a century before, his chiselled features would have been described as matinee-idol looks. He seems a little too perfect and Xander wonders if he dyes the flecks of grey into his temples, to make himself look more mature.

'And, look, I know how hard it is to accept that a relative or a friend has taken their own life ...' he says, tilting his head to make it look like he cares, but not getting there.

'Especially when you're pretty sure they didn't,' Xander says.

Danzig sighs. 'He sent me a suicide note,' he says.

'He didn't send it because he didn't write it,' Xander replies.

Danzig takes a breath. 'I knew your grandfather. Pete was a straight shooter –' he winces. 'Sorry, poor choice of words ... he was ... quite a character.'

'You knew him?'

'Met him, to be more accurate,' the older man says. 'He lectured a couple of times at Goulburn police academy. And did a couple of talks here and in Hobart. We were going to meet up for lunch before he ...' His voice trails off as he searches for the least inappropriate term.

'At his talks, did he give you the "Occam's razor is a double-edged sword" lecture?' Xander asks.

The commander looks puzzled. 'Can't say I recall that one,' he says.

'Oh, it's a doozy,' Xander says. 'Occam's razor is the theory ...'

'I know what Occam's razor is, Alexander,' the commander says. 'Not all cops are dumb.'

Xander shakes his head at 'Alexander' but ploughs on. 'Yeah, well, Pete used to say that the smart criminal leaves enough clues so that the police go for the obvious answer,' he says, ignoring Danzig's evident growing irritation. 'That way, the real clues get ignored. Double-edged sword. Occam's razor cuts both ways.'

'I'd heard this about you,' Danzig says.

'Heard what?'

'You're one of those crime reporters who's gone native. Think you're a cop.'

'Not me,' says Xander. 'I know what real cops look like.' Like Pete, and maybe not you.

'I read one of your books,' says Danzig. 'Well, half of it.'

'I write true crime. You'd have known the ending.'

'And conspiracy theories are a waste of time, money and manpower,' Danzig counters. He takes another breath, clearing the anger from his voice. 'I understand you don't accept that it was suicide.'

'Not one hundred per cent, no,' Xander says.

'Well, let me assure you we'll keep an open mind,' Danzig says, rising from his seat and offering his hand, signalling the meeting is over. 'At least until the coronial inquiry. No need for any negative publicity around this before then. I assume we can count on you in that regard.'

Xander says nothing but nods and shakes Danzig's hand and turns to leave.

'And listen, buddy,' Danzig says. 'It's hard for us too when we lose one of our own. But you mustn't let it eat you up or cloud your judgement. And, of course, if there's anything we can do . . .'

You could always go fuck yourself, you patronising tool, Xander thinks, but says, 'Thank you. I appreciate it.'

Xander comes out of the front door of the police station pursued, he guesses, by sympathetic glances and knowing smiles from the cops and civilian assistants inside. He leans on the steel rail at the top of a disabled-access ramp. That's how he feels: disabled. Like he's lost a limb, or one of his senses has stopped functioning. He can't identify the feeling because it's so alien to him. He didn't feel this when his father died – probably because he was too young. And Nanna Kate? They could all see that coming from so far off that it was almost a relief when she finally let go. Almost, but not quite. As for relationships, he has wasted a lot of time waiting for the women in his life to call it quits because of his absences, even when he was there.

But Pete's death is different. So sudden, so inexplicable, so final. Is it the fact that he didn't call, didn't ask for help or say goodbye that makes Xander want to believe someone else pulled the trigger? The door behind him clunks shut and Xander thinks he's about to be joined by another platitude-spouting local, but it must have been someone entering. He glances back at the building. Raw concrete and brick, it looks like an architecture student's final submission that they never got around to finishing. If the intention was to not compete with the old colonial building next door, it achieves that in spades.

He catches his reflection in the doors. Dress as the person you want them to think you are, Pete would say. But Xander didn't want people to think about him at all, as he moved among them, picking up their secrets, trading information, sifting through their self-serving exaggerations and downright lies to find nuggets of usable truth.

As Xander turns back towards the street, he notices a shadowy figure half-hidden by one of the trees across the road in front of what looks like a bus terminal. The kid is small – not much over five foot – and his face is shadowed by the hood of his jacket. Camo pants and white trainers have Xander profiling him as a teenage boy. An abrupt shift in body language suggests he's realised that Xander is looking at him because he suddenly turns away and starts walking towards a bus that's trading old passengers for new outside the terminus. Xander's instincts tell him to follow, but he's distracted by movement in a car parked at the side of the road in a no-stopping zone. A Mark 2 Jaguar by the look of it, which would make it at least fifty years old. Due to its age, the windscreen is untinted and he can clearly see there's a couple arguing in the front seats. The man is older, maybe in his sixties. The woman opens the door to get out and the man grabs her arm. Xander is about to step forward and ask her if she's okay when she turns to the driver, then looks straight at Xander, saying something he can't hear. That's when Xander realises it's Althea. The man lets go of her arm and smiles at Xander, giving him a tiny acknowledgement wave. Althea gets out of the car and slams the door behind her. The car peels off in a grunt of straight six cylinders and a complaint, rather than a squeal, of tyres.

'You okay?' Xander asks Althea as she approaches.

'Yeah, sure, fine,' she says.

'What, or who, was that?'

'My landlord.'

'Late with the rent again?' Xander says, not buying it.

'Dishes in the sink,' Althea lies, knowing Xander knows she's lying. 'What are you up to?'

'Just about to head back to the hotel.'

'Where are you staying?'

'Abernethy Hotel on York.'

'Trendy,' she says. 'Why there?'

'Starts with "A and B",' he says. 'That puts it near the top of the list. And it's reasonable. I'll move into the cottage later, tidy things up.'

'You don't know anyone in Lonnie?' she says.

'Lonnie? Launceston ... no. We only came here for the fishing – usually went straight up the road and stayed there until our time or patience ran out, whichever came first.'

An awkward, expectant silence fills the gap between them. She is poised to speak, but the words clearly aren't lining up the way she wants. Xander tilts his head, inviting her to continue, although he genuinely doesn't care what she says. She is a cog in a machine, no more, but it's to his advantage to keep her functioning – at least for now.

'Look, I don't know ... but if you want to catch up for a drink ...' Regret is immediate in her face. 'It's no big deal. Maybe you'd prefer to be on your own,' she says. 'Or not. Whatever.'

'Are you going to say as long as we don't talk about Pete?'

'No.'

'Okay,' Xander says. 'I've got your number.'

'And I've got yours,' she says.

They eye each other in amusement – are they both going for the double meaning? At the very least, there's a recognition that their lives are now digitally intertwined. He looks up, drawn to the sound of the bus revving its engine as it turns into the street. Through its darkened window he sees a figure, face invisible in the shade of a hoodie, apparently looking straight at him.

CHAPTER 5

The calls and whoops of a new consignment of troops on R&R drifted in from the dusty streets of Vung Tau. The accents were unmistakably Australian, the tone celebration and liberation, tinged with the desperation of men who knew this was a passing relief from being expected to kill and hoping to avoid being killed themselves.

'You said the lockdown was only part of the reason you were here,' Pete McAuslan said to Donnie. 'What else can I do for you?'

'It's more, what can I do for you,' Donnie replied. 'I'm here to advise you in the strongest possible terms to stay the Hell out of Soul Alley.'

Soul Alley, the area of Saigon where mainly African-American soldiers had set up an unofficial R&R retreat, complete with bars selling soul food and playing soul and rock music. Prostitutes, drug dealers, deserters and arms dealers soon followed.

'There's an Australian deserter in there and I need to go in and get him out,' Pete said.

'That's not going to happen,' Donnie replied. 'I can't guarantee your safety – no, let me put this another way. I can guarantee that you are not safe. And you can't go in mob-handed or you'll start a civil war. It's my patch, so that means no go.'

'Even to arrest a deserter?' Pete replied.

'Deserters are ten cents on a dollar in there,' Donnie said, shaking his head wearily. 'What's the big deal with this one?'

'He skipped just after he fragged his troop commander in broad daylight. Tossed a grenade into his hooch then legged it. That makes him special in my book.'

'Have you ever been to Soul Alley?'

'Nope.'

'You know even we don't go in there?'

'We?' Pete asked.

'Military police. It's a no-go area. Invitation only – and that invitation needs to come from a Black soldier. And he'd better walk you in there, too, and make sure you walk out. And you better not be wearing any badges.'

'We have Black soldiers ...'

'Really? I thought you had a White Australia policy.'

'We put them in uniform before we even gave them the vote. Good fighters, great trackers ...'

'And I thought we were racist,' Donnie said. 'Look, just give me the soldier's name and I'll try to get him out.'

'It's okay, I can look for him myself,' Pete said.

'Not there, you can't. And if I hear you are anywhere near, I'll come in and drag you out in chains.'

'You reckon?' Pete said, making it sound like the challenge that it was.

'Anything to help an ally,' Donnie said, unsmiling. 'Just give me the name and I'll see what I can do.'

Pete thought for a moment then scribbled 'Jager (Johnny) Weighorst' into a small pocket notebook, ripped out the page and handed it to Donnie. Lucy approached with more drinks that she assumed they'd want.

'You two like brothers,' she said with a laugh.

'You mean I look like this broken-down excuse for a human being?' Donnie asked, feigning insult as he folded the note and tucked it into his breast pocket.

'No, I mean you are always fighting, fighting ... but then you are friends again.'

But Pete thought, not for the first time, that they did look alike. Like him, the American was thin but far from gaunt. His thick blond hair was short and neat, though full enough to have him frog-marched to the nearest barber if he'd been a Marine grunt. Thin lips, a sturdy chin and narrow nose, bent by neither nature nor fist, spoke of good genes, Nordic antecedents and maybe old money. His eyebrows were almost invisible and there wasn't the faintest wisp of any other facial hair. His skin carried the ravages of too little pigment in too much sun, and the occasional glass of bourbon, Pete knew. He looked as tall sitting down as he did standing, and his upright posture was decidedly military. Donnie Carrick had taken Pete under his wing when he first arrived. They had a lot in common – they were both volunteers rather than conscripts, both had signed up for second tours, both had chosen military police. But there the similarities ended. Donnie came from a long line of career soldiers. Joining up was inevitable for him, signing up for a regiment that would definitely be going to the war zone was part of his destiny too.

Pete had been a young Sydney policeman on the rise when he'd joined the army. He'd told people he simply wanted to 'do his bit'. But his fiancée, Kate, said it was his overdeveloped sense of caring for others. Young men whom he knew were being sent overseas and he felt the need to go and look after them. She told her friends she could wait for as long as it took for him to return because she knew she would be well looked after when he did come home.

'I'll see what I can find out about Mr ...' Donnie takes the note back out of his pocket and squints at Pete's scribble. 'Weighorst. And I'll see you tomorrow.'

'Tomorrow? You can work that fast?'

'Oh, not that. Didn't I say? I'm your lockdown liaison.

Helping with the transition. Your MPs ... Provos ... Logistics ... Intelligence ... they all said you're the man for the job.'

'Lazy fuckers,' Pete interjected.

'We're going to be seeing each other a lot more.'

'And what, pray tell, will we be liaising about?' Pete asked.

'We could start with giving Major Tang some suspects before he starts turning over the wrong stones himself.' Again, his eyes flicked towards Lucy.

'Copy that,' Pete said and they toasted each other, coffee cup clinking on Coke bottle.

CHAPTER 6

It was a longer walk back to his hotel than Xander thought it would be. Still wrestling with his conflicting thoughts – Pete's suicide or something else, and if something else, what? He trudges across the hotel lobby, patting his shirt pocket to check his pass key is there, barely aware of his surroundings. He almost jumps out of his skin when the desk clerk appears at his side.

'Mr McAuslan, you had visitors,' the clerk says in a thick Baltic accent, pronouncing Xander's surname 'Mack Owsland'.

'Visitors?' Xander asks, as if he didn't know the meaning of the word.

'A Russian gentleman and your mother.'

'My *mother*?'

'I think that's what she said,' the clerk replies, seeming worried that he may be saying too much. Or too little. 'I think, mother ... or sister,' he adds, to be on the safe side.

'Was she a dumpy middle-aged red-head, short, a ton of freckles on her face and a shocking choice in fashion ... and men, for that matter?' Xander asks.

'Well, she definitely short and maybe middle-aged,' the clerk replies, his face contorted by a half-smile, half-frown of apology. 'I see no freckles ... or men with her.'

'And?'

'And slim. No red hair either – you don't get so much in Asians.'

'Asian?' Xander said. 'My mother isn't Asian.'

'Maybe half-Asian?' the desk clerk offers, leaning back to get a better look at Xander's features. 'Okay, not mother. Mother-sister. Aunt.'

'I don't have an aunt,' Xander says. 'Please tell me you didn't let her into my room, ummm ... Anton,' he adds, reading the clerk's badge.

'*Fuck*, no,' Anton replies, practising his colloquial Australian and clearly insulted by the very suggestion. 'I wouldn't want my mother snooping round my room. Or my aunt.'

'Trust me, she wasn't a relative. What did she want?'

'She left you this,' he says, handing over a hotel stationery envelope, which had a prominent lump the size and shape of a pencil eraser in it. 'Then she left, just before your Russian friend arrived.'

'Yeah, about this friend,' Xander says, confused and irritated in equal measure. 'How do you know he was Russian?'

'Because I'm Russian,' Anton says. 'He heard my accent, we spoke in our language.'

'What did he want?'

'He asked if you were in. I checked. You weren't. He left.'

Xander immediately wondered about that. Did he really leave? Still aching from his encounter in his flat in Sydney, he is on full alert to the potential for intruder ambushes.

'You got CCTV here?' Xander asks.

'Like in TV spy movie?' the desk clerk says. 'No. No CCTV.'

'You got a phone? I mean, a smartphone?'

'Of course. I am not a peasant,' Anton says.

'Okay. Do me a favour. Next time either of these two come in here asking for me, discreetly take a picture.'

'Take picture? I don't know,' Anton says. 'Feels like invasion of piracy.'

'Privacy,' Xander can't help but correct him. 'I'll give you fifty bucks for each shot.'

'Fifty dollars?' Anton says, frowns then smiles. 'Portrait or landscape?'

Xander races up to his room, enters tentatively and, having assured himself no one else is in there, looks around. Nothing is out of place, which he finds strange as his ability to wreck a room within the first five minutes of arrival is legendary among the travelling press corps. Or was, when such a thing existed. Another tidy intruder, or maybe the same one. Or, more likely, it's exactly the way he left it.

His mobile rings. It's Althea.

'Hey,' she says. 'I just wanted to firm up our arrangements for later.'

'Great. There's all sorts of weird shit happening that I need to tell you about.'

'What kind of weird shit?' she asks in a tone slightly more intrigued than her family liaison voice.

Xander tells her about the encounter at the petrol station, which he'd started to tell her earlier, and the mysterious visitors to his hotel since.

'You sure it wasn't your mother?' Althea says. 'She might have heard about your grandfather's death ...'

'And wanted to be the first to dance on his grave? I don't think so. Also, my mother is not part Asian. Far from it.'

'Of course,' Althea says. 'Then who was the visitor?'

'Well, that's another fucking mystery,' Xander says. 'If this is a suicide, there seem to be a lot of other people involved. Mystery Asian woman. Foreign-sounding stalkers who may or may not be Russian. Kids on motorbikes.' Then he remembers the note.

'Hang on a second,' he says as he rips open the envelope. 'She left me a package.'

The envelope contains a computer memory stick and a message:

Tôi có máy tính xách tay. Cẩn thận. Anh đang gặp
nguy hiểm. Đó là tất cả về Alden.

He doesn't try to read it, even phonetically.

Alden? The name rings a bell, but a very faint one that isn't getting any louder the more he thinks.

'You there?' Althea asks, her voice distant and tinny from the phone lying on Xander's bed.

'Yeah, sorry,' Xander says, picking up the phone. 'It's a note from someone calling themselves Alden. It's in ... I don't know ... Vietnamese? English letters with lots of inflections on the top.'

'Alden? That's not a very Vietnamese name,' Althea says.

'According to the manager here she's Eurasian,' Xander says, mostly thinking aloud. 'Mystery woman leaves intriguing package. This is getting weirder and weirder.'

'Xander,' she says, 'you're thinking in headlines. Maybe you need to get your head down. Get some sleep.'

'I want to check out what's on this thumb drive,' Xander says.

'Sure, whatever,' she says. 'I'll see you later. Get some rest.'

'Yeah, okay. See you,' he says and hangs up.

He plugs the thumb drive into his laptop and immediately sees a familiar file structure. He realises it's pretty much a clone of Pete's computer drive. Then he remembers Gotyaback, software he installed on Pete's laptop that will reveal its whereabouts provided it's switched on and near a wi-fi service. He logs on to the mirror version on his laptop. The screen hesitates then demands a password, which he provides. He presses the 'find me' button but only gets a 'not available' message. The laptop is either switched off or nowhere near a wi-fi signal.

Going back to the thumb-drive files, Xander trawls through

the documents. There's not much there, just a few folders and sub-folders and some randomly parked documents. One is simply called 'Pictures' and it's basically a list of disorganised images, some with names like 'Vung Tau Christmas' followed by numbers; others are just series of digits. He double clicks on one and the screen fills with a monochrome image of two tall young men in army fatigues with their arms around a tiny Asian woman. Is she the Alden who sent the Vietnamese note? Unlikely. She'd have to be in her seventies now. The men are beaming with apparent self-satisfaction but she looks less than pleased to be having her picture taken, not exactly scowling at the camera but thin-lipped with her head slightly bowed.

Xander looks at the picture again. Is one of them a much younger Pete? Soon Xander is flicking through what turns out to be an entire gallery of old wartime pictures, some of the same young man on his own or in groups – and now he's certain he's looking at pictures of his grandad in his prime, that unmistakable shit-eating grin. Many are with the guy who was in the first picture.

They are all certainly taken in Vietnam during the war. Most of the other pictures are typical shots of young men trying to look like they are happy, or maybe trying not to. Some are mugging for the camera, posing, not-posing. And every so often a shot captures at least one nineteen-year-old in a corner with faraway eyes, thinking of what? Home? Wondering what was going to stop him from getting there? Wondering who he was now, having seen what he'd seen and done what he'd done?

It occurs to Xander that these images have revealed more about Pete's time in the army or Vietnam than he has ever told him in person. On the few occasions that Xander tried to tease out more information, Pete deflected and delayed. 'When the time is right ...' was all he'd say. Xander closes the file, wondering how significant any of this is, if at all. He looks up 'computer supplies' on the internet and checks the map results to see what's closest. He feels an urgent need to backup all of this material, although he's not sure entirely why. While he's searching for Pete's laptop, he may as well get something to store the information from the thumb drive, just in case. What's that smartarse line? Just because you're paranoid, it doesn't mean nobody's out to get you. He reckons that applies to conspiracy theories too. Just because they're crazy, doesn't mean there's no truth in them.

CHAPTER 7

Xander's trawl of the computer repair shops in Launceston, both on foot and by phone during a rest stop at a café, reveals that none of them have had a laptop handed in for repair by a tall septuagenarian called Pete or McAuslan or anything else. This is no surprise. But returning to his hotel from a different direction, he spots lights coming from a nearby shop called TazziTek. He recognises the name from an earlier unanswered phone call. Suppressing his disdain for deliberate misspellings, he opens the glass door, the view through which is completely obscured by garish posters and flyers advertising motherboards, computer chips and gaming laptops that look like the flight desk of spaceships (which, when attached to a futuristic video war game, they would become).

A tubby hipster in his late teens or early twenties, with a straggly beard but immaculately formed man-bun, looks up reluctantly from a phone that he's working on behind the counter.

'C'n I help you?'

'You do computer repairs?' Xander asks.

The man points to a handwritten notice listing hourly rates and call-out fees, then returns to the task in hand.

'I called earlier but you didn't answer. I thought you were closed,' Xander says.

'As you can see,' the young assistant says, gesturing to the brightly lit interior, its shelves laden with boxes of various sizes, some vividly eye-catching, others anonymously brown or white.

'I guess you must have been on a break,' Xander says.

'I don't answer the phone. People just want to ask questions,' the young man says. 'Oooh, my computer's broken. How do I fix it for free?' he adds in a high-pitched whiny voice.

'What if someone calls wanting a repair?' Xander asks.

'Website, online booking, dude,' the kid says. 'Now, do you want to buy something or are you just here to ask questions too?'

'Both,' Xander says. 'I'm looking for a backup USB SSD hard drive. One terabyte. And my name's Xander, by the way.'

'Mo,' says the kid. 'Short for Mohammed. And no, I'm not Muslim. My dad was a big boxing fan with limited world experience.' He quickly takes a box from a shelf and places it on the counter. 'This is your best bet,' he says. 'Made in China – none of your American shit.'

With his credit card two hundred dollars lighter, Xander asks: 'Questions now?'

'Fire away, bro.'

'Have you had an older guy, in his seventies ...'

'Hand in a Dell laptop for repair?' Mo finishes his sentence.

'Yeah, exactly,' Xander says, surprised but encouraged.

'Nope. You're the second person to ask today and the answer is still the same.'

'Who was the first?'

'Tall skinny guy with a fake American accent,' Mo replies.

'Fake?'

'It was pretty good, but it slipped a couple of times,' he says. 'Also, co-inky-dinky, there was a small Asian woman came in to buy a power cable, also for a Dell laptop ...'

'And a thumb drive?' Xander says.

'Correctamundo,' Mo says, impressed. 'Two, to be precise. Some curious shit going down, I feel.'

'Never a dull day in computer repairs,' Xander says with a smile.

'Word,' the geek says. 'If it's not saddos trying to offload old floppy disks, it's pervs wanting me to take nasty porn off their computers without telling me it's there.'

'You don't really like people, do you?' Xander says, still smiling.

'I like computers. They are logical,' he replies, handing Xander the new backup drive in a bag. 'Hope you find what you're looking for. But don't bother letting me know if you do. I genuinely don't care.'

CHAPTER 8

'Can we meet somewhere more ... appropriate?' Major Tang said, looking unapprovingly around Lucy's café, which was otherwise empty. 'This place is so public.'

'Lucy has gone for supplies and no one comes in at this time of day,' Pete said. 'But where did you have in mind?'

'Your office?'

'You mean that desk beside the American MPs' station and one door down from yours? Hardly private. Or ASLG ... Or Intelligence at FWMAO?'

'FW ... what?' Tang said.

'The Free World Military Assistance Organization offices in Saigon,' Pete said. 'Almost as much a misnomer as Army Intelligence.'

'Then my office,' Tang said, his toothbrush moustache bristling with suppressed irritation.

'You mean the one you share with the city cops and the airport police? In the same building as the Yanks?' Pete scoffed, only just managing not to smile. 'The place is riddled with spies.'

'And who would they be spying on?' Major Tang snorted. 'Each other?'

'Exactly,' Pete said. 'Those window seats don't just get handed out on merit alone.'

'Always with the jokes, Lieutenant McAuslan. I'm sure that's why some people like you so much.'

Some people, but not him. If rumours and Major Tang himself were to be believed he'd completed his tertiary education at the Sorbonne in Paris and the London School of Economics, where he had developed an unhealthy distaste for Socialists in all their many forms. As a result, he could access the best and worst of both European cultures – charming, insouciant and laid-back one minute, arrogant and patronising the next. He was a wiry man of typical Vietnamese height who eschewed the precise and crisply laundered formal uniforms of his peers in favour of the more relaxed combat style preferred by many of his Australian equivalents. However, his too-neatly trimmed moustache and carefully parted and seemingly lacquered hair gave the lie to any suggestion that he might be sloppy in his appearance. He dressed the way he did for a reason, whatever that might be.

'But you are right about spies in Vung Tau,' Tang announced in an exaggerated whisper. 'That is why we are locking the city down.'

'I get it, Major Tang,' Pete replied. 'All those troops coming through the ports, navy ships with sailors looking for shore leave, the munitions barges being towed up the Saigon River to Long Binh. And there are thousands of spies all around us coming in and out of the city at will. Waiters, farmers, cops, ARVN soldiers …'

'Maybe a farmer, yes. Or a driver, or ARVN soldier. But right here, there is someone passing information to the Vietcong,' Tang said.

'Like I said, spy central.'

'Not just everyday observation,' Tang responded. 'Someone is trading secrets acquired from individuals who are handling higher-grade intelligence.'

'You mean, like me?' Pete said. 'You're saying someone is spying on me? Or are you saying I'm a spy?'

'Not you, but the people around you,' Tang replied. 'Don't

assume there are no bad apples in your barrel. No foxes in your hen house.'

'Do you have any candidates?' Pete asked.

'Many. Too many,' Tang replied. 'But those who presented an immediate low-level threat have been ... um ... dealt with.'

Pete knew exactly what he meant, having been involved in joint operations with ARVN troops, only for the military police to rock up and drag half a dozen of them away for questioning, usually never to be seen again.

'I just need you to be extraordinarily discreet in your dealings with members of the local community,' Tang continued. 'No one is above suspicion.'

'Are you talking about Lucy?'

Tang merely shrugs.

'Why are you even telling me this?' Pete asked. 'And how do you know it's not me?'

'I have set a few traps. Laid some bait with very specific information.'

'What information?' Pete asked.

'You know I can't tell you that.' Tang smiled. 'But I'm wondering if you've heard anything about the proposed bridge for Xuan Loc.'

'I know the sappers are planning to build one, but I don't know exactly where or when.'

'Well, we picked up a Vietcong courier with documents that detailed the where and the when, and the how. Oddly, it had a note telling local commanders not to attack.'

'Well, that's a relief.'

'We think it's a double-bluff. They want us to think they won't attack so that we don't waste manpower defending it.'

'Looks like they win either way,' Pete said. 'You don't defend it and they attack, or you send half a division up there that could be fighting elsewhere and they don't attack.'

'We think they're bluffing. The courier was caught a little too easily. The secret message was a deliberate plant.'

'What does he say?' Pete asked.

'She,' Major Tang replied. 'She was a bar girl from one of these establishments.' He waves airily towards the world outside. 'But she is no longer with us. However, the good news is that, so far, you are in the clear.'

'And Lucy?'

'I think she's clean,' he says. 'But if it wasn't for your relationship with her, she'd already have been taken in for questioning. And I can assure you, for Vietnamese civilians, being questioned is almost as bad as being found guilty – especially for women.'

'Fair call, but what do I do?'

'Just be careful,' Tang said. 'And trust me. You are being closely observed.'

'Maybe that's a good thing,' Pete said.

'Perhaps,' Major Tang replied, rising from the table. 'Perhaps not. But be sure to alert us to any suspicious activity.'

CHAPTER 9

Xander had been into computers since he was a kid and Pete never tired of teasing him that he'd raised him specifically to be his private on-call nerd, setting up his laptop, fixing his connections, updating his software. Pete loved his laptop but Xander knew he was like one of those fast-car enthusiasts who wasn't interested in what was under the hood ... just as long as it went faster the harder you pressed the gas. And Xander is glad of his digital skills. Eventually, the recently purchased hard drive will be a clone of the one on Pete's missing laptop, which means Xander will have multiple backups including the thumb drive from the mysterious Vietnamese woman, the contents of which he has copied to his laptop. He photographs the Vietnamese note with his phone. Belt and braces, as Pete would say. But, for now, Xander just wants to load the backup drive, then see what Pete was reading and writing before death came collecting the rent. Within minutes, hypnotised by the blue progress line crawling across the laptop screen, he falls asleep.

The trill of his mobile phone has him sitting upright so quickly his head spins. He has slumped forward in what yogis might call a half-lotus, one leg tucked under the other thigh, the lower one completely numb. He clicks the call button on the phone and tries to say hello but can only groan. 'Ah ... Ah ...'

'You okay?' It's Althea.

'Yep ... argh ... leg asleep. Pins and needles.'

'Is this a bad time?'

'No ... aaah ... no, I'm good,' he says. 'How can I help?'

'Have you eaten?'

'I had breakfast on the plane.'

'That was, what? Twelve hours ago? There's a cute little restaurant in your hotel,' she says. 'Also, it's not really breakfast on planes, is it? It's barely food. How about I come over ...'

'No, not the hotel.'

'Oh, I'm sorry,' she says. 'Yes, of course. That sounds weird. I didn't mean ...'

'No, it's not that. It's just ... I don't ...'

'O-kaaay,' she says, elongating the second syllable. 'What's up?'

'There are spelling mistakes on the restaurant's website,' Xander says.

'Spelling mistakes?'

'They make me ... uneasy.'

'Menu spelling makes you uneasy?' she says, sounding like she's trying not to laugh. 'That would explain your problem with "Alexander" in Pete's email. What's the problem with the menu?'

'Dining has only two Ns. They have it with three. Twice.'

'And that affects their cooking, how?'

'Attention to detail?' he says, knowing how weak it sounds.

'Maybe this isn't such a good idea,' Althea says, probably hearing excuses rather than explanations. 'I just thought you might not want to be on your own.'

Silence. Yes, maybe he does want to be on his own. Then his stomach rumbles.

'It's fine, give me a call tomorrow ...' she starts.

'No. It's okay. Is there somewhere that stays open late?' Xander interrupts.

'Geronimo's?' she says after a moment's thought. 'They have a full menu. Spelled correctly, I believe.'

Xander types.

'Yeah, got it. Looks good.'

'See you there in an hour?' she suggests. 'From your hotel, turn right into Margaret, then left into …'

'Yeah, got that too,' he says. 'See you at eight.'

'Perfect,' she says. 'See you then.' And hangs up.

Xander stares at the map on his screen, etching the street names into his memory, then clicks on the link to the new hard drive. The files have all loaded. He logs into Pete's Gmail account on his own laptop and discovers that the day before Pete died, there was a reassuring email from his urologist, telling him that he's sure they've got the prostate cancer early, which is good, but he needs to come in so they can discuss treatment options. Another hole in the suicide theory, but it doesn't bring him any closer to finding out why Pete might have taken his own life or been the target of a killer.

He locks the new backup drive in the room safe and tucks the thumb drive in the back corner of the stationery drawer in his desk. The risk of losing the information is reduced if he splits the resources. The laptop comes with him. Belt and braces means you have to work twice as hard to lose your pants, Pete would say.

Thinking about his grandfather, Xander wonders again if he's making more of this than he needs to; creating a problem he can resolve to make up for not being there when Pete needed him. He should have called as soon as he got that email. Now he's putting two and two together and coming up with numbers that have fractions attached. Sure, his flat was broken into but, regardless of what Vella said, it was more than likely one of his guys. Criminals and property developers don't last long if they spill their guts whenever anyone challenges them.

Is this just his guilt feeding an over-active imagination? And that's not just regret, it's about knowing that he failed in Pete's eyes. Not as a journalist – Pete was proud of his achievements

– but the fact that he wrote lowbrow true-crime books and magazine articles. Even worse, he used Pete's connections in the police force and his reputation among the criminal fraternity to open doors that might otherwise have been welded shut. To begin with, it was without Pete's approval; after a while it was without his knowledge.

'True crime?' Pete had scoffed the one time they argued openly about it, during a trout-fishing outing. 'Is there such a thing? Who's going to tell the truth in a book when it could get them jailed, or worse?'

'Truth doesn't always rely on pure facts,' Xander had said. 'Exaggerations are okay if they give information a new life. There's no point in telling a story if no one is listening.'

'Surely there's no point in writing a story if you have to lie to get people to read it.'

'I don't lie,' Xander had said. 'It's just sometimes you have to skirt round the boring details.'

'The only true-crime story is a court report,' Pete said. 'You are taking minor-league criminals and turning them into celebrities.'

'I'm not glorifying what they did just by telling the story from their point of view.'

'Jesus, Xander. You're even lying to yourself,' Pete had said. 'Give it a break. You're scaring the fish. Trout can sense self-delusion.'

And that was it. Pete had made his point, planted the seed and, as usual, watered it with a gentle joke. It was never mentioned again but, yeah, it had taken root. Is this what he's doing? Concocting a conspiracy, inventing a crime, so he can make amends for having crossed one of Pete's lines? Xander shakes his head. The thumb drive is real, and so is the Vietnamese note from Alden, and the woman who delivered it, and the Russian who came to the hotel. There's been a crime, and that's the irrefutable truth.

Xander shrugs into his leather bomber jacket and pulls his

beanie over his ears as he slips out of the hotel's front door into the deepening chill of the Tasmanian night. Launceston is a former timber-trading town so the streets tend to be wide and straight in a series of interlaced grids, with some roads built wide enough to allow teams of oxen and dray horses to pass and turn. Later, there would be trams here. Later than that, the tracks would be ripped up and the trams retired. Launceston's layout was planned rather than allowed to grow organically, unlike its much older European and Asian counterparts with their twisting lanes. The intersections here are crossroads so the route to anywhere is a series of right and left turns, meaning you are always likely to end up on the intended street, if not at the target address.

As soon as Xander crosses the road he becomes aware of someone walking in the same direction at the same pace on the other side of the street. Pete's voice whispers in his ear: 'Don't look now ... listen to your instincts but don't act on them till you're sure.'

Judging from a couple of quick glances in the dim lighting, his pursuer is male, tall and thin, slightly stooped as if trying to disguise his height, but in fact just drawing attention to it. The man's face is obscured by a scarf and hat, so Xander has no chance of telling the colour of his skin, let alone distinguishing his features. He is dressed in a heavy overcoat – perfect for the chill conditions, but surprisingly unusual for this part of the world, where thick North Face parkas and Uniqlo puffer jackets are de rigueur. Xander slows down, but the man on the other side of the road doesn't. This means one of two things: either he's not being followed or, much less likely, he's being trailed by a pro, someone who understands the principles of the 'forward follow'.

Xander stops and looks in a darkened shop window, checking the reflection for signs of accomplices, just in case this is a planned mugging and he is being herded into an ambush. He sees nothing, which is odd, as the other man should still be in view. Further along the street, Xander uses the wing mirror of a parked ute to check. Sure enough, he has a tail again. But has he? Once again he wonders if this is his over-active imagination filling in the gaps in his awareness.

He's outside a pub called the Thirsty Camel, an unspectacular brick building that takes up one corner of Bathurst and Elizabeth streets. A laneway leads up one side and, turning the corner, Xander realises it emerges just ahead of him, forming the other two sides of the rectangle. Now that he's out of sight of the street, he breaks into a jog and turns into the lane, planning to double back so he can observe his tail's confusion. Xander runs around the blind corner and crashes straight into a small woman coming the other way, not so hard that either of them is knocked over, but the impact is enough to give them both a shock.

'Ooof! ... Sorry,' Xander says, reaching out to stop her from falling.

A security light comes on automatically, momentarily blinding both of them, but then he realises the woman, her face mostly obscured by a hoodie, is Asian.

'Chin loi,' she says – or at least that's what he hears – and they stare at each other briefly before she nods slightly, repeats 'Chin Loi', almost wistfully, and walks briskly on, down the laneway and around the corner. He takes a second to gather his thoughts and follows her out on to the main street.

'Hey! Hello!' he calls, but by the time he gets there, she has disappeared, a ghost. Xander backtracks along the laneway, completing the square back on to the street. A movement in his peripheral vision draws him to the tall figure in the coat walking off in the other direction. So much for his 'tail'.

The buildings lining the streets seem more compactly arranged as Xander nears Geronimo's restaurant. Launceston is a low-rise town and if there's a structure more than two storeys high, churches and the police station excluded, he hasn't seen it yet. Geronimo's is opposite a park and next to the Tasmanian Aboriginal Centre where a poster on the wall says: 'Australia Day – Yes, let's celebrate invasion, murder, rape, theft'.

The restaurant looks as inviting in real life as it does on its website, Xander notes with surprise. He is five minutes late and Althea has already secured a table in the corner. She stands up and waves.

'Sorry I'm late,' Xander says, sitting down. 'I thought I was being followed.'

'By whom?' she says.

Xander notes her impeccable grammar before he registers that she is wearing what can only be described as a fashion tracksuit, deep blue with silver trim, smart-casual taken to an extreme. She's made an effort, but not too much, presumably just in case he gets the wrong idea.

'Good question,' he says. 'I was sure I was about to be mugged by a bloke I thought was following me. Then I was almost bowled over by a small Asian woman.'

'You were mugged by a small Asian woman?'

'Very funny,' he says. 'I think she was Vietnamese. Said something like "Chin Loi". I don't know. Languages aren't really my thing.'

Althea takes out her phone, taps the screen a few times, holds the device closer to his face and says, 'Say it again.'

'Chin Loi,' Xander says, knowing exactly what she's doing and slightly disappointed to have been out-geeked by not thinking of it first.

'Chin Loi,' repeats a female voice on the phone. 'Sorry.'

Althea holds the phone so he can see the screen. It says: 'Xin Loi is a Vietnamese phrase meaning "Sorry" in English. Click here for pronunciation.'

'You got many Vietnamese in Launceston?' Xander asks.

'A few,' Althea replies. 'There are at least three restaurants – one just two blocks from here. Maybe she was just on her way to work.'

'Yeah, for sure,' Xander concedes. 'I probably worried her more than she did me. But, on the other hand, there's this note ...'

He takes the folded hotel envelope out of his pocket and opens the note on the table.

'It came with a thumb drive that has a lot of Pete's files on it, pictures mostly,' he says. 'With any luck we might not need Pete's laptop.'

Althea shapes to say something. The slightest frown forming on her brow, but then she smiles indulgently, like a mother whose child has just uttered its first swearword.

'Order first,' Althea says as she slides a menu over the table. 'It'll save the waiter from interrupting your excellent story about your near-death encounter with a Vietnamese dish-jockey.' She takes the note and tucks it deep inside her bag, zipping the pocket closed. 'I'll take this into the station and get it translated ... discreetly,' she says with a conspiratorial frown.

Xander rolls his eyes, knowing Althea is determined to distract him from what she thinks is a pointless investigation, and looks at the menu.

'You eat here often?' he asks. 'These are Sydney prices.'

'Only when work's paying,' she says with a laugh. 'The boss asked me to keep an eye on you.'

'And here was I thinking it was my natural charm.'

'I'll let you know as soon as it turns up,' she says.

A waiter approaches and Xander panic-orders fish and chips while Althea goes for a salad with haloumi fries. They almost order two glasses of the same red house wine so decide on a bottle of slightly better stuff instead.

'It wasn't suicide,' Xander says as soon as the waiter has sashayed off to the kitchen. 'Not because of prostate cancer, anyway. I read his emails. It hadn't spread and he was already discussing a fix with his doctor.'

Althea tilts her head, listening but not hearing, then smiles.

'A lot of the older guys in that station remember your grandad,' she says. 'There's a lot of respect there. They don't want it to be suicide either.'

'Yeah, it's hard to take ... harder if it wasn't.'

'Tell me about Pete,' she says. 'Sounds like you were close.'

'Close?' Xander says. 'Phew! Yeah, yeah, we were close ...'

He feels an unfamiliar wave of emotion surging through his body and he knows she must be able to see it shining in his eyes. Xander coughs and smiles with relief when the waiter arrives with the wine. The opening and pouring give him a chance to compose himself; the first gulp clears the catch at the back of his throat.

'Pete was more than a grandad to me. He was a mentor, and inspiration and a pretty good substitute for my dad.'

'Your father ...?'

'My dad was a cop too. Got between a knife-wielding wife-beater and his victim.' Xander smiles grimly. 'It was nothing heroic, just stupid. Apparently, after he had disarmed the guy and was cuffing him, she picked up the blade and stabbed Dad in the back seven times. Shit happens. She wouldn't be the first victim of a violent relationship to attack the guy trying to save her. He died, so Pete and Nanna Kate came out of parental retirement and raised me.'

'What about your mother?'

'She was already long gone. Ran out on us just before I started school, long before Dad was killed. Last heard of she was living somewhere in Queensland with a prison officer and a whole new family. She offered to take me back after Dad was killed but Pete told her and her husband to get fucked – his actual words, if I recall.'

'And your grandmother ... Kate?'

'She died when I was at uni. Breast cancer. She wasn't old. They married young. Pete used to say he was a child bride.'

'And you and Pete were all each other had?'

Xander nods, the full import of that hitting him like a swinging punchbag, stopping his wine glass halfway to his lips.

'Having no dad at home, I got picked on at school. It was Pete who got me to stick up for myself,' Xander says, eventually. 'The first time I got bashed, Pete spoke to the self-defence trainer at his station and he suggested Wing Chun ...'

'Is that the one for smaller people ...?' she asks and, from the look on her face, Xander can see she immediately regrets it.

He lets her off the hook. 'Yeah, smaller, and women, too – anyone who can't afford to take too many hits before they get their own shots in,' Xander says. 'They taught me how not to get hurt, then how to hurt the other guy. Then Pete taught me how to look like I could hurt them if I wanted. Turns out that's usually enough.'

'Really? How do you do that?'

'First, you pick a spot where you could hit them and inflict serious damage. The throat is a good option. People see right away that you aren't looking at their face or their hands and subconsciously ... sometimes consciously, they wonder why and there's only one answer to that. If they drop their chin, or raise their hand protectively, you know it's game over.'

'And if they are too dumb or drunk to take the hint?'

'He had a stack of good lines,' Xander says, smiling at the thought. 'Like "you can go straight to jail or you can go to hospital first, then jail – your choice".'

'Awesome. I'm going to remember that one,' she says. Her laughter starts deep within her and rumbles out as she throws back her head.

Another time, another place, thinks Xander, maybe. He's not telling her the other part of the story, the part where they don't get the hint and don't read the signals and all they can see is someone smaller than them, short and slightly built, who is giving them shit when he has no right to. That's when it kicks off. And that's the part Xander relishes most – that they don't realise what they're dealing with until it's too late.

'Of course, if they are off their tits on ice, all you can do is grab the nearest piece of furniture and smash them with it. But I'm guessing you wouldn't have much use for that in family liaison?'

'I don't plan to be in the sob squad forever,' she says.

'Sob squad? Nice.' Xander looks askance at her. 'Hey, are you doing your family liaison thing now?'

'No, not intentionally.' She smiles. 'Well, maybe a little. But I'm genuinely interested.'

'Okay, what's your story? You joined the police ... why?'

'I honestly don't know,' she says with a wry shake of her head. 'My mother was a community aid lawyer and I spent so much time in court watching her I could have qualified myself. Should have. Maybe still will. But I needed something real – less talk, more action.'

'But they put you in the sob squad.'

'Life is what happens when you're busy making plans,' she says.

'What about your father?' Xander asks.

'Let's just say that sometimes having no father is better than having a shit one,' she says. 'Anyway, why are you so convinced that Pete didn't take his own life. Or, I should say, "were convinced"? You had made up your mind before you got here.'

'He sent me an email, said he had something to tell me about his past. Something he'd never told anyone. It had to do with Vietnam, which is a coincidence ...' he says, gesturing towards her bag.

A look passes over Althea's face. A memory?

'You okay?' he asks.

'Yes, of course. I was just thinking – I read somewhere – that people make bad choices in a moment but spend a lifetime regretting them.'

Her wry smile has a sadness to it and Xander wants to dig deeper but the food arrives, giving him a perfect chance to reset the conversation once the waiter has gone.

'Look, I have an ulterior motive for meeting you.'

'I suppose that makes us even,' she says. 'Go on.'

'I don't think I can persuade your boss to investigate Pete's killing, not on my say-so.'

'It's bad enough having a suicide on our hands,' she says. 'But a cop killing might be too rich for local tastes. He has told me to actively discourage any thoughts in that direction. His words. Sorry, "actively and forcefully" to be precise.'

'Which means ...?'

'It means, I can't help you,' she says, her tone adding 'obviously'.

'Can't or won't?'

'Does it make any difference? It's not going to happen,' Althea says. 'If there was a killer, what are the chances that he or she came from Tassie?'

'Almost zero,' Xander concedes. 'This has all the hallmarks of a fifo hit.'

'Fly in, fly out,' she concurs. 'Exactly. Mainland victim, mainland perp. Sounds like it belongs in the "not our problem" basket.'

'It's still a crime committed on Tasmanian soil.'

'Only if we ignore the overwhelming evidence that it was a suicide,' she says. 'I don't know what you expect me to do. I can't launch a murder inquiry on a feeling, especially someone else's. And I can't do it in Sydney or Melbourne. Actually, I can't launch a murder inquiry at all. Way above my pay grade.'

Xander pauses, wondering whether or not to press on.

'Look, I would really appreciate it if you could make some

discreet inquiries for me with the airlines,' he says. 'Look for single males from Sydney or Melbourne, who flew in then flew back out again.'

'Xander, Launceston is just a commute from Sydney and Melbourne. Half the passengers would do that.'

He raises a finger to interject. 'Also, they will have hired a car and notched up the mileage from here to Mole Creek and back. You could check with the airlines and the rental car firms.'

'Is that all?' she says, her voice laden with sarcasm. 'Or do you need more for your next book?'

'Umm ... they could be Vietnamese,' he says with a diminishing smile. 'Or Russian.'

'Xander, I'm not a detective, remember?'

'No, but you have a badge.' He pushes the plate of largely untouched food away from him. 'I can dig around but it will be quicker and easier for you.'

'You know I can't do that,' she says. 'Danzig would string me up if he found out. He doesn't want me or anyone else in the force spending a moment more of our time than we need to on this. He says it's a suicide and doesn't want to hear anything to the contrary.'

'But if he heard what's happened. It's just a couple of phone calls.'

'It's a lot more than a couple of calls,' she says. 'If I do it without permission ...'

'No one will find out,' he says.

'Everybody knows everybody here,' she says. 'My job would be on the line. Don't make an issue of this, Xander. I was just starting to like you.' She pushes her seat back. 'Excuse me, I need to go to the ladies.'

Left alone with his thoughts, Xander pieces together the few facts that he has. The pictures of Pete in Vietnam, the Vietnamese woman he'd bumped into in the street, the possibility Pete had flown overseas recently and didn't even tell him. And this other Vietnamese woman, maybe the same one, claiming to be his aunt. He looks at Althea's bag, wondering if he dare attempt to retrieve the note, then remembers he has a picture of it on his phone. Does the translation app work with written words too? He opens the image of the note, drops it into Google Translate and fractions of a second later words in English appear on his screen: 'I have laptop. Be careful. You are in danger. It's all about Alden.'

About Alden? Not from her or him? That name is ringing a bell again, but it's still barely a distant chime and he certainly isn't making any connections with Pete's long list of friends, colleagues, or the many people he's arrested and sent to jail. The answer must be in Pete's files. He needs to get back to the hotel room and find it.

'Sorry, Althea,' Xander says as she returns from the bathroom and takes her seat again. He stands and tosses a fifty-dollar note on to the table. 'I need to check something out. Next time, eh?'

The look on her face suggests there may well be no next time.

'Please, Xander. Sit down,' Althea says, grabbing his arm. 'This is embarrassing.'

He sits, but only because the minuscule disturbance to the otherwise relaxed vibe of the place has drawn the attention of some other diners. Althea takes a huge breath and looks down.

'You aren't thinking rationally. Let's just take this step by step and …'

'Rationally? That note, the Vietnamese one, says I'm in danger. And it's not from Alden, it's *about* Alden, whoever the fuck he or she is.'

Althea looks confused and glances at her bag. Xander's raised voice and strong language silence the other conversations in the restaurant as if a switch has been tripped.

'Sorry,' he says. 'If you aren't going to do anything about this, I'll do it myself.'

He grabs his jacket and laptop and heads for the door. Glancing back, he sees her reach into her bag and unzip the pocket with the note in it. He's relieved that she's not going to pursue him out of the restaurant like a jilted lover. He stews over his frustrations with Althea all the way back to his hotel, annoyed at her for not doing what he wanted, pissed off with himself for pushing too hard and allowing it to get to him. He is better than that. If a reporter can't persuade, cajole or seduce people into saying or doing things they don't want to say or do, they may as well just copy passages from press releases.

Xander barely notices the brisk walk home, albeit by a different route, but when he passes his keycard over the reader on his room lock, clicking it to green, the brass safety loop will only let it open a few inches. There's someone inside.

CHAPTER 10

Pete and Lucy were leaning in so close he could feel the heat of her body rising to his neck. It was 10 p.m. and the bar was closed and empty but they were still speaking in murmurs, like they had secrets they didn't want God or ghosts to hear. Laughter, shrieks and music trickled in from the nearby bars that had barely launched into their illicit nightly revelries. Curfew was 10 p.m. but there were always stragglers who would chance their arms with an extra hour or two of fun and games, especially if tomorrow would bring that painful truck ride back to the base at Nui Dat. Pete and Lucy sat tight to a marble-topped coffee table on rickety bentwood chairs, knees brushing thighs, fingers feathering on the backs of hands. He looked at his watch.

'Donnie's late ...' he said.

'You'd rather be with him?' she teased.

'Course not,' he says. 'It's just unlike him. He said he'd be here for last orders. But hey, there's a war on.'

'You see him every day,' Lucy said. 'Is he your boyfriend now?'

'Very funny. I need to talk to him about Major Tang, what he said.'

'Your other boyfriend ...'

The door eased open, its hinges complaining. Donnie entered, ducking instinctively under the low lintel. 'Whose boyfriend are we trashing now?' he said, by way of greeting. He kissed Lucy's cheek a little too closely to her lips for Pete's liking, while grabbing his shoulder.

'Yours,' Lucy said, looking pointedly at Pete as she sashayed off behind the bar to get them all beers.

'Tang was in earlier. Says there's a lot of chatter about the bridge at Xuan Loc,' Pete said. 'He's wondering if we've heard anything.'

'Straight down to business, buddy?' Donnie said. 'Must be important.'

'They intercepted a courier. Local girl carrying all their plans.'

'Which were?'

'That we're building a bridge at Xuan Loc so we're going to need to establish a forward support base there.'

'And are we?' Donnie asks. 'Building this bridge?'

'Not you, us. And yeah. Tang is getting nervous. Wants us to put a whole fucking battalion up there. The VC courier, they killed him … her … before she could be questioned, but they know she was from around here.'

'Why's he so skittish? Okay, it's advance warning of troop movements, but building a bridge across a river isn't going to go unnoticed.'

'The weird thing is the notes with the plans were telling VC commanders not to attack the bridge builders.'

'Excellent news,' Donnie said. 'I may celebrate with one of those beers heading in this direction as we speak …'

'You are building a bridge at Xuan Loc?' Lucy asked, plonking three opened beers on the table. 'For a road?'

'Sure,' Pete said, uncertain if he was giving too much away, especially in front of Donnie.

'Don't worry about defences …' Lucy said, running her finger and leaving a trail of nothing in the sweat on the outside of her bottle. 'You won't need them.'

'What?' Pete laughed. 'If we don't have defences the VC will just destroy us.'

'They won't attack,' she says, looking him in the eye, expecting to be believed.

'The VC?'

She shook her head. 'Not till you are finished.'

'And you know this, how?' Donnie said.

'Because Vietnamese people are not stupid.'

'Okay,' Pete says. 'I'll buy that.' Donnie nodded his agreement. 'But why does that mean they won't attack?' Pete asked.

'Do you think you are going to win this war, Pete?' Lucy asked.

Pete shrugged, unable or unprepared to offer an answer.

'Donnie?' Lucy challenged.

Donnie smiled. 'We have the biggest, strongest, best-equipped army on the planet,' he said. 'I think we can get the job done.'

'You *think?* The Vietcong, the Hanoi government, General Giap, they *know* they are going to win,' Lucy said.

'Okay ... maybe ...' Pete replied.

'Not maybe. They know. Then why would they stop you from building a bridge for them? For us?'

Pete looked at Donnie for support but the American merely coughed and looked away, amused.

'Maybe the chatter is happy talk about the nice new bridge you are going to build for us poor Vietnamese,' she said before taking a dainty sip from her beer. 'I need to close up,' she added, getting up and going behind the counter, where she started switching off lights and locking store cupboards.

The classic sounds of a fist fight intruded from the street. Australian voices, mostly, and at least one American accent. Some were egging the combatants on, others were trying to calm them down.

'Shall we?' Donnie said.

'And end up as punching bags for both sides?' Pete replied.

'It'll sort itself out. My great-grandfather was a cop in Glasgow, Scotland, between the wars. He told me they'd wait till the fighting died down then take the losers to hospital and the winners to jail.'

Right on cue there was a thud that sounded like a side of beef being hit with a sledgehammer, a louder thud as something or someone hit the ground, and a cheer mixed with more reasoned calls to end the combat. Soon the shouting and singing faded as the group moved on to another bar or their beds. Punch-ups between American and Australian troops were not unusual, and frequently started over either girls or heated discussions about their different tactics.

'Did I hear an American accent there?' Donnie said.

'Now that your blokes have to stay in uniform, makes them an easier target.'

'Another in-depth discussion about our contrasting military strategies, no doubt,' Donnie said.

'Your problem is your "come and get us" approach,' Pete said. 'You let the enemy know you're around and trust your superior firepower and fly-boy support will get the job done.'

'Better that than sneaking around like the enemy you're supposed to be fighting,' Donnie replied. 'Where's your dignity and honour?'

'Out in the jungle, looking for your tactics.'

There was a brief contemplative silence, interrupted by the creaking music from the speaker, squeaking its own tune as it rocked back and forth.

'Can I ask you a question, Major?' Pete asked with fake formality.

'You just did, Lieutenant,' Donnie answered with a smile. 'But you're on a roll. Fire away.'

'Why are we here?'

Donnie looked at him askance. 'This isn't a meaning of life question, right?'

Pete shook his head. 'I mean why are we here … in this war? America and Australia, Korea, the Kiwis … the Thais?'

'Keeping the world safe from Communism?' Donnie offered.

'Maybe Communism is keeping the world safe from us,' Pete said, the words sounding glib even to him as he uttered them.

Donnie merely raised an eyebrow, indicating that he didn't buy that and he didn't think Pete did either.

'You've heard what's going on in Laos and Cambodia?' Pete continued.

'If you mean the carpet bombing of the Ho Chi Minh Trail? Not officially, no, so it's not happening.'

'If half the stories we hear are true …' Pete says, a tremor of horror in his voice.

'If they don't want to be in the firing line, they shouldn't let Uncle Ho use them as a supply route,' Donnie said, and now it was his words that had a hollow echo in Pete's ears.

'Now, you boys stop fighting,' Lucy said, appearing stealthily from the shadows and plonking down two cold 33s, the condensation forming instant rings on the table. 'No fighting in here.' Standing behind Donnie's chair, she draped her arms over his shoulders and kissed the top of his head. Pete looked her in the eye, as if to say 'what's going on here?' She answered him with a wink and a smile that Donnie couldn't see.

'You want to know why you are here?' she said. 'You are here to drink my beer. Now do your duty or I call the QC.'

QC. Quan Cahn. Vietnamese Military Police – although foreign troops had other uses for the initials, some of them homophobic or racist or both, all of them insulting. With that, she picked up two empties with one hand and saluted theatrically with the other, before returning to the bar. Pete could have sworn she was exaggerating her wiggle as both he and Donnie watched her waltz around the end of the counter. When she was out of sight, they looked at each other and smiled.

'That's why we're here,' Donnie said. 'To save people like Lucy from a world that would crush them like flowers under a tank track.'

CHAPTER 11

Xander bangs on the door, having checked the number to make sure it's his room. An English voice inside says, 'Hang on. Sorreee!' Xander lets the door close fully so that it can be unhasped from its safety chain on the inside, then it's opened to reveal a tall, thin man, about forty years old with narrow features and a mop of curly, vividly golden curls.

'I'm really sorry, mate,' he says, smiling broadly, his accent more Mockney than Oxbridge. 'I came to the wrong room, and bugger me, my card opened your door. All these rooms look the same. Only realised I was in the wrong place when I opened your wardrobe and noticed none of the clothes were mine.'

Xander looks him up and down. He is sharply dressed in a well-tailored suit partially revealed by what looks like an expensive overcoat. In other words, every inch a businessman and certainly not your typical sneak thief.

'Didn't even have time to take my coat off,' he says. 'Just as well you got here when you did, before I laid waste to your minibar.' He smiles engagingly and opens the door wide, inviting Xander to enter. 'This *is* your room, isn't it?'

Then it clicks. The accent is different but the body shape is the same as the man who was looking into his car in Mole Creek and, most likely, attacked him in his flat in Sydney.

There must be something in Xander's eyes, a flash of recognition, because the man quickly reaches inside his coat, pulls out a gun with a silencer attached and points it at Xander's heart.

'Come in and close the door,' the man says, gesturing with the gun. His accent has fled England and landed in Eastern Europe.

Xander's mind is churning possibilities and probabilities. In a strange way he's relishing the opportunity to get even with his attacker, although the presence of a firearm is less than welcome. However, in their first encounter he didn't get the chance to draw on the hours upon hours of repetitive martial arts routines that had drummed the best moves for attack and defence into his subconscious. He hasn't forgotten them now. Facing a firearm, unarmed, his instructor said your best weapon was surrender, the next best was surprise. This guy only knew Xander as a victim, so surprise might be easier to achieve than if he'd been able to put up a fight in their first encounter. Angry, tired and a little drunk, surrender wasn't on his drop-down menu of options.

'What do you want?' Xander says, stepping forward, his hands half-raised in submission, creating time and reducing space for what would come next.

'I told you, come in and shut the door.'

Xander looks over his shoulder as if judging his chances of escape.

'You'll never make it,' the man says. 'Long, narrow hotel corridor. Shooting fish in a barrel.'

He's using none of the voices he'd used in their previous encounter and, judging by his current accent, is almost certainly the Russian-speaking visitor Xander had missed earlier. Xander briefly wonders which is his real accent. Time for part two of the move – distraction.

'You're a man with a thousand voices,' Xander says.

'Not a thousand, mate,' he says, slipping now into his very convincing Australian drawl. 'But enough to get by,' making it sound more like 'enaff ter git boy'.

He does this for fun. Xander allows his eyes to flicker over the man's shoulder then quickly come back to lock his gaze, as if he's seen something he doesn't want the man to know he's seen. All he wants is a moment of doubt and he gets it when the man smiles an 'I'm not that stupid!' smile but turns his head fractionally as if listening for whatever might be behind him. It's not a conscious move, just an instinctive reaction to a possible threat, and it's all Xander needs.

Next step and the most crucial one. Get out of the line of fire. In close combat, that means getting the weapon to point in a different direction, something Xander achieves by grabbing the top of the gun with his right hand – which has the added advantage of possibly hindering movement of the slide and hammer – and twisting it away from him. The man's left hand comes across to try to force the barrel back and the silencer gives him extra leverage. But Xander weaves his left arm over his assailant's right, then under his left, and twists. Now the gun is pointing at the floor, which is when Xander headbutts the intruder, feeling a satisfying crunch as his brow contacts the bridge of the gunman's nose. The gun drops, the man's hands fly up to his face and are immediately covered in his blood. Xander kicks the gun across the floor and it's game over. The man sees the gun disappear under the bed and clearly decides Xander will get to him before he can get to it. He stoops and bull-runs past Xander into the corridor, blood dripping as he flees. Xander retrieves the pistol from under the bed, which takes longer than he'd hoped, and by the time he goes back out into the corridor the man has gone, leaving only a breadcrumb trail of blood spots towards a fire exit.

Xander closes the door and locks it, then walks briskly over to the window and sees, in the street below, the shape of a tall, thin man in an overcoat, walking quickly, holding his face with one hand, closing his coat against the cold with his other. He then turns up a sharply shadowed laneway and disappears. Xander quickly goes to the wardrobe and immediately sees that the safe door is open and the backup hard drive is gone.

But that's okay because he still has Pete's files on his laptop. He checks. They're all there. Also, there's the cloned files on the thumb drive the Asian woman left for him ... unless that too has been stolen. Belt and braces. He rushes over to the desk and pulls open the drawer. He quickly finds the thumb drive, and plugs it in. As he's watching it load, it occurs to him that the slim device looks slightly different. He's not sure how, it just doesn't look like the one that fell out of the hotel envelope. He's watching its tiny light flickering on and off, questioning his memory, when his heart stops. He pulls the thumb drive out, but looks in horror at his laptop screen as it flips, flashes and seems to be dying before his eyes.

He tries to turn it off but no amount of prodding, unplugging or key combinations will stop the machine from eating itself. A message says 'you have 10 seconds to insert the rescue password' and the time counts down in large red numerals. At the appointed time the screen is blank. This is the kind of thing that happens when your computer is infected with ransomware and you don't pony up with the Bitcoins.

'Fuck ... fuck ... fuck,' Xander curses his laptop, lifting it, looking at every angle as if it might reveal a secret magical switch that he knows doesn't exist. His heart surges as it occurs to him that his assailant could easily come back. He grabs the gun and steps briskly to the door, which he deadlocks then swings the brass safety hasp over its hook and puts a chair under the handle like he's seen people do in movies. He thinks about calling Althea but he's too tired to contemplate the hours of questioning, not to mention suspicion, that would surely ensue. And he needs to decide whether or not to tell her about the gun. Instead, he heads for bed, making a brief detour via the minibar. As he pours himself a whisky, skipping the mixers, he wonders what could possibly be so important in Pete's documents and pictures that would merit two break-ins and physical assaults, one with a gun, not to mention industrial-grade computer espionage related to something that his grandfather had never even spoken about.

And then there's Pete's death, either at his own hand or someone else's. At least that makes sense. Maybe it wasn't that Pete didn't want to talk about his time in Vietnam. Did something happen then that he had to keep a secret for the best part of half a century? Maybe he couldn't say too much, and he definitely can't now. Xander lies back on the bed, residual adrenaline competing with fatigue and alcohol, trying desperately to fix some of the images from Pete's files in his mind.

Deep in the mix there's a version of Pete that he never knew, and a mysterious Vietnamese woman calling him from the past, and he doesn't know how to reply. But at least he knows this truly is a crime – he's just not sure exactly what the crime is.

CHAPTER 12

The first thing Xander does when he wakes the next morning is to perform his daily routine of Wing Chun kata, the now life-saving close combat that was his inheritance from the small kid who didn't want to be targeted by bullies anymore. He almost succumbs to another excuse not to do it but then logic kicks in. Will getting himself ready for another attack make a difference to the outcome? Perhaps. Will taking his dead computer to the repair shop thirty minutes sooner make it more likely to be fixed? Probably not. Half an hour later, exercised, stretched, showered and dressed, he takes his laptop to Mo at TazziTek, who declares the device 'bricked'.

'It's deader than disco,' he says, holding the slender thumb drive that did the damage gingerly between two fingers as if it was contaminated with a physical virus. 'From what I can tell from this, you have infected it with some weapons-grade ransomware,' Mo says. 'My malware detection apps went apeshit as soon as I plugged this in.'

'I didn't infect it ...' Xander protests.

'You plugged the thumb drive in, my man,' Mo says, inappropriately cheerily. 'It's hardly an act of God. You got backup?'

'Not anymore,' Xander says, annoyed.

'If it's any consolation, whoever did this was a pro,' Mo says. 'My guess, before they bricked your laptop, like days ago, maybe weeks, they somehow loaded a keylogger on it, and they've been tracking every word you've written, every password you've punched in.'

Xander's stomach sinks. He suddenly feels vulnerable and exposed.

'I have some good news, though,' Mo says.

'I could use some.'

'I have a reconditioned Windows laptop going second-hand for half the list price.'

'Reconditioned? What does that mean?'

'I cleaned the dried semen off the screen and keyboard.' He tilts his head to let Xander know he's joking. 'Seriously, all the previous owner's files have been deleted and the disk has been reformatted. It's got the latest version of Windows, some freeware word processing and it's fully loaded with two different antivirus programs. I'm guessing you didn't have any on this,' he gestures to the dead laptop.

'Always thought they were a bit of a scam,' Xander says. 'Like drug dealers – they provide the stuff that makes you sick then sell you the cure.'

'And people say I'm cynical,' Mo says.

'What was wrong with this?' Xander says, pointing to the second-hand laptop.

'Nothing. Bloke gave it to me to sell on consignment. His girlfriend persuaded him to convert to Apple.'

'Another lost soul,' Xander says.

'My sentiments exactly,' Mo replies, reaching under the counter for the replacement device's charger. 'There was a time when PC didn't mean "politically correct". Now we are the digital dinosaurs trudging towards oblivion, awaiting an Apple-shaped comet to crash-land and wipe us all out. Now, would you like a carry case with that?'

Settling into a nearby café that not only has wi-fi but a wall socket into which he can plug his new laptop, Xander emails his editor to tell her he's taking some of the accrued time off that they've been begging him to use up. It's not that they don't want him in the office, just that they won't have to pay him out at time-and-a-half at some future date.

Then he tries to call Althea but either her phone is off or she isn't taking his calls. He leaves a voicemail, basically apologising for being a dickhead and appreciating that his fight isn't hers. What he doesn't say is that he still thinks it should be. Or that there was a man with a gun in his hotel room when he got back the previous night and they should look out for a someone with an atomic blonde bubble-cut wig, one, maybe two black eyes and one broken nose. That information, vital though it may be, can wait until he finds out if he's been forgiven.

Xander logs into his cloud storage and changes his passwords. At least all his stuff is there. But it hits hard when he realises he's lost all those pictures of Pete in Vietnam, a huge part of his grandfather's life into which he'd only been allowed the briefest of glimpses. Xander hadn't even known those pictures existed. All intended to be part of his memoirs, obviously, but also part of his life that he never discussed with Xander. Were they linked to the story he'd wanted to tell Xander before he told the world?

Xander crosses his fingers and tries to log into Pete's Gmail with the new password he installed. It refuses. He tries the 'forgotten password' button but it won't connect to his email address. Was this more of his cyber ninja stalker's handiwork, erasing any information that might lead to . . . who? Oh, yeah, some mystery man or woman called Alden. Xander closes the cover of the laptop slowly and solemnly, like he's lowering the lid of a friend's coffin for the last time.

Thinking of which, the logistics of Pete's departure are another issue he's got to deal with. He needs to arrange for Pete's body to be flown back to Sydney or Melbourne. The two forces, army and police, both of which he served with distinction for many years, both want to help with his funeral. The first one to offer to pay for the body to be flown back can have the funeral; a pragmatic resolution that he knows would have amused his grandfather.

'How much do you think they think I'm worth, Xander, dead or alive?' he can hear him ask, before collapsing in an avalanche of croaky laughter.

His phone rings – it's Althea Burgess.

'Hi ... Althea ... good to hear from you,' he says. 'Look, I'm sorry about ...'

'Nobody matches that pattern,' she says, talking over him, her voice a gust of icy wind.

'Sorry?' he replies.

'No male passenger, from Melbourne or Sydney, arrived in Launceston in the seventy-two hours before your grandfather's death, then hired a car that would have taken them to Mole Creek and back, then left,' she says.

'Right,' he says. 'Thanks. Look, I just wanted ...'

'No female Vietnamese either,' she adds, abruptly. 'I understand you are flying back to Sydney, tonight or tomorrow,' she says. 'Have a safe flight.'

'Althea, wait,' he says. 'I'm trying to apologise.'

Silence.

'Hello?'

'So apologise,' she says. 'I know you hot-shot city journos don't have much time for police, especially here in the sticks ...'

'It's not like that ...'

'It's exactly like that,' Althea says. 'Come on, then. Let me hear it.'

'Okay, I am sorry for walking out on you last night. I was tired and I wasn't coping with my grandfather's death ...'

'Apology accepted,' she says.

'Hey, Althea, can you do me a favour?'

Silence.

'Could you maybe check that name, Alden?' Xander starts to spell it.

'Unbelievable!' Althea says. 'Have a nice flight home.'

And with that there's a blooping sound on his phone as she hangs up and is gone. He didn't get the chance to tell her about his late-night visitor, and he's guessing she wouldn't be too receptive to hearing the news so long after the event. He also didn't get to tell her that he's changed his plans and won't be flying back to Sydney right away. Xander almost throws his phone at the wall, but his arm is restrained by one of Pete's myriad 'life laws' tugging at his sleeve: 'Whenever you are pissed off with someone, ask yourself if they meant to make you angry or if it was an accident. Was it them or was it you? Is there anything you can do to fix it, or is this just another burnt sausage on the barbecue of life?'

The last part of this homily frequently changed, making the preceding lecture worth sitting through countless times. 'Another zit on the chin of existence,' was one. 'A flat tyre on the road to contentment,' was another. 'A hang-nail on the fickle finger of fate,' was a particular favourite of Xander's.

He texts Althea. 'I've been a tool. I hope you'll understand why and forgive me. Thanks for trying to help.'

But then there are the circumstances surrounding Pete's death and Danzig's reluctance to investigate. 'Never ascribe to malice anything that can just as easily be explained by stupidity,' was another of Pete's favourites.

Danzig. Maybe now he can get him to take Pete's death seriously – if he hands in the gun and silencer, Danzig won't be able to ignore him any longer. Xander calls the police station and eventually gets through to Danzig's PA.

'Commander Danzig's office. How can I help you?' a woman with a practised calming voice asks.

'Hi. It's Xander McAuslan, I'd like to come in and speak to Commander Danzig, today if I can.'

'Can I ask what it's regarding?'

'It's regarding Pete McAuslan. I'm his grandson.'

'I know who you are, Mr McAuslan, and I'm sorry for your loss. But Commander Danzig is very busy so if you could just tell me ...'

'Look, I need to talk to Danzig, okay? It's important.'

'Hold on a second,' the voice is laden with weariness, letting Xander know that he is near the wrong end of a very long queue of requests for urgent discussions. 'I'll see if he's available ...'

There's a click on the line followed by some jangling music that Xander surmises is deliberately irritating to deter impatient callers. The music stops with another click. 'I'm afraid Commander Danzig is terribly busy at the moment and is likely to be tied up for the next few days. If you could give me your number, I'll ...'

Xander hangs up and gathers up his newly acquired laptop and phone, pays for his coffees, then heads back to the hotel. Assuming the Launceston police are working the percentages rather than the facts, one of which being they didn't know Pete like he did, is it so surprising that they want to wrap this up as a suicide? Moreover, it's a problem that chance has lain on their doorstep. It's highly unlikely that there's going to be a series of killings of police, retired or otherwise, or anyone else in Launceston. In the unlikely event, in their view, that this turns out not to be suicide, then it's a blood feud that's been imported from the mainland like a blight on their apples. It certainly isn't a straightforward murder-robbery. There are more conveniently located places with richer pickings than a holiday cottage outside a tiny town no one has ever heard of. And nothing else of Pete's is missing. His expensive Breitling watch and his wallet stuffed with credit cards and cash were handed back to Xander along with his overnight bag, although the gun, obviously, had been impounded. Not their cop, not their crime. Everything points to suicide, so why fight it?

His first task is to convince Althea that the threat is real so he sends her an email.

Hi Althea

Didn't get the chance to tell you I had an intruder in my room last night. He had a gun, which I now have in my possession (long story, happy ending). I'd really like you to take it off my hands and show it to Danzig. Maybe then he will understand that I'm not bullshitting.

Xander could and should wait for a response but that's not in his nature. He's fucked if he's going to wait for some multilingual psycho to hunt him down again. If anyone's going hunting, it will be him.

His phone rings again and he checks the screen. It's his office.

'Xander speaking,' he says, wondering, half-hoping they have a job for him to do while he's in Tasmania, so he can justify staying on a little longer.

'Xander, sweetie,' the familiar croak of his editor, Stella McGear's voice rasps in his ear. 'Tell me, you don't happen to have lost your laptop have you?'

CHAPTER 13

Pete had grown to hate the drive from Vung Tau to Saigon and especially back again. It wasn't just the rough-as-guts road, or that he'd occasionally have to veer off to allow a convoy of military vehicles to pass unhindered. It was the mixture of tedium interspersed with bouts of anxiety when he realised he was alone on the track, and therefore a prime target for a sniper, land mine or ambush. Or all three.

He could have grabbed a seat on a chopper out of the airfield, or on a speedboat up the Saigon River, but there was always the problem of how to get around once he got there. And then how to get back if he couldn't bum a ride home.

Once a week he had to check in with the Australian Army Intelligence guys at the headquarters of the pompously mis-named Free World Military Assistance Organization in District 10, if only to establish his bona fides as a floater between the Australian MPs, Intelligence and Logistical Support. But he liked the FWMAO building, which was very French Indochina, with a low, flat podium supporting three floors and two elegant towers. It reminded him that this city had once been a hub of civilisation rather than a focal point of a war.

He also didn't mind being there as it tended to feature a hubbub of voices wrangling the incoming and outgoing troops from Australia, New Zealand, South Korea, the Philippines and Thailand. It was also where the flows of non-military support like medical supplies, transportation, construction and agriculture were traffic-managed.

Pete was usually glad to see the Intel guys, and they him, as his stories from the den of iniquity that was Vung Tau never failed to entertain, but this morning was different.

'Muldoon's on the warpath,' one young officer said. 'Watch your back.'

The space around them cleared when the aforementioned Major Muldoon spotted Pete and called his name, cornering him in the main office.

'We had a platoon of our sappers ambushed by Vietcong two days ago on their way to clear passage for an American convoy,' Muldoon said. 'Know anything about that?'

'Should I?'

'Charlie must have known they were coming. As a so-called liaison, you were one of the few soldiers outside the immediate planning group who were aware of the operation.'

'I knew they were planning it. What's your point?'

'What's your point, *sir*?' Muldoon scolded. 'Who else did you tell about this?' he continued in a tone that was just one bright light in the face short of an interrogation. 'Who could have told the VC we were coming?'

'Apart from the Yanks?' Pete said, to not even a flicker of amusement from the officer who was two ranks his senior but barely a year older than him. 'And I know our ARVN allies leak like old buckets used for target practice. But with a fair percentage of them being patriots caught on the wrong side of the war, their loyalties would be divided, wouldn't they?'

'I heard you were a bit of a commo,' Muldoon said, sniffing to punctuate his speech rather than because of any tropical allergy. He was a round-faced, dumpy man whose unfulfilled promise to himself to eat less and exercise more meant his uniform was the right size for the man he hoped to be. His discomfort in the heat added to his general air of irritation. His barely controlled hair would have tested Vidal Sassoon, let alone the brigades of army barbers who'd fallen in that battle.

'Some people – and I'm one of them – are concerned about you moving between us, Logistics and the Provos, not to mention our allies,' he said. 'Picking up bits of information here and there.'

'It's kind of my job, isn't it? Liaising does involve talking to people.'

'Well, it depends who you are liaising with. I'm worried about pillow talk with that whore who runs your so-called office in Vung Tau.'

Pete blinked and could feel his hands itching to clench into fists.

'You know, if you'd care to repeat that some time when we are both off duty, I'd be happy to engage in a frank and free discussion with you,' Pete said eventually, murmuring through a smile. 'Maybe somewhere quiet where we wouldn't be disturbed.'

'There's no need to take that attitude, Lieutenant McAuslan,' the Major said, visibly leaning away from Pete. 'We just want to get to the bottom of this. It could have been an innocent comment ... a slip of the tongue ...'

'To my whore in Vung Tau, you mean, you charmless cunt?' Again, his smile belied his fury.

'And I'd caution you to remember our respective ranks.'

'Well, when you're done getting to the bottom of the shit in your brain, *sir*,' Pete said softly, 'feel free to go fuck yourself and don't forget to grease up the horse you rode in on.'

The major took a breath. They both knew that, with no witnesses to the content of this conversation, any complaints against Pete for abusing an officer would harm the complainer more than him. All anyone watching would have seen was Pete smiling and talking too quietly for anyone to hear.

'About this Weighorst fellow?' Muldoon said after a brief

staring contest, clearly glad to have something else to discuss. 'Any progress?'

'Apparently he's hiding deep in Soul Alley and our American friends don't want us upsetting that particular apple cart,' Pete explained.

'Not good enough, McAuslan,' Muldoon said. 'Our soldier, our problem, our fucking apple cart. Get it done.'

With that, Muldoon walked out, smiling at having won at least one small victory. In fairness, Pete could understand his concerns about security. When information means life and death, careless words are like stray bullets. Pete had no idea how the VC had acquired the info they'd have needed to set up an ambush in exactly the right place at precisely the right time. Luckily, the would-be attackers had been accidentally flushed by an infantry patrol and found themselves trapped in an unintended pincer movement with the advancing sappers. It could have been a lot worse, but it was bad enough, just for what might have happened and, pertinently, how the enemy knew the platoon was coming.

The Weighorst thing bugged Pete too. The Intel major was right – their deserter, their problem. He decided to swing by Long Binh on his way back to Vung Tau, phoning ahead to make sure Donnie would arrange for him to get into the massive US Army base – more like a small town, really – about five clicks from the Bien Hoa military airbase.

With about fifty thousand troops and support staff on its massive campus, Long Binh was bigger than many country towns in Australia, and with much better facilities. Bars, a cinema, bowling alley, craft workshops, even massage parlours, maybe it was to remind the enlisted men what they were fighting for, Pete thought as he stop-started through the afternoon chaos of bicycles, buses and military vehicles that converged on the city centre then dispersed again on the spokes of Saigon's intersecting traffic wheels. Elegant and wealthy Vietnamese women were being ferried from one bridge game to the next coffee date on pedal-powered tri-shaws called cyclos, seemingly unaware that there was a war on. Their less fortunate countrywomen balanced baskets of produce on *quang ganh,* long bamboo shoulder poles with a basket suspended at either end. Some even managed this feat of strength and skill while riding a bicycle.

Pete needn't have bothered calling ahead, the gateman waved him through peremptorily, safely guessing that a tall white man in an Australian uniform posed little or no threat to the security of the camp or its inhabitants. When Pete pulled up outside the 18th Military Police HQ hut, Donnie was overseeing the loading of three truckloads of MPs. When he had banged the door of the last truck to send it on its way, he turned and smiled broadly at Pete.

'What's up?' Pete said, genuinely baffled. 'You got a riot on your hands in the city?'

'Big win in the Delta,' Donnie said, like he was reporting a football score. 'No ARVN involvement so the Marines went in clean and found themselves the proud captors of a couple of hundred POWs and civilians. Hard to tell which is which. Our boys will sort them out. And we need the MPs to guard the flank in case Charlie circles back.'

'Shit, you really are a fighting unit too?'

'Sure are. I wasn't here at the time, but if it wasn't for the resistance our guys – our MPs – put up during Tet, we'd all be eating with chopsticks right now and waving Chairman Mao's *Little Red Book.*'

'That would be *Das Kapital,*' Pete said. 'The Viets are Stalinists, not Maoists.'

'Same-same,' Donnie said. 'Now, you said you wanted to talk.'

'I need you to get me into Soul Alley,' Pete said. A passing Black grunt, having overheard, stopped open-mouthed but then thought better of whatever he was going to say and moved on.

'And I need you not to ask for that, old friend,' Donnie said.

'Exceptionally high-risk, extremely low potential reward. That would be a "no".'

'I'm not asking for permission,' Pete replied. 'Help, yes. But I'm going in, with or without you.'

'Pete . . .' Donnie looked concerned. 'Listen to me. That is not a good idea.'

'This whole fucking war is not a good idea,' Pete replied. 'But we all have orders and mine are to find Weighorst. Consider this a courtesy call.'

He turned to leave.

'How long have we got?' Donnie asked.

'Some time in the next week would be good,' Pete said.

Donnie's brows furrowed as he calculated the logistics and risks. 'Leave it with me and I'll see what I can arrange,' he said. 'I guess it's about time we had a look in there ourselves.'

CHAPTER 14

Stella McGear's mention of his laptop drops a dread bomb into Xander's gut. Stella is a good friend but a straight-to-business kind of boss, so this would not be idle chit-chat.

'Funny you should mention it,' he says in a tone devoid of amusement, 'but my laptop is toast and I've lost a lot of my files. Why do you ask?'

'It seems someone has sent your friend Mr Vella notes on a story you were working on. A very damaging story.'

'Oh.'

'Yes, "oh". And he's also been sent copies of emails you sent to some of your contacts that were very uncomplimentary about him and suggest you were out to get him.'

'Okay, I suppose I was,' he says. 'He *is* an evil piece of shit.'

'Yes, but, sweetie, that's an indication of intention to damage his reputation,' McGear says. 'If he sues for defamation, any defence of absence of malice or fair comment goes out the window.'

'Shit!'

'Shit indeed,' she says. 'If he comes after us, it could cost the paper millions, if we had millions. In reality it could shut us down, especially in this climate.'

'What do I need to do?'

'Look, there's no easy way of saying this, but there was some pretty colourful language on your emails.'

'And?'

'And we are overdue for another round of redundancies.'

'Vella wants me sacked?' Xander says, thinking none of the highly abusive terms he'd used to describe the former criminal had not been said to his face.

'Not Vella. Our lawyers. They say we need to get in front of this before he issues any threats. Put some distance between us.'

'And me?'

'All your holiday pay, a decent redundancy package and no restrictions on you working elsewhere.'

'Oh. Shit. Right. That's way past "Can I freelance?",' he says. 'I suppose I don't have any choice.'

'None of us do, sweetie,' she says.

'Okay, let me think about this,' he says.

'Nothing to think about, sweetie,' she replies. 'You can go with our blessing and pockets of dosh, or you can just go. The lawyers say it's a sackable offence.'

Xander falls silent. With no Plan B, no bargaining chips, he has nothing to say. He knows Stella well enough to guess that she has already considered and rejected any arguments he might have had.

'Do you have any idea who would want to do this?' she says, the aching silence proving too burdensome. 'And how they got a hold of your files?'

'Someone broke into my flat the night before Pete died, remember?' Xander says, deciding not to tell her about his more recent encounter with the Russian.

'One of Vella's crew, do you think?'

'Maybe. Probably not. Who knows?' He knows exactly who did this even though he's not sure why.

'And are you okay? Are you safe?' she says, concern colouring her voice.

'Yeah, all good, Stella,' he says. 'Just working out what to do about Pete's funeral.'

'Well, be sure to give us plenty of notice. Everybody will want to be there for it.'

'Could be tricky,' Xander says. The thought of endless consolations and rose-tinted recollections sinks to the pit of his stomach and instantly firms up his plan. 'I'm thinking of here, in Tassie.'

'Okay,' she says, disappointed. 'You could always arrange a memorial service here.'

'Yeah, or just a wake, maybe. That's more Pete's style,' Xander says. 'Anyway, I guess you don't need me back there any time soon.'

'We'll look after you, Xander. Anything you need,' she says.

Except a job, Xander thinks but says, 'Thanks, Stel, appreciate it,' and hangs up.

***

The 762 bus from Launceston to Mole Creek operates once a day in either direction, transporting country schoolkids to the city and back again. Having decided to return the hire car and start using Pete's ancient Volvo, and with Althea unlikely to be in any mood to offer transport, this is the cheapest way for Xander to get to Mole Creek where Pete's car is parked outside the cottage. Xander opens his laptop and manages to zone out most of the squabbling and giggling around him but can't avoid the gaze of an Asian girl who has knelt on the seat in front of him and is peering over the backrest. He guesses she must be between twelve and fourteen years old or she wouldn't be travelling to senior school.

'Wotcha doin'?' she asks.

'Working,' he replies.

'Wotcha workin' on?'

'A report,' he lies.

'What's the report about?' she asks.

'Annoying kids on school buses,' he answers.

'Bullshit,' she says.

'And kids who swear,' he says.

'Are you doing a report on me?'

'As we speak.'

'But you don't know who I am.'

'Facial recognition,' Xander says. 'I secretly took a picture of you.'

'No, you didn't.'

'I did.'

'Show me!' she says, still unconvinced.

'Can't.'

'Why not?'

'It's private,' he says.

'But it's my picture, so it can't be private,' she protests.

'No, it's your face, but my camera, my laptop, so it's *my* picture,' he explains.

'That is so fucked,' she says.

'Don't ever get famous, kid,' he says.

'Yeah, but I'm gonna be famous,' she responds.

'For what?' Xander replies.

'I dunno,' she protests. 'I haven't decided. Gimme a break. I'm just a kid.'

'Okay. Good luck with that.'

'Are you a . . .' she hesitates over the word, drawing its strands together. 'A pedophiliac?'

'Paedophile,' he corrects her.

'Yeah, that.'

'No,' he says. 'Why do you ask?'

'My mum says pedo . . . whatevers are old men who take pictures of kids like me.'

'I'm not old,' Xander replies.

'How old are you?' she asks.

'Thirty-four,' he replies.

'You're old,' she says, turns around and slides back into her seat.

Xander feels positive and amused for the first time since he got to Launceston, even when the bus stops in Deloraine and his new friend and her buddies gather near his window, point at him in unison and chant 'pedo ... pedo ...' like a soccer crowd.

As he rolls sedately into Mole Creek, his safe school-bus dawdle giving him time to think and take in the countryside, it occurs to Xander what a strange little town it is. Picturesque and laid-back, it's also teetering on the edge of nature 'red in tooth and claw' as the saying goes, not to mention its own brand of cryptozoology. Just out of town there's a giant Tasmanian devil at the gateway to a conservation reserve and visitor centre. The devil is a very real and ferocious little fucker that eats dead wallabies and other carrion, using the effective technique of a bunch of them ripping it apart, by all pulling in different directions. Just like journalists.

Then there's the Limestone Ridge Hotel – the Ridge, to locals – which is all about the Tasmanian tiger, a striped marsupial that's more dog than cat and more kangaroo than dingo, and which some people say isn't as extinct as it's generally believed to be. For starters, the pub landlady would swear on a stack of bibles that she's seen one, and no one who drinks there would ever challenge that assertion. The hotel's timber-lined walls and small side rooms take patrons back to a time when tourists travelled here to visit the caves about ten minutes further on by car. The limestone caverns speak to an era when the less conservation-minded would snap off the point of a stalactite to take home as a souvenir.

Along a track in the modestly named Sensation Gorge, the caves had been visited once by Xander and Pete, an experience Pete had declared was equivalent to smoking opium in a Saigon brothel – worth the effort for curiosity's sake but not something you necessarily needed to repeat. It's a memory that now strikes Xander as one of the few times Pete ever mentioned Vietnam.

Xander doesn't recognise any of the faces in the bar and none of them recognise him, apart from Rob the barman, a rangy skeleton of a man with a moustache that threatens to wander off on its own even as you watch his lips move. He also sports an ageing hippie comb-over, with the front hair grown long and pulled back into a ponytail to hide an exceedingly unhip bald patch.

'Sorry about your pop,' Rob says, his lilting accent having more than a whiff of the Welsh valleys to it. 'Can't believe he ...' He stops, there are no euphemisms that won't seem patronising, insulting or both, so he chooses not to employ any of them. 'He seemed okay. Came in every other day for lunch here, the past few weeks. Sometimes for dinner.'

Xander knows the elevated pub grub simplicity of the Ridge's menu suited Pete to a tee. 'Nothing too fancy, nothing too shit' was all he required, although his definition of 'not too fancy' embraced fish tacos and sashimi as well as the Tassie tiger pies made in the hotel kitchen. Xander presumes the contents were something other than their name suggested.

The surroundings are simple yet weirdly exotic. An over-abundance of lacquered pine is mostly obscured by paintings, posters, framed prints of ancient pictures and even a 3D representation of the ill-fated thylacine. This is Tassie tiger country, all right, even down to the labels on the local Cascade lager.

'You hear anything?' Xander asks Rob as he passes him the low-alcohol ale he's ordered as a concession to road rules and his liver. The barman shakes his head. 'Like, I know you hear *everything*,' Xander says.

'True,' the barman replies. 'But nothing on Pete. Sounds pretty straight up and down,' he says as he goes off to serve another customer at the far end of the bar.

The chalkboard specials menu on the wall announces the soup of the day is pumpkin. Always fucking pumpkin, all the time, everywhere, but, inspired by the blackboard, Xander wonders where he could get hold of a whiteboard, just so he could map out all the tangled strands of this mystery.

'Hey, Rob,' Xander asks the barman as he passes with a tray of freshly washed glasses. 'Does the name Alden mean anything to you?'

'Ooooh, Alden?' Rob says, thinking aloud. 'Maybe. Not the kind of name you'd forget, but, no, I can't place it.'

'Yeah, I feel the same,' Xander says.

'There was one odd thing, the other day, now that you mention it,' Rob says. 'Tall bloke with a strong Queensland accent came in asking if Pete ever worked here ... you know ... writing or whatever he was doing. I told him he always sat at that table over there, near the power point. Nothin' there now, of course. But I always said to Pete, he should get a laptop with better batteries ...'

'And he said, belt and braces, right?' Xander ventures.

Rob nods and smiles. 'Exactly,' he says. 'We're having a chat and this bloke is asking if Pete ever left his laptop here, like, for safe-keeping, and I'm saying not to my knowledge. And this Asian woman comes in and he's like, gone. Outa here like a stiff breeze. Coulda been a coincidence but ... I dunno ... it looked like he spotted her across the bar.'

'Asian woman?' Xander asks.

'Totally,' Rob replies. 'Small, but. And fully kitted in motorbike leathers. I mistook her for a kid at first. Almost asked her for ID, then, like, I realised she was about my age, fiftyish, maybe older.'

Processing the connection between the Asian woman who claimed to be his aunt at his hotel, and the one he'd bumped into in Launceston, and the biker who'd interrupted his chat with the man who was looking at his car at the gas station, Xander falls silent.

'You all right, mate?' Rob asks.

'Yeah, sure. When was this?'

'Coupla days ago. Like, when you came back to the cottage, I s'pose.'

Xander slips back into his thoughts. The Russian, the Vietnamese woman, and Pete. Obviously there's a strong connection. Xander's clear distraction with weightier concerns has Rob scanning the bar for customers. To the barman's relief, there are a couple of rescuers, both holding up $50 notes to get his attention. Raised eyebrows and a nod are his wordless farewell as Xander takes a sip from his beer and decides that no drink is better than something that's halfway to nothing, settling the schooner precisely back on the ring it had left on the bar.

Back at the cottage, Xander steels himself to go in but can't. There are too many memories in there for him to cope with right now. He grabs the car key from its usual hook on the back of the front door as he decides to return to Launceston, check out of the hotel and come back with all his gear and clothes. Maybe he'll be ready by then. The Volvo's starter briefly whines its protest at being awoken from its long slumber but once it gets going it's a pleasant enough drive back to Launceston, although it brings back too many raw memories of Pete. The road to their hiking track. The real estate agent's window where they first spotted the cottage. The supermarket where they argued over the relative nutritional value of instant pot noodles over packaged macaroni cheese kits. These recollections sting his eyes but Xander is in no hurry to let them go, or to get back to town, unlike the idiot in the black SUV behind him. Lights flashing, horn beeping, the 4WD keeps surging towards his tail, pulling back only when its grille seems to fill Xander's rear-view mirror. The road is a strand of twisty climbs and dips punctuated by the occasional short straight stretch. Xander is reluctant to pull over just to let an entitled psycho in a Range Rover go past, but peace and quiet come at a price.

'All right, all right, keep your hair on,' Xander mutters, as he slows down on the first stretch of straight road that he comes to, allowing the more modern vehicle to pass. Only, instead of racing off to the next corner, the vehicle slews in front of Xander's car and stops, forcing Xander to stand on the brake to avoid slamming into the Range Rover or the ditch.

The Volvo stalls and shock freezes Xander momentarily, processing what just happened and how close he came to a serious accident, when he sees a tall, thin man coming round from the driver's side. He's dressed in a long black coat like a character from *The Matrix*, but incongruously has a tourist beanie, complete with an embroidered slogan promoting Tasmania, pulled down over his ears.

Thinking, not thinking, that he is about to apologise, Xander turns the handle and lowers his window.

'What the fuck do you think you're doing?' Xander says. 'You could have ...' His final words are stopped in mid-syllable by a leather-clad fist punching him in the mouth. The pain immediately brings tears to Xander's eyes and that's when he sees the plaster across the bridge of his assailant's nose, only partially covered by aviator shades. Finally, he notices the gun pointed straight at him. Xander doesn't know much about cars but he's guessing a thirty-year-old Volvo would not have bullet-proof doors or windows.

'That's for last night,' the man says in a familiar Eastern European accent that Xander is now sure must be his real voice. 'Now hand it over or tell me where it is or I start with kneecaps and move on to elbows.'

Xander's head is still reeling from the punch but he knows this is no time to be a smartarse.

'Do you mean Pete's laptop?'

'No, a signed copy of your last shit book,' the man says. 'Of course I mean your grandfather's laptop.'

'I don't have it.'

'Wrong answer,' the man says, pulling back the pistol's slide to chamber a round.

'But I think I know where it is ...'

'Keep talking ...'

'Well, not where it is but who has it.'

'Name?'

Xander momentarily toys with the idea of giving Althea's name to lead the Russian into a trap, but he couldn't live with himself if she came to any harm.

'Wait!' the man says. 'First you give me your car keys, your phone and my gun. Very slowly and grip-first or I start shooting like an American traffic cop.'

'Sorry, no can do. I handed your gun into the cops,' Xander lies.

'Seriously?' the man says. 'Do you know how fucking hard it is to get a silencer in this country?'

Xander shrugs. 'I don't really do guns,' he says almost apologetically. 'Anyway, you seem to have another.'

Xander slowly reaches for his car key, from the ignition, and then his phone, in the central console of the car. He hands them to the gunman, who hurls the car key into the scrub beside the road and then punches a number on Xander's phone. One of his pockets buzzes then stops. He hands Xander's phone back to him.

'Now you have my number,' he says. 'And I have yours. Now, who has the laptop?'

'Alden,' Xander says.

'Alden?' the man says, as if he knows the name. 'This is no time to be taking the piss.'

'Okay, then maybe it's the Vietnamese woman who's been stalking me,' Xander says.

'Fucking bitch,' the man says, shaking his head. 'She's not stalking you, she's stalking me, idiot,' he says, pronouncing it *eedi-yoat*. 'Everywhere I go, she turns up. I thought you were supposed to be some shit-hot researcher. You are useless at even being you.

I should just kill you now, do you a favour, save you from a life of failure and disappointment.'

The man Xander now mentally calls the Russian shakes his head in frustration, then opens the car door. 'Get out of the car.'

'You can't kill me,' Xander says. 'Then Danzig would know for sure Pete didn't kill himself and you'd never get off the island.'

'Danzig? Pah!' the Russian says, smirking dismissively. 'Danzig is shit-for-brains, very shit-for-brains. Out of the car!'

'If you're going to shoot me, you need a plan, like you had for Pete,' Xander says as he slowly swings his legs out of the vehicle and stands. 'Something to cover your tracks.'

The Russian takes a step towards Xander, clenching his fist, clearly thirsting for revenge. But he stops. Perhaps he doesn't want to get too close again, now that he knows Xander's capabilities. But then he hears the rumble and purr of a motorbike that rolls to a stop about two car lengths from them.

It's the biker kid from before, or more precisely, the woman who claims to be his aunt. Slowly she unzips her leather jacket to partially reveal what looks like pale-grey metal armour but Xander quickly realises is the fake brushed aluminium of a laptop case pressed against her chest.

The Russian raise the pistol and points it at the rider's head. The momentary hesitation as he calculates his chances of making a clean hit through the motorbike helmet is enough of a delay for Xander to grab his arm, twist his wrist and force him to drop the gun. But this time, before Xander can kick it away, the Russian stands on it and they are reduced to what is effectively a standing arm wrestle.

The motorcyclist watches briefly, then zips up her jacket, clicks the bike into gear and roars off in the direction of Launceston. Infuriated, the Russian finds an extra boost of energy and pushes Xander over, grabbing the gun from under his own foot. He points it at Xander while anxiously watching the motorbike disappear around a corner.

'You can't even *hurt* me, or anyone else, or the cops will have to take me seriously. And then what?' Xander says. 'Looks like you are fresh out of moves, buddy. Or should I say "Alden"?'

'Fuck! You are the most stupid …' The Russian runs out of insulting epithets. 'We are not finished, you and me. Not even close.'

Then he sprints off to his 4WD, doubtless knowing he has little chance of catching the motorbike, which is already out of sight, but obviously feeling he ought to at least try. 'Good luck finding your keys,' he says over his shoulder.

Xander watches the SUV lumber into the first bend before he starts looking in the sun-scorched scrub. It takes no more than fifteen minutes and Xander is halfway back to Launceston before he realises he should tell Althea about all this. He pulls over and calls her but gets no response. No surprise there. She'll be telling some old dear that Tasmania's finest will do their best to find her cat. Even if she isn't, she might not want to talk to him. Should he call Danzig? What's the point? The station commander has already pigeon-holed him as an overwrought relative. And these stalkers – the gunman and the Asian woman who has the laptop … or *a* laptop … are operating on a whole different level to your average Tasmanian toerag.

Instead, he pulls over and writes Althea a long text – three in fact, due to the word limit on his phone – and heads back to his hotel, obsessively checking his rear-view mirror for SUVs and motorbikes. Should he duck and run back to Sydney? Or should he pursue the most intriguing mystery he's encountered in years, and one that has dropped right in his lap?

'Don't let fear hold you back,' he hears Pete say. Quickly followed by another of his well-worn aphorisms: the easiest way to get an answer is to start asking questions.

Pulling into the Abernethy Hotel carpark, the Volvo stops with a judder and sigh. The old beast hasn't been serviced in years. Pete said the car was like an old lady who was convinced she had cancer but wouldn't go for a test because as long as she wasn't tested, she didn't have it. As long as the Volvo's engine kept turning over, then it wasn't dying, Pete reckoned. He called the car Cleopatra, Queen of Denial.

Xander is heading for the back door to reception, where he has left all his gear, when he hears footsteps and what sounds like a man screaming 'ca-a-a-a-a-a-nt'. Then there's a thud that he feels rather than hears, then darkness.

CHAPTER 15

'Do you have any idea what's really going on in Soul Alley?' Pete asked Donnie before the American had even seated himself on the other rickety bentwood chair at Pete's table. Between them was a slightly skewed stack of bulging manila file folders.

'I told you. It's a no-go area,' Donnie said, signalling to Lucy to bring two drinks.

'That would explain all this,' Pete said, gesturing to the folders. 'Drug dealing, selling arms to the enemy, prostitution, people trafficking, deserters, pimps, and the cherry on the cake: money laundering.'

'Who says?' Donnie replied.

'Your lot do. I asked our Intelligence guys, they asked your Intelligence guys and this is what we got,' Pete said. 'It's Sodom and fucking Gomorrah, there.'

'Allegedly,' Donnie said, taking his turn to gesture to the folders. 'There is no proof or we'd be through there like shit through a pig. And we gotta let our Black brethren have somewhere to let off steam or there would be riots. We get enough of them back home.'

Pete looked at the files, opened a couple of them and scanned their top sheets, then shook his head. 'Right under our fucking noses,' he said.

'Sometimes you have to choose not to see what you see, not to smell what you smell,' Donnie said. 'What else is on your mind, Pete?'

'Major Tang came by again,' Pete said.

'What did he want?' Donnie asked.

'He started off asking if we'd read the Pentagon Papers,' Pete says. 'He was almost smug. "Hoist on your own petard," I think was his actual phrase.'

Back in the USA, the *Washington Post* had been carrying stories on a massive leak of state secrets that had exposed decades of lies by the American government to justify the war – the one in the middle of which Donnie and Pete found themselves.

'I read 'em back in DC before anyone even knew they existed,' Donnie said. 'It's shit-ugly embarrassing.'

'Shit-ugly embarrassing,' Pete said, tapping the pile of folders. 'Like this. Imagine if all this crap about Soul Alley got out.'

'Don't even think about it,' Donnie said. 'If all the moms and dads in America knew what their boys were up to ...'

'Copy that! And when are we going in?' Pete asked.

'I don't get you ...'

'We said a week,' Pete said.

'*You* said a week,' Donnie said. 'I said I'd see what I can do.'

'Okay, but if you don't do something soon, I'm going in myself.'

'Okay ... okay! I'll set it up,' Donnie said. 'We'll go in like tourists and hope we come out alive.'

Pete looked at the stack of folders and shook his head. 'This war does strange things to people,' he said eventually.

'All wars do,' Donnie replied. 'It doesn't take long for the thin veneer of civilisation to be stripped away.'

'What I don't get is the level of cruelty,' Pete said.

'Theirs or ours?' Donnie asked, flicking over the cover of a folder and wincing at a glimpse of its contents.

'Good point,' Pete said. 'But I was thinking of them. I heard they bury traitors alive – or people accused of helping us – rather than wasting a bullet on them.'

'"They" being Charlie?' Donnie says. 'Not our ARVN buddies?'

'I don't know,' Pete replies. 'They're basically the same people. Same families, sometimes, just caught on different sides. I guess it's all that stuff about dehumanising the enemy. We do it too. Brainwashing young guys till they're ready to do the unspeakable.'

'You mean like that horror show at My Son? They're calling it My Lai in the papers back home now,' Donnie said, then, almost to himself. 'That stink isn't going anywhere, anytime soon.'

'We captured a VC kid, once,' Pete added after a pause. 'Can't have been much older than sixteen. He started crying, begging us not to eat him.'

'He thought you were going to eat him?' Donnie said, eyebrows disappearing into his flop of blond hair.

'That's what he'd been told. Don't let them take you alive – the Australians eat their prisoners.'

Donnie considered this for a moment.

'How'd he taste?' he eventually asked, with a grin, and both men laughed. In the background, Lucy shook her head and sighed.

There was a murmur of hushed conversation from the corner where a young Australian infantry officer was earnestly trying to convince a pretty young Vietnamese woman that he would come back for her. She was crying. Maybe she could tell he was also trying to convince himself.

'A lot of hearts being broken in this shitstorm,' Pete said. 'One way or another.'

'True,' Donnie replied. 'And sooner or later you have to accept that the best thing you can do is make sure it's not yours.'

CHAPTER 16

'Oh, there you are,' a nurse with short black hair with green highlights and an Irish accent to match sing-songs to Xander, as he lies in a hospital bed, trying to open his eyes while she grips his upper arm a little too tightly. 'I won't be a minute.'

Xander, who seconds before had been lost in a drug-enhanced reverie about driving Cleo the Volvo across the Nullarbor with Pete's coffin in the back, opens his eyes fully and realises the grip on his bicep is not the nurse's hand but the sleeve of a blood pressure tester, a sphygmomanometer, to give it its correct name, a trivial fact he recalls for reasons he can't comprehend. Likewise, he can't understand why he's in a hospital bed with a thumping head pain and aching sides.

'Where ... how did I get here?' Xander asks.

'Ambulance,' she replies.

'And how did I end up in an ambulance?' he says wearily.

'You were attacked by a man with a golf club.'

'Ouch! How bad is it?'

'Twenty-three stitches in a head wound. Bad enough for you?'

'Wow! Somebody really wanted to hurt me.'

'Wanted to kill you, more like,' a uniformed policeman, sitting on a chair in the corner says.

'Maybe, but I'm alive,' Xander replies, without looking up.

'You were saved, at least from further injury, by a small Asian woman,' the policeman says in a contemptuous tone that suggests it might have been better to have died.

'Jesus, will this never end,' Xander says. 'Did you get her name?'

'No,' the cop says, slightly confused. 'She left before I got there. Apparently she jumped the guy from behind, kicked him in the nuts and they both ran off.'

'And you know this, how?'

'The hotel desk clerk saw some of it. He's the one who called us.'

'Then it wasn't her who attacked me? The Asian woman?'

'Don't think so. My money is on the man seen running away with a golf club in his hands and blood all over his trainers.' The policeman didn't need to use a sarcastic tone – his words did all the heavy lifting. 'But, hey, I'm not a detective.'

'Could I get a drink?' Xander says. 'Please?'

The nurse holds a mug with a bent straw up to his lips and he awkwardly draws some water onto his parched tongue.

'Does Althea know I'm in here?' Xander asks.

'DS Burgess?' the cop replies. 'Why would she?'

'DS?'

'Detective sergeant,' the cop says. 'I thought you were supposed to be some shit-hot crime reporter.'

'I know what DS stands for,' Xander says, 'but ... fuck ... I'm confused.'

'Concussion,' says a young female doctor – at least, younger than Xander, he guesses – who enters and studies a clipboard she's pulled from a rack at the foot of his bed. 'How are you feeling?'

'Great. Terrific. Good to go,' Xander says.

'That'll be the head injury talking. And the dehydration. At least there's nothing broken, according to the X-rays, and no sign of internal injuries.'

'Look, I'm fine.'

'So you say. But you needed twenty-three stitches on the back of your head. The good news is there is no sign of fractures or swelling on the brain, but right now you need to rest.'

'I'll be okay,' Xander says but closes his eyes for a moment to spare them from the bright hospital lights, then he's gone.

***

The first face to swim into Xander's focus when he wakes again is Althea's.

'I'm sorry,' she says as he opens his mouth to speak.

'For what? Was it you?'

'For not taking you seriously. And being too wrapped up in my own shit to keep an eye on you.'

'I don't need a babysitter.'

'You think?' Althea says, gesturing to the bed and room.

'They say I was saved by the Vietnamese woman ... or at least, an Asian woman.'

'This woman?' She shows him a blurry picture.

Xander waits for his eyes to adjust then realises it's the picture that's slightly out of focus, not him, but there's no doubt in his mind that this is the same woman he bumped into on the street. He nods minimally, the action setting off landmines in his head. 'Where did you get this?'

'Concierge at the hotel says you owe him fifty dollars,' Althea says with a weak smile.

'And the guy who attacked me ...?'

'He won't get far. We have good descriptions. Skinny, spiky ginger hair, lots of bad tatts.'

Xander half-smiles.

'If it's any consolation, we now have a prime suspect – that's if it's determined that someone killed your grandad.'

'His name is Ralphie and he didn't kill Pete,' Xander says.

'How can you be so sure?'

'Because he was busy threatening me in a pub in Sydney when Pete died.'

'Oh,' she says. 'Well, that's only going to confirm Danzig's theory that this whole business was imported from the mainland. We'll get him when he tries to leave – unless he has some way of getting on a fancy yacht, which I doubt.'

'Don't be so sure. Ralphie is a low-rent crim but he's well-connected,' Xander says. 'Hey, the cop who was in here before said you are a detective sergeant.'

Althea stops, open-mouthed.

'Are you?' Xander asks.

Althea sags and sighs with a weary smile. 'I used to be. But I overreacted when a senior colleague put the hard word on me.'

'You reported him?'

'No, I kneed him in the nuts and cuffed him to the roo-bar of his four-wheel-drive. Calling me DS, pretending they forgot I got demoted, that's their way of taking the piss.'

'In-jokes,' Xander says. 'All about inclusion and exclusion.'

'Listen to you, Sigmund Freud.'

Xander touches his heavily bandaged head. 'Got a mirror?' he asks.

'You don't want to see. It looks like a half-arsed attempt at a turban.' A pause. 'I got the texts you sent before your … incident,' Althea says, then lowers her voice to a whisper. 'We picked up the gun from your hotel room. It's in safe custody now.'

'I should hope so. It's a hit man's special. Ruger Mark IV with a silencer attached.'

'Listen to you,' she says. 'I thought you said you didn't do guns.'

A red flag pops up in Xander's mind. Did he ever tell Althea that he 'didn't do guns'? He shrugs it off, putting it down to his drug-addled memory.

'I read the name on the handle and looked the rest up on the internet,' he says. 'But I can't see how the Russian would have risked trying to bring that into the country.'

'Meaning?' She looks concerned.

'The gun must have been here already. Illegal trades,' he says. 'And with Tasmania's history, that's a problem for you guys.'

'Pete brought *his* gun in,' Althea says, defensively.

'He'd have brought it on the ferry. Maybe when he brought Cleo over. Less security.'

'Cleo?'

'Cleopatra. She's an ancient Volvo estate car that we use when we're in Mole Creek. Pete parked her in the long-term car park at Launceston airport when we were both back on the mainland. It was only $40 a week to leave it there, so a lot cheaper than hiring a car when we came back.'

He registers that Althea has looked at her watch a couple of times.

'I should get out of here,' Xander says, sitting up and pulling ineffectually at the sheets.

'The doctors say you'll be good to go after they've checked you over,' she replies. 'But you shouldn't drive anywhere for a while.'

'Just as well I didn't get a chance to check out of the hotel,' he says.

'Actually, you kind of have,' she says. 'I've got your stuff in my car. I can drive you to Mole Creek or ...'

'Or?'

'Or you could come and stay with me for a few days. Till we're sure you can drive yourself.'

'Your husband okay with that?'

'We've got plenty of room and he's not my husband,' she says with a sad smile.

'Partner, boyfriend, whatever ...'

'None of the above,' she says.

'Well, I know he's not an invisible friend,' Xander says. 'The guy I saw you with in the car. Your landlord, you said – which, by the way, I didn't believe and still don't.'

Althea tilts her head and offers a half-smile.

'What?' Xander exclaims. 'Did I miss something? You live with someone. That guy I saw you with in the old Jag?'

Althea looks down to her lap.

'My former university tutor, my occasional mentor, a Supreme Court judge, a friend and, whether you believe it or not, the man to whom I pay real rent in real money,' she says. 'It suits us both to allow people's imaginations to run with our ... um ... situation, wherever they want to take it.'

'Won't he mind me being there?'

'He probably won't even notice. He's out a lot. Academics, judges and gay men tend to live in worlds of their own, and he's all three.'

'Young female cop lives with older gay judge,' he says. 'You don't read that too often in the accommodation ads.'

'He helped me out of a spot of trouble at uni,' Althea says, then falls silent and Xander senses she has already given too much away.

'Trouble?'

'There was an incident. I was dealing with a lot of guilt.'

'What happened?' he asks, hoping it sounds more like concern than curiosity.

'We ... people ... were just messing around. Girl ended up in a wheelchair. I was there, maybe I could have done more to stop it. Geoffrey stepped in.' She sighs and shrugs, changing gear. 'There's a room if you want it. Plenty, actually. No pressure.'

It's tempting. Being suddenly out of work, Xander doesn't know how many more nights in the hotel he can afford before his credit card collapses under the strain.

'You said you brought my stuff,' he says. 'I don't suppose ...?'

'This?' she says, producing the laptop from under the bed. 'Don't overdo it.'

'It'll do me more harm sitting here not able to even check the cricket scores,' he says as he removes the laptop from its case and passes her the cable so she can plug it in for him.

'Okay, I gotta get back to work,' she says, rising and turning to the door. 'Let me know when you've been freed and I'll come and pick you up.'

'Sure, yeah,' says Xander but his attention is already occupied by the log-in screen on the notebook. When he looks up again, Althea has gone. She wouldn't even have reached the car park by the time Xander calls her on his mobile.

'Hey, Althea. Can you come back for a minute? You'll want to see this.'

***

Jaidn Mulvaney can't believe his luck. Waiting at Launceston airport for his dad to get off a much-delayed flight from Melbourne, the fourteen-year-old spots what looks like a laptop sitting unattended and, it seems, abandoned on a table. He watches it for ten minutes to see if anyone comes back for it, most likely some fat businessman sweating bullets as he keeps a planeload of tourists waiting, he expects. But no one comes. People with trays laden with snacks and soft drinks, as if wherever they are going won't have 'proper' food, head for the apparently unoccupied table then veer away when they see the laptop, thinking it's a placeholder for an unusually trusting customer.

Jaidn gets himself a Coke Zero and moves to the table with the laptop on it – guarding it in case some more adventurous soul takes it before he can – waiting and hoping. Two hopes. One, its owner is already in mid-flight and isn't coming back to claim it. And two, it isn't a fucking bomb.

After the last plane that the laptop owner could possibly have been on has left, and another delay on his dad's flight has flashed on to the arrivals screen, Jaidn tentatively opens the lid of the notebook. It sparks to life and a message says it doesn't recognise his face and asks him for a password. Shit! He wishes Tina was here. Tina has a memory stick that has software on it that could open just about any password-protected computer in seconds. Or so she says. He's never seen it.

He tips the laptop up and looks at the base. He grins. Written in tiny letters on a slim piece of masking tape is '1972Minh'. Could it really be so easy? It is. Who needs Tina or her memory stick when there are so many dumb people in the world?

Once he is in, and after many furtive glances around the café looking for anyone who might have lost a laptop, Jaidn decides that, should the owner turn up unexpectedly, he'll tell them he was trying to discover their identity so he could get the laptop back to them. But it's weird. Even if that had been his intention, there's nothing there. No documents, pictures, music or emails. It's like the owner decided to leave the laptop stripped of anything of value, just for someone like him to discover and make use of. People do shit like that, he read somewhere. Random acts of kindness, they call it. He goes into Gmail but it won't let him log in, even with the password stored in the memory. Okay, Tina, he thinks, that's one point for you.

The only non-standard software on the computer is an app called Gotyaback, probably some sort of cheap antivirus he's never heard of, but it doesn't block him from hooking up to the internet via the airport's free service and watching stuff on YouTube, so he isn't too worried about it. With his oversized, over-ear, Bluetooth headphones paired with the laptop, Jaidn isn't aware of very much at all, apart from the music and booming sound effects and action on the movie he's streaming. He's certainly not aware of all the other customers quietly being ushered away from nearby tables. Suddenly the earphones are snatched off his head and a screaming man pulls him off his chair, throws him face-first to the ground and secures his hands behind his back with cable ties while six other men in airport police combat gear point very real-looking guns at him.

Jaidn goes through a comprehensive range of emotions at this point. Shock, confusion, fear, physical pain, relief at seeing his father at the edge of a crowd being held back by uniformed police, and shame when he realises he's wet himself.

*

'That location software is amazing,' says Althea. 'Maybe I should install it on you.'

They are carrying Xander's bags up stone steps into a large 100-year-old terrace house with balconies in a toney area just south of Launceston city centre and barely two blocks from the general hospital. St John's Road is a broad, tree-lined boulevard – at least at this end – and would offer a straight run from one side of the city to the other, were it not punctuated by a small park, doubtless added to divert ferry-bound truckers and local hoons.

The house, with its recently painted bright-white iron-lace balustrades, looks like a boutique hotel from the outside. Beyond its substantial oak front door it bears a passable resemblance to a trendy city flat – all white walls and polished timber floors, except with ceilings high enough to accommodate another level. The black cast-iron fireplace that Xander glimpses as he passes a room that he assumes to be the lounge, looks original. The dimmable LED downlights less so.

Althea leads him up lacquered dark wood stairs to a room at the back of the house. It contains a wide single bed – or small double – a wood and woven rush chair, reminiscent of the one in Van Gogh's painting of the room at Arles, an antique dresser and a window that's obscured by timber slat blinds. They say nothing until they are in the room and Xander, exhausted by his injury, the treatment, and the climb up the stairs, sits on the bed. Only then does he pick up the conversation, as if there had been no interruption.

'The same geo-location interface that tells the world where you are when you upload a picture, for instance, tells you where the laptop is when you can't find it,' Xander says. 'Was there anything else on the laptop?'

'Nothing so far, according to the lab boys at the station. All the folders were clean and the files incinerated, whatever that means.'

'It means there's nothing there and no trace that there ever was anything,' Xander says. 'You delete a file and it leaves a shadow that can still be read. Trash the same file and it could stay there until it's over-written by another one. Incineration pretty much wipes it clean. How's the kid?' he adds, feeling slightly guilty that he might have traumatised the boy when he alerted Althea and she passed the message on to the airport cops.

'Young Jaidn is safely at home, I'd imagine,' she says. 'The airport guys kind of overreacted – but when you think what the stakes might have been … His father was all piss and wind, threatening to sue us for wrongful arrest until we explained that boy's lucky not to be charged with attempted theft, not to mention accessory to murder.'

'Oh, so it's murder now?' Xander says, teasing.

'That was just to put the wind up him. Danzig is even more convinced now that this is all about you and not about Pete,' she says, smiling wanly. 'Dinner's at seven,' she says, dropping his backpack on the chair. 'Geoffrey would like to meet you. Don't be late, he has a thing about punctuality.'

'I thought you said …' Xander protests.

'Seven,' she reiterates. 'No need to dress up.'

***

'I understand you're a bit of a writer?'

Xander instantly parses the comment to pinpoint which word is intended to be more patronising: 'understand', 'bit of a' or the tincture of amusement behind 'writer'.

'And I understand you are a bit of a judge,' Xander says with an insincere smile.

Geoffrey Dreevers looks insulted for a moment then roars with laughter and claps his hands. 'I can see you are going to be fun,' he says.

Xander reckons Dreevers is somewhere in his sixties but with the demeanour and dress sense of someone with another decade on the clock, his white hair adding to the illusion of dodged retirement.

'Althea tells me you think your grandfather was … err … bumped off, if I may be so crude,' Geoffrey says, in a cultured Australian accent, somewhere between Barry Humphries and Clive James. Xander looks at Althea, who half-shrugs. Of course she'd have told her mentor and friend, her eyes say.

They are in the dining room, which furthers the impression that the house could, and possibly should, be a small hotel. It was certainly designed for more gracious times, with the décor tending towards art deco florid restraint rather than the Scandinavian minimalism of the rest of the interiors. Althea has cooked up a vast bowl of bucatini in a pungent puttanesca sauce so aromatic that Xander suspects it might really be a sneaky takeaway. Having checked that Xander was okay to drink after his 'incident', Geoffrey has decanted a more than passable chianti to accompany the 'whores' pasta'.

'Pete would never have committed suicide,' Xander says. 'I know you hear that all the time, but there are people, when someone tells you they took their own lives, inside you go, "oh, yeah … that fits". Pete was not one of those people.'

'And you've been attacked before?' Geoffrey says. 'I mean, since you came to Launceston.'

'I've been beaten up, run off the road, threatened with a gun ... two guns, actually, and had my flat and hotel room broken into, all by the same Russian c—' He stops before the profanity.

Althea looks at him gratefully. This is the wrong time and place for the word that's tipping the edge of his tongue.

'But then your guardian angel saved you from the thug with the golf club,' Althea says.

'Yeah, I've been thinking about that,' Xander says. 'Maybe she is my aunt, like in Aboriginal communities where they call older women auntie as a sign of respect. I know my dad was an only child. Pete would have mentioned it, otherwise.'

'Is it significant that your assailant – the one armed with guns rather than golf clubs – is Russian, do you think?' Geoffrey asks.

'I don't know,' Xander says. 'Someone trained him and I'm guessing it wasn't ASIO.'

'Guessing?' Geoffrey says. 'In my limited experience of espionage and intrigue, I find it's rarely a good idea to make assumptions.'

'All I know is this guy was a professional, highly trained, unlike the standover merchants I've encountered in Sydney and Melbourne,' Xander says.

'I see,' Geoffrey says. 'Can you think of any reason why a foreign power, and specifically Russia, or even a Balkan state, would want to kill your grandfather?'

'Not a clue,' Xander confesses. 'But then there's the Vietnamese woman who had my back. I mean, shit, is there any connection between Vietnam and Russia, apart from the fact that one of them is still Communist and the other used to be but really, really hasn't been for thirty years?'

'None that I can think of,' Althea says.

'And you have no idea who or what this is all about?' Geoffrey asks.

'I've got zip on that,' Xander says. 'Apart from the note from the Vietnamese woman. It said it was all about Alden.'

'Alden who?' Geoffrey asks. 'Or who Alden?'

'Beats me,' Xander says. 'I haven't had much time to research it. Althea says there's no one with a police record and all Google came up with was expensive shoes, a long-dead Australian theatrical manager, a character in *The Quiet American* – the Graham Greene novel – and an author of post-apocalyptic fiction.'

'Would anyone kill for a pair of shoes?' Geoffrey asks.

'Depends on the shoes,' Althea says. Both men look up at her and are met with an amused smile. Geoffrey nods to her and she starts ladling the pasta into white dishes.

'Now, do you know how puttanesca sauce got its name?' Geoffrey asks, mischievously.

'Putana, meaning hooker in Italian,' Xander says with smug satisfaction. 'I believe it was because the prostitutes of Naples' Spanish quarter could rustle it up quickly between customers.'

'That is the PG-rated theory,' Geoffrey says, nodding to recognise Xander's knowledge. 'Personally, I sway between the notions that the garlic prevented their clients from kissing them on the lips – unlikely in Italy – or that the anchovies removed the taste of sweaty Italian dick from their mouths.'

And it is at precisely this point that Xander realises the night is likely to be long but highly entertaining.

The next morning he awakes with a dusty Sangiovese dullness but having otherwise survived. His head is throbbing more from the excess of northern Italian reds than brain damage from the attack by Ralphie, at least he hopes so. Geoffrey turned out to be an amiable and knowledgeable host who, in his capacity as a part-time lecturer in criminology, had read Xander's books. There is no greater flattery, Xander knows, than having your own words quoted back at you.

'That was a night,' Xander says as he sits at an empty kitchen table and Althea unwraps the bandages to check his dressing.

'You and Geoffrey seemed to hit it off,' she replies.

'He's smart and funny,' Xander says.

'And wise,' she says. 'Do you remember him telling you to move on, drop your obsession with Pete's death.'

'Yeah, that's okay for him to say. Pete wasn't his grandfather.'

'What would it take for you to drop it?' she says.

'I dunno. I suppose, just for someone in authority to come out and prove Pete definitely killed himself,' Xander replies. 'But even then, what's going on with this Russian and the Vietnamese woman. Why Pete? Or me?'

'I made a few calls while you were still snoring and farting in the spare bed this morning,' she says. 'We now have a suspect both for your mystery aunt and the theft of the laptop. Asian woman caught on Hobart airport security video working on what looks like the same laptop that sparked young Jaidn's magpie tendencies. Same woman as in the picture the hotel clerk took. And we have a name. Trang Linh.'

'Name means nothing to me,' Xander says, frustrated. 'You got any other leads on her, like where she was going?'

'Flew to Sydney, then caught a flight to Saigon. Then we kind of lost her in the bureaucratic shitstorm of two nations' police forces that wouldn't know how to deal with each other even if they wanted to. Which they don't. I've sent you links to video files for you to look at later, in case you recognise anyone.' She shows him the gauze from the back of his head. What little blood there is on it has long been dry.

'Leave it off,' Xander says. 'Let it air.'

'You've got a bit of a landing strip shaved on the back of your head,' she says, trying to suppress a laugh.

'I'll buy a beanie in town,' he says. 'They seem to be all the rage here.'

It dawns on Xander that he and Althea are now working together, rather than her watching him while he struggles to sort the truth from useless facts. She with her empathy training, he with his journalists' cynical, best-friend schtick – they are a perfect match. 'Any relationship based on fake friendship has a rock-solid foundation of mutual distrust,' was Pete's view of close connections between cops and journalists.

The scrubbed timber table is big enough for a medium-sized commercial operation and Althea plants a large white plate containing a Jenga stack of buttered toast and a French plunger of hot coffee.

'Best I can do at short notice,' she says.

'Breakfast of champions,' he replies.

They sit side by side, each with their laptops fired up. Watching the Hobart airport videos on Althea's computer, Xander confirms that the Asian woman who stole, then abandoned, Pete's laptop is the same person who has been following him.

'She hired a motorbike,' Althea says. 'That's why we didn't pick her up in the rental car places.'

'What make?' Xander says.

Althea checks her notes. 'Triumph American?' she says, then looks unsure. 'Or American Triumph?'

'Right first time. That confirms it. She was definitely the kid on the motorbike too.'

'Good,' Althea says. 'Your stalkers are currently off the island.'

Xander responds to her broad smile with a querulous look.

'The Russian has gone too. I'm sorry I didn't read your message about him bailing you up on the road,' Althea says. 'If it's any satisfaction, they found the SUV in the Launceston airport car park. It had been stolen earlier in the week, although God alone knows how. These things have all sorts of electronic security.'

'A scanner, probably,' Xander said. 'He would have been standing near when the driver 'beeped' the car lock. His scanner would have picked up the signal and replicated it.'

'People can do that?'

'These people can. They have technology you'd only ever find in a sci-fi movie. It was the same guy I found in my room,' Xander says. 'He'd wiped my hard drives and tricked me into bricking my laptop. But he still hadn't found Pete's laptop. That's why he drove me off the road yesterday.'

'Why didn't you tell me right away?' she says.

'I tried. You weren't in a listening mood.'

'Yeah, well, shit is what happens when you're trying to be human.'

'I thought he was working with the Asian woman, at first, but no,' Xander says. 'She saved my arse twice ... and the laptop. Was there any sign of him on the airport videos?'

'No, but we know the name he used when he flew back to the mainland,' Althea says. 'Sidney Reilly.'

Xander laughs so abruptly, the coffee he's been sipping comes out of his nose. Eventually, when he's dabbed himself dry, he says, 'Fucker has a sense of humour.'

'Tell me,' she says, annoyed by his superior knowledge.

'Sidney Reilly aka *Reilly, Ace of Spies*,' Xander says. 'TV series about a real person, born in Russia, who spied for the Brits during the First World War and the Russian Revolution afterwards. Starred a young Sam Neill.'

'Are you for real?' Althea says. 'Who would know that kind of shit?'

'Someone who'd been in our cottage and wanted me to know,' Xander says. 'The DVD was on Pete's desk. And maybe they also want me to think that they're a fucking spy to mess with my head.'

'Seriously, Xander?' Althea says. 'A spy? Maybe you should leave this to ASIO.'

'I know ASIO people,' Xander says. 'These stakes are way too small. It's just a European guy, an Asian woman and a retired, now deceased, Aussie cop. Not enough in this for them. They'd flick it to the plastics and they'd put it under a pile of missing person reports. These guys dream of a big drug bust. A container full of cocaine. Great images for the nightly news.'

Althea nods. 'I know the plastics too,' she says.

The 'plastics' – the Australian Federal Police, thus named for a variety of reasons. Some said it was because of their plastic name tags, others related it to the time when they accidentally left 230 grams of plastic explosives in a suitcase at Sydney airport after a sniffer-dog-training exercise. The abandoned suitcase was later given to a woman as a replacement for a bag that had been irretrievably damaged in transit. When she handed it in to her local police station, it had to be evacuated until the bomb squad had cleared the building. Whatever its roots, the name 'plastics', and the low regard in which the force was held by 'real' cops, were unlikely to change.

'Okay, let's assume this guy is messing with your head. Why would either of these two have travelled all the way to Tasmania to steal information and kill an old, retired cop?' she asks. 'Was Pete working on some international drugs case? Or people smuggling?'

'He was fully retired,' Xander says. 'He said he was writing his memoirs, which made sense for him to be doing now. You can only write the really good stuff about people who are dead or locked up permanently. Live criminals pretty much skate, and then they hit you for defamation.'

'By the way, I checked Nopers, and there's no Alden, first name or last, with a criminal record or outstanding warrant,' she says. 'Nobody active, anyway.'

Nopers. Xander recognises the acronym: the National Police Reference System, or NPRS, allowed interstate police to check names and criminal records of 'persons of interest' across all Australian borders.

'Thanks for trying, anyway,' Xander says. 'And don't forget I've got a new admirer. Ralphie.'

Althea's phone vibrates so she leaves him to his thoughts while she checks it. She turns back to him. Eventually, reluctantly, she breaks the silence.

'Danzig wants me off the case,' she says. 'He says we can't keep the lid on Pete's suicide for much longer,' she replies, air-quoting suicide.

'Oh, so *he's* still calling it suicide? Even after all this shit with the laptops and the guy who has now attacked me twice and plans to kill me as soon as he can work out how to do it?'

'I've tried, Xander, I've really tried,' she says. 'Danzig doesn't want to entertain the idea that Pete's death was a hit. As far as he's concerned, all the other stuff is a problem you brought over from the mainland and no crime has been committed. Also, now it looks like your stalkers have flown the coop.'

'Fuck this,' Xander says. 'I'm going to see him. Tell him about the intruder and the guns. That might get him over the line.'

'He'll just dig in even more. I know him,' Althea says. 'You know, there's something weird about the way he's blocking this. Like he doesn't want to know. Let me have another shot at him first. Oh, and by the way, he needs you to do something about Pete's ... um ... remains,' Althea says.

Silence.

'Can't decide,' Xander replies eventually. 'Melbourne or Sydney? Burial or cremation? I know Pete really wouldn't give a damn. Funerals are for the people left behind, he always said. Actually, not cremation ... he was against that, carbon footprints and all that.'

'You could always bury him here,' she says. 'You said he loved the peace and quiet.'

'Yeah, I'd been thinking that too.' Xander laughs. 'It's not like he would know or care. Pete always said the thing the dead people and stupid people had in common was that neither was aware of their condition.'

'I can put you in touch with a company that specialises in low-impact burials,' Althea says.

'Low impact?'

'Environmentally responsible ...'

'Is there such a thing?' Xander asks. 'Oh, of course you would know. Sob Squad to the rescue.'

She smiles and punches his arm. 'Unless you want to be able to visit him when you go home.'

Home? Xander is not even sure where that is. His scruffy little flat in Surry Hills feels like it's been violated. He could move into Pete's place. Might have to, to sort out his stuff. He wonders if the intruder, stalker, spy, whatever, has already been through it. He'd almost be disappointed if he hadn't. At least it would be tidy. And there's the cottage.

'You know what,' Xander says. 'I reckon Pete would be happier here. Me too, for that matter. I'll check with his brief. See if he left any instructions.'

'Cool,' she says. 'I'll make some calls. By the way, the techies cracked Pete's phone ...'

'You mean they took it down to the morgue and put his thumb on it.'

There's a brief silence, then: 'They got into his phone and found this picture on it. What do you think it means?'

Xander looks at the picture on her computer screen. It looks like a man lying in the fetal position on a timber floor. He recognises the floor and the furniture, but the man's face is distorted so much by his obvious agony that it takes him several seconds before he realises he's looking at himself.

'The fucker sent this to Pete?' Xander says rhetorically. 'That's probably how he got him to send the so-called suicide note. Told him he would do me again if he didn't.'

'At least you're safe now,' Althea says. 'He's gone.'

'Am I?' Xander says. 'I don't think the Russian was working

alone. Someone here got him the gun – two guns – and he seemed to have a lot of local knowledge. Google Maps will only tell you so much.'

'Another conspiracy theory, Xander?' Althea says. 'How about I try to persuade Danzig to put a couple of detectives on the case? There's enough evidence now. You should just lie low.'

'What happens if I stop looking for these bastards but they haven't stopped looking for me?' Xander says.

'I'd better get to work,' she says after a moment. 'You can stay for a few nights more if you want, but I can't leave you in the house alone. Geoffrey would have a fit.'

'A journo in a judge's house,' he says. 'I can't promise I could resist the temptation to have a sniff around. I'll get my stuff and head back to the cottage.'

It only takes seconds for Xander to grab his gear as it's mostly still in his bags. As they leave, Althea takes a scarf from a hat stand by the front door. He sees the letters UNT and for a moment thinks that he's only seeing part of an obscenity. Althea notices his surprise.

'What?' she says, following his stare.

'Your scarf . . . UNT.'

'University of Northern Tasmania,' she says. 'You wouldn't be the first to add a letter.'

She takes the scarf off and hangs it up again. 'It's not that cold,' she says. 'I'll drop you off at the hotel and you can pick up your car.'

The look on her face as she replaces the scarf on the hook is like that of a child hiding a broken toy. Whatever the reason, he suspects he's not getting the full picture. Maybe she's dealing with her own demons, just as he is his. But now he needs to know what or who those demons are.

CHAPTER 17

Her expression when she caught him looking at the university badge nags at Xander all the way to the hotel car park, but he says nothing. What was that? She played it as another dumb joke about the lettering but there was a moment of obvious anxiety.

Driving into town for breakfast, Xander spots a sign for the library. It's only a block and a half away. The building is another effort by Tasmanian architects to contrast the faded beauty of the town's older buildings, Xander thinks as he parks near the disappointingly modernist block, its near brutalist straight lines almost offset – but not quite – by a metallic frill tumbling down one corner.

Inside, it's a different story, he discovers. Glass, timber and subdued lighting create an altogether less confronting ambience and he is already smiling as he approaches an overweight woman of about forty who is stacking books in a trolley marked 'returns'. With glasses and greying curls – not entirely natural, judging by the way they seem to move in one direction while her face goes in the other – she is a librarian from Central Casting. She is uncomfortable about her size, he notes, as she unconsciously tugs at tight points of contact of her silk floral blouse.

'Good morning, can I help you?' she asks pleasantly.

'Hi. I need to access some newspaper files,' he says. 'Do you have them here? I'm looking for the local paper, mostly.'

'We have all the newspapers,' she says. 'Going back one hundred years, some of them. Every newspaper in Australia.'

'Here?' he says, guessing the building is too small to accommodate every paper ever printed. 'Oh, you mean on microfiche.'

'Listen to you,' she says with a laugh. 'Are you a time traveller, just landed from the twentieth century?'

Xander shrugs, not quite comprehending.

'They're digitised,' she says with an eyeroll. 'Are you a member?'

'Of what?'

'Of the library,' she says.

Xander rummages in his bag for the second wallet in which he keeps his 'other' cards – things like Medicare, health fund and frequent flyer memberships. He extracts his library card and passes it to her.

'City of Sydney,' she says with a disappointed smile. 'Very colourful.'

'No good?' Xander asks.

The librarian shakes her head although her curls barely move. 'Would you like to join?' she asks.

'Sure. What do I need?'

'Are you a resident?'

'No. I mean, yes,' he says in quick succession. 'I have a cottage in Mole Creek.'

'Do you have any proof? Like utility bills? Or a driving licence with that address on it?'

He makes a show of thinking, even patting his pockets as if he might have forgotten where he put his non-existent proof of local worthiness. Then he gives up and shakes his head.

'It's okay,' she says soothingly. 'I can look something up for you if you can give me some idea.'

'All right,' he replies. 'I'm looking for some background on a local judge ... Geoffrey ... Deevers?'

The woman has gone behind the counter and has her fingers

poised over the keyboard. 'Dreevers?' she corrects him, leaning back from her computer. 'Is this some kind of joke?'

'No,' Xander says. 'Why would it be a joke?'

'Why do you need to know about Judge Dreevers?' she asks.

'I'm a journalist. I'm following a lead,' he says, half-hoping she will be intrigued by a hot-shot reporter from the big smoke. 'Sniffing out a story.'

The librarian gets up and offers Xander his impotent library card. 'Maybe you should sniff elsewhere,' she says. 'You true-crime bloggers are becoming a major pain in my substantial arse.'

'I'm not a blogger,' Xander says, genuinely offended. 'I'm a real journalist and an author. You probably even have a couple of my books here.' The librarian looks at his library card suspiciously before sitting back down and typing his name into her computer.

'Xander McAuslan?' she asks, looking up from the display on her screen. '*Killers of the Cross? Bury My Heart in Kurnell Sands?*'

'For my sins,' Xander replies, suddenly ashamed of endeavours that had hitherto been a source of pride. 'Can you help me?'

'Park yourself over there,' the librarian says, pointing at an unused computer terminal. 'It'll get you into the archives.'

As he searches for stories about Judge Geoffrey Dreevers, Xander realises that this could be a tangent that will take him to all the wrong places, but he senses Althea hasn't been entirely honest with him. He also gets the feeling that she owes Dreevers, big time, so it's worth a little exploration. Every newspaper in Australia for the last one hundred years, the librarian had said. She wasn't exaggerating and it turns out there's no shortage of information about the judge.

Sifting through newspaper files and random reports that had found their way online, Xander discovers that Dreevers was born in 1950 and, although he avoided the draft, as a student he travelled to Vietnam for a month, purportedly as a journalist on a fact-finding mission for a left-leaning organisation called Friends of All Vietnam which was later revealed to be solidly anti-war and pro-Hanoi.

Shortly after the war, he had studied for a year in Moscow on a scholarship. It turned out Geoffrey had been a member of the Communist Party all along, a forgivable misstep for a young idealist that he'd corrected when he resigned from the Friends very publicly after stories started to emerge from Vietnam of the 're-education' camps set up after the war.

Occasional op-eds in Tasmanian newspapers and articles in legal journals saw his rise through the ranks of the judiciary coincide with a steady rightwards drift politically, although clearly not too far in that direction. He was frequently described as both hard-line on violent crime and left of centre, especially in cases he was hearing that involved female or Indigenous defendants.

'All-round good bloke,' Xander says to himself. But would his Vietnam wartime connections help him get in touch with a Russian hit man? And why would he want or need to? And where did Althea fit into all this? He logs out and approaches the librarian who is busily scanning the bar codes on returned books.

'Find what you were looking for?' she asks with an engaged smile.

'Yes and no,' Xander replies. 'Why did you ask if this was a joke?'

The librarian's smile all but disappears, but she says nothing.

'I'm curious about something that happened a couple of years ago. A university prank that went wrong. It involved Dreevers and a student called Althea Burgess.'

The librarian nods.

'There's nothing about it in the records.'

'There wouldn't be,' the librarian says. 'It was all hushed up.'

'Is there anywhere I could get more detail? Find out more?'

She smiles. 'I know where the victim is, if that's any help.'

'Really? Where?'

'Right now she's upstairs reading to our Kindy Club kids. She's easy to spot. She's the one who can read ... and she's in a wheelchair.'

***

There are people with whom the fates have dealt harshly who can forgive the accidental – even deliberate – harm done to them. Tina Everista is not one of them.

'That fucking bitch Althea Burgess destroyed my life,' she says, gripping the armrest of her wheelchair as if she's worried she might explode out of it. 'And then she walked away like I was nothing.'

Her demeanour is in stark contrast to the sweet young woman who only moments before was reading a picture book about a bouncing koala to a semi-circle of enraptured pre-schoolers. Xander notes that she is unusually thin for someone who is wheelchair-bound, even those who follow carefully controlled diets. Readily accessible anger may be the answer, he concludes as she launches into a full-tilt demolition of Althea's character.

'I was the star student in our law class – straight As – and Althea was probably my best pal, but she was always, I dunno, jealous of me, I suppose,' she says wistfully, as if she is still processing the end of their friendship.

'Anyway, we were doing an end-of-term satirical sketch thing – as students do before they discover they are not the smartest people in the universe – and she thought it would be hilarious to re-enact the bucket of blood scene from *Carrie* without telling me,' she says. 'Except the whole bucket came down and broke my back.'

'You sure it was her?' Xander asks.

'We were rehearsing the skit for the end-of-term concert.

She calls out "stop" as I'm walking across the stage. I look down and there's an X marked on the floor and I look at her and she's grinning at me and then pulls a rope ...'

'And then?'

'And then I woke up in hospital and my parents were crying because they'd just been told I would probably never walk again. And here I am.' She bangs the armrests of her wheelchair for emphasis on each of the last four words. 'If she'd just said she was fucking sorry ...'

Two little girls, identical twins by the look of them, walk past with their mother. 'Bye, Tina,' they say in unison, waving.

'Bye, sweethearts,' Tina says, her fury quickly suppressed like a stifled yawn. 'See you next week.'

'Are you sure it was Althea?' Xander says after they move out of earshot.

'As sure as I'm sitting here knowing I'll never have kids of my own,' she says as the twins and their mother disappear behind book racks. 'Why else would my so-called best friend not visit me in hospital, if it wasn't because of guilt? There was another girl who looked a bit like Althea and they went after her, made her life Hell, until she very reluctantly proved that it couldn't have been her.'

'Why reluctantly?'

'At the time, she was supplementing her student loan by working in a massage parlour giving hand jobs to fat businessmen. She really didn't need that little piece of information to get out. Her parents disowned her. Another life ruined by that fucking bitch.'

'How come they didn't go after Althea?'

'They said the accident and the drugs in hospital had messed with my memory and I was imagining it was her. Also, she had an alibi. But I know ... and she knows.'

'What was her alibi?'

'She said she was with her tutor at the time and he swore blind it was true.'

'Her tutor?'

'Guest lecturer, really. He was a pretty successful lawyer. Now a judge, so he had cred with the cops.'

'Geoffrey Dreevers?'

'You've heard of him?'

'Heard of him? I had dinner with him last night.'

'Oh, shit. You're one of them ...' Tina says, turning her wheelchair and shaping to propel herself away.

'I'm not one of anyone,' Xander says, grabbing the chrome armrest support, but letting go when Tina glares at his restraining hand. 'There's a lot of strange shit happening in my life right now and I'm trying to find answers.'

'Well, you're looking in the right place,' Tina says. 'Althea is the queen of strange shit.'

'I believe you. But why would Geoffrey, a rising star in the legal profession, risk his career by covering for a student involved in a prank that went horribly wrong?'

'Beats me,' Tina says. 'Ask him or Althea. It's not sex, if that's what you think. He's gay.'

'She told me.'

Tina laughs. 'It's true, but I wouldn't take anything that cow tells you at face value.' She looks at her watch. 'Sorry, I gotta go. I have an adult literacy class and I can't be late. We're doing clocks.'

As she wheels away towards the lift, Xander tries to sell himself the story, the guts of it, twenty-five words or less.

'Gay lefty judge pulls student out of a hole and she becomes his beard,' he says to himself. 'Gonna need more than that. A lot more.'

CHAPTER 18

Xander has passed the Mole Creek Cemetery so many times he's almost forgotten it's there, tucked into the junction of Caveside Drive and the prosaically named Cemetery Road. Like Mole Creek itself, it's sparsely populated, but functional and neatly laid out, with plenty of room for new residents. The incumbents tend towards flat, polished granite slabs, and Xander briefly wonders if they are there to ward off burrowing Tasmanian Devils, if such a threat exists.

Pete's solicitor had responded immediately, with condolences and the old cop's funeral instructions, a print-out of which Xander holds in his hand.

> If you are reading this, I am more than likely dead, so you can pretty much do what the fuck you want with me. However, if I may express a preference – and assuming I have been denied my true destiny of a shallow grave on Kurnell Sands or the boot of an abandoned car – I want as little fuss as possible.
>
> No religion – that would be hypocritical, and if it turns out there is a God, she'd surely see through it. A quiet burial – not cremation, please, as I might change my mind about being dead, not to mention it having an embarrassing carbon footprint. No police or army uniforms, just family, which means my dear boy Xander and any women who've

been foolish enough to share my bed in the past few years.

Make the coffin as cheap as you can find – cardboard is good – and don't bother with a stone (on the other hand, if you can't resist, I would like the inscription to read 'He loved and lived the best he could'). I have left $2000 in my account specifically for a massive piss-up in the hostelry of Xander's choice. All welcome. Enjoy.

Pete's late-life embrace of environmentalism had surprised Xander at first, but when he realised his grandfather had lived through the decades of humanity's steepest decline into self-destruction, it all made sense. Back in the sixties, being Green had been a hippie fad, just another reason to rebel. In the twenty-first century, it seemed like the only hope for humanity's survival. Pete hadn't needed the *I Ching* to know which way the wind was blowing.

In the shadeless cemetery only the permanent residents are escaping the heat. A defiant breeze throws up a puff of reddish dust before it too lies down to rest. Xander and Althea – he in jeans and a clean T-shirt, she, incongruously and unknowingly against Pete's wishes, in full dress uniform – look on as the same mechanical digger that had prepared the ground for Pete's final resting place lowers the simple pine coffin through a top layer of clay into the cool darkness of loam beneath. Althea had explained that if Pete was concerned about his final carbon footprint, cardboard coffins weren't going to cut it as they had to be shipped from the mainland, so local recycled timber would have to do. Xander is surprised at her attention to detail, even in family liaison. He notes the last remnant of a thread that once held her sergeant stripes in place. On a second glance he can see the outline of the chevrons.

She catches his eye and shrugs wistfully. 'Life is shit and then you get demoted,' she says.

Xander tosses a handful of earth on to Pete's coffin, then pours the mortal remains of a bottle of single malt on to its lid.

'Is that allowed?' Althea asks as the cemetery workmen conspicuously look away.

'Who's going to complain?' Xander replies. 'Although Pete would have called it a terrible waste of a decent drop.'

'No doubt,' says Rob the barman, who had ridden down from the pub on what looked like a specced-up mountain bike, his ponytail streaming behind him. 'But there's plenty more where that came from.'

If Pete had truly wanted a simple funeral, his wishes are being recognised in spades. It's unsentimental and functional with this minimal number of mourners and only Althea's uniform surrendering to any notion of pomp and circumstance. Xander has seen more fuss accorded to a family pet, but he's done his grieving alone in the dark hours of the night and in moments during the day when the memories of Pete sneak up and surprise him. And he knows he has more grief to come, with the emotional tripwires of forgetting that Pete has gone, then the shock of remembering.

'Drink?' Rob says as Xander gives the workers a nod and they start filling the grave. They toss his bike into the back of Althea's 4WD and drive silently to the pub where the landlady is relieved to see them, if only so that Rob can return to his bartending duties. Althea has left her jacket, hat and tie in the car and slipped her badge in her pocket so she only looks a bit over-dressed for the pub, rather than a threat to all the drink-drivers ensconced therein.

With Rob back at work, Xander and Althea park themselves on bar stools, just to be sociable.

'Is it over now, do you think?' Xander asks.

'Is what over?' Althea responds.

'Whatever it was that got Pete killed and me attacked?' he says. 'And I don't mean by Ralphie. That's a whole other story.'

'Are you sure?' Althea asks, sipping at a non-alcoholic ginger ale.

'I'm pretty sure all this stuff with Pete and his laptop has nothing to do with Ralphie and Trackie Vella,' Xander says. 'We've got two suspects, one male, one female, both foreign, neither believed to still be in Tasmania or even Australia, for that matter. Trang Linh is back in Vietnam, and the Russian – if that's what he is – has flown back to Melbourne, under his joke name of Sidney Reilly. His final farewell fuck-you, let's hope. The files he was so keen to get his hands on have disappeared – maybe he has a copy and maybe he hasn't – and nobody really cares why Pete died or how. Except me.'

'I care,' Althea says. 'But there's not a lot I can do. Danzig is putting a lid on this and locking it. And nothing we say now is going to change anything. Nobody's in danger and there's nothing more to lose.'

'Except I'll never know what it was that Pete wanted to tell me.'

Althea strokes his forearm then squeezes it.

'It's funny when people go,' Rob says. 'You remember all the things you meant to ask them but never got round to.'

'Tell me about it,' Xander says. 'All that time Pete was in Vietnam, never told me anything about it. Not a word.'

'There's a lot of Vietnam vets like that,' Rob says. 'They don't want to talk about it because, I don't know, they must be worried where it will end up, I suppose, emotional, like.'

'I see a lot of that,' Althea says. 'People scared of their own feelings, especially men. It's not that they don't want to cry, they're frightened they might not be able to stop.'

'I feel bad that Pete never had anyone to talk to about his time in Vietnam,' Xander says, nodding from his beer glass to Rob, who pulls a clean one out of the chiller and starts pouring. Rob looks at Althea who gives the slightest shake of her head.

She's driving. 'He never went to any of the reunions or caught up with other vets. He must have been carrying a lot of pain.'

'You sure?' Rob says. 'About not connecting with other vets, I mean.'

'Why do you ask?' Xander says.

'He had a mate used to come and visit. They'd start off, like, chatting about the fishing and hunting then get round to talking about Vietnam sooner or later. And then they'd get all solemn and quiet.'

'This mate?' Xander says. 'Does he have a name?'

'Laurie?' Rob says, doubting his memory. 'No, Lorenzo. That's it, Lorenzo.'

'You listen in to everyone's conversations, do you?' Althea asks.

'Part of the job,' Rob says. 'Keeping an ear open for them as have had too much or, like, if there's a fight about to kick off.'

'You should be a copper,' Althea says.

'How do you know I wasn't?'

'Lorenzo, does he live locally?' Xander asks.

'Walls of Jerusalem,' Rob says.

'Fuck! Israel?' Xander says, prompting laughter from both Rob and Althea.

'It's a national park, south of here,' Althea says.

'I reckon Derwent Bridge was his, like, point of contact,' Rob says. 'It's about two hours down the Lyell Highway.'

'Point of contact?' Xander says. 'What does that mean?'

'Lorenzo is a funny old bugger. Living off the grid, like, in a hideaway in the bush and all that,' Rob says. 'He sometimes walked here. Ten hours it would take him, he reckoned. Maybe more.'

'I thought people weren't allowed to live in national parks?' Althea says.

'They're not,' Rob says. 'I suppose that would be part of living off the grid.'

'We could drive down, see if we can find him,' Althea says.

'Just what I was thinking,' Xander says.

'You might want to leave the cop car and uniform at home if you do go,' Rob says. 'Living alone with no contact with the outside world can make people a bit, like, twitchy with figures of authority.'

CHAPTER 19

When Donnie Carrick had accused Pete of 'sniffing around' Soul Alley, what he'd meant was that he'd heard he'd been asking questions, not that he'd actually been there. Pete had never set foot in the place, so when he and Donnie ventured in, accompanied by two African-American MPs, Dook and Poinder, all of them in civilian clothes, he looked more like a rubber-necking tourist than a military cop.

A loud Hawaiian shirt and khaki shorts was Pete's default dress code when he wasn't on official business, so he fitted in perfectly with the generally dissolute ambience of these streets and lanes filled with loud music, bright colours and exotic smells. Donnie, by way of contrast, looked ill-at-ease, as if he needed the constrictions of a uniform to be truly comfortable. Or maybe it was the Smith and Wesson tucked in the rear of his pants, like a TV version of a Miami drug dealer.

Dook and Poinder were trying, and mostly succeeding, in masking their high-alert anxiety with forced camaraderie that included much back-slapping and dapping – the elaborate ritualised handshakes that let crackers know they were excluded from whatever was going on, as if the colour of their skin wasn't signal enough.

Night this close to the equator came abruptly, as if there was one switch that extinguished the sun and fired up the neon signs imported from Thailand – like half the street girls – and the lights inside the bars and cafes. Pete found comfort in the darkness. The dark was where bad, illicit things happened, so that was where he was needed, and feeling needed was as primal an urge for Pete as food, sex and shelter was for the rest of his species.

They passed cafes with blackboards outside offering 'the best soul food in Saigon' or 'the best collard greens this side of Georgia'.

'These Viet chefs are magicians,' Dook said. 'I swear, I had the best grits I ever had right here and I don't even care for grits.'

'I feel ya,' Poinder said. 'I don't know how these guys who've never left 'Nam know what we like.'

'They got spies in the Big Easy,' Dook said, and they both laughed as they weaved their way between café tables, street food stalls and women with 'you know you want it' eyes.

The girls outside a bar called Li'l Sista were so young they made Pete feel like a truant officer. He was fascinated, entranced perhaps, that such a place as Soul Alley could even exist, when it was known to be such a den of iniquity and a refuge for deserters and criminals. But that was part of the fascination. What forces were at play here that allowed such obvious disregard for the law and social mores?

They stopped outside a bar called China Doll. From the country music sliding into the street, riding the plaintive notes from a pedal steel guitar, Pete reckoned the name of the bar had more to do with the Slim Whitman song than women from the other side of the South China Sea. But then again, maybe not.

Was that how they viewed local women? Perfect creatures that they could own, who would never give them shit? Never betray them with hearts of stone? Whatever the reason, this was clearly not a Black-only bar, which became evident as soon as they ducked under the low timber doorway and their eyes adjusted to the lack of light. The flushed and sunburned faces looking at them inquisitively, possibly fearfully, were clearly not exclusively

African-American. Neither were their Australian accents.

'Anybody here know Johnny Weighorst?' Pete said loudly, earning warning glances from his three companions. 'Australian sapper?' he continued, undeterred.

The response was almost non-existent, little more than mutters, mumbles and whispers.

'I need to find him 'cos I owe him some money,' Pete said.

'Give it to me, digger, 'cos he owes me a shitload,' said a skinny Aboriginal soldier sitting between two women at a high table topped with scratched and faded red plastic.

Pete looked at his companions and was greeted with smiles of both congratulations and irony. Got a result first time. Lucky. They moved around the Australian soldier.

'Get this man a beer,' Pete said. 'My round. And the girls?'

'You can order any shit you like for them, they'll still get Saigon tea,' the soldier said. Saigon tea, the alcohol-free, overpriced beverage soldiers were obliged to buy if they wanted female companionship in many clubs and girly bars. Dook moved to the counter. Pete noted he had cash in his hand, no wallet, just to make it harder for the pickpockets, he presumed.

'Tell me about Johnny Weighorst,' Pete said.

'He's a fucken racist, woman-hating bastard,' the Aussie replied. 'I'm no grass, but that fucken piece of shit took my girlfriend off me then beat her up.'

'Your girlfriend? Like them?' Donnie asked, looking at the girls, his tone suggesting he didn't think any relationships in Soul Alley could be purely romantic.

'Fuck you, you seppo shithead,' the Aboriginal man said. 'She was my girl. And she got beat up bad. Her sister,' he adds, gesturing to the girl on his right, who nodded.

'Hospital,' she said. 'Very bad.'

'Can I ask you your name?' Pete said.

'You can ask,' the squaddie said.

'Okay, what's your name?'

'Fuck off,' the man said, then laughed uproariously at his own joke. The girls chimed in with their tinkling geisha laughs.

'Billy Bunnerong,' the soldier said when he'd stopped chuckling. 'You after Weighorst for real?' he asked, as if it were a trade-off for revealing his identity. 'You go careful, hear. That fucker is connected.'

'Connected, how?' Donnie asked.

'Your lot,' Billy replied. 'The fucken drug dealers and loan sharks, pimps and other lowlifes you brought here.'

'Who you with, Billy?' Pete asked.

'Three Troop,' he replied.

'Tunnel Rat,' Pete said with a nod and a smile.

'My bloody oath,' Billy replied with a grin.

'Does this Weighorst come around here much?' Donnie asked.

'Sometimes, but he doesn't stay, not since he got rollin' with the big boys,' Billy said.

'And where *would* we find him?' Pete asked.

'Not here, that's for sure,' Billy said. 'These cunts, they got apartments in the city. Fancy hotel rooms. They are like Mafia, brother. Weighorst is a collector. He comes in, picks up the baksheesh from the pushers and pimps and buggers off with a couple of girls, like a fucken ghost.'

'These big boys …?'

'Yanks, Pommies, Frogs, Russkies …'

'Russians? Are you serious?' Pete asked.

'Serious as a dose of the clap on the first day of R&R,' Billy replied. 'It's the whitefellas that run the show here. The Yanks, none of them look like you or me,' he said, looking pointedly at Poinder and Dooks. 'We just the customers. The victims.'

'And the girls?' Pete asked.

'They the product, just like the drugs and guns. All the money goes back to whitey.'

'What you're saying is, none of this is your fault,' Donnie said, a statement rather than a question.

'Don't you be lookin' down your nose at me, you seppo cunt,' Billy said, up off his stool. 'I know what you lot do. Pick up a village girl and take her on patrol then shoot her at the end. Fucken drover's boy, ain't it.'

'That's bullshit,' Donnie said, suddenly looming over the much smaller Australian.

Billy took a half step forward but one of the women grabbed his arm and whispered in his ear. He smiled and nodded.

'Look, boys, I'd love to help, but I'm on a promise here,' he said to Pete and Donnie. 'It's been a pleasure but yarnin' to you ain't gunna compete with what they're plannin'.'

'What about Weighorst?' Pete asked.

'Kick down enough doors and you might find him. Kick down too many and you never will.'

And with that he was dragged into the dark recesses of the bar, putting up only token resistance to the girls' abduction before the trio was enveloped by the smoke and gloom of the interior.

'What now?' Pete asked. 'We know Weighorst is around.'

'Well, we sure as Hell won't be kicking down any doors,' Donnie said, to assenting nods from Dook and Poinder. 'We have no idea of how high or deep this goes.'

'How deep can it go?' Pete asked.

'You mentioned the Tunnel Rats. Are you familiar with the Cu Chi tunnels, up in the iron triangle?' Donnie said.

Pete nodded. 'Heard about it. It was our sappers discovered it.'

'So they say,' Donnie said. 'Level on level, and just when you think you've got to the bottom of it all ... another damned level. It's like that here, dealing with the locals. And when they start talking to each other ... It could be in Enigma code.'

'You've got interpreters,' Pete said. 'Like we have.'

'Some of them tell it straight, some of them leave stuff out, some of them tell us complete bullshit because they're on the other side,' Donnie said. 'It's what you or I would do if some other asshole country invaded ours.'

'What happens now?' Pete asked. 'I have a feeling Weighorst will already know we're here.'

'For sure,' Donnie said. 'And that means we'll see him when he wants to be seen and not before. Like I said, I'm not about to re-enact the Civil War here just for the sake of one Australian deserter.'

'Fair call,' Pete conceded. 'And right now?'

'We find a bar with some brothers in it, drink beer, eat soul food, listen to some decent music and go home and work up a plan,' Donnie said. 'No doors will be kicked by these boots tonight.'

'Amen to that,' said Dooks.

'All of it,' said Poinder.

'And you can tell me what the Hell a drover's boy is,' Donnie said.

CHAPTER 20

There is something about driving a reasonable distance, stuck in a vehicle with someone, even someone pathologically reticent, that can lead to unplanned honesty, Xander thinks as he and Althea navigate the twists and turns of the road up into the mountains and south towards Derwent Bridge. A motor car, a metal and glass capsule hurtling at inhuman speeds, isolated by speed and technology from the world around it, can be like a travelling confessional. Proximity leads to intimacy in a cocoon of silence. Unheard and unobserved, disturbed only by road rumble and music from the playlist on the phone of whoever got to the Bluetooth feed first, or in the case of Cleo's ancient dashboard, the cassette player. Xander knows all about car-seat confessions, having used them many times himself in the past. 'Let me drive you to your next meeting ... or lunch ... or assignation ... or flight ...' and often enough the previously uncommunicative passenger can't wait to unload everything they've been trying not to say, trusting the seclusion and the illusion of privacy. Maybe it's simple logistics – you can't replace words with facial expressions when the person you're talking to is looking in the same direction. Eventually the silences get too awkward for most people.

'I've never heard you mention a partner,' Althea says, as she slows too much for a corner that wasn't as severe on the way out as it seemed on the way in.

'That's because I don't have one.'

'No wife, girlfriend or boyfriend? Right now, or never?'

'Are you checking me out?' Xander asks, amused.

'I'm checking that a friend has someone to talk to after their grandfather died,' Althea says as she slows and manoeuvres round some days-old roadkill.

There's a long wordless interval, filled by Tom Petty and the Heartbreakers' 'Won't Back Down'.

'Fuck, your music is so *old*,' Althea says eventually.

'Not my music, Pete's,' Xander says. 'But if you want to play yours, you have to let me drive. That's the rule.'

Another wordless musical interlude follows. 'Tom Petty's estate sued the Trump campaign for using this song at rallies,' Xander says eventually.

'His estate?' Althea says.

'Yeah, he died of an accidental opioid overdose,' Xander says. 'Ironic when you think. Anyway, his people told Trump's people they didn't want the song used to promote Trump, because Tom Petty fucking hated him and all he stood for. But Trump's people said the stadiums have the right to play it cos they paid for it, so fuck you.'

'And this is important, why?' Althea says.

'Because it proves that you can't always get what you want,' he laughs. 'The Stones sued him too.'

'People don't vote because they like a song,' Althea says. 'If they do, we are all screwed if Abba ever run for office.'

Another silence. Then . . .

'I've had two serious . . . um . . . as in, long-term relationships in my life,' Xander says. 'One was with a journalist, the other was with a cop. Both women. In that way, if no other, I was consistent.'

'Were they similar? I mean, personalities?'

'Apart from in one regard, they could not have been more different. One was studious, serious, political and committed.

The other was a piss-pot party girl who just wanted to have fun.'

'The cop, right?'

'Saying nothing,' Xander replies, saying everything.

'Why'd you break up with them?' Althea asks. 'Or they broke up with you?'

'I couldn't live up to the ideals of the political one and I couldn't keep up with the excesses of the other woman.'

'How long have you been rehearsing that line?' Althea says. 'And what was the one thing they had in common?'

'They both wanted to fix me. Make me more positive, less cynical and reckless. They didn't realise that being cynical doesn't mean you are broken or unhappy. It just means you have low expectations, which is fine because you are rarely disappointed.'

'And reckless?'

'I'm like Tom Petty ... I don't back down.'

Althea looks at his face to see if he is joking and almost drives onto the verge.

'That's the trouble with these travelling confessionals,' Xander says. 'You'd better have said your prayers.'

'Aren't you Mr Quotable Quotes,' she says.

'It's my job,' Xander replies. 'Okay, your turn.'

She thinks and sighs. 'As you know, I'm sharing a house with Geoffrey. He's lovely.'

'And a Supreme Court judge, you say, which is awesome ... and kind of unexpected.'

'It is.' She smiles as Linda Ronstadt hits the heartbreak notes on *Desperado*. 'Both.'

'I saw you arguing in the car, outside the police station?'

'Oh, you saw that,' she says. 'It was nothing ...'

It was *something*, but Xander doesn't press the issue. They have at least twenty-four hours together and now is not the time to start exploring cracks in their relationship, such as it is.

'How did you hook up with Geoffrey?' he asks, aware that he's planting a landmine.

'You know, police forces can be old-fashioned and sexist organisations, and this one is no exception,' she says eventually. 'Dating colleagues can be high-risk – it can get very ugly, very quickly if it doesn't work out, and you can't be too stand-offish or you get tagged a snob or a dyke. Or both. And while being seen as gay is no big deal, it leads to confusion with the women who really are gay,' she continues. 'It's just not fair on them, or you. So I went for the oldest trick in the book – a marriage of convenience, you might call it.'

'You're married?' Xander says. 'Okay. Wow!'

'We're not,' she says with a laugh. 'I'm living with an older gentleman who just happens to prefer the company of young men and doesn't want everyone to know it.'

'Even in this day and age?' Xander asks.

'He's old school. This was the last state to legalise homosexuality, remember? And before they did, he was heading for what turned out to be a stellar career in law. He's made it now, but some habits are harder to shed than others.'

'You are his beard and he is your ... what?'

'Like I said, my landlord ... and dearest friend.'

The road from Launceston to Derwent Bridge passes through patchwork farmland overprinted with giant circles from rotating irrigation pipes. Then, just after the Poatina hydro power station, to the west of Great Lake, it zig-zags brutally up into heavily forested hills. Althea drops a gear to take the bends at survivable speeds, ever aware of the potential for traffic coming the other way, especially trucks and motorbikes that might have underestimate the effect of gravity. Xander, normally impatient with slow drivers, doesn't mind her caution. This is her patch, after all, and these are her roads.

Derwent Bridge isn't so much a holiday village as a launching pad for trips into the surrounding bush to access the numerous lakes and hiking trails that lie in every direction. It boasts a couple of cafes that sell basic but hearty meals, a pub that is fundamentally a drinking barn trying to elevate the cuisine to something approaching city restaurant standards, a small gas station with a shop, some upmarket chalets, and a scattering of powered sites for caravans and motor homes. This is not the kind of place you go to sit around the pool all day, especially since there isn't one. This is where people go to sleep after they've hiked the hills and fished the lakes. There are a few motorbikes too, some high-clearance, all-terrain jobs and a couple of low-slung tourers, although none are the Triumph ridden by the Vietnamese woman, Xander notes to his relief, before he reminds himself that she has fled the country.

'How do you want to handle this?' Althea asks as they enter the extravagantly vaulted cathedral of the Derwent Bridge Explorer Hotel's bar, lounge and restaurant.

'This?' Xander asks.

'When we ask questions, am I a cop or are you a journalist? Or both? Or neither?'

'We could say we are on our honeymoon,' Xander suggests, with a sly half-smile, knowing it will rile her.

'In separate rooms?' she says. 'Oh, and by the way, that ain't changing.'

'I'll tell them we had a fight,' Xander says. 'Because you wouldn't let me drive.'

Althea rolls her eyes and sighs.

'We'll just tell them we're looking for friends of Pete's,' he says, now serious. 'Passing on the bad news.'

'That's a plan,' Althea says as they reach the bar, where a gauntly striking young woman wearing a checked flannel shirt open over a white singlet waits to serve them. Her nose ring and straight, black goth hairstyle give her a contemporary but timeless look. Her broad smile speaks to North American dentistry and self-confidence. Chloe turns out to be Canadian, just there for the season, working her one-year extension to the tourist visa that foreigners get if they take a job in the boondocks for a few months. She hasn't heard of Lorenzo and doesn't know any Vietnam vets, although a bunch of them came through on a motorbike tour a couple of weeks back.

'Something you never forget, 20 seventy-year-old psychos,' she says. 'Starting like they're going to drink the pub dry – all bullshit and bravado – then falling asleep in the lounge after dinner. But kinda sweet and polite. Asked me if Canada had troops in Vietnam. I said I didn't know but there's a lot of Vietnamese in Canada. They seemed to like that.'

'Any locals join them?' Xander asks.

'Are there any?' Chloe asks. 'Are any of the locals really local? Not many born and bred in Derwent Bridge, from what I can tell. Most people here are passing through. Whether it's for two hours, two days or two years, nobody's here to stay forever.'

She spots the look of disappointment that passes from Xander, to Althea and back again. 'This person you're looking for ... what was the name again?' she asks.

'Lorenzo,' Xander says. 'Vietnam vet, friend of my grandfather. My late grandfather.'

'Recently late,' Althea adds.

'A walking oxymoron,' Chloe says, handing them their drinks, Cascade lager for Xander, a prosecco for Althea. 'Oh, and sorry for your loss. That was inappropriate.'

'You're not a full-time barperson, are you?' Xander says.

'Bar person? You're clearly not from around here,' Chloe laughs. 'Majored in Film Studies at Boston. Taking a break but kinda looking for work at the same time. And, hey, if you want me to ask anyone in here that qualifies as local if they've heard of ... what was his name again?'

'Lorenzo,' Xander and Althea say in unison.

'You guys are too cute,' Chloe says. 'Newlyweds, right?'

'Not even close,' Althea says, too quickly.

'Anyway, enjoy your drinks and I'll see if anyone has heard of your friend,' she says and heads back down the bar, collecting empties as she zeroes in on another customer.

Xander and Althea take seats opposite each other on the heavy timber benches at even heavier tables scattered randomly across the room. If the Limestone Ridge Hotel was a frenzy of pine, this is a former forest of dark and heavy hardwood. The furniture, the bar, walls and ceilings are ironwood, or cheaper timber stained to look like it. A thick noise-absorbing carpet prevents it from being an echo chamber. A log fire crackles away in a brick fireplace and chimney in the centre of the room, prompting Xander to immediately search for sprinklers in the web of criss-cross rafters in the ceiling. A CD jukebox sits neglected in the corner, the room's only concession to plastic and chrome. The vintage advertising signs on the wall are more rust than metal.

'The bedrooms are pretty basic,' Althea says. 'I got us the last two ensuites.'

'I'm sure they'll be fine,' Xander says.

'TripAdvisor was hilarious,' Althea says with a chortle. 'One lady was complaining about dinner starting too late ... at 6pm. What Launceston is to Sydney, I guess Derwent Bridge is to Lonnie.'

'Launceston isn't so bad,' Xander says as he looks up and sees Chloe chatting to a middle-aged couple dressed casually in outdoor gear but not, like some of the other inhabitants of the room, as if they are about to tackle the north face of Annapurna. They look over in Xander and Althea's direction and shake their heads.

'Should we be letting her do our leg-work?' Althea says.

'She's a trusted member of the community and it's kind of

her job to talk to people,' Xander says. 'We start interrogating customers and they could all just clam up. Lorenzo is flying under the radar. Let's see what she comes up with.'

Xander and Althea are just finishing their drinks as Chloe comes past with some cleared dishes from another table.

'Nobody's heard of anyone called Lorenzo,' Chloe says. 'And it's not the kind of name you'd easily forget.'

'Okay, who's the most local of these non-local people?' Xander says. 'And I mean that you haven't asked already?'

Chloe thinks for a minute. 'There's always Johnny Spanners, I suppose ...'

'Johnny Spanners?' Althea repeats, incredulity dripping off every syllable.

'Yeah, he's been around a while. Got a little workshop round the back of the gas station. He's like a bush mechanic, I think you call them here.'

'That figures,' Xander says as Chloe smiles apologetically and hefts her tray of stained crockery towards the kitchen. Xander slips a ten under his glass and he and Althea pull their jackets tight as they exit into the chill wind and darkening skies of late afternoon in the mountains.

Passing the Kookaburra Kaffe, Xander shudders at the misspelling, and skirting round the gas station and its shop selling soft drinks, snacks, spare fanbelts, and not much in between, they hear Johnny Spanners before they see him, metallic hammering punctuated by vehement curses emanating from a lean-to shed at the back of the garage. There they find a man in his late fifties, head under the hood of an old Holden saloon car, wrestling with a wrench attached, it appears, to a bolt on the side of an engine. He taps the wrench with a hammer and it slips off its seating. He curses in what sounds like German, retrieves the wrench, then notices he has visitors.

'Mr Spanners?' Althea says.

'It's Spangler,' he replies in a medium-strength German accent. 'And you are?'

'My name's Xander. Xander McAuslan,' he says. 'And this is Althea.'

'Okay, now I know your names, but I still don't bluddy know who you are,' Spangler says. 'Enlighten me, please.'

'We are looking for someone,' Xander says. 'Lorenzo?'

'Two questions,' Spangler says. 'Why are you looking for this ... Lorenzo, is it? And why are you asking me?'

'Lorenzo was a friend of my grandfather, who has recently passed away,' Xander says.

'And we were told you've been around here the longest,' Althea continues.

'By the same bluddy person who told you my name was Spanner?' Spangler says.

'Sorry about that,' Althea says.

'It's okay. Sometimes I am Spangler, sometimes I am Spanner,' he says. 'When I first came here people got my bluddy name wrong then they thought Spanner was my nickname because I am mechanic, so I became bluddy mechanic, so it became my nickname.'

Xander and Althea look at each other, their eyes asking the same question – how nuts is this guy?

'Anyway, I do not know anyone called Lorenzo. Sorry. Bad luck. Why do you ask?'

'We were told he was based here ... near here,' Xander says. 'Comes here for ... you know ... basics.'

'Right place for bluddy basics, that for sure,' Spangler says with a laugh, then turns serious. 'If there was someone here called Lorenzo, I would know. So sorry.'

He turns back to the engine, picking up the hammer and wrench.

'You're not really a mechanic, then?' Xander says.

'I do a bit of this and that. I know more than the people who bring their vehicles in here when they are broken,' Spangler says. 'That's usually enough.'

'Use a ring spanner. And try tightening it first,' Xander says. 'Give it a tap in the other direction.'

'You bluddy serious?'

'Just a couple of light taps,' he says. 'A trick my grandad taught me.'

'He was mechanic?' Spangler asks, taking a ring spanner out of a jumbled toolbox.

'He just knew a lot of shit,' Xander says. 'Told me he got that from a sapper – an army engineer – in Vietnam.'

Spangler looks pointedly at Xander, then attaches the wrench and taps lightly as if trying to tighten it even more. Then he reverses the effort. The bolt turns a little. He gives it a few more taps and a couple of twists, as if to make sure this trick has really worked, then turns back to Xander and Althea.

'This bluddy Lorenzo,' he says. 'Tell me more.'

'Don't know much,' Xander says. 'He'd be in his seventies and he's like ... I dunno ... a survivalist? He's apparently living off the grid in the bush near here, so it's no surprise if you don't know him. And he's a Vietnam veteran, like my pop. They were friends.'

'How long are you here for?' Spangler asks.

'In Derwent Bridge?' Althea says. 'At least until tomorrow.'

'And your bluddy name again?' he asks Xander.

'McAuslan.'

'McAuslan, same as your grandfather?'

Xander nods.

'Go and sit in the café, McAuslan,' Spangler says. 'Drink coffee, eat cake.'

'Okay,' Althea says. 'Why?'

'Just go sit,' Spangler says. 'I need some bluddy time.'

Xander can see Althea is about to ask what for, but he touches her arm and gestures back towards the café.

'Tell him Pete's dead,' he says. 'You know where we are when you want us,' and they leave, walking back through the carpark between the gas station and the café.

'Do you think he knows more than he's saying?' Althea asks.

'Maybe,' Xander says. 'Or maybe he's just on commission from the café. Sends all his customers there while he Googles how to fix their cars.'

'I can see why your girlfriends wanted to make you less cynical.'

Xander pauses briefly then walks on, purposefully looking straight ahead. 'Don't look now,' he says, 'But did you notice that black crew-cab ute with the hard top on the rear tray?'

'They all look the same to me,' she says, then looks back and spots the vehicle immediately, a massive, dark intruder in a herd of uniformly white SUVs.

'I said not to look,' Xander hisses.

'That's never worked for me,' she says. 'What about it?'

'I'm sure the driver slid down in the seat as we came past,' he says. 'I couldn't really see because of the tint on the windows.'

The Ford Ranger, the largest of all consumer 4WDs, rumbles to life behind them and they turn to watch it as it pulls out towards the exit. The driver is no more than an indistinct shape in the car's interior gloom.

'Get the number?' Xander asks.

'Couldn't make it out,' Althea says. 'The plate was caked with mud.'

'Yeah, weird,' Xander says, ''cos the rest of the truck was spotless. Maybe you can call it in, just in case.'

'With no number to give them? That'll make me popular. And we've had this discussion already ...'

'You don't have to say you're doing it for me. Just suspicious activity.'

Althea sighs and finds a number in her speed-dial list. He listens as she asks the person on the other end of the line to let her know if there is any suspicious activity related to a black Ford Ranger travelling between Derwent Bridge and Launceston. Xander catches her eye while she's listening to the response and she pouts in a way that makes something stir deep inside him. He smiles, but inwardly he's telling himself to keep his head in the game.

CHAPTER 21

It takes a couple of hours and several cups of coffee before Spangler emerges in the Kookaburra Kaffe with news that Xander and Althea have long since given up on. There are worse places to wait. The café tends towards functional rather than fancy, and to call it a family restaurant would be erring on the side of culinary romanticism, but to describe it as a roadhouse, truck stop or greasy spoon would be a serious disservice to a place that clearly has its charms. The tablecloths are, in fact, plastic sheets, protecting craftwood surfaces. But the food is dominated by thick slices of bread and generous serves of fries, all of which hit the spot, judging by the happy hikers tucking in at a nearby table.

'Just what you need after a few hours trudging across misty mountains,' Althea says as platefuls of potato wedges and burgers are delivered to their heavily sweatered neighbours.

'I was thinking what great hangover food it would be,' Xander says. 'That ute in the car park? You don't think ...? The Russian?'

'I don't recall us being tailed by a giant ute. Do you?' Althea says.

'There was no rear-view mirror on my side,' Xander replies. 'And these trucks are everywhere. You wouldn't even have noticed.'

'Maybe it was somebody who'd had a drink,' she says. 'Felt guilty or exposed when I looked at him. Simple as that.'

'Because anyone can tell you're a cop under all the fake fleece, beanie and puffed duck feathers,' Xander says with a smile.

'Maybe. I like to think I have a certain bearing.'

A gust of cold air has them look up at the entry door for the umpteenth time. Finally, the half-familiar figure of Johnny Spangler slouches in, waves peremptorily at the serving staff and joins them at their table.

'Three questions,' he says immediately, unfolding a piece of paper on which are scribbled notes that Xander can't read from his angle. He looks at Xander. 'What was your grandmother's name?'

'Kate,' Xander says immediately.

'Okay,' Spangler says, peering at his own writing as if he's seeing it for the first time. 'Ah, yes. What was your grandfather's favourite drink?'

'Laphroaig single malt whisky,' Xander replies.

'I got malt whisky but I suppose whatever you said will do,' Spangler concedes, then turns to Althea. 'And you, are you a Parks and Wildlife officer? And remember if you say no and it's a bluddy lie you can't prosecute.'

'I'm not and, by the way, that's bullshit,' she says. 'You've been watching too many movies.'

Spangler shrugs. 'Okay. I don't care,' he says, producing a larger piece of paper from his inside pocket. 'You got bluddy boots – walking boots?' he asks Xander.

'Of course,' Xander says.

'Not of course. You should see people turn up here expecting to walk the trails in high heels or ugg boots. Blokes in thongs – you'd think we were at the bluddy beach.'

Xander points to his feet. He is already wearing the lightweight hiking boots he kept at the cottage for his fishing trips with Pete.

'Okay. Here is plan,' Spangler says to Althea. 'You drive McAuslan to here ...' He points to an X drawn on the paper he'd produced earlier, a photocopy of a tourist map. 'Look for car park on left for Frenchman's Cap track. Don't stop there. Drive on maybe 200 metres where there's another sign for the bluddy track and a stopping place. Pull in there.

'You –' he points at Xander '– walk 200 metres further on to Stonehaven Creek sign then cross to north side of road and walk 10 metres into bush until you can't see bluddy road no more.

'Drop him off by 7 a.m.,' he says to Althea. 'Come back here. I will call the man you call Lorenzo – that's not his bluddy name, by the way – he does not want to see you.'

'Not Lorenzo?' Xander says.

'Is who you are looking for,' Spangler says as he bobs his head from side to side and shrugs. 'She drop you off. You walk into bush, he will find you and meet you there. You,' he says to Althea, 'drive back here. You give me your number, I will call you for picking up McAuslan.'

'When will that be?' she asks.

'When McAuslan and ... Lorenzo are done, I suppose,' Spangler says, almost revealing Lorenzo's real name. 'Maybe tomorrow, maybe day after. They tell me, I pass on bluddy message. Oh, and I need you to leave your phone with the lady,' he says to Xander. 'She don't bring it to me, no Lorenzo.'

'Is that okay with you?' Althea asks Xander.

'If you want to meet him, it better be,' Spangler says. 'If she don't come back here straight after drop-off with your phone, I don't make signal and he don't come for you. We clear?'

Both Xander and Althea nod their agreement.

'Seven tomorrow,' Spangler says, tapping the map. 'Don't be bluddy late. He won't wait.' And with that he shuffles over to the counter, picks up a takeaway coffee that's waiting for him and heads straight outside without even looking in Xander and Althea's direction.

***

The chill night air seems to carry darkness with it, rather than the other way around. Shadows lengthen and deepen gradually, but a sudden breeze drops the temperature starkly and has the denizens of Derwent Bridge, and the transient tourists, wrapping themselves tighter in their artificial second skins as if to protect themselves from the predators emerging from their lairs, somewhere in the deepest reaches of the surrounding bush. Or maybe in the next hotel room or cabin.

Xander and Althea sit by the fireplace in the Explorer Hotel lounge, the guttering flames tricking the light on their faces. They are both content in their silence, woozy from the heat, as well as their hearty meal and the drinks that preceded and followed it. Althea's passing frown catches Xander's eye.

'Are you okay with being left out of the meet with Lorenzo?' Xander asks.

'Look, to be honest, I'm kind of relieved,' she says. 'I'm a cop, remember? Even if I'm off duty, I'm supposed to report people who are breaking the law. And living in a UNESCO-listed national park is breaking the law, even if he is off the grid.'

'UNESCO,' says Xander. 'Impressive. But if not to play cop, why are you here?' he says, trying to make it sound less of a challenge.

Althea stares into the flames and takes a sip from the glass of red wine she's brought from the table.

'I don't know, Xander,' she says. 'Partly, I think, because you have been getting the runaround from ... well ... you know who. Partly because I think you might still be in some sort of danger. And partly because I'm intrigued. According to you, we've got people running around with guns, hacking computers, faking suicides, killing people.'

'According to me?' Xander says. 'You doubt it? What about the gun I gave you?'

'Sorry, I meant your side of the story,' she says. 'And Danzig says the gun is proof it was a mainlander looking for you.'

'What do *you* think, Althea? And why are you really here?'

Her silence hangs like a dull ache.

'If this is even only partly real ...' she says eventually.

'If?'

'Shit, Xander, whatever is going on here could turn out to be the most interesting thing that ever happens to me, now or ever, okay?' she says. 'But if it all turns out to be just a wild goose chase led by a grief-stricken fantasist, then you may as well take my career into the woods with you tomorrow and bury it.'

'Did Danzig tell you to come with me?' he says.

Another long silence. Eventually she looks at him and gestures with open hands, beseeching.

'Why else would I be here? But he just told me to stick with you to keep an eye on you. Keep you safe. He doesn't know about Lorenzo.'

'Good. And I think it's good that you don't get directly involved with Lorenzo or whatever the fuck his name is,' Xander says.

'Do you want me here?' she says. 'I can drive back to Lonnie right now. Slowly, though, to save the wildlife.'

'No, don't go.' He takes a deep breath, pauses. 'Listen, I met Tina Everista the other day.'

Althea looks at him and blinks once, then holds his gaze.

'Not your biggest fan,' Xander says.

'Why would she be?' Althea says. 'I ruined her life.'

'You own that?'

'I don't have any choice,' Althea says. 'But there's nothing I can do about it. I can't fix her. I can't undo what happened. It was just dumb bad luck.'

'You could apologise. Admit it was your fault.'

'Could have when it happened. Probably should have. But now, that would just open things up. Risk ruining another life, maybe another two if you count Geoffrey's reputation, and what's the point in that?'

'Is that why you stick around with Geoffrey? Because you owe him?'

'That's pretty cynical, even for you,' she says. 'I live with Geoffrey because he is the kindest, smartest man I have ever met. Some people are just good, Xander.'

'He lied,' Xander says. 'Even if it was to protect you.'

'Says the journalist who never stretched the truth,' she says. 'I lied; he backed me up. He didn't see any point in me screwing my life up over a stupid prank that went wrong. I agreed.'

Xander says nothing and looks into the flames.

'Have you never made a mistake that fucked things up for someone else?' she says. 'There must be something.'

He shrugs his concession.

'Go on,' she says.

'I once ran a story about a guy who had pled guilty to passing obscene online messages in an online chat room. Something about how he'd like to fuck a girl in a school uniform. The paper ran it under a headline that he was planning to rape a schoolgirl. According to him, he was just airing idle, if pretty disgusting, fantasies with someone he clearly thought, from the transcripts, was a 34-year-old woman. Turned out it was a hairy-arsed 55-year-old male police sergeant with a nice line in entrapment.'

'What happened?'

'The offence was using public telephone lines to plan a crime. The judge said if he'd said the stuff in public, there would have been no offence, but on the internet he was bang to rights. He found him guilty. He didn't go to jail, but he was put on the sex offenders list. His girlfriend walked out, he lost his job, his landlord kicked him out of his flat and he was beaten to a pulp in the carpark of his local pub. On a positive note, the hairy-arsed cop kept up his record of one conviction a week.'

'Even so,' Althea says. 'Come on! Wanting to have sex with a schoolgirl?'

'Two words. Chrissy Amphlett.'

'Who?'

'Lead singer with The Divinyls.' He watches her expression for any sign of recognition. 'A kind of punky pop band of the late twentieth century?'

She shakes her head.

'Big hit was "I Touch Myself", which she sang onstage – and in the videos – in a Catholic schoolgirl uniform.'

'Omigod, I know that song,' she says. Then, 'School uniform. Britney Spears. "Baby, One More Time"!'

'There you go!' Xander smiles, but it fades. 'This man whose life I helped to fuck up, okay, he could have been a bona-fide fully paid-up paedophile, but he was probably just a loser who got careless on the internet.'

'It's hardly your fault,' she says. 'I mean, he was a bit of a perve.'

'I was naïve. Turns out in just about any other jurisdiction in the English-speaking world the case would have been tossed for entrapment.'

'But it wasn't. And you could always apologise,' she says, almost but not quite keeping the sarcasm out of her voice.

'I would but he topped himself,' Xander says. 'No suicide note, just a photocopy of my story in his fist. Best I could do was run a story asking how come the cop was getting away with this.'

Silence feels like the only option and they both welcome it, especially Xander; after all, Althea belongs to a profession that mostly hates him for ruining the career of the policeman who led the investigation.

'I guess that kind of trumps putting a girl in a wheelchair,' Althea says, eventually.

'I guess it does,' he says. 'Most people, especially women, don't respond ... um ... positively to that story. "Fuck you, Xander," is pretty much the standard response.'

'I'll pay that,' she says. 'Better to err on the side of caution.'

He snorts a laugh and nods.

'What?' she says. 'Why is that funny?'

'It's not funny. Just real,' he says. 'I'm really bad at relationships so I tend to err on the side of caution.'

'In what way?'

'I pick up all the wrong signals, think there's something there when there isn't. Then when I think there's nothing ...'

'Welcome to the human race,' she says. 'You need to go with your instincts.'

'And what if they're wrong?'

'Just don't try it with friends,' she says. 'Real friends don't fuck.'

'I usually trip over my guilt long before I get to that,' he says.

'What have you got to feel guilty about?'

'I know they're going to end up feeling disappointed, like they've wasted weeks, maybe months on me, when I knew all along the relationship was going nowhere.'

'You knew?' she says, one eyebrow cocked. 'How could you possibly know?'

'Experience,' he says. 'The kind of women I'm attracted to seem to want to find a part of me that isn't there. I can fake it for a while but they suss me out sooner or later.'

'Suss what out?'

'My psychologist said it was fear of abandonment. Something to do with my mother pissing off with another bloke, then my dad dying when I was young.'

'That'll do it, I suppose,' she says. Then, surprised, asks, 'You saw a shrink?'

'My bosses insisted. I was putting myself in unnecessary danger, they said. And that meant I was sometimes putting my colleagues at risk too. Photographers and the like. They said it was something to do with work health insurance but it was just my bosses' excuse to make me get my shit together.'

'And what did the psychologist say?'

'Fear of abandonment and a subconscious need to relive the attack on my father, while hoping to achieve a better outcome,' his sardonic tone implies the air quotes he would never employ. 'Pretty standard stuff.'

She nods, more to indicate she is absorbing this than agreeing. Xander spots something in her frown.

'Have you ever seen a shrink?'

'I don't need to. I've got Geoffrey.'

Althea's phone buzzes and she looks at the screen. 'I'd better take this,' she says, clearly relieved, and moves off to the next table.

This meeting with Lorenzo the next morning. The elaborate screening and the demand that Xander trust this complete stranger – this strange stranger – while not being trusted himself. Is this another risk he really doesn't need to take, and relishes because of that? He looks over at Althea, phone pressed to her ear, doing a lot more listening than talking.

His attention is caught by an item on the late TV news, on a screen on a nearby wall. The sound is off, but according to the words scrolling across the bottom of the screen a cyclist has been badly injured in a hit-and-run just outside Mole Creek. The vision shows the mangled remains of what was once a fancy mountain bike.

Althea says her goodbyes and rejoins him, her smile evaporating as she follows his eyeline to the TV. Xander is looking around for someone to turn the sound up but the news item ends and a new unrelated report is already on screen. Althea looks alarmed and concerned.

'That was my mate in traffic,' she says. 'They found a Ford Ranger in a carpark in Deloraine.'

Xander mirrors the concern in her face. Deloraine is a small town between Launceston and Mole Creek.

'The ute was damaged down one side.'

'Shit, that bike …!' Xander says. He pulls out his phone and finds the number of the Limestone Ridge Hotel. The phone rings several times before a male voice answers.

'Hi, could I speak to Rob, please?' Xander asks.

There's a long silence.

'Hello?' Xander says.

'No, mate, I'm sorry, you can't. He's not here.'

'Is he okay?'

'Why do you ask? What have you heard?'

'I just saw a report on TV,' Xander says, alarm evident in his voice. 'It's Xander McAuslan. Pete's grandson. Rob was at my pop's funeral the other day.'

The man on the end of the phone sighs. 'Look, Rob's in a bad way. He's in hospital in Launceston. Some bastard cleaned him up on his bike. If one of the locals hadn't seen it, God alone knows. Bloke in the ute stopped, reversed, then drove off as soon as he saw there was someone coming.'

'Is he going to be all right?'

'Hard to say, mate. I'm no doctor but the ambos weren't hanging around getting him back to Lonnie. Call the hospital. Or the cops, if I were you.'

'Thanks, I will,' Xander says and hangs up.

'Rob?' Althea says, having heard half the conversation.

'He's in hospital,' Xander says. 'It was him.'

'Omigod,' Althea says, shock turning her face a ghostly shade of pale.

'It's the fucking Russian,' Xander says, then registers Althea's sceptical frown. 'Who else would it be?' he says. 'You need to get back to Launceston. You'll be safer there.'

'Are you still going to meet Lorenzo?'

'Now more than ever,' Xander replies. 'Tomorrow, you could just drop me off, check in with Spangler, then head back to town if you want,' he says.

'I want to check up on Rob,' she says. 'If you're right about the Russian, maybe I need to arrange police protection for him. I'll give the station a call.'

'Good idea. I feel like we got him into this.'

'And what exactly is this "this" that we got him into?' Althea says.

'Fucked if I know,' Xander says. 'I'm hoping Lorenzo will give us a clue.'

CHAPTER 22

One of the few benefits of being in a widely and often wildly disliked role such as military police was that Pete could wander the streets of Vung Tau at night as and when he liked, at the very least using the excuse that he was rounding up strays who'd missed the 2200 curfew. This particular evening, he noticed that, although the time to down their beers, disengage themselves from their hostesses and make their way to the Badcoe Club was still at least an hour away, the streets around Lucy's were quiet, as occasionally happened if there was a major exercise afoot up-country, or if a gap had accidentally occurred in R&C assignments – Rest and Convalescence, the Australian equivalent of R&R.

To Pete's surprise, Lucy's was also quiet, with no music spilling from the creaky speaker and no one there to hear it if there had been. Then he noticed, sitting in a shaded corner, slumped over a table like a pile of brightly coloured rags, one of the girls from the next-door bar. They knew each other as she occasionally came in to get away from the furtive fumblings of drunk squaddies or to help out when Lucy's was busy, or both.

'Lucy not here?' Pete said, lapsing into the perfunctory English that Anglos used when talking to foreigners and small children.

'She taken,' Xuan said, rousing herself blearily from her half-slumber. 'Should I close up?'

'Taken?' Pete said. 'By who? Where?'

'*Quan Cahn,*' the girl replied. 'Military police,' she translated unnecessarily.

'Australian, American or Vietnamese?' Pete said, panic rising.

'Vietnamese,' she answered, her brow furrowed.

Pete called out to her to close up, as he ran out of the bar and jumped into his Jeep. Weaving between donkey carts, wobbly bicycles laden with produce, weird little Daihatsu three-wheeled vans and ambling pedestrians, he drove one-handed as he kept the other on the horn between gear changes, as if whoever had arrested Lucy would be able to hear him coming and leave her be till he got there.

He wheeled into the stony courtyard formed by the combined military police office's prefabricated, temporary-looking edifice in front of a two-storey stone building that would have been built by the French. The wide painted sign revealed that it was the Military Police Station for Vietnamese, American and Australian forces, each with offices side by side. The nondescript wings at either end closed the other two sides of the small yard. The Jeep grunted and clattered to a halt as he stalled rather than parked it.

Pete jumped out of the vehicle then, realising he was in hyperactive mode, gathered himself and marched briskly into the office, saluting the two guards posted at the door perfunctorily and receiving a surprised stiffening to attention in response. Their surprise was partly due, he realised, to the fact that he was wearing bush shorts, one of his extensive collection of garish Hawaiian shirts, and combat boots. It's doubtful if the room he entered would have been bright and welcoming during the day but now, with night having already fallen like a trapdoor, it was a gloomy cave with small pools illuminated by lamps spotlighting a scattering of desks around its perimeter. The room, stacked with folders and drab green communications equipment, its walls peppered with letter-sized memos, lists, reminders and warnings, was half-familiar to Pete. The Provos office was just next door but he had made a point of avoiding spending any significant time there, so much so that he was a stranger to each new intake of office-bound MPs.

Off to the side, one soldier typed deliberately on a small portable machine, using all his fingers but slowly, resisting the urge to rattle out his document in a quarter of the time it would take using two-fingered hunt and peck. Pete stopped at a table placed front and centre, which was clearly intended to be some kind of reception, although it had no signs to indicate this. Having checked that the intruder into his personal space wasn't a superior officer, the savagely crew-cut corporal behind it affected a studious lack of interest as he scribbled on a ledger. Pete knocked the table so hard with his knuckles that the corporal visibly jumped with surprise and the others in the room fell silent. The corporal looked up and sighed.

'Do you have a prisoner here called … um … Trang Minh?' Pete asked.

'And you are …?'

'Lieutenant Peter McAuslan,' Pete replied.

'What the fuck is this? Hawaii Five-O?' a voice said from the gloom. There was laughter and Pete briefly regretted not having embedded himself more solidly in the military police HQ, such as it was.

'Do you have any ID?'

Pete patted his pockets, knowing there would be nothing in them to establish his authority.

'Pete,' an Australian voice came from another corner. 'Do you mean Lucy?'

Pete turned to face the questioner, he knew the voice and he recognise the bulk. The giant busting out of his combat fatigues was an Australian sapper he knew as Lorenzo who, with his beard, hair and headband, looked like a refugee from the Grateful Dead.

197

'Yeah, Lucy,' Pete said.

'ARVN have got her,' Lorenzo said, gesturing to the door and the corridor beyond. 'Brought her in two hours ago.'

'And you are telling me this now?'

'Mate, you're the MP. I thought you must've known.'

'What the fuck are you doing here anyway, Lorenzo?'

'Our guys need some wiring and shit. I got seconded from the Dat,' Lorenzo said, gesturing with the screwdriver and a mysterious piece of Bakelite he held in the other hand. 'I get here and everybody needs something done.'

Pete turned back to the American corporal. 'I need you to get a message to Major Donnie Carrick. He's probably with your guys at the airfield. Tell him Lucy's been arrested.'

'Major Carrick? I'll get him a message in the morning, okay?'

'Not okay,' Pete said. 'Do it now.'

'And why would I do that?' the corporal said.

'Because if you don't, and I tell him you refused to help when you could have, you are going to be spending the rest of your tour cleaning out latrines,' Pete said.

The American corporal looked over to Lorenzo who nodded.

'I'll see what I can do,' he said. 'It's pretty late.'

'He'll want to know ASAP,' Pete said. 'And that's all *you* need to know.'

Pete pointed at the phone on the corporal's desk and waited until he had picked it up before he walked through to the adjoining office where three Vietnamese soldiers sat around a cluster of weathered timber desks.

'Hi, you have a woman called Trang Minh in custody?' he asked.

All three of them looked at him blankly.

'Any of you speak English?'

'Some,' a tall skinny man with glasses and spiky hair said. 'Do you speak Vietnamese?'

'I don't need to, with smart cookies like you around,' Pete said. 'Trang Minh, aka Lucy. Is she here?'

'She is being held for questioning,' Spiky Hair said.

'On suspicion of what?' Pete asked.

The three looked at each other, but said nothing.

'Look, I am an Australian MP – like you, only higher rank. Much higher. I am also investigating Trang Minh. I hope your questioning doesn't ruin the weeks of work I have put into this.'

The trio look at each other again, now more than slightly alarmed but trying not to show it.

'You don't look like MP,' Spiky Hair said eventually. 'How do we know you aren't just some bullshit person?'

'I'm off duty,' Pete said, looking down at his civvy shorts and shirt, then quickly added, 'was.' He looked over at Lorenzo who had followed him into the Quan Canh office. 'Hey, Digger,' he said. 'I need someone to vouch for me.'

Lorenzo said something in surprisingly fluent Vietnamese and the local soldiers looked at Pete with something between alarm and respect. Pete, for his part, was suddenly ashamed that he had never learned enough of the local language to understand more than the very basics. But then Lucy's English was immaculate, something that allowed him to be lazy with her mother tongue.

Spiky Hair said something to Lorenzo, there was a brief exchange in Vietnamese, and the Australian sapper turned to Pete.

'She's been arrested on suspicion of spying,' he said. 'She was dobbed in by someone, said she was passing on gossip from her bar to Charlie.'

'Lorenzo, mate,' Pete said. 'Can you explain to these gentlemen that I need to interview Lucy right now? No questions. No delay.'

'Umm, that's going to be tricky, Pete,' Lorenzo said. 'She's a Viet civilian and she's their prisoner. Their ball game, their ball.'

'You are aware of their preferred method for interrogating female suspects around here, aren't you?' Pete asked.

The widening of Lorenzo's eyes told Pete he knew exactly what he meant.

'Ask them. If I try, they'll just pretend they don't understand and stall.'

Lorenzo turned to the three QCs and spoke in tones that suggested to Pete he was being polite but firm.

'On what authority?' Spiky Hair responded, looking disdain-fully at Pete, who suspected his English was much better than he was letting on.

'Major Tang,' Pete lied. 'He told me to get here and question her myself. Call him, he'll confirm it.' Pete hoped he could count on his counterpart's notoriety for being uncontactable. 'If you can't get him, he's probably on his way here right now.'

Spiky Hair spoke to the other two, watching Lorenzo out of the corner of his eye and muttering, clearly in the hope of not being fully understood. The smaller of the three men sighed and eased himself out of his chair, strolled to a door at the back of the room and exited.

'What's happening?' Pete asked Lorenzo.

'They're preparing an interview room and bringing her up,' Lorenzo replied. 'Your new best buddy wants to sit in.'

'Okay, fair enough,' Pete said after a moment's thought. 'And you too, okay?'

'It's not like I have anything better to do.' Lorenzo shrugged. 'The wiring here hasn't killed anyone ... yet.'

The door at the end of the room opened and the QC grunt who'd left moments before gestured to his boss that they should follow. He led them to a side room with bare walls, flaking plaster and a ceiling fan that circled wearily above a small weatherworn table where Lucy sat, upright and defiant, one wrist handcuffed to the back of a bentwood chair.

'Lucy,' Pete said. 'Are you okay?'

'As well as can be expected,' she said, nodding towards her handcuffed wrist.

Pete noticed the clear impression of finger-shaped bruises on one of her forearms and a bruise on her right cheekbone, its redness forcing its way out from under her natural skin colour.

'Did you do this?' he said to Spiky Hair, gesturing to her face.

'No, but I would have if I'd had to,' he replied. 'I'm told she resisted arrest.'

Lucy scoffed audibly.

'Just to be clear,' Pete said. 'If you or anyone in this God-forsaken hole touches a hair on her head, I will hold you responsible.' He emphasised the point with an angry finger in Spiky Hair's face. 'I will hunt you down and gut you and feed your flesh to your dogs and make you watch while they eat.'

'Pete ...' Lorenzo said, shaking his head slowly.

Lucy sagged. This was not making things easier for her. Spiky Hair gestured to one of the other soldiers and nodded towards the door. One of them unlocked Lucy's handcuff and gestured for her to stand.

'Interview over,' Spiky Hair said. 'You go now.'

'What the fuck?' Pete said, reaching for a side-arm he immediately realised wasn't there.

'It's okay, Pete,' Lucy said. 'I'll be okay.'

'You fuckers ...' Pete roared as Lucy was led through the exit at the back of the room.

'Easy, Pete,' Lorenzo said. 'Come back later ... in uniform.' When he'd calmed down was implied.

Spiky Hair half-smiled, keeping his anger and contempt at bay. For him, emotions were understandable, but responding with more emotion was weak.

Pete watched the door close behind Lucy and wondered if he'd just made her plight a hundred times worse.

CHAPTER 23

Morning is a bleary rush. Xander and Althea had retired early and to separate rooms, but he slept badly. Looking at her sunken, dark eyes, Xander assumes that she too has been trying to make sense of what has happened. Breakfast is consumed on the run, and their checkout is delayed by the arrival of a minibus full of Japanese hikers, meaning Xander and Althea have to race to the pre-ordained drop-off point to make it in time.

'All your movements will be observed,' a message scrawled in Sharpie on the back of Spangler's map said. 'Any deviation from the plan will result in the mission being aborted.' This is not Spangler-speak so Xander assumes it was dictated by the mysterious Lorenzo. Having no idea of how long the next part of the journey will be, let alone where it is going, Althea insists on Xander taking two large bottles of water in his day pack. She also hands him a day pass allowing him to enter the park, downloaded from the internet and printed at reception.

'A pass? Really?' Xander asks. 'I have a feeling I'm not going anywhere that a Parks and Wildlife inspector is likely to ping me.'

'Belt and braces,' she says.

'You'd better take my phone,' he says. 'Or Spangler won't make the call to Lorenzo.'

She slips his mobile into her pocket and they hug but don't kiss, a possibility that momentarily hangs like their breath in the cold morning air.

'It's not too late to pull out,' she says.

'Why would I do that?'

'Maybe there's nothing to be gained. It's all settled. They've won, but you haven't lost.'

'They?'

'The Russian. Danzig. Whoever else wanted Pete's files.'

'And Rob?'

'Could just be coincidence. They do occur,' she says.

Xander looks at his watch. 'I gotta go,' he replies and walks along the gravel at the roadside. He hears the car start and the crackle of rubber on stones as Althea pulls back onto the bitumen. The road is too narrow and the bend too severe for her to even think about hanging a U-turn so she drives past, looking for somewhere safer. Xander looks up to see her watching in the rear-view mirror, her hand briefly raised in a tiny wave.

The road is lined with cable-and-post crash barriers and Xander crosses over and walks on the other side until he reaches the Stonehaven Creek road sign, which is facing away from traffic coming from Derwent Bridge, as was the sign for the Frenchman's Gap track. Drivers from Derwent Bridge, in the other direction, would hit the main car park before they got to the little pull-in spot.

Xander scrambles down the roadside embankment and across a small gully. He pulls himself up the other side with the help of a hanging branch, and weaves through bushes and trees, trying to estimate 10 metres in half-steps. The dawn cacophony of bird song is occasionally replaced by the braking and acceleration of the odd truck and tourist minibus negotiating the looping bend far behind him. He's sure he hears Cleo's grumbling engine as Althea drives back to the village, but it could be anyone. The traffic is as invisible to him as he must be to passing drivers.

The low winter sun is barely skimming the treetops but soon it will be high, forcing its way through the foliage. Xander reaches a gap in the trees and checks his watch. He's right on time, so he sits on a fallen log and calculates how long it will take Althea to get back to Spangler's and then for the bush mechanic to contact Lorenzo. In the meantime, he entertains himself by imagining how he would write this story, assuming he gets a chance to write it. Will it be about an old man being killed because of what he can remember about the past, or is it about a gung-ho young journalist who, through a series of screw-ups, draws friends, family and strangers into a criminal conspiracy to erase information that he's not even aware that he possesses?

The guilt descends again and he slumps forward as if already making himself a smaller target for the slings and arrows he knows he deserves and which are surely coming his way. Come-uppance is long overdue. Who the fuck does he think he is, palling it up with known criminals then expecting to be able to expose them publicly and get away with it? Maybe Danzig was right in one regard, if no other: he's gone native, starting to think he's a cop.

Supposing, just supposing, Pete did take his own life – and that's another rich seam of guilt to mine – if this is something Xander's brought from the mainland he has now put his own safety, the safety of a Vietnamese woman who bizarrely claims to be his aunt, and now Rob the barman, in jeopardy. And there's Althea, too – even if that's a risk she takes as a cop, although maybe not so much in family liaison.

In a way, Xander is happy to be far from civilisation and all the stress and confusion. But here he is, on a mission to meet someone he doesn't know, chasing facts that may lead nowhere. There possibly isn't even a story to follow, and he doesn't have a newspaper to publish it in if there was. But then maybe *he* is the story. Maybe it *is* something that has followed him from the mainland. What if the Russian was looking for *his* files, not Pete's? If that's the case, this little wilderness adventure could be a huge waste of time.

He's becoming increasingly irritated at himself and deflated as the minutes tick away. And now he's wondering how he's going to get back to town if he gives up. Xander gets to his feet, checking his watch and picking up his day pack. He momentarily forgets that Tasmania doesn't have bears when a huge figure erupts from the bushes and turns towards him. It turns out to be a camo-clad, bearded man who stands squarely between two trees and looks him up and down.

'Xander?' Lorenzo says.

'Yeah ... hi ... you must be ...'

'Follow me!' Lorenzo orders and disappears back into the bush.

Xander walks to the spot where Lorenzo last stood and squeezes through a gap between two silver banksia, then has to quickly duck under the branches of a fir tree. He sees Lorenzo's shape ahead of him and bobs and dodges his way through the undergrowth until he finds himself in a small clearing. His first impression confirms that Lorenzo is a big man, tall and broad shouldered, which is evident inside his lightweight camo jacket. He is also wearing a military-style bucket hat, below which hair is sprouting in every direction. His eyes are obscured by aviator shades, but even they can't restrain his voluminous grey-and-ginger eyebrows. His bushy orange-and-silver beard completes the mountain-man image, but Xander can tell this is no weekend warrior. He seems to be carrying minimal clutter in his many pockets and his army-issue pants are tucked into khaki gaiters above his lightweight boots. Gaiters, Xander thinks, means they're going to be walking through scrub. He is about to speak, but Lorenzo hushes him with a finger to his lips.

Xander realises Lorenzo is sizing him up too and is gratified that he seems to generally approve of his choice of kit, judging by the frequent nods. Then Lorenzo reaches forward and tucks the vivid red collar of Xander's jacket away, folding it in on itself.

'Not exactly stealth colours, old son,' he whispers. 'Now, put these on.'

He hands Xander a black eye mask – the kind you get in business class on aeroplanes – and a black beanie. Xander is confused.

'If Charlie captures you, you won't be able to tell them how to get to my hootchie if you don't know.'

Xander now strongly suspects his grandad's friend is completely nuts, but does as he says anyway. He's come too far to quibble over eye masks and beanies. Xander puts them on and then feels Lorenzo tugging at the front of the beanie to pull it down over the mask.

'Okay, this is how this is going to work,' Lorenzo whispers. 'I'm going to hook your hand into the back of my belt and you're going to follow me. When I say "duck" do it and stay ducked till I say "up". If you feel yourself falling just hold on. I've had better men than you try to pull me down and I'm still standing.'

'Why are we whispering?' Xander says softly.

'Why do you think? So Charlie can't hear us.' He feels a tug on his fingers and suddenly he is stumbling forward, trying to find a rhythm for his feet amid the stones, twigs and tree roots beneath them.

They walk north, Xander can tell by the feel of the flicker of early morning warmth on his right cheek and the occasional babble of the Stonehaven Creek in the same ear. The 'duck' and 'up' instructions work reasonably well, apart from two occasions when Lorenzo belatedly says 'up' and one where he forgets to say 'duck'. It's only sensing Lorenzo's movement that has Xander lowering his head before he walks face-first into a low branch. After about ten minutes of walking over rough ground, passable but clearly not an established path judging by the rocks and branches that challenge Xander's ankles, the incline starts to rise. Lorenzo stops and tells Xander he can take off the mask and hat.

Xander blinks several times, adjusting to the light before it occurs to him to don his shades. Once he can see, he realises he is in an area of trees and bushes that's fairly open yet completely covered by the leafy canopy.

'The next stretch is a bit of a climb and I'm guessing you have no fucking idea where we are so it's okay,' Lorenzo whispers.

Xander opens his day pack and pulls out a bottle of water. He offers it to Lorenzo, who says 'You first' in a voice so soft that they might have been in a church. Xander can't tell whether he's being polite or cautious and decides it's probably both. He takes a long pull at the water then passes it to the big man who wipes the top with his sleeve then pours the water into his mouth without his lips making contact. Lorenzo hands the bottle back to Xander then nods and walks off into a gap in the trees. Xander stows the water bottle hurriedly and follows. Immediately they are climbing again. A breeze is rustling the highest leaves on the trees but not a breath of it is reaching ground level. Xander is grateful for the shade; even in late autumn, walking uphill is warm work.

Up and along one ridge, down a small scramble and then up again, they are following no discernible path as far as Xander can tell but, surefooted and certain, Lorenzo seems to know exactly where they are going, neither hesitating for a second to get his bearings nor pausing before a change in direction.

After an hour of steady hiking, up and down slopes and screes, but always ultimately getting higher, Lorenzo stops and raises his hand.

'Listen!' he whispers, then urgently, 'Get down!' He throws himself to the ground and commando crawls under a bush. Xander does likewise then looks over at Lorenzo who is pointing at the sky. 'Fucking drone,' he whispers. 'Didn't know Parks and Wildlife were using them.'

Xander looks up but can see nothing, however he can hear an insistent buzzing that cuts through the natural hubbub of the bush.

'How do you know it's Parks and Wildlife?' he asks.

'Because they are illegal for civilians,' Lorenzo says.

The buzzing passes overhead in one direction then crosses again at right angles.

'Have they seen us?' Xander asks.

'Doubt it,' Lorenzo replies. 'If they had, they'd have stopped. They're probably working grids or maybe just trying out their new toys. Give it five minutes then we can move.'

Xander is glad of the opportunity to rest. For a man who must be in his seventies, Lorenzo has remarkable agility and stamina. There were uphill sections where Xander had struggled to keep up.

Shortly after they resume their hike, they come to the outer limit of a fringe of the trees and Xander realises they are looking down into a bowl-shaped chasm.

Lorenzo disappears under a bush and emerges with a length of rope, which he starts reeling in as if he was hauling an invisible boat to shore.

'Done much abseiling?' he asks Xander.

'Abseiling?'

'Or rappelling ... you know, like abseiling but with nowhere for your feet?'

'Fuck, Lorenzo,' Xander says. 'Not much call for either in my line of work.'

'Ah, well, first time for everything,' Lorenzo says, then laughs at the look on Xander's face, and shakes his head as his final tug reveals a rope ladder attached to a pulley on a metal stake driven into the stony ground underneath a bush.

'I'll loop a rope round you and you can use the ladder as hand-holds,' Lorenzo says. 'Don't try to put your feet on the rungs. Just prop them on the rock face. There's enough grip there to stop you from falling. And there's me. I ain't gonna let you fall cause there's no way I can carry you out of here.'

Xander gingerly lowers himself over the edge of the drop

which, before he decides not to look down again, he estimates to be about 20 metres. Once he gets the hang of it, the descent is relatively smooth. Only once do his feet slip and he feels the tug of the rope looped under his armpits, across his chest and around his shoulder blades.

'You okay down there?' Lorenzo calls.

'All good,' Xander replies. 'Nearly there, I think.'

A few metres more and Xander finds his feet on solid ground, and feels a surge of both relief and satisfaction, at least until he looks down and realises he is only halfway down the cliff on a ledge that's only about a metre wide. Lorenzo joins him in a shower of pebbles, gravel and dislodged vegetation, having abseiled from the top. The big man immediately starts pulling on a thin cord and the rope ladder slides down the rock face towards them. A tug on the rope that he rode down to the ledge releases it and it falls in a heap at his feet.

He looks at Xander, quizzically. 'You gonna wear that all day?' he says.

Xander looks down at the rope wrapped around his chest and feels even less adequate than he did at the top of the cliff. Shrugging it off, he follows Lorenzo round the edge of a rocky outcrop where, to his relief, the ledge widens considerably. Xander is taking in the view of the bowl-shaped gorge beneath them when he realises Lorenzo has disappeared. To add to his sense of dislocation, there's a strange, muted ululation coming from a bush towards which he'd last seen Lorenzo walking. Xander approaches the bush and the strange sound stops. He stares at the bush for several seconds before the edge near the rock face moves and Lorenzo's face appears.

'You'd better get in here before some cunt spots you,' Lorenzo whispers. 'Then we'll all be fucked.'

He pulls the bush aside – it turns out to be woven into a camouflage net – and Xander follows him into a dimly but sufficiently lit cave where two dogs are eyeing him suspiciously, if not malevolently.

'That's Crosby on the left and Stills on the right,' Lorenzo says. 'They're basenjis. Great hunting dogs and they don't bark, they sing.'

'Oh, that was the weird sound,' Xander says.

'Yeah, barking would have Parks and Wildlife here with a swat team. But yodelling? That just sends them off to try to identify a new bird species.' Lorenzo looks at the dogs; they are on full alert. 'Hold out your hand and let them sniff it and they'll be fine. They don't get many visitors.'

Xander does as instructed and one by one they sniff his hand. Then, as if they have learnt everything they need to know, they lose interest and turn away to a dark corner of the cave. This gives Xander a chance to take in his surroundings which, as his eyes adjust, are revealed to be bizarrely impressive.

The illumination is from arrays of LED lights fixed to bookshelves on two walls. Heat, of which he is suddenly aware, comes from what looks like a wood-burning stove, its chimney starting off on a normal upwards direction then lurching off along the cave roof into the intense gloom of the cavern's far reaches.

There are two comfortable chairs, a table, a bed and a small bar fridge that chunters away happily in a corner. This is the ultimate 'man cave'. He is suddenly aware that Lorenzo is watching him and gets the feeling that his host is not so much seeking his approval as looking for a sign that he appreciates what's going on here.

'I love what you've done with the place,' Xander says eventually.

Lorenzo laughs uproariously and it rings around the walls of the cave. In their beds, the dogs prick up their ears. Laughter is not a sound with which they are familiar.

'Have to say, if I'd known about the scramble down the rock face, I might have suggested a meeting in the hotel,' Xander says.

'That was never going to happen,' Lorenzo says. 'I can't afford to be seen around town too much. Now, coffee or beer?'

'I'll take a coffee, if you've got one.'

'Of course,' Lorenzo says, taking a blackened, six-sided Bialetti stove-top coffee maker from a shelf and unscrewing the top half to load it.

'What was with all the whispering?' Xander says, aware that they are both now talking normally.

'Force of habit, I suppose,' Lorenzo says. 'Back in Vietnam, when we were on patrol we wouldn't raise our voices above a whisper for days on end. Otherwise they knew we were coming. Our voices and the smell, if any of us had been naïve enough to use soap in the days before. Speaking of which, the head is round to the right.'

'The head?'

'Latrines. Toilet,' Lorenzo says. 'It's the next cave along. But you'll need a torch once you get in there.' He gestures to a headband light on a shelf. 'Be careful you don't slip. It's a long drop.'

Xander can see Lorenzo grinning in the gloom. He's not sure if he means the cliff or the toilet. Probably both.

'By the way, Johnny Spangler said Lorenzo isn't your real name,' Xander says. 'What's the story there?'

'Your grandad was the last person I knew who called me that,' Lorenzo says. 'Let's just stick with it for now.'

'Works for me,' Xander says. 'I didn't even know you existed until a couple of days ago.'

'There's a lot you didn't know about your grandad,' Lorenzo says. 'A Hell of a lot.'

CHAPTER 24

'Spangler said Pete's gone,' Lorenzo says. Xander has returned to the cave unscathed and they are sipping freshly brewed coffee from white enamel mugs with blue rims and trims on their handles. 'What was it? Heart attack? Or cancer? I know he was worried about some results.'

'He was shot. One bullet in the side of his head.' Xander registers the shock on Lorenzo's face. 'Sorry. I thought you'd have heard.' He warms himself at the wood-burning stove.

'Mate, I'm so out of touch here that if they ever do a dementia test on me, I'm fucked – I have no idea who the prime minister is, or what day it is, for that matter,' Lorenzo says. 'But ... wow ... shot ... by the way, sorry for your loss and all that. Sorry for mine, too.'

'The cops say he shot himself,' Xander mumbles. 'But there's no way.'

'What do you mean?'

'I reckon he was killed by someone trying to cover something up.'

'Shit, really?' Lorenzo says. 'I don't want to be rude, son, but that sounds like a denial and conspiracy theory cocktail you've got there.'

'Yeah, I wonder about that too.'

'Why do the cops think it's suicide?'

'They have a suicide note – well, a text message, actually.'

'But you think it's bullshit?'

'Since it happened, I've been attacked three times by an armed Russian and once by a wannabe Australian crim. Had all my computer files stolen or wiped – Pete's too – and stalked by a middle-aged Vietnamese woman who's been telling people she's my aunt.'

'Okay,' Lorenzo says, lengthening the vowels as he rises from his chair and opens a small cupboard. 'This is going to take something stronger than coffee.' He produces two glasses and a bottle of single malt whisky. 'Right, tell me the whole story, from the very beginning.'

'It's a long story,' Xander says.

'Look around, son. I don't have a TV.'

***

They have made a serious dent in the bottle by the time Xander has finished relating the events of the past two weeks, especially since Lorenzo has prodded him for every nuanced detail and tangent. When Xander mentions the hit-and-run attack on Rob the barman, Lorenzo sits back and breathes deeply.

'I like Rob,' he says. 'He's a good bloke ... for an ex-copper.'

'Okay, your turn,' Xander says. 'How did you know Pete?'

'I was a sapper in Vietnam,' Lorenzo says. 'An engineer. Your pop was a provo – provost – military police, in other words. I assume you knew that?'

Xander shrugs. 'Some. He barely ever mentioned the war. It was like he wasn't even there.'

'He was there all right,' Lorenzo says. 'That's where we met. He seemed to cope with it all. Me, a bit less so. But sometimes you're too busy being fucked up to notice how fucked up you are. By the time I realised, I had blown up my marriage, lost touch with my kids, made some seriously self-destructive relationship choices and made myself unemployable along the way. One day, I looked around and realised I'd got old and it was too late to do anything about it.

'Some of us deal with it in different ways. Or don't. Me, I met Pete again. Started walking around here. Hiking. It helped to clear my head when the complete arse I had made of my life was bothering me too much. Bivvied down in the gully there a couple of times, then one day I scrambled up here and found these caves. Know much about geology?'

Xander shakes his head again. 'Not much call for it, even in Sydney's underworld.'

He realises that Lorenzo is typical of people who've spent a little too much time in their own company. When the chance to talk to another human being presents itself, the torrent of words is hard to stem.

'Tasmania has the longest and deepest caves in Australia. Even so, these shouldn't really be here,' Lorenzo says. 'This ridge is an outcrop from the limestone formation around Mole Creek.'

'King Solomon's Caves,' Xander says.

'Exactly,' Lorenzo says. 'Anyway, I started spending more and more time up here and it became a bit of a hobby ... no, an addiction, really.'

'And this helped you get your head together?'

'That and Pete. He talked me back from the edge and it was him that suggested the walks. This –' He gestures to their surroundings. 'This was just a distraction – something to fill in the void left when all the guilt and shame had been put to bed.'

'It's quite a distraction,' Xander says, looking around.

'As an ex-sapper, I am pretty good at adapting things. "We make and we break," that's our motto,' Lorenzo says. 'It became a challenge to see how comfortable I could make this. The stove came first, then the pipes to funnel the smoke into natural breaks in the rock – inspired by the Cu Chi tunnels in Vietnam, if you must know. God knows where it comes out – I've never been able to find it. Then I found a couple of underground streams for fresh water and to drive little generators to power up batteries for the lights.'

'I guess solar panels would be a bit obvious,' Xander says.

'The hardest part was carrying all the gear up here under cover of darkness,' Lorenzo says. 'You can't use lights or you'd be spotted, quick-as. As for humping it up here in daylight, try explaining to a Parks and Wildlife officer why you've got a dunny seat and six lengths of PVC piping attached to your backpack. Some stuff I took to the top and lowered down. The rest I carried up through the valley – the Ho Chi Minh Trail, I call it. Did you know it was Vietcong women who drove the supply trucks up those narrow mountain passes, at night with no headlights? Amazing people. Fucking amazing.

'Anyway, I accidentally became self-sufficient up here. Sappernuity, they call it in the engineers. Fixing things that don't work, building things that shouldn't work but do. Once you find an outlet for that, the urge to go back to town drains away pretty quickly. Eventually I gave up my rented pad in Melbourne. I've got everything I need here. Every couple of weeks I trek down to Derwent Bridge to collect my laundry and supplies from Johnny Spangler, order anything I need on the internet and pick it up from him next time. He gets cash from my pension and we're sweet.

'About once a week I'll take the dogs for a night hunt, rabbits and foxes mostly and the occasional wallaby or deer, even a wild goat. They're all pests – well, maybe not the wallabies, but you can get a licence to hunt them to keep the numbers down, so I guess it must be okay. I use night-vision goggles, which feels a bit like cheating but, hey, you gotta do what you gotta do.'

'Do you have a gun licence?' Xander asks.

'Fuck no,' Lorenzo scoffs. 'Then they'd know who I am. I use a crossbow. It's silent and I'm pretty good with it. They don't suffer.'

'And you say Pete got you into this?'

'Not directly,' Lorenzo says. 'But yeah, I suppose.'

'So you kept in touch after Vietnam?'

'Nope,' Lorenzo says. 'I was going through a rough patch and one of the veterans magazines said there was holiday accommodation going, discounted for vets ...'

'The Mole Creek cottage ...' Xander says.

'Exactly. We met at the hand-over, keys and stuff, and realised we knew each other. It was awkward at first, but we went for a drink, had something to eat ... Pete never left. Turned out we both needed someone to talk to who knew the shit we all went through. Me especially.'

'When was that?' Xander asks.

'About three years ago, I suppose,' Lorenzo says. 'Ironically, I was going there with serious thought of topping myself.'

'Three years?' Xander says. 'Pete never mentioned you.'

'That was the deal. He didn't talk about me, I wouldn't talk about him. He was pretty good at keeping secrets.'

'Tell me about it,' Xander says.

'Your pop told me a lot about what happened to him back in Vietnam and what has happened since – although I have to say there were some areas he wasn't keen to get into. He was based in the seaside town of Vung Tau, where we all went for our R&C. His day job was escorting visiting officers and dignitaries to Checkpoint Charlie – halfway to the main army base at Nui Dat – or up the river to Saigon. His night job was rounding up the drunks who'd broken the twenty-two hundred hours curfew in Vung Tau.

'His story did not take in Khe Sanh or Long Tan,' Lorenzo continues. 'He was not that kind of soldier. And ... I don't know how to tell you this ...'

'Go on,' Xander says. 'He's gone and I'm way beyond being surprised.'

'Pete had a woman in Vung Tau. A Vietnamese woman called Lucy,' Lorenzo says. 'Not her real name, but she ran a bar called Juicy Lucy's so everyone called her Lucy. I guess the bar named her, rather than the other way round. Lately Pete had gotten obsessed with what happened to her.'

'Which was?'

'After Pete came back, Lucy was killed by an Australian deserter with a chip on his shoulder. Executed. Pete said it was the first crime in his career that affected someone he cared about, and it was the only one worth a shit that he hadn't solved. The grub who killed her, Johnny something, he had a grudge against Pete and a limp from being shot in the leg by one of Pete's mates. They found his gun dumped in a trash can near the bar.'

Xander processes this, probing the story for obvious holes, gaps that would have been big enough to send Pete on a potential wild goose chase to Vietnam.

'To be clear, a man with a grudge against Pete kills his ex-girlfriend a year later? Weren't these Tour of Duty romances ten a penny?'

'Not this one,' Lorenzo says. 'This was different. Lucy had a baby ... a little girl.'

He looks at Xander, waiting for the penny to drop, then nods when he sees the look on Xander's face.

'Holy shit,' Xander says. 'My mystery aunt?'

'I'd stake my pension on it,' Lorenzo says. 'Pete didn't like to talk about it, but I know he left a kid behind in Vietnam – or, at least, a pregnant lover – and he told me he sent money for the girl to Lucy's sister for years. Right up into her teens.'

'I don't know ... It just doesn't seem right,' Xander protests.

'Yeah. I know he adored your grandmother ...'

'Kate ...'

'Yeah, Kate,' Lorenzo says, confirming to himself that his memory is still functioning. 'But I reckon the relationship with

Lucy was the real deal too. Why else would he fly to Vietnam to follow up a fifty-year-old cold case?'

'When was that?'

'A few weeks ago ... closer to a month or so,' Lorenzo says. 'He'd been online to the War Memorial website, just looking to confirm dates and names for his book, I suppose, and finds something. I'm not sure what – he was keeping it close to his chest – but next thing he's on plane to Vietnam.'

'I knew he'd been overseas and I guessed Vietnam, but he never mentioned it,' Xander says. 'He sent me an email, the day before he was killed. Said he had something to tell me but needed it to be face to face,' Xander says. 'Could it have been as simple as he needed to tell me that he had an affair and a secret love-child?'

Lorenzo shrugs. In the half-light in the cave he looks even more bear-like than he did when he crashed out of the bushes, so much so that Xander's sometimes still surprised when he speaks.

'And Pete said this was the only case he never solved? Or the most important, anyway,' Xander says.

'He did.'

'But then you also said it was an Aussie deserter with a grudge.'

'Like I said, Pete had been digging around and the more answers he found, the more questions he got,' Lorenzo says.

'Did he find out anything worthwhile in Vietnam?'

'We met up shortly after he got back,' Lorenzo says. 'He was excited and frustrated. He'd tried to connect with Linh – his daughter – but she was up-country, working as a tour guide, apparently. But he did meet up with Major Tang – he was the ARVN liaison back in the day.'

'Arvin?' asks Xander.

'A.R.V.N. – Army of the Republic of Vietnam, aka the South Vietnam Army,' Lorenzo says. 'Part of Pete's duties was to check with Tang that everything they were doing in Vung Tau was okay, and vice versa.'

'Did he get anything from him?'

'Tang told him Lucy had information she wanted to give him, Tang, before she died. She wanted safe passage out of Vung Tau but she never got a chance to pass it on.'

'Sounds all a bit *Casablanca*, doesn't it?' Xander says. 'Papers of transit and all that.'

'You're not far off the mark,' Lorenzo says with a laugh. 'Tang was a Vietcong spy. That's how he survived the reprisals after the war. While all the others who'd worked with us and the Yanks were carted off to re-education camps, he scored a cushy job in the civil service on account of having worked for Hanoi the whole time.'

'Jeez, Pete must have been really fired up after hearing that.'

'And there's more.' Lorenzo lurches off his seat and disappears briefly into the darker reaches of the cave. He returns clutching a large children's scrapbook that is only just retaining its contents. Xander can see the edges of documents and pictures trying to escape from between the leaves of the vividly coloured binder. Lorenzo sits back down and opens the scrapbook on his knees.

'Look at this.' He hands Xander a small black-and-white picture of two tall white men in army fatigues with a tiny Vietnamese woman in between them.

Xander recognises it immediately. 'This was on Pete's computer, before all the files were wiped.'

'Yeah, I know,' Lorenzo says. 'He scanned it from this. That's Pete on the left, and Lucy of course, in the middle.'

'Who's the other guy?' Xander asks. 'He appears in a few other pictures of Pete's. Or appeared, I should say – they're gone now.'

'That's Donnie Carrick, an American. He was Pete's best friend, all the time they were in Vietnam. Those three hung out together a lot.'

'What was his relationship with Lucy?' Xander says. 'Maybe some rivalry there?'

'Uh-uh.' Lorenzo shakes his head. 'Donnie loved those two, both of them, like a brother. And he was straighty-180, a very moral dude. Pete could be a little wild when Lucy wasn't around. Donnie was always the one who pulled him back into line.'

'You sound very sure.'

'I was there too,' Lorenzo replies. 'Who do you think took the picture?'

'And this Carrick, guy ... Pete never mentioned him. Is he still around?'

'That's my point. Pete goes back to Vung Tau, tracks down Major Tang and asks him about Lucy's death. Tang gets all mysterious and clams up, tells him to talk to Carrick, and to do that he needs to go back to Australia. Carrick is military attaché or some shit at the American consulate in Canberra.'

'You are kidding!' Xander says.

'Me no kid, kid,' Lorenzo says with a laugh.

'And did he?'

'No idea. Me and your pop weren't exactly Facebook friends telling each other and the world what we had for breakfast.'

'Why would Carrick know anything different about what happened to Lucy?'

'Carrick was military police,' Lorenzo replies. 'He was there when it happened. Pete had already gone home. It was Carrick who told him he was a dad and that Lucy had been killed. Pete said that if Carrick didn't know the truth, no one would, because Carrick did the investigation and he'd have done it right for her. For both of them.'

The last tendrils of sunlight that had snuck in through the gaps in the camouflage netting had retreated into the gathering gloom outside.

'I think I know the name of the person who's behind all this,' Xander says after a long silence. 'Someone called Alden.'

'Who? What?'

'Linh, my mystery aunt, in her note said this was all about Alden,' Xander explains. 'Mean anything to you?'

Lorenzo leans back with his eyes closed, clearly thinking, computing, cross-checking the names in the card files of his memory. Eventually, he sits up but shakes his head.

'Alden?' he says. 'That name ... I've heard it before ... can't place it.'

'Yeah, me neither,' Xander says. 'Maybe Pete mentioned him in passing and it's stuck. But I tell you this, we find this Alden, and I reckon we've found our killer. And maybe we'll find out why this fucking Russian is hunting me like I was the last Tassie tiger.'

CHAPTER 25

'Have a gulp of this, it'll put some hair on your chest,' Lorenzo said as the Elektra hissed and burped its approval.

Pete took the coffee and smiled his thanks before leaning back into the shadows of the closed café. It had been twenty-four hours since Lucy was detained and he had shut up shop and parked himself at their usual table, waiting for her return, growing more anxious with every tick of the electric clock that flicked numbered cards on rotating spindles. Click, 8.10 becomes 8.11. Clunk and flicker, all three cards flip forwards as 8.59 becomes 9.00. He was glad of Lorenzo's company. The sapper said he was there for a routine clean of the coffee machine, but Pete suspected he was making sure he was all right after the confrontation at the police office.

'She'll be okay. They know she's connected,' Lorenzo said. 'They wouldn't dare hurt her.'

'What are the Provos saying?'

'The QC are telling them nothing and they're telling me even less,' Lorenzo said. 'Best just to sit quiet. Ride this one out.'

'I'm just worried that I might have made things worse. I've already had my arse kicked twice this morning.'

'Twice? Or once on each cheek?' Lorenzo's attempt at humour misses its mark.

'Logistics and Intelligence have both had a go. One for interfering in a legitimate local investigation, the other for abusing and threatening two Allied personnel.'

'Two?'

'The spiky-haired Viet and the Yank corporal.'

'Oh, yeah, forgot about him. If anyone asks me I'll say you were provoked.'

'How about saying I didn't do it?'

'Happy to commit perjury wherever possible … but, mate, there were about a dozen witnesses.'

Pete considered this, nodding. He was glad to have distractions from the dreadful mental images of what could be happening to Lucy. His thoughts strayed to the story of the young woman who had been travelling from village to village to teach locals how to retrieve Allied landmines without getting blown up themselves, passing them on to their cadres for re-use against enemy forces. She had been captured and died in custody. He assumed it wasn't suicide.

'How come you speak the lingo?' he asked Lorenzo, trying to bump the darker thoughts out of his head.

'School of Engineering organised it before my second tour. A very cute teacher at uni gave me the basics and I took it from there,' he said. 'It looks complicated, but I suppose I have a talent – once you realise that the written form was created by a French priest, it kind of makes sense.'

'If you say so …'

'That's why U and Y are pronounced "ee" like the French do. So Nguyen' – he spells it out – 'is "nyween", not "new-yen".'

'Fascinating …' Pete lied. 'Do you think they might just disappear her? I mean, she's never seen again and they say she was being taken somewhere … got lost in transit.'

The door creaked open and Pete stiffened, feeling for his side-arm despite having no idea who he was going to shoot or why. He recognised the shapes in the doorway long before he could see their faces. He leapt out of his seat to hug Lucy, but she flinched and held back.

'Are you okay?' Pete said. 'Did they hurt you?'

'I'm fine,' Lucy replied, squeezing his hand. 'Just tired. I need to sleep.' She squeezed Pete's hand again then slowly but purposefully walked through to her living quarters. Pete made to follow her, but Donnie grabbed his arm and stopped him.

'She's exhausted, buddy,' Donnie said. 'She's had a tough twenty-four hours.'

'Hey, I might just head off,' Lorenzo said, clearly feeling awkward that his chaperoning of Pete was no longer required. 'Those booby-traps aren't going to disarm themselves.'

'Thanks, mate,' Pete said, and Donnie slapped Lorenzo on the shoulder, a silent acknowledgement that he'd done his bit.

'Why was she arrested in the first place?' Pete asked as the door closed behind the sapper.

'It comes down to information the VC are getting about ARVN actions,' Donnie replied. 'And it seems to be coming from your side.'

'My side?'

'Our Intelligence guys leaked a fake report to your Intelligence guys and then ambushed the Vietcong who turned up to a party that didn't exist.'

'Did you get anything useful out of them?' Pete asked, knowing the captured combatants would have been questioned to within an inch of their lives, and maybe beyond.

'They work in cells,' Donnie said. 'They don't know where the people they got information from got it. All we learned was that it was someone on our side working in Vung Tau, who either gave the information up accidentally or passed it on deliberately.'

Pete thought for a moment. 'Am I a suspect?' he asked.

'Are you?' Donnie responded.

'Fuck off, Donnie,' Pete said. 'How did you get her out?'

'I tracked down Tang, who's been keeping his head down. He said she was accused by one of the papa-sans in a bar – one of them near here. Seems like he had his eye on this place and saw an opportunity to get Lucy out of the way.'

'A business rival? Really, as simple as that?'

'Don't worry. Tang doesn't take kindly to being used in that way. He'll make sure the fucker pays.'

Pete nodded. Donnie wasn't given to foul language normally, so he had no doubt he was fired up about Lucy's arrest.

'By the way,' Donnie added, 'your tantrum in the police station didn't really help Lucy at all.'

'Oh, you heard about that?'

'Everybody's heard about that, my friend. How long have you been here? You know how important face is to these guys.'

'Yeah, you're right,' Pete said. 'I've been wondering how much damage I did, blundering in like that.'

'Well, here's something that might stop you beating yourself up,' Donnie said, tossing a manila envelope on the table. 'Go on, open it.'

Pete leaned forward, unclipped the flap and pulled out an eight-by-ten black-and-white photograph showing a white man surrounded by Asian women at a table laden with half-finished bowls of food and bottles of beer.

'Is that him?' Donnie asked.

Pete reached into his pocket for his wallet. Inside he had a passport-size picture of a man in uniform.

'Yeah, that's him,' Pete said. 'That's Weighorst.'

'Well, he's no longer your problem, or mine, for that matter,' Donnie said. 'This was taken in Bangkok less than a week ago. He's skipped and I can't imagine why he would ever crawl back here.'

'Bangkok?' he said.

Donnie nodded. 'He'll either find himself a lovely Thai girl – probably with an extended family up-country – or he'll end up in a canal in Pat Phong, especially if he tries to pull any of the shit he did here.'

'Where did you get this?' Pete asked.

'Hey, I'm a cop too,' Donnie said, rising and clapping him on the shoulder. 'And I never reveal my informants. That's one less thing for you to worry your pretty little head about. And one less reason for us ever to wade into the cesspool of Soul Alley again.'

'Good work, mate,' Pete said, looking at the picture again. 'Can I hold on to this?'

'Of course. Send it to your people in Intel, it might calm their frayed nerves. Catch you later for a beer and debrief.'

Donnie left in a gust of humidity from the street as Pete examined the picture. He was still studying it a couple of hours later when Lucy emerged from her bedroom.

'Who's that?' she said, draping her arms around Pete's shoulder and kissing the top of his head.

'The guy I've been looking for,' Pete said. 'Looks like he's decamped to Bangkok.'

'Thai girls for sure,' she said. 'Longer faces. And Thai beer, too.'

He silently ceded to her superior knowledge of the visual features of South-East Asian women but there was no mistaking the bottles: Singha beer, Thailand's national drink.

'I guess I'd better get this to the Intel guys, ASAP,' Pete said. 'They're going to be less than pleased that bugger's got away.'

He was sliding the picture back into the envelope when Lucy grabbed his arm.

'Wait,' she said. 'Have another look.'

He shrugged and removed the picture from its cover.

'You see what's on top of the food bowls?'

Pete looks at the picture closely. 'Chopsticks. So what?'

'Thais don't eat with chopsticks so much. They use fork and spoon,' she said. 'And the beer?'

'What about it? It's Singha beer.'

'All labels facing the camera. Every one. Funny, huh?'

Pete studied the picture with renewed focus.

'The framed picture on the wall?' he said.

Lucy looked at the photograph. 'It's the Thai king and queen.'

'Yeah, but look around the edges. There's a lighter shape where a bigger picture used to be. That's just been hung there. Look at where your picture of the Eiffel Tower used to be.'

On the wall there was a distinct dust shadow around the framed portrait of the English Queen.

'You think someone has tricked Donnie?' she said.

'It would have to be someone with the smarts and resources to fake this whole set-up,' Pete replied. 'And a good reason. I'll call Donnie when he gets back to his office. It won't be for a couple of hours but he'll want to know. And he is going to be seriously pissed off.'

CHAPTER 26

The darkness that fell while Xander and Lorenzo unpicked the threads of Pete's life is now a glittering cowl, an endless dome that stretches halfway to infinity. Lorenzo switches off the interior lights and rolls back the camouflage net, all the better, it strikes Xander, to remind them of their insignificance in the great accident of the universe. He passes Xander a lit doobie.

'Where'd you get this?' Xander asks.

'I'd love to spin you a yarn about a hidden valley with marijuana plants the height of palm trees, but I bought it off a guy on the way to the farmers market in Launceston,' Lorenzo says. 'Pure supercharged hydro, I reckon.'

Xander stifles a cough as the smoke slams against the inside of his lungs and nods his confirmation of the potency of the herb. They sit in silence for a few minutes, cogitating, contemplating, trying to remember how to speak.

'The arsehole who said there are things we know, things that we know we don't know, and things we don't know that we don't know got that right, at least,' Lorenzo says, then thinks. 'I may have mixed that up.'

'Nope, you were right,' Xander replies. 'Donald Rumsfeld. US Secretary of Defence, twice. He was the youngest to ever have that job when he got it under Ford, and the oldest when he was hired by George W Bush.'

'Wow, you know a lot of shit,' Lorenzo says.

'Knowing shit is my job,' Xander says. 'There's a fourth part of that he missed out – things that we choose not to know. But as he was the guy who took us into Iraq over weapons of mass destruction that didn't exist, that's hardly a surprise.'

'Do you think there's an element of that with Pete? Not wanting to know?'

'You mean, like me refusing to believe he committed suicide?' Xander asks.

'Well, no, I didn't mean that. I meant Pete and his hunt for Lucy's killer. But now that you mention it ...'

'There's too many other elements for the attacks on me just to be a coincidence,' Xander says. 'Why would anyone steal a suicide victim's laptop? Okay, maybe they were after my files and thought Pete might have a copy. But on the same night that he chose to take his own life? Come on! There's something bigger going on. Something we know that we don't know.'

'No, things we know we don't know are like how pigeons find their way home,' Lorenzo says. 'This, we don't even know if we don't know it. The answer could be right under our noses so we could know it but not even know we know it.'

Both men collapse in giggles that seem to last for lifetimes.

'Shhhh! The neighbours,' Lorenzo says, and that sets them off again.

'I know what it is that we don't know,' Xander says when they have both stopped chuckling. 'We don't know why Lucy was killed. Answer that and we'll be closer to finding out who killed Pete.'

The mention of Pete's murder is as sobering as a bucket of ice water in the face for both men.

'This Russian,' Lorenzo says. 'Does he seem like a pro?'

'Hundred per cent,' Xander says. 'He does voices – accents – but I reckon that's mostly for fun. I've encountered him three, maybe four times; he's a trained fighter, he has access to weapons and is as cool as. But he messes around too much. It's like he can't help it, but he needs to fuck with you.'

'That arrogance could be his weakness and therefore your strength,' Lorenzo says.

'Copy that,' Xander replies. 'I wouldn't mind crossing him again, for Pete if not for me.'

'I don't think you have any choice,' Lorenzo says. 'If you want to get to the truth about what happened to Pete and Lucy, you won't be able to go round him. You'll have to go through him.'

And Xander says nothing because he knows it's true.

They hear the drone before they see it, the distant insistent buzz growing suddenly louder as it clears the ridge behind them. 'Son of a bitch,' Lorenzo says as he quickly stubs out the joint and rolls back the camouflage net. He and Xander peer out through gaps in the foliage into the night sky.

'There!' Xander says, pointing at a flashing red light. They watch as the drone tracks back and forth and then from side to side across the valley below them and then buzzes over the opposite ridge.

'He's doing grids again,' Lorenzo says. 'He thinks we're around here but he doesn't know where.'

'He?' Xander asks. 'It couldn't be Parks department?'

'I'm not sure Parks even have drones, and if they did they'd never put them up at night, scaring the crap out of half the nocturnals and all the nesting birds. No, this is your Russian friend, for sure. Tomorrow, before first light, I'm going to take you out along the Ho Chi Minh Trail. I'll put you on one of the regular walking tracks and you can make your own way back to Derwent Bridge from there. It's a long way round, but if that bastard's drone comes back when we're hallway up the cliff, we're fucked.'

'What if he comes back when we're on the trail?' Xander asks.

'I'm taking the crossbow. That'll be one dead drone.'

CHAPTER 27

The descent to Lorenzo's 'Ho Chi Minh Trail' is less perilous and a lot quicker than the climb to the cliff above Lorenzo's cave, not least because Xander is neither blindfolded nor having to hang on to the older man's belt. Once again, his companion sets a cracking pace, but manages to step lightly for someone of his considerable bulk. It occurs to Xander that Lorenzo might be happier fighting a real war somewhere, rather than simply evading Parks and Wildlife. But then he recalls the sudden and extended silences that punctuated the previous night's reminiscences about Vietnam. But they weren't all horror stories. Lorenzo – whose real name turned out to be Gordon – even told Xander how he got his nickname.

'It was a stinkin' hot day and we were trying to move a truck that had snapped its axle on Kangaroo, the helipad at Nui Dat,' Lorenzo said. 'The only way to move it was to repair it and that was taking hours, getting in the way of flights in and out, screwing up ops, stuffing up supplies. The sun was ripping down and I could feel the skin lifting off the back of my neck. My old giggle hat – that's what we called bush hats – wasn't doing it so I draped a towel over my head and tied an old elastic snake belt round it. Then this desk jockey officer walks past and says, "Who the fuck do you think you are, Lawrence of fucking Arabia? Put your bush hat on." And my skipper, who's working under the truck, slides out, and says, "As a matter of fact, he is Lawrence of Arabia so why don't you fuck off before we put a spanner in your hand and make you do some work for once in your privileged life." The rest of the fellas were pissing themselves and I was Lawrence, then Lorenzo, from that day on till I shipped out. That's how I knew you were Pete's grandson – no one else alive calls me that.'

Lorenzo has been silent all the way down to the valley floor, occasionally stopping Xander with a hand gesture, listening then moving on. When they reached a fringe of trees with the outline of a well-trodden path beyond, Lorenzo unexpectedly hugs Xander.

'You're a good bloke and your grandad was very proud of you,' he says in his combat whisper. 'I'd like to catch up with you when all this shit is behind you. But don't come looking for me. I will find you.'

He hands him a piece of paper, folded neatly into a small perfect square. 'That's the number of my satellite phone. Just ring it twice then hang up and I'll know it's you and call you back. Any more than that, I'll know it's someone else or you're pissed and wanting a chat, and I'll ignore it. Take care of yourself. The track back to Derwent Bridge is that way.'

Xander looks in the direction Lorenzo is indicating and sees a trail dwindling along the valley before rising dauntingly towards the horizon, a mere scratch on the side of the hill. When he looks back to thank Lorenzo, he has gone and not even a quivering branch betrays his recent presence. Xander gets a sense that the people both helping him and trying to harm him are operating at a completely different level of subterfuge than he's ever encountered before, even among big-city crims.

It takes three hours for Xander to reach the road, merrily greeting fellow trekkers as they pass, but only for the first hour. After that he can barely raise a smile, let alone muster a friendly wave, as the physical exertion and the previous night's alcohol-induced dehydration take their toll.

Xander sags with relief when he gets to the Frenchman's Bridge car park and the old yellow Volvo is sitting there, an anachronism amid a mob of shiny, roo-barred, over-powered and underutilised SUVs. Althea is leaning against the driver's door.

'Well, if it isn't Bear Grylls,' she says with a laugh, enfolding him in an unexpected hug.

'Paddington Bear Grylls, maybe,' Xander says. 'I need looking after.'

'I brought coffee. That's a start,' she says, handing him a paper cup that he's surprised to feel is still warm.

'Been waiting long?'

'Lorenzo and Johnny have a very basic but effective communications system,' she says. 'Lorenzo apparently watched you all the way then called Johnny when you were about an hour away. He called me, and here I am.'

Xander takes a long pull on his coffee and takes Althea's place against the door of the car.

'What's he like, this mysterious Lorenzo?'

'He's like a fucking talking bear. If you saw him in the street, you'd think he was a derro. His clothes are half-combat, half-bushwalker, all camo. He has this huge beard and eyebrows like you've never seen. He'd be 190 centimetres, easy and fitter than most men his age, I reckon, or mine for that matter. Oh, and he hunts game with a crossbow,' Xander says. 'One of a kind.'

'And he camps in the bush?'

'In a cave and I can't tell you exactly where ...'

'You probably shouldn't, me being a cop and all that.'

'I was blindfolded for most of the way in. And I couldn't tell you how we got down onto that track.' Xander gestures back to the path and the gap in the trees from which he'd recently emerged. 'Any developments while I was away?' he asks, not expecting much of an answer, barely thirty-six hours having passed since they last saw each other.

'A lot, actually,' she says. 'Rob didn't make it.'

'Shit! He's dead?'

'Heart failure,' she replies. 'The docs said he'd been weakened by years of drug abuse. Decades, they reckoned. He'd cleaned himself up, but the damage was done. The hit-and-run was just the last straw.'

'It's still a crime, though? Right?' Xander asks.

'For sure. And the Russian is the prime suspect, but he's already back on the mainland. Flew out yesterday under what we think may be his real name ...'

'Which is?'

'Alexei Alden.'

'Alden?'

'He's Russian-Maltese. Alden is a pretty common name in Malta.'

Xander thinks, trying not to jump to the obvious conclusion but failing.

'What's up?' Althea asks.

'Trackie Vella is Maltese. I wonder if Alden was working for him.'

'Could be.'

'Are you sure he's left?'

'Pretty sure. We have him on CCTV boarding a plane to Melbourne. Why do you ask?'

'Lorenzo's place was buzzed by a drone a couple of times yesterday and last night. Lorenzo says Parks and Wildlife don't use drones.'

'They didn't, but there have been reports of someone living wild near the Walls of Jerusalem,' she says, her voice heavy with irony.

'Lorenzo ...'

'That would be my guess. It was Johnny Spangler who told me,' she says. 'A Parks and Wildlife crew had been in asking questions just yesterday.'

'Then maybe we'd better get back to town before people start putting two and two together and coming up with four point zero.'

They drive in silence for a while, Xander behind the wheel, Althea waiting for him to describe what happened with Lorenzo.

'Anything you want to share?' she says eventually. 'Was Lorenzo any help?'

'He knew Pete really well in Vietnam. Better than I knew him here.'

'How come? You said you two were really close.'

'Not enough for him to tell me he had a lover in Vietnam. And she had a kid by him.'

'What!?'

'My mystery aunt, I suppose.'

'Holy Hell,' Althea says. 'He knows this for sure?'

'He has all these files … pictures, mostly. Pete, his girlfriend Lucy, and an American called Caddick or Carrick or something. I wrote it down. It seems Pete's lover wanted to trade information for safe passage out of Vung Tau, but before she can tell the Vietnamese Army contact, a Major Tang, that she knows the name of a spy, she gets killed by an Aussie deserter who had a grudge against Pete.'

'And Lorenzo knows who it was?'

'They know who it was, but they don't know why. The information she was going to pass on died with her, but Pete got obsessed with finding out. Writing his memoirs must have triggered it. The only significant case he hadn't solved, he told Lorenzo. But this guy Carrick or whatever, they were big mates back in the day and …'

Althea's phone pings. She pulls it out of her bag and studies the screen in rapt silence.

'Interesting?' Xander says, forcing himself to keep his eyes on the road.

'It's from NSW police. Alexei Alden is a known associate of Vella's, he's a former GRU – that's Russian Intelligence ...'

'I know what GRU is,' Xander says.

'And he's now a gun for hire. Vella is suspected of having used him to eliminate rivals but nothing could ever be proved. They've got him on CCTV in Sydney Airport ...'

'I thought you said he flew to Melbourne?'

'Did I? Maybe he did, then jumped on a connection to Sydney. It's almost as quick and if he was making sure he wasn't followed ...'

'You said you saw footage of him getting on a flight to Melbourne.'

'Like I said ...'

'How did you know it was him?'

'How do you mean?'

'You've never seen him.'

'CCTV from the hotel.'

'My hotel doesn't have CCTV.'

'From the hotel in Mole Creek,' she says, throwing her hands up in exasperation. 'Fuck sake, Xander. Rob said he'd been in there? What's with the third degree?'

Xander drives in silence for a moment, distracting himself from the thoughts bubbling in his head by focusing on the road.

'Sorry,' he says eventually. 'I guess I'm freaked out by all this. Jumping at shadows.'

'Yeah, well, just don't jump down my throat when things don't add up the way you want them to.' She leans forward and presses play on the ancient tape player in the console and Bruce Springsteen is 'Born to Run' all over again.

'Kill me now,' Althea says. When Jackson Browne comes on, suggesting drivers don't let the sound of their wheels make them crazy, she switches off again.

'Was it hard to find Lorenzo's cave?' she says.

'I guess. At least for me.'

'But the drones didn't spot you?'

'Lorenzo reckoned if they'd seen us they would have held their position for a while, taking pictures and fixing the location.'

'Why is he living there? Is he on the run or something?' she asks.

'From himself, maybe. Like a lot of Vietnam vets, he was messed up by what he saw and did there. Now that he sees the Vietnamese as people, rather than the enemy, the guilt must be pretty overwhelming.'

'Do you think that's why your grandad didn't talk about it?'

'That, and the fact that he left a kid and a secret lover behind – albeit a dead one,' Xander says. 'You wouldn't have to scratch the surface of war stories too deep before all that started to come out. Speaking of which, what's the connection between Alden and Auntie Linh turning up?'

'Is there one?'

'She had the laptop Alden was looking for. That's a connection.'

'Or a coincidence.'

'My train doesn't stop at that station,' he says. 'Coincidence is the last resort of the logic-impaired.'

'Was that one of Pete's little sayings?'

'Nope. I thunk that one up all on my own. But, yeah, Pete believed that behind every coincidence there was a couple of intersecting but separate strands of fact.'

'Give me a for-instance,' Althea says.

Xander thinks for a few seconds. 'Okay, a man and a woman both work in IT and like art house movies. They go to a brand-new bar, they meet, they hit it off, they get it on. Is that coincidence?'

'Sounds like it to me.'

'Okay, but they read the same magazines because they have similar interests, tastes and have the same cultural backgrounds. That increases their chances of having similar jobs, which means they would work similar hours and read the same reviews of bars, which increases their chance of going for a drink at the same bar at the same time and, guess what . . .'

'They have similar interests so that increases their chances of hitting it off,' she says. 'I get it.'

'So what's the connection with Linh turning up at the same time as Alden? And then warning me about him?'

'Interesting,' she says. 'Pete was trying to find out what happened to his lover . . .'

'Lucy.'

'Lucy. He travels to Vietnam and stirs things up there. Linh gets wind of it and follows him back to Australia to help solve the mystery. He is her father, after all. Meanwhile, Alden comes looking for Pete, to find out if he's helping you with your story about Vella. They both end up at Pete's cottage around the same time. That's the coincidence.'

'You could be right,' Xander says. 'There was no earlier time that they could have crossed paths because Pete wasn't there.'

'That's it! Maybe there's no connection between Linh and Alden,' Althea says. 'They just happened to turn up looking for Pete at the same time.'

'That's starting to sound awfully like a coincidence, and an unlikely one,' Xander says. 'Linh took the laptop. Then tried to warn me about Alden.'

'How about Linh borrowed the laptop to copy the pictures and stuff – we know she did that – then Pete gets killed and she warns you,' Althea says.

The slightest shake of Xander's head suggests he's not fully buying it.

'What are you going to do now?' Althea asks.

'What do you think I should do?'

'Honestly, I think you dodged a bullet with Alden – almost literally – but he's back on the mainland now, if he's even still in

Australia. I would just let it lie. What's done is done. The local police are looking for him, and so are the cops in Melbourne and Sydney. He's going to have to keep his head down and he can't come back here. If he does, and he's caught, we can nail him for killing Pete too.'

'Is it safe for me to go back to Sydney?' Xander asks.

'I wouldn't. You've got a place here. No point in turning yourself into bait.' She looks at him pointedly. 'Unless that's what you want.'

They fall silent while Xander wrangles the balance between caution and gravity as they follow the twists and turns of the road down the mountainside.

'We can always listen to your music if you've got a cassette,' Xander says with a smug smile.

'What's a cassette?' she says, pressing 'play' again, and they let the echoes of a different time in their lives and other peoples', wash over them, each in their own thoughts as they roll back towards Launceston.

'I might head over to Mole Creek, to the cottage,' Xander says as he pulls up at Althea's front door, a solid hour of vintage rock and zero conversation later.

'No way, compadre,' Althea says. 'You're exhausted and, I'm guessing, hungry. Come in, rest and eat, then convince me why it can't wait till tomorrow.'

Xander turns off the engine and follows her up the steps and into the house, his car door closing with a rusty crunch rather than a clunk.

'Hey,' Xander says to her back. 'Did you ever catch Ralphie?'

'Who?' Althea says as she stops and turns.

'The ginger guy with the bad tatts who attacked me with the golf club.'

'Oh, him?' she says. 'He's in the wind. Probably back in Sydney.'

'I was just thinking,' Xander says. 'Why would Trackie Vella hire a professional like Alden, then send an oxygen thief like Ralphie to back him up?'

'Belt and braces?' she says, as she continues into the house.

Xander pauses by the car. There's a tingling sensation at the back of his neck, a shiver caught with nowhere to go, that tells him danger may be near. But he smiles as he realises he's totally okay with that.

***

Xander sits on the saggy single bed in what he has mentally christened the 'Arles room'. He can hear water running but no voices. Geoffrey must be out. Xander contemplates his predicament. Alden almost certainly killed Pete and was clearly looking for information. Or, at least, wanted to know what information they had. But if he thought Pete had information on his computer, why kill him? He would only do that if he thought Pete knew stuff, secrets that Vella didn't want shared. And if this was about Trackie Vella, why wasn't he, Xander, lying under six feet of Tasmanian clay? He's the one with the knowledge in his head. Forget the laptop. He's done all the digging. He's the one who knows stuff. The files may be deleted but he only needs to retrace his steps to put them back together again. It would take time but it's far from impossible. Was Alden trying to find out how much he knew before he killed him too? That would work, but then, how many people would Alden have to bump off to be sure the information was safe? This all feels like overkill, literally. And in any case, Pete's laptop seemed to be the Holy Grail in this quest.

Althea taps lightly on the door, but doesn't wait for a reply before entering.

'I ran you a bath,' she says.

'Do I need one?'

'I thought you might like one after your efforts in the wilds,' she says with a smile. 'And, to be honest, you are a bit whiffy.'

He follows her through to the main bedroom and its massive ensuite bathroom, all white glazed subway tiles and polished chrome fittings. The bath is modern, in a scallop shape, huge, and three-quarters full of sudsy water.

'Now, that is a bath,' Xander says.

'One of the benefits of living with rich, gay men,' she says. 'They don't stint on fixtures and fittings. Now hop in and I'll get you a towel.'

'Speaking of whom ...?'

'Geoffrey? He's at a conference in Adelaide. You won't be disturbed.' She walks to the door. 'I'll get you that towel.'

Xander waits till the door clicks shut, then undresses and climbs into the bath. The water is luxuriously warm, the scents of lavender and vanilla, he guesses, instantly relaxing. Xander makes a conscious decision to enjoy it and dismiss any negative thoughts that threaten to intrude on this blissful interlude. He doesn't stand a chance. The brain's beta waves, triggered by warmth and relaxation as he slides under the bubbles, take his thoughts laterally. What if it was something Pete knew about Vella that he didn't? Pete was still in the police when Vella was getting started. What if Alden didn't mean to kill Pete? And what was it Althea said? 'I thought you weren't a gun person ...'

The door opens and Althea enters carrying two towels, her hair tied up in a ponytail and wearing a knee-length silk robe with a red-and-gold dragon motif embroidered down one side. Xander says nothing but believes this may be the sexiest human being he has ever seen.

'You brought two towels?' is all he can think to say.

'We shouldn't waste hot water,' she says. 'Didn't you know we're in the middle of an environmental crisis?'

She places the towels on a shelf and allows the robe to slide off her shoulder and form a crescent on the floor at her heels.

'Now, is that a periscope or are you just pleased to see me?' she says.

***

Face-up, lying on a creeper trolley under a jacked-up Nissan Patrol, Johnny Spangler contorts himself into an awkward twist as he tries to tighten a nut he hopes will hold the transmission in place long enough to get the vehicle to Launceston and a proper mechanic. A pair of shiny shoes and neatly pressed khaki chino shins appear beside his head.

'I said a bluddy hour,' he says. 'Wait in the café.'

'Sind sie Herr Spangler?' says a voice.

'Who wants to know?' Spangler replies.

'Manners, Herr Spangler!' the voice says, continuing in an accent he recognises immediately as East German. 'I asked first.'

Spangler starts propelling the creeper from under the SUV but one expensively shod foot stops it.

'Tell me what you know about the man who calls himself Lorenzo,' the voice says.

CHAPTER 28

The shouts and laughter of Australian voices percolated from the bar next door. It was business as usual in the rest of Vung Tau as Pete waited for Donnie to arrive. Their conversation that morning had been more businesslike than usual, but that was hardly surprising, Pete thought. He'd just informed Donnie that the picture of Johnny Weighorst in Bangkok was probably a fake, as confirmed by Army Intelligence, and the person who gave it to him may well have been the spy that Major Tang had warned him about.

Donnie had said he'd look into it, then sent a message via Logistics to meet him in Lucy's at closing time. That time had come and gone, and while the bar sat empty apart from her and Pete, next door the men were getting drunker, clearly trying to loosen the shackles of memory and fear. The women – girls, really – were getting louder, bolder, shriller, each finding their own siren song as they timed their teases and taunts. They needed to make sure the diggers spent as much as they could on Saigon tea – the overpriced, under-proofed beverage of choice for the bar girls – but not so much on beer for themselves that they'd lose the urge to follow them to a sweaty cot, one in a row divided by dangling sheets, to complete the main transaction.

The sounds of the night ebbed and flowed as Lucy swept the floors and carried the dust of the day out into the back yard. Pete had tried to help but she had shooed him away. This was women's work. Instead, he cleared the empties off tables and stacked the crates ready for collection. For some unfathomable reason, this was men's work that won Lucy's approval as she nodded on her way back outside with another panful of dirt. Squeals of fake delight and roars of bravado from the adjoining bar almost drowned out her scream from outside, the piercing edge of a nightmare.

'Lucy!' Pete said aloud, dropping beer bottles into the sink, where they dribbled and foamed like unhappy endings. Pete didn't realise how drunk he was until he tried to follow her out into the yard where her cries were audible but muffled. He had to pause for a moment and get his balance before he entered the lane behind the café, where she was being held, kicking and wriggling, by a tall man in battle pants, a green singlet, and an art gallery of tattoos. He'd reduced her yells to mumbles by clamping his massive fingers over her mouth. At least two other male figures were lurking in the shadows.

'Okay, guys,' Pete said, one palm raised, the other reaching for his side-arm. 'We all know this isn't going to end well for you. This might be a good time for you to let her go and fuck off back to the cesspit from which you oozed.'

'Hey, McAuslan! I hear you're looking for me,' an Australian voice said from the darkness. Its owner stepped into the light of a single unshaded bulb that illuminated the small yard.

'Weighorst?' Pete said, squinting in the half-light.

The man nodded and smiled. 'You are way too fucken smart for your own good,' he said.

'Let her go,' Pete said. 'Then we can talk about you giving yourself up.'

It was a ludicrous suggestion and Pete knew it but he was playing for time and looking for an angle.

'Let her go? Man, I am so not ready to do that,' Weighorst said with a snort of derision. 'I'm here to get my compensation for the trouble you have caused me. And I'm thinking some Juicy

Lucy pussy. As for my boys here, well they've been on, let's say, minimum wage for a while.'

Pete looks around the yard. There must be another four of them, apart from Weighorst and the man holding Lucy – who seemed to have exhausted herself and stopped fighting.

'Okay, just to be clear, if you touch a hair on her head, I will hunt you down and kill you in as slow and painful a way as I can think of, capiche?'

Which was exactly when someone smacked a length of timber behind his knees and he went down like a kicked deckchair. This was the cue for the others to pile in and punch and kick him towards oblivion.

Pete felt no pain, just the jolts of kicks and blows, but sensed blackness closing around him. Then a gunshot emptied the air of the grunts and curses of his assailants and replaced them with a scream from Lucy. As it echoed away, and car doors slammed, gears crunched, and tyres squealed, Pete was aware of being lifted up gently and held.

'Sorry, buddy,' Donnie said. 'I should've been here sooner.'

Pete looked up and saw Lucy's tear-streaked face next to Carrick's. Then he blacked out.

CHAPTER 29

When Xander wakes, the surprise of realising he is in a strange bed is replaced by the sensory overload of an aroma of hot coffee, the sensation of her soft body against his as she slides back into his warm shadow, and her whispered imprecations to stay.

'I can call in sick,' she says. 'We can stay in bed all day.'

'Hmm. Tempting,' he says. 'But I need to get back to Mole Creek sometime.'

She snuggles up to him and tries again but her radio alarm clicks into life.

'... the mayor said they had no plans to reopen the venue. Meanwhile, in news from Northern Tasmania, a popular Derwent Bridge mechanic has died in an accident in his workshop. Local sources say it appears a support slipped as he was working under a vehicle. Authorities are trying to contact his family in Germany before releasing his name. He had no known family locally. In sport ...'

'Johnny Spanners,' Xander says.

'Shit,' Althea says. 'I probably need to get up there ASAP.' She pronounces it 'ay-sap'.

'Much need for family liaison when there's no family here in Australia?' Xander says, without thinking.

'These communities are families,' she replies, as she rolls out of bed and checks her phone on the bedside table, using her

249

thumbprint to unlock it. 'We're expected to be there.' She runs to the shower.

'Should I come ...?'

'Fuck no,' she says. 'Get dressed and get your bags,' her muffled justification for haste lost in the torrent of her shower and a gust of billowing steam.

Her mobile phone starts buzzing periodically. First with a phone call. Then with text messages. Xander stares at it for a moment, but his desire to trust and be trusted gives way to natural and professional curiosity. He flips the phone over and reads the texts. The first says: 'DS Burgess. Make your way to Derwent Bridge immediately. Call me en route.' The second reads: 'Sarge, DB accident may not be an accident. SOCO on way.' Another says: 'Burgess. Call me now. DD.' Xander hears the shower being switched off and replaces the phone so it's lying face-down.

'I'm sorry but you don't have time to shower,' she calls from the bathroom. 'Get your things from your room. We're leaving in ten.'

She checks the messages on her phone as he grabs a towel discarded on the floor the previous night.

'Will I see you again?' she says minutes later, pink and damp in a neatly pressed suit as they meet up in the hallway. 'See, as in ... you know ...'

'Do you want to?'

'I didn't think I'd be a one-night stand,' she says.

'Don't all relationships start with one night?' he replies.

'Oh, this is a relationship now?'

'You tell me,' he says. 'I'm not complaining, but I didn't expect any of this.'

'You think I did?' she says with a mischievous smile. 'Plan it, I mean?'

'What I mean is, shit is going down too fast to even think.'

'Johnny Spanners? It's an accident. That's all.'

He can't tell her that he knows it's more than that, because then he'll have to admit he was looking at her phone. But why is she lying to him? There's a feeling in Xander's gut that he doesn't want to address until he's had a chance to process the events of the past few days. He certainly doesn't want to discuss it with Althea, who seems to be playing her own game of truth or dare.

Outside at the Volvo they part in a series of awkward moments. A look ... a hug ... kisses on the cheeks, then the lips.

'Althea,' he says. 'You're an amazing woman and I'm lucky to have met you. I want to get to know you better, I really do, but ...'

'It's okay. We can take our time. But I worry about you. It's an accident, but if you're right and it wasn't, maybe you would be safer back in Sydney.' She looks down. 'I don't want to be the reason you put yourself in harm's way.'

'The guilt thing again,' he says.

'Something like that,' she says and kisses him again, more perfunctorily this time, and gets into her car. She closes the door, starts up and pulls away, looking back and waving before she drives off.

Xander stands in the street, wondering exactly what just happened. Two texts referring to her as a detective sergeant. Isn't that joke inappropriate for a death call? But then she's still insisting that it's an accident, despite what the text messages said.

St John's Street takes Xander straight into the centre of town and he drives circuits, scanning passing cafes for signs of something other than bacon and eggs on their specials boards, although all he really needs is coffee and free internet. Anything edible will be a bonus.

Having found a place that ticks three boxes – coffee, internet and a Cleo-sized parking space outside – he orders the first thing he recognises on the menu and logs into the café's promised high-speed internet connection. He wants to clear things with Vella but there's no point in calling him before noon – Trackie is a night person. Not wanting to use up the credit on his pre-paid phone, he WhatsApps Marnie, former girlfriend but current Sydney cop.

'WhatsApp? Really, Xander? What are you? Fifteen?' a surprisingly clear voice emanates from his earbuds.

'Whatever happened to "Hey, how are you?" or even just "hello"?' he says. 'And I wouldn't be able to connect if you didn't already have it.'

'Part of the job these days,' she says with a sigh.

'Mine too. Encrypted at both ends.'

'Like that's not suspicious from the get-go,' she says.

'Look, I need to know if Trackie Vella's hit man is still here in Tassie. If you could give me a heads-up ...'

'Vella?' she says. 'He's gone straight.'

'None of them ever go straight. It's not in their DNA.'

'Yeah, true,' she says. 'But the word is he's using lawyers rather than standover men these days. There are no hit men on our radar.'

'You sure? How about Alexei Alden? Maltese-Russian.'

'That's an exotic combination, Xander,' she says. 'Not the kind of profile you would forget.'

'I'm told your guys, the Vics and the Feds are turning over rocks to find him,' he says, the Vics meaning Victorian police. 'He's a pro.'

'Yeah? Well, I must have missed that memo,' she says.

'And I was attacked by one of Vella's thugs. A scrawny scrote called Ralphie ...'

'Ralphie Emerson? I heard he was on the outs with Vella. He forgot they'd changed the rules and threatened a building manager with a baseball bat.'

'Ralphie is quite the sportsman,' Xander says. 'He used a golf club on me.'

'You okay?'

'Damaged pride is the only long-term injury. I reckon he's on his way back to Sydney. Maybe Ralphie and this Alexei Alden are working together.'

'Doesn't sound like Ralphie. He couldn't maintain a friendship with his reflection. I'll check and maybe get back to you.'

'Maybe?'

'Your credit at the Bank of Marnie is well overdrawn, babe. Don't push your luck.'

'Hey, before you go, have you ever come across a cop here in Launceston called Althea Burgess?'

'DS Burgess? Yeah, I've met her. Odd fish, if you ask me.'

'Well, is she a detective sergeant or has she been bumped down to family liaison?'

'Burgess? She's a high-flyer and doesn't she like you to know it. At least, she *was* three weeks ago when I met her on a forensics course. To hear her you'd think she invented fingerprints.'

Xander falls silent. A garish artist's impression of a Tasmanian tiger on one wall seems to be mocking him, laughing rather than snarling.

'Zan? You still there?' Marnie asks. 'Oh, jeez, don't tell me you've fucked her.'

'No ... well ... look, it's more complicated than that.'

'You fucking root rat,' Marnie says. 'You are fucking hopeless.'

She clicks off and Xander stares at his phone, briefly, then goes online to read reports of Johnny Spangler's death. According to one story, a recently filed online update, the old bush mechanic was crushed under a car he was working on when a support slipped, but now there's a theory that it may have been deliberate. Police are investigating a report by a foreign tourist who saw Spangler arguing with an older man and had provided a detailed description.

'The suspect was wearing a mixture of combat gear and bush-walking clothes, all in camouflage colours,' says the report. 'He had a huge beard and bushy eyebrows. He was 190cm, looked fit and strong for his age and had a crossbow strapped across his shoulder. Police believe he may be living in a cave somewhere in or near the Walls of Jerusalem national park.'

Xander pulls up with a start. The description not only fits Lorenzo, but matches almost exactly the way he'd described him to Althea.

'Is she feeding them this shit?' Xander asks himself a little too loudly. But he knows the answer before he's even uttered the words. He digs out the emergency number Lorenzo gave him and calls, letting it ring only twice, as instructed. Then he waits. Lorenzo doesn't respond by the time Xander has finished his breakfast and second coffee. He wonders about this foreign tourist who reported the argument with Johnny Spangler. Could it be Alden? Maybe he isn't back on the mainland, after all.

Xander feels sick. Althea has been lying to him, this he knows. And spying on him too, for that matter. But why? And for whom?

CHAPTER 30

Pete had lost track of the days. It wasn't the injuries that kept him somewhere between coma and consciousness, it was the morphine they were pumping into him to deal with the pain. Truth be told, he was blissed out, most of the time. The proper bed in a real hospital with a procession of nurses from the beautiful to the briskly efficient – or both – would have been enough to put him on cloud nine, but it was the high-grade opiates that kept him there when his broken ribs and collar bone and busted jaw ached.

Pete felt Donnie's weight, the mattress moving and springs complaining as the American sat on the end of the bed, before he opened his eyes and his friend's face swam into focus.

'And he's back,' Donnie said, squeezing Pete's leg. 'How are you feeling, buddy?'

'Like someone removed my brain and replaced it with the insides of a cushion,' Pete said.

'Well, that's exactly what they did,' Donnie said. 'And apparently your IQ has gone up twenty points.'

Pete laughed then grimaced and howled comically as his ribs took issue with the sudden increase of lung activity. Then he was serious.

'How's Lucy?' Pete asked.

'She's fine. Just a bump on the head,' Donnie said with a smile. 'She's thinking of selling the bar and moving to her sister's in Saigon, out of harm's way. In fact, that's the plan for you, too.'

'You're sending me to Saigon?'

'Your people are sending you home – back to Australia. You're done here.'

'What?' Pete protested. 'Why?'

'You're in worse shape than you think – but you'll feel it soon enough. Also, it's been reported that you shot one of your comrades in arms,' Donnie said. 'Not a good look for an Aussie MP or whatever you call yourselves.'

'Provos,' Pete said. 'And did I? I'm pretty sure I would remember.'

'No, you didn't,' Donnie said. 'I did.'

'Okay,' Pete said slowly. 'But how come I'm the one being cashiered?'

'You're not,' Donnie said. 'Full pay and pension while you serve out your time training new recruits in Sydney. Maybe even a promotion.'

'I still don't get it.'

'It's all about ass-covering,' Donnie said. 'If Weighorst surfaces again, we're officially saying he was shot in self-defence. If anyone challenges that, you can legitimately say you were defending yourself. I mean, look at you. Whereas I ...' He rolled his eyes. 'Look, basically, we're not supposed to shoot our allies, okay?'

'And what do you need from me?'

'If push comes to shove, I need you to say you shot this Weighorst clown, even though everyone knows you didn't ...'

'And some people know *you* did?'

Donnie nods again. 'For reasons that are pretty obvious, we want to keep this under wraps.'

'What about Weighorst?'

'He seems to have sunk back into Soul Alley. Don't worry, we'll get him.'

'Soul Alley? I thought you said you shot him.'

'I did, in the leg. They have their own medics there.'

'When do I ship out?'

'Soon as you are fit to fly. And don't worry about Lucy. I'll keep an eye on her.'

'I'll bet you will,' Pete said, trying to smile.

'It's not like that, old buddy,' Donnie said. 'We are all friends. I'm fond of her, of course, and she of me, I think. War is Hell and there are always losses on both sides, but you don't have to be a complete asshole.'

Pete closed his eyes and felt the weight shift off the end of the bed as Donnie left. War is Hell, he thought, and in so many ways. He was lucky not to have suffered the ignominy of dying in a bar fight after surviving so many real battles.

Leaving Lucy was going to kill him in a different way, but they'd both known this day would come eventually. He tried to look on the bright side – he was going home to Kate, and he'd had enough of this man-made hellhole and this war that they were surely going to lose.

Even so, something about this just did not seem right.

CHAPTER 31

The smell of bleach and disinfectant in the cottage carry a whiff of betrayal as Xander thinks back to his first meeting with Althea. He'd sarcastically said her cleaners were experts in destroying evidence. He'd had no idea how close that was to the truth. He'd ignored three phone calls from her while he was in Launceston, but takes the fourth now that he is safely home.

'Hey, how are you going?' she asks. 'Want to meet for dinner tonight?'

'You still in Derwent Bridge?'

'Yeah, but we're wrapping up soon.'

'Thing is, I'm taking your advice ...'

'How so?' she says.

'I'm on my way to the airport,' he lies. 'I'm on the next flight back to Sydney.'

'Oh.'

'It was your idea,' he says.

'Yeah, I know,' she says. 'Just kinda disappointing.'

'I can't win here.'

'You can if you stay,' she says. 'Stay and you get the jackpot.'

'Tempting,' Xander lies again. 'But it sounds like the Russian is still around. Or maybe he flew back.' He can't bring himself to repeat the elaborate, calculated mendacity he suspects created the name Alexei Alden.

'They think it might have been deliberate,' she says. 'Johnny Spangler. But they think it was Lorenzo, not Alden.'

He wants to scream 'Stop it. Just stop fucking lying.' But for as long as she believes that he hasn't worked out that she's been playing him then he's just a little safer.

'Look. I gotta go. They're calling my flight.'

'Call me when you get there,' she says. 'Let me know you're okay.'

He doesn't say what he's thinking and instead just mumbles, 'Will do. Bye.' And clicks off.

'What now?' Xander asks himself as he looks around the room. What would Pete do?

The room is tidier than he expects – but then the Russian has probably been through here at least once. The desk is clear and the blood stains have been removed by the cleaners with efficiency that would be the envy of a serial killer. The saggy sofa, where he would sleep off the first half of whisky nights until his aching back would drive him to his bed, looks less dusty than it has in years.

He looks around, not exactly seeking inspiration, but finding some nonetheless. On one wall hangs a display of cute inspirational wooden plaques that would normally carry saccharine, positive messages like 'Home Sweet Home' or 'Home is Where the Heart is' or 'A Mother is the only friend you'll ever need'. But a pal – possibly a girlfriend – of Pete's had some specially made for him with lines from TV cop shows and movies. Like 'Get off your ass and knock on doors' or 'Kick ass and take names' or 'Be Careful Out There' and 'Do you feel lucky, punk?' all done in ironically flowery fonts on pastel colours.

One in particular catches Xander's eye: It says, 'Follow the money'. That's when it occurs to him that the Russian may have wiped all of Pete's computer files, but he couldn't erase a bank's credit card records. Two minutes later, aided by Pete's credit card number and using the password that he could never persuade Pete to change, he is looking at all his grandfather's transactions for as far back as he could ever possibly want to go.

He starts at three months earlier and works forward, feeling he is intruding but knowing it's exactly what Pete would have wanted him to do. His first quick scan for larger sums reveals a payment for more than $3000 to Vietnam Airlines. Then there's the Myst Dong Khoi hotel in Saigon and Palace Hotel in Vung Tau and an obscure reference that turns out, with help from TripAdvisor, to be a restaurant in Long Than village. From what Lorenzo told him, that's where Major Tang now lives. Then a taxi ride to Saigon, another night in the Myst, a much smaller charge on Vietnam Airlines, presumably for changing his flights, and then ... nothing, except 48 hours later he's eating in a fancy restaurant in Canberra. But then not, it seems, as the charge is cancelled.

Xander calls the Long Than restaurant listed on the credit card. The phone rings several times and Xander is about to give up when the phone clicks and a female voice answers.

'Xingxau,' she says, followed by a stream of Vietnamese that Xander assumes is the name of the restaurant.

'Hello. I don't suppose you speak English, do you?'

'Of course,' she says. 'How can I help you?'

'Oh great ... hi ... look, I know this is a long shot but, do you know a Major Tang? I think he might be a customer in your restaurant.'

'Not Major Tang,' she says. 'I know Colonel Tang. Is that who you are looking for?'

'Yes, yes, of course. Colonel Tang. Do you have a contact number for him?'

'Yes, but I shouldn't really ...'

'It's okay. I'm an old friend.'

'An old friend who doesn't know he is a colonel? I don't think so.'

'Okay,' Xander says. 'Can you pass on a message? Tell him Pete McAuslan's grandson called.'

The girl on the end of the phone hesitates.

'Then he can choose whether or not to contact me.'

'Okay,' she says. 'Give me your details.'

The information exchange concluded, and a promise to pass on his number and name extracted, Xander returns to the credit card charges.

Why does a fancy restaurant charge you then cancel it? Because you complained about the meal? Unlikely. Xander has eaten there a couple of times and the food and service don't leave any room for complaints. No, someone else insisted on paying. Someone with a generous entertainment allowance from their employers, or Pete would never have allowed them to pay. Definitely not a journalist, not with the Fourth Estate's fifth-rate expenses budgets. Xander would lay odds this meal was at the expense of the US Consulate and, specifically, Donnie Carrick.

The next date and the one after that show two visits to the War Memorial museum and Xander decides it's time he took a trip to the nation's capital himself.

As he drives back to Launceston, Xander wrestles with his increasing doubts over Althea, the principal one being why she has been lying to him. It seems to have started on day one, when she told him she was family liaison – for whatever reason – and then maybe just became harder for her to undo the fiction, especially when they got romantically involved. Is it as simple as that? A first-date lie based on a belief that you will probably never see this person again. Xander had once told a girl he was a vegetarian as he suspected anything else was a deal-breaker if he was going to have a one-night stand with her. Three months later, after a long and largely meat-free relationship, she walked out on him when she caught him in a café eating a bacon sandwich.

But there's more to this that's bugging him. Pete used to say that love may be blind, but lust turns you into the Pinball Wizard – deaf and dumb as well. Only in this context, it's dumb as in stupid.

'There are three reasons good people do bad things,' Pete told Xander early in his crime-writing career. 'Money, sex and power, or combinations thereof.'

Neither money nor sex seem to be an issue for Althea and Geoffrey. That leaves power, and Xander wonders what control Althea has over Geoffrey, or vice versa. And, again, why? Althea has been playing him, for sure, stringing him along to avoid him digging too deeply into Pete's death. But why would she or anyone else do that? Was she trying to protect him? Keep him out of harm's way? She said as much. She didn't want to be the reason he was in danger, which he would be if he stayed in Tasmania to be with her. But why would he be in danger at all? The more facts Xander nails down, the less logical any of this seems. And Althea is right at the heart of this conundrum.

He sits at a table and opens a blank page on his laptop, creates two columns and types 'Pro' at the top of one and 'Con' at the head of the other.

Under 'Pro' he types 'She likes me' and 'She's a cop'.

He hesitates but only briefly. Under 'Con' all his doubts and suspicions come tumbling out in a torrent of perfectly spelled, impeccably grammatical but nonetheless gut-churning words: 'She's probably lied about her police rank ... she probably gave the newspapers the description of Lorenzo ... she could be lying about Alden ... she injured her best friend and covered it up.' Another statement seems to appear magically on the screen, as if ghost-written by his subconscious: 'I never told her I wasn't a gun person – I only said that to the Russian.' Finally, just as his silenced phone buzzes into life with a text, he types, once again, this time under cons, 'She's a cop.'

He looks at his phone. It's a text message from Marnie. He reads it and reads it again. Then he returns to his laptop and changes 'could be' to 'is definitely' in the line that says she might be lying about Alden.

Xander reads the text message again. Marnie's texts tend to be devoid of conjunctions or adjectives and have few verbs, as if she were sending an old-style telegram where every additional word cost a few cents more.

'No Alexei Alden on any database. Vella knows nothing, says Ralphie Emerson gone rogue not working for him. Blames you for that. DCMICU.'

Don't Call Me, I'll Call You – their code for whenever Marnie felt she was being used or her job was getting in the way of their friendship, or vice versa. Either way, the Bank of Marnie was closed, at least for now. Unfamiliar emotions jostle for attention. Embarrassment and shame at being duped take centre stage, anger at Althea for doing it, and confusion about her apparently orchestrating the cover-up of Pete's murder are also competing for the spotlight.

Xander looks at his list and tries to recall every odd reaction Althea ever had or strange question she may have asked. Did she keep him busy while the Russian broke into his hotel room? Or give him enough real information to keep him on the hook for her lies? Or tell the Russian where he'd be at any time for one of his 'accidental' encounters? Or suppress the information that would make police treat Pete's death as murder? Or, good God, kill Rob the barman as he lay in hospital?

It all starts from their first encounter. She told him she was family liaison, rather than a detective sergeant. Now he gets it. She was certain he would accept the facts as presented and move on. Giving her true rank would have raised his suspicions – they don't send detectives out on death knocks unless they are conducting an investigation, and that's the last thing she wanted him to think. Once he stuck around, everything after that was to put him off the scent. The best con men and women leave as much truth as possible in their lies so that the mixture of facts and fiction muddies the water if people become suspicious. Occasional truths are hooks on which to hang your fabrications.

But why would she go to such elaborate lengths, risking her career and possibly even jail, to cover up a story that seems to have its roots fifty years ago in a country with which she has no apparent connection? And why has she teamed up with a Russian hit man to the extent that she is concocting elaborate stories about who and where he is?

Obviously, Geoffrey has a hold over her from the incident with Tina Everista. He got her off the hook. But what's his role in all this? Applying his cynical, sceptical journalist logic to this, pushing all nascent conspiracy theories to the side, Xander reaches the same conclusion by whatever narrative path he follows. Geoffrey Dreevers is Alden, the man who killed Pete's lover Lucy, or had her killed.

Why he had Pete killed is easy. A high-profile judge could not allow a serious indiscretion, even from half a century ago, to blot his reputation. Jesus, a judge in Sydney went to jail because he lied about who was driving when he was caught speeding. Geoffrey has the leverage with Althea to get her to do his bidding, the wherewithal and probably the contacts to hire an out-of-town hit man, and the motive to erase every trace of whatever Pete was about to reveal. Now it all makes sense, or as much sense as extreme craziness can ever make.

CHAPTER 32

Lucy was wiping tables distractedly, but she looked up in fright as a stooped, shuffling figure filled the doorway. Then she squealed in delight as she realised it was Pete. She rushed over and smothered his face with kisses, oblivious to his winces and yelps of pain, before gently leading him to a seat by her table.

'You survived ...' she said. 'Thank God.' She looked him up and down; between bandages and casts, she could see he was in his field uniform – a rare sight, even when he was on duty.

'You too,' he said, squeezing her hand.

They sat in a silence that ached for words, neither wanting to broach the obvious.

'You'd look nice in your uniform ... if you didn't look so awful,' she said with a sad smile.

'Regulations ...' he said. Lucy didn't need the details. She'd seen enough soldiers on their way back to Australia to know what the uniform signified.

'You're going back to Australia,' she said, trying to sound matter-of-fact. He nodded.

She looked at him. Freshly shaven, his hair neatly trimmed and his uniform looking as if it had been ironed on to his body while he was in it. She bit her lip and shook her head, tears glistening as they gathered before rolling down her cheeks.

'Pete, I need to tell you something ...' she said.

Pete reached out to comfort her, squeezing her arm as three infantrymen of no discernible rank burst through the door and paused as their eyes adjusted to the gloom from the brilliant sunshine outside.

'Fuck me, mate,' one of them said, eyeing Pete. 'Whose fucking chopper did you fall out of?'

One of his companions elbowed him solidly in the ribs as he snapped to attention.

'Sir! Sorry, Sir!' the second man said, saluting. 'Didn't mean to interrupt. We can go.'

'Sir!' the other men said in unison, as they too saluted.

'At ease, fellas,' Pete said. 'And take a seat. Lucy could use the business.'

Lucy looked askance at him. 'Don't go anywhere,' she said to Pete. 'We need to talk.'

She led the three soldiers to a corner table, taking their orders and fetching them beer. By the time she got back to Pete, he'd been joined by Donnie.

'Hi, Luce,' he said. 'Look who's been demoted to driving this sad apology for a cripple around.'

Lucy smiled thinly, her breathing controlled. 'When do you leave?' she asked, the tears gone from her eyes but still catching her voice.

'Pretty much now if we're going to catch the last chopper to Saigon,' Donnie said, extending his arm to help Pete get to his feet. 'Said your goodbyes?'

Pete grabbed Lucy's hand and pulled her to him, hugging her, kissing her cheek and whispering, 'I love you ... always will ... no matter what.'

Lucy pushed him away. 'Piss off, you sentimental fool,' she said. 'Go home to your wife and your kangaroos.' And she turned and walked back to the bar.

Donnie shrugged and helped Pete to the door. Pete paused and looked back, but Lucy still had her back to him and was already chatting to the soldiers. If he had looked for just a second longer, he would have seen her shoulders shudder as she started to sob.

CHAPTER 33

The number that flashed up on the screen of Xander's phone as he sat in the back of a cab heading for the War Memorial museum in Canberra had an 84 prefix, so he was about to reject the call as probably an offer of financial advice he didn't need, or an opportunity to provide all his bank details to a complete stranger to 'secure his account', when he remembered it was the code for Vietnam.

'Mr McAuslan?' a slightly shaky male voice on the other end of the call said.

'That's me.'

'Good afternoon. My name is Tang, Colonel Tang. I understand you want to speak to me.'

'I do. Would you like me to call you back? This could be expensive.'

'Not for me,' Tang said with a chuckle. 'I am afforded certain privileges by a grateful government. Now, how can I help you?'

'I know you knew my grandfather. Pete McAuslan. You met during the war.'

'The American War, yes, that is correct.'

'He had a friend. A woman friend. Lucy ...?'

'Trang Minh? Yes, I remember her well. Now, Mr McAuslan, can I stop you there. You are going to ask me who killed Minh, am I correct?'

Xander hesitates. 'Yes, but why did you assume ...?

'Because that's what your grandfather asked me. And my answer would have been the same – an Australian deserter called Weighorst.'

'Okay,' Xander says slowly. 'You said "would have" ...'

'Mr McAuslan, I see you are a very successful and highly regarded author of true-crime books ...'

'I wouldn't go that far ...'

'You do on your web page,' Tang says with another chuckle. 'And on Facebook. My point is, how would you like to write a book about a spy who worked for all sides in the American War – South Vietnam, the Vietcong, the Americans and ... um ... another foreign power?'

'Not Australia?'

'No, not Australia. But I think your readers would find it fascinating.'

'I'm sure they would,' Xander says, caution competing with his instinct and hope that there may be something in this. 'What would be in it for you?'

'Bring me to Australia. We can write the book together. I can live out my declining years in your wonderful country.'

'You mean you'll be a refugee?'

'After the book came out, a refugee for certain, my young friend,' Tang says. 'Contact your publisher, get us a deal and send me a ticket, as easy as that.'

'Okay. But how do I know you have a story to tell?'

'Because I will tell you who really killed Trang Minh and, more importantly, why. Call me on this number when you are ready to write my story.' And with the slightest of clicks, the phone went dead.

***

The War Memorial and its museum sit one kilometre away at the other end of a broad and straight avenue from where the relatively new Parliament seems to squat on the old building so they become one. It's as if the museum is there to remind the politicians that war comes at a cost. It's not romantic, neither is it merely pragmatic – people get killed, often horribly.

Browsing its website on the cab from the airport, he discovers belatedly that the War Museum's research centre asks for two weeks' advance notice of any projects, partly because there are mountains of files or, more realistically, serried ranks of folders and bound volumes that, viewed from above, must look like trenches of paper with timber and aluminium ribs.

The tired-looking young man behind the first desk that Xander encounters sighs long and a little too loudly as he approaches. His podgy features are mottled patches in shades of pink and peach with the occasional red blot. His hair looks like it hasn't been washed in a week, plastered in an old-fashioned short back and sides with a parting that reveals a dandruff storm gathering on his scalp like the first snows of winter. His Australian infantry uniform is immaculate, however, although devoid of any badges of rank or distinction. Instead, there is a shiny black badge that declares him to be 'Pte Wilson – Temp research assistant' with his name and the word 'Temp' added by a home-made stick-on label.

'You need to make an appointment. Two weeks in advance,' he says, peering at a large computer screen that takes up most of the space on his small, grey-painted metal desk.

'I know, but …'

'I don't see one,' Wilson replies.

'I haven't made one,' Xander says.

'Then you'll have to come back when you have.'

'I'm not really doing research –' Xander begins.

'Then why are you here?' the young soldier retorts before Xander can explain.

'I just need to ask a couple of questions.'

'That's research. Make an appointment. Two weeks.'

'You really don't like this job, do you?' Xander says.

'Not my choice,' Wilson replies.

'Cheer up. Even the badge that says you're temporary is temporary.'

'I know. I added the temp bit myself to remind people. I shouldn't be here. I'm not trained for this but they're short-handed.'

'I know how it feels. I used to be a journalist – a reporter – then they put me on computers,' Xander lies.

'A journalist? I thought you said you weren't doing research.'

'I'm not. My grandfather died recently and I need to check something.'

Wilson looks at him slightly askance, but not saying 'no'.

'He was here a few weeks ago. His name is ... was ... Pete McAuslan. They're saying he committed suicide, but I don't believe it. I need to know what he was looking into.'

'Okay,' Wilson responds cautiously, but with evident growing interest. 'Can you spell the surname?'

Xander does and Wilson types it into his computer. He reads the screen intently.

'Yeah, here he is,' he says, adding another short flurry of keystrokes. 'A provost in Vietnam – military police – served with distinction ... two tours ... went back to Oz and trained recruits for a while.' Wilson sits back, nods and smiles. 'Yeah. Funny old bloke. And I mean funny as in amusing.'

'That's Pete all right,' Xander says, the brief narrative fitting the scant knowledge he had of Pete's military record. 'I don't suppose you can tell me what he was here for?'

'He was asking about someone called, let me see ...' Wilson clicks and scrolls with his mouse. 'Jager Weighorst – a real colourful character.'

'Colourful in what way?'

'Deserter, suspected of fragging his troop commander ...'

'Fragging?'

'Tossed a live grenade in his hooch ... tent.' Wilson studies the screen again. 'Here we go. Accused of beating up your grandad so badly he had to be medivacced back to Oz. Your grandad, that is. Oh, this is interesting.'

Xander watches impatiently as Wilson devours the words on his screen. 'About a year after your grandad came home, Weighorst was accused by American Military Police of murdering a female Vietnamese civilian,' the young soldier says eventually.

'My grandad's ... um ... girlfriend, I'm guessing,' Xander says.

'Go, grandad!' Wilson says, then winces apologetically at his inappropriate joke. 'There's a reference to another file but it hasn't been digitised yet and the physical version seems to be in transit, so we're kind of stuck.'

'Make an appointment for two weeks from now?'

'Something like that,' Wilson says. 'That code is for a file that we don't have in-house. We'd have to request it.'

Xander sits in silence for a moment, processing.

'You okay?' Wilson asks.

'Yeah, just thinking,' Xander says. 'Sometimes the answer you expect isn't the one you want. Can I ask another favour?'

'Fire away.'

'Do you have any files on anyone called Alden?'

***

'Hold on, please, I'll just put you through.' Xander registers embarrassed surprise that the American Embassy receptionist speaks with an Australian accent, but then she would, given that they can't import all their office staff from the USA. There's a trickle of classical music that he almost recognises before it's cut short by a voice that's most definitely American.

'Xander? Xander McAuslan,' the voice says. 'Great to hear from you, son.' Xander immediately places the accent as 'educated Southern' – Bill Clinton with a little more gravel and gravitas.

'And good to hear you too, General Carrick. I wasn't sure I'd get through.'

'Call me Donnie,' he says. 'General is a title I left behind way back. I can still use it, but only for formal occasions and when I need to scare the shit out of some jumped-up pen-pusher. And, hey, I'm sorry about Pete. Glad I got a chance to catch up with him before ...'

'He was killed,' Xander finishes the awkward sentence, creating an even more uneasy momentary silence. 'But he did come and see you here? I thought he might have.'

'We had a fine time together ... all those years just drifted away. He didn't tell you?'

'I didn't even know you existed until a couple of weeks ago. Pete never spoke about the war.'

'Sounds like Pete.' It's Donnie Carrick's turn to insert a pause into the conversation. 'If you don't mind me asking, how *did* you hear about me?'

'Oh, let's just say a mutual friend of yours and Pete's,' Xander says, suddenly feeling an inexplicable need to be cautious.

'Hey, did I hear you say "here" as in Canberra?' Donnie emphasises the second syllable of Canberra, as Americans often do.

'Yeah. I'm just looking into Pete's service record. Filling in some gaps.'

'Pete was one of the good guys. That's all you need to know,' Carrick says. 'You around tomorrow? Maybe grab some lunch?'

'Pomegranate?' Xander replies, immediately regretting naming the same restaurant where Pete had dined on someone else's expense account.

'You've done your research,' Donnie says, his tone altering slightly. 'Pete said you were the real deal. He was mightily proud of you.'

'Twelve-thirty?' Xander suggests, keen to cut the conversation short. 'I've got a four-thirty flight out.'

'Sounds good to me,' Donnie says. 'See you there – I'll get my girl to book it. I gotta go, son. Deal with a marine who thought an Asian massage parlour in Fyshwick was the sands of Iwo Jima.' There's a click and with that he is gone.

Xander smiles, just at having spoken to someone who knew Pete. He has his own friends like that, people you don't meet from one year to the next but when you do, it's as if the last time was only yesterday.

He thinks it's time he found out more about his prospective lunch companion so hits the internet and a simple name search brings up a stack of newspaper reports, mini biographies and citations. Donnie Carrick has had an immaculate military career taking him from Vietnam to Grenada, both Iraq wars and Afghanistan, as well as several disaster relief and peace-keeping missions. After he retired from the military he joined the diplomatic corps with a number of senior postings to the top US embassies in the world, including London, Paris, Beijing, Berlin and Moscow. Even so, the hallmark of his career seems to have been modesty and humility. He's always the guy behind the guy in the picture, Xander thinks. His rise through the ranks has been unspectacular but steady, making Xander wonder why he's in Canberra. Australia is a step down from most of the places in his CV. Has he blotted his copybook in some way?

Xander's attention is drawn to the flat screen TV fixed to the exposed brick wall of his 2.5 star motel. A police raid is being conducted at a half-familiar location in the bush somewhere. It's with a growing sense of dread and guilt that Xander realises he is looking at a human chain of police and parks officials ferrying all

Lorenzo's worldly goods to a platform attached to a pulley system to lift them up the side of the cliff behind the caves. Xander lunges for the remote and turns up the sound in time to hear a detailed description of Lorenzo, again, almost word for word how he'd described him to Althea.

The vision cuts to a press conference in what looks like Derwent Bridge, where David Danzig is talking to the camera with a phalanx of police and parks officers behind him. Althea is immediately behind Danzig, in a prime spot.

'The suspect is being sought in connection with two murders,' Danzig says. 'Local mechanic Johnny Spangler and retired police officer Peter McAuslan who was found dead in his cottage in Mole Creek a week ago. The suspect's name is Gordon Flax and he also goes by the name Lorenzo.'

'The public has been warned to call police if they see the suspect and not to approach him, as he is armed and extremely dangerous,' the newsreader says.

'Yeah, well you got that right,' Xander says to the TV as the newsreader segues seamlessly to a story about gay penguins at a zoo. As he switches off the TV, Xander is now convinced that Althea and Judge Geoffrey are working together to cover up the facts about Pete's death and, probably, Lucy's too. But why would Dreevers, a one-time anti-war agitator, have had anything to do with the death of a Vietnamese civilian?

How about Geoffrey goes to Vietnam, gets involved in a messy relationship with a local woman, Lucy, it all goes wrong and he gets someone to kill her? No, that would take too long to play out. He was only there for a month and, anyway, he's gay. Okay, maybe she discovers this, back then that was a crime that could have put the kybosh on his legal career, so he has her killed before she can tell anyone. That's believable, if only just. And if that were the case, it's problem solved until fifty years later when Pete starts digging around. Now Geoffrey, as a judge, is even more vulnerable and the revelation that he had killed a Vietnamese civilian to cover up his sexuality could destroy him. Then he gets his old mates in Moscow to help out and calls in his tab with Althea when Xander turns up asking the right questions about Pete's death.

It all makes some kind of sense, but not much. And it's dependent on quite a few stretched coincidences. Xander wonders how precisely he could prove it even if he knew for sure that it was true. Once again, Pete is at his shoulder, reminding him that it's better to test your theories to destruction than have them pulled apart in court. His wrists aching from his research, he presses the voice recognition button on his laptop and starts to dictate his thoughts.

'Theory 1 [full stop] Pete killed himself,' he says, and the words trail across the screen as if by their own volition, punctuation included. 'Counter theory: Pete wouldn't. And if that was the case, why are others being killed?

'Theory 2. It's a coincidence and this is all about Trackie Vella trying to kill my story. Counter theory: Not likely as the story is dead and people are still being attacked and killed and, anyway, Trackie would be boasting about it, to me if no one else.

'Theory 3. Judge Dreevers is and always has been a Communist. Something happened in Vietnam and he killed Lucy or had her killed to cover up the crime. Pete starts digging. The Russians kill Pete and steal all the information that was on his laptop.'

Xander sits back and reviews the words on his screen and nods.

'Dreevers gets Althea to step in and head me off at the pass, trying to convince me it was suicide,' he continues. 'I don't buy that and, when I don't let it go, she's trapped by the lie. Meanwhile, the Russian working for Dreevers is getting ever more desperate to get the information and is prepared to kill anyone who gets in his way or who might expose him as the killer.'

'Counter theory,' Xander says into the machine. 'Is Dreevers' career worth all this mayhem? Those stakes aren't very high. Is there something about him we don't know? And where does my Vietnamese aunt come into all this? Did she find out they were coming after Pete – who was her father, after all? And where does the Australian deserter ...' He checks his notes from earlier. '... Weighorst fit into all this?'

Maybe General Carrick will have an answer to some of these questions, Xander thinks as he closes the laptop lid and turns towards his bed. He'd better have, before more innocent civilians are killed.

CHAPTER 34

It was one of those Vung Tau nights when you could smell the heat, as much as feel it. The humidity crept under your clothes then lay there, an invisible, inescapable sheen on your skin. The trick was to stand still, very, very still, so as not to expend one micro-calorie of energy that you didn't have to, thought motor-pool driver Jensen 'Bax' Baxter. Let the sweat run where it would, movement just made it worse.

Cicadas were chirruping like a choir of love-sick frogs, meanwhile a white man with a Black voice was singing 'Lean on Me' from a cracked radio, a whole block plus half a world away. Bax felt like he was being serenaded by his Jeep. He took a long pull on the joint that an undernourished kid on an oversized pushbike had just sold him for a dollar, and sat back on the wheel arch. It was good weed and it would get him through another dry night.

A scooter, one of those Italian contraptions that sounded like a sewing machine on Dexedrine, passed, the sweep of the headlight briefly catching the windscreen of the Jeep. The scooter went to the end of the street and turned, briefly silhouetted by the light from the bar where his cargo, a major and a lieutenant-colonel, were boozing it up, bar girls dangling off them like Christmas decorations. Lean on me, all right.

There was something about the rider that got Bax's attention. He was taller than your average local. Way taller. Bax had never met a Viet that would qualify for a ride at Disneyland. This guy was military – probably Australian, considering this was their turf. Bax wondered briefly what a soldier was doing on a scooter. He was momentarily blinded as it turned and its headlight swept across his face. He stepped back into the shadows and by the time his eyes had adjusted, he was looking at the red brake light as the bike was pulled up on to its stand, across the road from Juicy Lucy's bar at the foot of the street. The rider sat on the scooter and seemed never to take his eyes off the entrance.

The bar was a known no-go area for any American soldiers without clover leaves on their epaulets signifying their senior rank. Maybe it was different for Aussies, or this guy was an officer. Or both. Word was a high-ranking American military cop had it under his protection. Earlier, idling in the shadows, Bax had watched a woman – a manager or the owner – busily locking up for the night. The other bars were still going strong, music, shouts, and the occasional drunk tumbling out into the street, but the sign for Juicy Lucy's was extinguished abruptly from inside. As the street outside descended into shadow and remote neon glow, the Australian officer got off the scooter and limped heavily to the door and entered, his frame filling the small, Asian-dimensioned doorway. Yeah, he was an Aussie all right – the camouflage was indistinguishable in the half-light and the badges were too far away to recognise, but the bush hat – the giggle hat, they called it – looked like the American boonie but didn't have the bullet loops around the crown. Muffled voices seeped from the bar, raised; the tone was anger but the words were indistinct. In any case, Bax's thoughts had drifted on a marijuana cloud to other trivialities. Then he heard two loud pops. Gunfire, for sure. Small arms, probably a handgun. He reached across the passenger seat for his M-16 assault rifle and cradled it in the crook of his arm, more for show than anything, in case his passengers came out, alerted by the noise.

The officers didn't appear, but the Aussie exited from the bar, limped painfully straight to the scooter, heaved it off its stand and rode off.

'What did you do in there?' Bax mutters to himself, peering into the darkness. But it gives him nothing. He senses, then sees his passengers looming out of the half-light in the other direction, just in time to drop his smoke and extinguish it beneath his heel, wasting half of a decent doobie.

'Okay, Baxter,' the older of the two officers says. 'Get us back to Ben Hoa.'

'Sir,' Bax says. 'I think an Australian soldier just went in there and shot someone.'

The two officers look at Juicy Lucy's then at each other.

'That's sounds like a whole heap of none of our fucken business,' the older man replies.

'And since we're not actually here ...' says the younger one.

'Not anywhere near ...' says the older one. 'Ben Hoa, Lance-Corporal, and try not to hit every damned pothole like you did on the way here.'

'Do my best, sir,' Bax says as he swings behind the Jeep's oversized steering wheel. 'Mission accomplished, Colonel?'

'Just drive, lance,' says the senior man, looking over at the darkened bar again. 'Just drive.'

***

Pete had just finished telling a classroom of junior infantry officers about the dangers of non-combat life in Vietnam when a corporal from signals appeared in the doorway, clearly content to wait until the lecture was finished. The young soldiers in his class had already mentally wandered off, despite Pete's best efforts to round up their interest and corral it somewhere worthwhile. They and he knew they were unlikely to ever set foot in Vietnam now that

Australian troops were being withdrawn, so his lecture on moral rectitude and personal hygiene was more pointless than usual.

'Never forget, life and love are sexually transmitted diseases,' he said to a murmur of unenthused laughter. 'Class dismissed.'

The dozen or so raw recruits tumbled out of the classroom in a jostle of jokes and jibes. The signals corporal handed him a folded sheet of manila paper.

'Telex from Saigon, Sir,' the corporal said, sympathy seeping into his voice.

'Is this bad news?' Pete asked. 'Do they want me back?'

'Wouldn't know, Sir.'

'Are you saying you didn't read this?' Pete asked.

'Can't read, Sir,' the youth said. 'That's why they give me this job.'

'Fuck off before I put you on a charge of being a smartarse while in uniform,' Pete said. The youth smiled, turned, and marched away with exaggerated formality for a few steps before resuming the sauntering slouch of the unobserved digger.

Pete looked at the unprinted side of the telex. Was he going to have to tell a brother, wife or girlfriend that another young Australian had paid the ultimate penalty for being born on the wrong day and losing that life-and-death lottery? He sighed and turned it over.

September 2, 1970
US Forces Command HQ
Saigon

Pete,
Apologies for doing this by telex but phone calls are impossible and a letter would take too long and, I guess, might invite too many questions on the home front.

I'm sorry to have to tell you, Lucy has died, killed by an

intruder in her bar a couple of days ago. From the reports I have read, it sounds very like your old nemesis Weighorst. Maybe I shouldn't jump to conclusions but a motor-pool driver saw a man with a limp in an Australian uniform walk in after she had closed for the night. There were raised voices, shots, and the man walked out and rode away on a scooter. Some girls from the bar next door found her later that night. Why would Weighorst do it? Maybe he was looking for you or me and decided she would be a good way to get at both of us. Either way, trust me, I plan to hunt him down like a dog and put him out of his misery.

There's something else you need to know – you have a baby, a girl. Maybe you knew already but Lucy always said she hadn't told you. Her name is Linh and I have arranged for her to go and live with Lucy's sister in Saigon. I will send you the address if you want to help out, and knowing you, you will. Lucy would never take money from me but I think her sister may have a different view on financial assistance.

So that's it, good buddy, you've lost a lover and gained a daughter. Let me know if there's anything I can do. Condolences again. Telex me back on this number.

Your friend

Donnie Carrick

Pete read and re-read the telex, hoping he had misunderstood the content or missed a crucial word that would make all of this untrue. Then he closed his briefing-room door from the inside, leaned his back against it and wept as he had never done in his life.

CHAPTER 35

'You okay, son?' Donnie asks, mopping up the last of his Paris mash potatoes with a haemorrhaging chunk of perfectly undercooked steak. 'You've gone quiet all of a sudden.'

'Thinking about Lorenzo,' Xander says. 'He was so happy up in his cave and doing no harm. I hope the cops go easy on him when they find him.'

'If they find him,' Donnie says, eyebrows raised. 'I don't have any influence in that sphere or I would be happy to help.'

Xander nods. His lunch companion is an impressive-looking character. Some people are diminished and bent by the years. Others, like Donnie Carrick, grow into their acquired wisdom. Sure, the blond hair from the wartime photographs is now silvery grey, and the flesh that once barely contained an ounce of fat has filled out a little from the days when he last stood in front of Lorenzo's camera. But a decent diet and regular exercise – or maybe some fantastic new pill the US military had that they weren't telling anyone about – had meant maturity hadn't taken too much of a toll.

Xander smiles. In fact, he hadn't been thinking about Lorenzo at all. He's been silent because he's wondering how much to tell Donnie about Althea and Alden, the Russian, Vella, Geoffrey, Johnny Spanners, and his Vietnamese aunt. The temptation has been great, just to unburden himself with someone who knew some of the characters involved and had no emotional investment in the others.

But Pete always said the best way to get people to talk was 'Suck don't blow'. And he felt so burned by Althea that he wasn't sure who he could trust, regardless of how they came across. In any case, Donnie was happy to reminisce about Pete and what he was like when he was young.

'He had that ... that thing ... starts with L means you don't give a shit and you're Australian.'

'Larrikin?'

'Yeah, larrikin. Pete was the larrikinest guy I ever met. Not crazy, just a little bit wild. It was Lucy who calmed him down. Or me. I would tug his chain before he could do too much harm to himself or anyone else. He called me the Quiet American because I was so boring, compared to him, anyway.'

A fleeting look of concern and regret passes across Donnie's face. Xander has seen that look many times before, usually in people who realise they may have said too much and hope it hasn't been noticed. What was it? Telling Xander that his grandfather had a dark and wild side?

'Look, I have to be honest here, I have an ulterior motive,' Xander says, leaning in so he doesn't have to raise his voice over the murmurs of other diners on the restaurant's leafy terrace. 'It seems Pete was trying to find out why Lucy was killed. Major Tang told him she was planning to pass on some information but was killed before she could do it. He told Pete that if anyone knew why she died, it would be you. Because you investigated it, right?'

'I should thank him for the vote of confidence, but you're not telling me anything I haven't heard before,' Donnie says. 'I had the same conversation with Pete right here in this fine establishment. And I'll tell you the same as I told him. I'm one hundred per cent sure it was Weighorst who killed Lucy. A tall Australian with a limp and a grudge. There's no other possible suspect. I mean, you're looking at the guy who gave him the limp.'

'And the information Lucy was going to trade with Tang for a safe ticket out of Vung Tau?'

'Yeah, I've been wondering about that too,' Donnie says as he proffers a half-finished bottle of chianti and Xander nods for him to pour. 'The first thing you have to ask is, was Tang telling the truth? He was a wily old fox and probably still is. After that, you have to realise that this was the beginning of the end in Vietnam … certainly for people who'd been on good terms with the Allies. A lot of people were rushing for the exit, including your guys, and a little information could be worth a lot – and everybody had a story to tell. I'm guessing Lucy might have had information that would have put her in a better spot than she was in.'

'But she didn't tell you?'

'I was her friend but I was also the enemy. She needed to get some brownie points with Charlie quick smart, just in case she was rounded up as a collaborator.'

'And Tang was the real spy …'

'He sure was, pompous little fucker. He had us all fooled.'

'Does that mean Weighorst killing her was just a coincidence?'

'Probably not. He had a track record, don't forget. He killed an officer who was giving him a hard time,' Donnie says. 'What are the three pillars of murder? Motive, means and opportunity? Weighorst had all three in abundance.' He pauses. 'Who gave you all this stuff? Lorenzo?'

Xander nods cautiously.

'Okay,' Donnie says. 'You should know that there was a spy – not just Tang, someone else – operating around Lucy's bar, and Lorenzo's name was in the frame for a while.'

'Lorenzo?' Xander says, unable to hide his surprise and disappointment. 'You think Lucy was about to tell Tang that Lorenzo was the spy?'

Donnie's look and gesture are half-question, half-confirmation.

'But you said it was definitely Weighorst,' Xander protests.

'Weighorst pulled the trigger,' Donnie says. 'But did he really benefit from the killing? Maybe someone set it up for him. Maybe he was covering up for some of his people in Soul Alley. That place had all sorts of shit going on, starting with gun- and drug-running and all the way up to money laundering. We cleared it out at one point but we never got the bosses, just the pimps, whores and low-level dealers.'

Xander ponders this for a moment, absently pursuing a sliver of carrot around his plate.

'Do you know Geoffrey Dreevers?'

'The judge in Tasmania?' Donnie asks after a moment's thought. 'I met him once. A conference in Darwin about who gets to prosecute American soldiers who commit crimes on Australian soil. He was a real hardliner if I recall. Wanted them all flogged first then sent home in irons.'

'Did you know he visited Vietnam when you were there? Round about the time Lucy died?'

'I had no idea. He never mentioned it.' Donnie looks confused. 'When you say visited . . .?'

'He was part of an anti-war movement. Somehow got himself on an observer trip.'

'Yeah, we had a few of those come through,' Donnie says. 'Jane fucking Fonda, for a start, although she never came south of the DMZ, or we'd have shot her on the spot.'

'Where do you think the Russians figure in all this?' Xander asks.

'Do they figure at all?'

'It was a Russian who killed Pete and took out other people I know and who's had a couple of shots at me.'

Donnie considers this for a moment, then leans in again.

'Look, the Russians were bankrolling the North in Vietnam,

for sure, but that was fifty years ago. Now? There's a lot of ex-KGB roaming around, offering themselves as guns for hire. Maybe your guy is freelancing. A mercenary is the most dangerous man on the battlefield,' Donnie says. 'Any deluded idiot can risk their life for a cause – whether it's a religion, a country, or a political movement – but someone who does it for money and no other reason, and is better than average at it? You are talking truly professional in every sense.'

'Okay, but who is picking up the tab for this "professional"?' Xander asks.

'Someone with something to hide,' Donnie says, and Xander's thoughts immediately flit to Althea, Geoffrey and maybe even David Danzig as Donnie calls for the bill.

'If Major Tang was a spy, how reliable do you think he is?' Xander asks.

'In what sense?'

'He wants me to write his memoirs. A tell-all book by a guy who spied for everyone, a triple, quadruple agent, if you like. If it's even half-true, it'll be pretty sensational.'

'Would they let him? Vietnam is still pretty much under Communist control.'

'He wants a ticket to come here and live out his last few years in comfort,' Xander says.

'What's in it for you?'

'Maybe a bestseller. Who knows? But at the very least he's promised to tell me who killed Lucy.'

Donnie nods but says nothing, frozen in mid-motion, his credit card halfway out of his wallet.

'What do you reckon?' Xander asks. 'What are the chances that he actually knows?'

'But we know already,' Carrick says eventually. 'It was Weighorst. Don't forget that Tang is a professional liar. He's an expert in telling people exactly what they want to hear.'

'Yeah. You're right,' Xander says, deflated. 'But it might still make a great yarn, even if it isn't true. And even if he just confirms it was Weighorst, knowing why might explain everything.'

'Yeah, well don't be surprised if he doesn't come through,' Donnie says. 'After all, he could be a prime suspect himself.' He pauses. 'You know you really do have a Vietnamese aunt, a kid Pete had while he was over there?'

'Yeah, Lorenzo told me.'

'And you know she had been in touch with Pete just before he died?'

'I didn't know that,' Xander admits. 'But it makes sense.'

'Did it ever occur to you that she might have killed Pete?'

Xander sits up with a jolt. This is one theory that has never occurred to him.

'Pete was her father ...' he says.

'A father who abandoned her mother, was possibly the cause of her being killed, if indirectly, and left her to grow up as a "Child of the Dust". That's what they call the children left behind by foreign soldiers. Mixed-race kids who never quite fit in.'

'You think Linh could have killed Pete out of revenge?'

'I don't think anything, son,' Donnie says. 'I just know you have walked into the middle of a clusterfuck of epic proportions. Want my advice? Tell Tang to take a hike and keep your head down for a while. Hand your information over to the police and let them do their job. Go back to Mole Creek and stop turning over stones – you never know what's going to crawl out and bite you.'

Xander nods and smiles grimly. He doesn't say what he's thinking: that the police are a major part of the problem and he won't be handing them anything.

CHAPTER 36

Sitting on a giant circular sofa in the Canberra Airport departure area, when the flight advisory display changes to 'flight delayed' Xander pulls out his laptop, fires it up and logs into the free wi-fi. Immediately the computer announces the arrival of an email, which only briefly distracts him from analysing his lunch with Donnie Carrick. He's struck, and somewhat confused, by how his grandad's former best friend was seemingly able to pluck theories out of the air without ever landing on any one with certainty. Maybe they teach them that at diplomat school.

The idea that his aunt Linh might have killed Pete seems ludicrous but it also fits three of the crime pillars Donnie mentioned: motive, means and opportunity. And it ticks that other box, that most violent crimes are committed by someone close to the victim. But it doesn't fit with any of the other events, including the theft of Pete's laptop and the mayhem carried out by the mysterious Russian. Xander sighs and shakes his head – he feels further than ever from finding out the truth.

'Xander! Xander McAuslan!' He looks up and sees a shortish, slightly overweight, but immaculately dressed woman with unnaturally auburn, short hair walking briskly towards him across the airport waiting area. 'How are you, Zan?' she says. He stands and she pulls him into a genuinely warm hug. It takes him a moment before he recalls she is his former newspaper's chief political reporter Nicole Swift.

'Hi Nicole. How are you going? I haven't seen you for years.'

'I'm more or less permanently parked here in Canberra,' she says. 'Don't get up to Sydney much. More to the point how are you?'

'I'm good, thanks.'

'How long are you in Sydney? We should catch up for a bite, a drink maybe.'

'I'm just dropping in to check my flat. I've got a midday flight to Launceston tomorrow. We ... I've got a cottage near there. Mole Creek.'

'Oh, yeah, I heard about your grandad,' she says. 'Shame, he was a riot. But suicide? Really?'

'Not really. No.'

'Oooh, I sense a story.'

'Yeah, well, I'm chasing up a few leads.'

'Curiouser and curiouser,' she says. 'Where are you sitting?' He shows her his ticket. 'Other end of the plane. Go on, we've got a few minutes before the flight. Give me the bullet points.'

'Way too complicated for that,' Xander says.

'Okay, why are you here? Who did you see? What did you find?'

Xander smiles. Nicole's terrier-like energy and determination got her the job over candidates who were more experienced and better qualified, on paper at least.

'I went to the War Museum ...'

'Of course.'

'And I had lunch with an American diplomat called Donnie Carrick.'

'A diplomat? You moving into the international politics beat?'

'He was Pete's best friend in Vietnam, during the war. We're trying to piece together who killed Pete's lover, then we might be closer to finding who killed Pete.'

'Pete had a lover? In Vietnam?' she says, exaggerating her wide-eyed surprise.

'And there's more ... turns out I have a Vietnamese aunt.'

'What is this,' she says. 'True crime or a soap?'

'I'm beginning to wonder myself.'

'We should catch up, either here or there,' she says as an echoey voice announces a flight departure. The only word Xander picks up is 'Sydney'. A male voice calls out her name and she turns and waves.

'Gotta go, hun,' Nicole says, briefly kissing his cheek. 'Let me know if there's anything I can do.'

'Of course, yeah, stay well,' he says as she picks up her bag. 'Oh, there is one thing. Have you ever come across anyone called Alden? Alden something or something Alden?'

She stops and thinks. 'Alden? How do you spell it? Like Alden Pyle in *The Quiet American*?'

'Yeah, exactly,' Xander says although he can barely speak. 'Like *The Quiet American*.'

'I'll keep an ear open,' she says as she turns away. 'Send me your email address.'

Xander has barely processed this when his phone buzzes and rings an unfamiliar tone. It takes him a moment to work out that it's a WhatsApp call from a number he doesn't recognise. He presses the answer button.

'Hey, my man. Bad time?' It's the unmistakable voice of Mo from TazziTek.

'No, you're good. I'm waiting for a flight.'

'To or from?' says Mo.

'To Sydney, then Launceston. There are no direct flights.'

'This arvo?'

'No. I'm swinging by to check on my flat. I'll be back tomorrow afternoon.'

'Call in on your way through, bud. And bring two hundred and fifty dollars cash.'

'What for?'

'Because I've got something you're gonna want, and that's how much it cost me to get it for you. See you tomorrow.'

As Mo hangs up, Xander realises the plane is boarding and the queue has dwindled to the last couple of stragglers. He packs up his laptop and phone and momentarily thinks a smartly dressed young woman at the coffee stall is talking into her suit lapel. Xander laughs at himself and shakes his head. Paranoia feeds itself, he knows only too well. The steward returns his smile as he shows his ticket at the gate.

***

The train from Sydney Domestic to Central is fast, clean and efficient, certainly the latter for Xander, whose flat is barely a five-minute walk from the station. His fellow passengers in the side-facing section between the connecting doors and the stairs are a motley bunch who range from irritated businesspeople talking animatedly into their phones to overladen backpackers belatedly wondering if they really needed to bring every item of clothing they own in their multilevel rucksacks. A tall, dark-haired man in a smart but not overly expensive suit gets on the train just before the doors close. Sydney trains are double-deck affairs, with entrance sections at the doors and short stairways leading to the upper and lower decks. The man hesitates. The seats next to the doors are all taken, the passageway crammed with suitcases and backpacks. He looks briefly at the two sets of stairs and chooses the lower deck, taking an outside seat, facing back towards Xander.

Is the man following him or is it just paranoia again? Xander looks away then looks back. The man appears to be studiously typing a text message into his phone. Still, there's something about him. He seems out of place. He doesn't have an overnight bag or briefcase, yet he boarded the train at the Domestic Airport.

Who travels by air, even interstate, and doesn't have at least one bag?

Xander switches his phone to video record, then holds it up to his ear as if he's making a phone call. The side-facing seats mean his phone's camera is pointed back down the train. He gabbles randomly about the weather and football scores to make it look authentic to someone watching from half a train carriage away, but not – it would seem – to a Swedish backpacker sitting next to him who looks up in alarm, as if he's just realised he's sitting next to a serial killer, then looks away. Xander plays the video. The mystery man appears and disappears from shot thanks to the gentle rocking motion of the train, but Xander's blind filming is reasonably on target. The whole time he was pretending to call someone, the man was staring straight at him.

When they get to Central Station, Xander waits until the last moment and stands as if to exit. The man leaps out of his seat and takes the steps two at a time. However, as they both exit the carriage, Xander does a quick 180 and allows himself to be pushed back inside by a gaggle of uniformed schoolgirls. The man still has just enough time to get back on the carriage, but both he and Xander know his cover has been blown. As the train pulls out of the station, the man turns his back and reaches for his phone while Xander feels slightly insulted that he hadn't merited a better-trained tail. An Indian woman in a sari and puffer jacket, surrounded by bulging shopping bags and a crammed shopping trolley, is sitting opposite his now-occupied seat. She smiles her sympathy as he clutches a strap and hangs on.

The next stop, Museum Station, a slightly longer walk back to Xander's flat than from Central, is a relic from Sydney rail's past, and has no escalators. Xander find himself at the bottom of the exit stairs at the same time as the Indian woman from his carriage.

'Would you mind?' she asks, gesturing to the handle of the

shopping trolley. 'It's too heavy and the lift ...' She looks around as if hoping an elevator will magically appear.

His laptop case over his shoulder, his overnight bag in his left hand, Xander grabs the handle of the shopping trolley and half-bumps, half-carries it to the top of the steps.

'You are very kind,' she says as they get to the turnstiles at the exit.

'No worries,' Xander replies. He walks away, but looks back when he stops to cross the road, and sees the woman take a roll of cling film from her bag and wrap some of it around the shopping trolley handle. That's a bit rude, Xander thinks as he examines his hand. He's not that sweaty.

Xander spends the first five minutes back in his flat making sure he's alone, and the next five opening windows and blinds to let some light and air in. A quick check of his mail – some non-urgent bills and offers of things he doesn't need or desire – and he settles himself down with a mug of plunger coffee to focus on what he knows and what he believes about Pete and Lucy's deaths. He grabs his A4 notepad and draws two columns. This time instead of pros and cons, as he did with his analysis of Althea, he writes 'Known' and 'Unknown'.

Under 'known' he writes 'Weighorst killed Lucy' and next to it in the adjacent column adds 'Why?' Then he writes 'Pete didn't kill himself' and next to that, again, 'Who killed him?'. 'Major Tang was a spy' under 'known' is joined by 'Who for and why?' under 'unknown'. On the left, he writes 'The Russian killed Rob and Spangler' and next to that 'What's the Russian connection?' On the left he writes 'Alden is the Quiet American'. On the right he scribbles 'Is Donnie Carrick?'

Without being fully aware of what he's doing or why, Xander draws circles around 'Quiet American', 'Donnie', 'Russian', 'Major Tang' and 'spy'. He looks at his handiwork for a moment then grabs his phone and searches for recent calls. He clicks on the

Vietnam number that Tang called him from, clicks on the phone handset symbol and lets it ring. Vietnam is four hours behind so he knows there's no chance it's the middle of the night there, but the phone rings out anyway. That can wait, there's another call he needs to make. A much trickier one. He checks his notebook for the code for switching off the privacy function on his landline and then dials Althea's number. He wants her to know he's in Sydney.

It rings a couple of times, then clicks as she picks up.

'Hi, it's me,' he says.

'Xander? How are you?' she says. 'Where are you?'

'In Sydney.'

'I can see that.'

'At my flat. Just keeping my head down,' he says.

'Good idea. We're worried about you.'

'We?'

'The police. Geoffrey and I. Everybody.'

'No sign of Alexei Alden, then?'

'Turns out that's not his real name, but anyway, it's not him we're worried about. It's Lorenzo. We think he killed Johnny Spanners.'

'Really? Are you sure?' Xander says.

'We did some digging. Turns out Lorenzo was suspected of spying in Vietnam.'

'Lorenzo was a spy? He really doesn't seem the type.'

'That's what spies do, convince people that they're okay and on their side and no threat.'

Xander falls silent, rage bubbling inside his chest. He can feel the heat as his face reddens.

'Althea, I know you've been lying to me,' he says.

'What?'

'You're not family liaison. You're a detective sergeant and all that stuff about being demoted – it's bullshit.'

Silence.

'Got nothing?' Xander prompts her.

'Saying I was family liaison was Danzig's idea. Pete was a special case and so were you – a journalist and author and all that – so I wanted to look after you. Danzig said no at first. Then he said to say I was family liaison and not to tell you I was a detective sergeant or that would make you think there was more to Pete's death than just … you know …'

'Suicide,' Xander offers. 'Come on! How stupid did you think I was? You must have realised I would find out sooner or later.'

'There wasn't supposed to be any later,' she says. 'We thought it would be a meet and greet. Shoulder to cry on and then we'd send you back to the mainland with Pete's body.'

'And I screwed it up by refusing to believe Pete took his own life?'

'Well, it looks like you were right all along. And by the way, I'm having my doubts about Danzig. Why was he so keen to shut all this down?'

'This thing about Lorenzo being a spy … where did you get that?'

'Geoffrey, mainly. When Geoffrey was young – much younger – during the Vietnam War, he was a bit of a commo. He reckons he met Lorenzo there, in Saigon, along with some high-ranking Vietcong. In a place called Soul City or something like that.'

'Soul Alley,' Xander says before falling silent again, but mentally noting that this fits with everything he's learned about Geoffrey and his radical past.

'Seems Lorenzo was caught in a compromising situation there, blackmailed into doing the Vietcong a few favours, then once you've done one favour they've got you. The favours get bigger, more frequent, until they don't even have to ask. That story he told you about someone calling him Lawrence of Arabia? That was all BS. Lorenzo was his codename.'

'Really? Is that so?'

'Geoffrey says that's what they do. Spies. They seduce you, make you fall in love with them. Wait till you see the stuff we pulled out of his cave. Years of spying. Decades of it. That's your next book, right there. Never mind Colonel Tang's biography.'

'Is that what happened to you? You crossed the line once to pay Geoffrey back for helping you out, then he had you and you helped him to cover up Pete's murder?'

'What the fuck are you talking about, Xander? We think Lorenzo had Pete killed because your grandad discovered all this when he was looking into Lucy's death. We think Lorenzo hired the Russian – or called in a favour – because he liked Pete and couldn't do it himself. He must have told Lorenzo what he'd found and it was all getting a bit too close.'

'You're saying I've been duped by Lorenzo?' Xander says.

'We've all been fooled,' Althea replies. 'The Russian was covering Lorenzo's tracks, then he was covering his own when he tried to get the laptop back, or at least erase all the files.'

'What about my aunt? Where does she fit into all of this?'

'Without Pete's files we can't know for sure, but it seems she became aware that Pete was investigating the death of her mother, and so she turned up to help. Or just to meet him. Pete was her father, after all.'

Xander can almost hear the pieces of the jigsaw clicking together in place. Everything Althea has said makes some kind of sense, so he is disarmed when her voice takes on a familiar smoky texture, as if she's breathing directly in his ear.

'Are we okay? You and me?'

'Sure, yeah. Did you get any of this from Donnie Carrick?'

'Who?'

'He's an American diplomat, served with Pete in Vietnam.'

'Never heard of him,' Althea says. 'I can run some checks if you want.'

'No, it's okay. Just another blind alley.'

Xander's mind is racing. If she doesn't know Carrick, how did she know about Colonel Tang's approach?

'Babe. When are you coming back to Lonnie?'

'I've got a flight about lunchtime tomorrow, but I'll be heading straight down to Mole Creek.'

'Can I come visit? I'm missing you. Maybe we can sort it all out then.'

'Sure,' he says. 'That would be great. Give me a couple of days to sort things out and I'll call you.'

'I'll bring the champagne.'

'And a whiteboard, I reckon,' he says.

'Seriously?'

'Not seriously,' he says. 'Except the wine. Do that.'

'No problem.'

'See you then, then. Talk soon. Bye.'

'Bye,' an innocent word delivered in a breathy Salome promise before she hangs up.

Xander realises that he's hit one of those points where you don't tell the person you're interviewing how much you know in case it results in them pulling down the shutters. So he didn't challenge her on the fact that he can't recall ever telling her that he wasn't 'a gun person'. He only said that to the Russian. And he's pretty sure he never told her about Tang's approach to write his biography. He only said that to Carrick.

As for Lorenzo being behind this, Xander replays their conversations in his mind, or at least those he can remember. At what point was he being pumped for information? When exactly was he being misdirected with lies? A fact here, a detail there, each of them tipping the balance away from the falsehoods and fabrications. Xander had been able to confirm most of what Lorenzo had told him, but did that make him honest or a highly accomplished liar?

One thing he knows for sure is that he can't trust anyone in this whole clusterfuck that's taken over his life. Xander checks his door is triple-locked then collapses on his bed. He falls asleep immediately, dreaming of strange old Vietnam vets in caves in the Walls of Jerusalem. In his dream, Jesus is there – having been delivered by drone – along with Lorenzo, Pete, Lucy, his aunt Linh and Johnny Spanners. They all want to leave the cave but its entrance is blocked by Althea and the Russian. Xander wakes several times in the night, but every time he falls asleep again, he's back in the same dream. The last time, before he wakes, Pete is holding a double-edged broadsword, like the one Mel Gibson wielded in *Braveheart*, with the words 'Occam's razor' engraved on it.

In the morning he performs his Wing Chun kata with renewed intensity, at first feeling self-conscious as he catches a glimpse of himself in a mirror, perched one foot with the other raised, like a parody of the Karate Kid's signature praying mantis move. But as the meditative powers of the exercise take hold and he becomes increasingly aware of his body as well as the forces it can tap into, he moves through the sequences with the grace and confidence of a ballet dancer.

CHAPTER 37

Mo is unexpectedly cheerful when Xander sidles into the computer shop after looking both ways down the street then over his shoulder as he entered. Xander had been both relieved and disappointed that there'd been no welcoming party for him at the airport. The drive to TazziTek had been uneventful. But right now, he guesses, Pete would be quoting John Wayne, saying it was too quiet.

'Wassup, my man,' Mo says. 'You're sneakin' around like a cat that smells dog.'

'It's been a stressful time,' Xander says. 'What have you got for me?'

'Straight down to business,' Mo says with a wry smile, reaching under the counter to produce a USB memory stick. 'This little baby would normally cost twenty bucks but my special, one-day-only offer ... two hundred and fifty dollars.'

'Seems a bit steep.'

'That's what it cost for me to get it from the backpacker who just got back from a trip to Vietnam. Said her tour guide, who apparently is your aunt, told her to bring it here and I would give her two hundred and fifty dollars and pass it on to you.'

'Linh,' Xander says. 'Would have been cheaper to have Dropboxed the files.'

'Yeah? How did computer backup work out for you last time?'

'What's on it?' Xander asks, reaching into his computer bag for his wallet.

'No idea. It would be a breach of privacy and trust for me to have looked.'

'Yeah, right,' Xander says, counting out five fifties that he had liberated from an ATM at the airport. He hands them over, adding an inquiring tilt of his head.

'Okay, I had to check there were no viruses on it, knowing you aren't exactly Bill Gates in that department.'

'And?'

'No malware but there are a couple of files that are password protected.'

'Shit!'

'When I say "are", of course I mean "were",' Mo says. 'I thought I'd save you a trip back here to unlock them.'

'What's on them?' Xander asks.

'Funny thing, there's a point where the urge to find out takes second place to a need to not know.'

'I wish I had that choice,' Xander says as Mo hands him the USB stick.

Tempted to check in to the nearest café with internet, Xander decides instead to wait until he's in the relative safety and obscurity of the Mole Creek cottage. That deer fence and the airlock gates will slow down unwelcome visitors, if not deter them completely.

He's aware that paranoia is starting to win its battle with logic and common sense, arriving in his thoughts disguised as both. He'd felt foolish checking under Cleo for car bombs and tracking devices, just as he does now, scanning the street for Taswegians who might not be simply going about their daily business, as if a spy would be wearing a trench coat, fedora and Ray-Bans in the morning's rising heat.

He's no more relaxed on the drive back to Mole Creek. Every vehicle that catches up with his slower, older car feels like a tail when it nears and a threat as it passes. He is relieved to finally get to the cottage and relative safety, and opens the doors at both ends of the house to let the air through, then fires up the modem. It's ADSL rather than broadband, but it serves its purpose, even if it takes a minute or two to connect him with the outside world. Having logged in, despite two failed attempts at the modem's unnecessarily complex password, his laptop immediately bloops the arrival of a new email. It's from Tim Wilson at the War Memorial museum.

> Hey Xander,
>
> Turns out the reason the other file you wanted was in transit was because your grandfather called for it before and it was still on its way back to records. The gist of it is that your Australian Army deserter, Jager Weighorst, was jailed and executed for drug-running in Phnom Penh, Cambodia. The file has a 'do not contest' note from the Army and Foreign Office. They'd just left the poor bugger to his fate.
>
> The strange thing is, his appointment with the firing squad occurred three months before he's supposed to have killed your grandad's girlfriend. Weird, huh? Couldn't have been him after all. I can scan it and send it over if you want. Just let me know.
>
> Tim Wilson

Xander is dazed. Weighorst didn't kill Lucy. But why is Donnie Carrick so sure it was him? Surely, he would have known about a deserter, even an Australian one, being executed in a jail in Cambodia? Xander looks at his phone and the memory stick, trying to decide which one to consult first. Eventually he tells himself the memory stick will still be there when the phone call is over, so he pulls up Colonel Tang's number and dials again. There's an overlong silence during which nothing seems to be happening and he's fighting the urge to hang up when the phone is then picked up.

'Hello?' a soft female voice says tentatively.

'Hi. Good. You speak English,' Xander replies.

'Of course,' the woman says. 'I see you are calling from Australia. Is it about my grandfather?'

'Major ... I mean Colonel Tang? Yes. May I speak with him?'

'I'm afraid that is not possible.'

'Later, maybe. Tell me a good time and ...'

'My grandfather passed away last night.'

'Passed away?'

'We think it was a faulty heater. It was only serviced yesterday and now ... he fell asleep and never woke up.' Xander hears a suppressed sob.

'Jesus wept!' he says. 'Oh, and I'm sorry for your loss.'

'May I ask who is calling?'

'Xander. Xander McAuslan.'

'Oh, the writer. You were going to write grandfather's book.'

'That's me.'

'Then I'm sorry for your loss also,' she says. 'Now I'm afraid I have to go. As I'm sure you will appreciate, there is much to do.'

Xander says his goodbyes and hangs up. His first instinct is to call Donnie Carrick. He would want to know his old sparring partner had died. But an urge for caution grips Xander. Can it be purely coincidental that Colonel Tang died the day after Xander told Donnie that Tang was planning a tell-all book? And then the fact that Alden was the name of the Quiet American in the Graham Greene novel, and Carrick said Pete called him the quiet American. That would be one hell of a coincidence, even if nothing about it makes sense. Pete said coincidence was often the logical confluence of two or more strands of events, more likely to be inevitable than unforeseeable.

Remembering Pete has him reaching for the memory stick and the entry in his notebook naming the files that Mo had unlocked. One of them, entitled *The Bullshit Chronicles*, is an ordered account of Pete's professional life from his decision to join the NSW police force to his signing up to serve in Vietnam. Xander doesn't read it in detail but gets a sense that this is a well-organised, if not particularly vivid, account of Pete's life. However, it's incomplete and right at the end of the document, in the middle of a sentence that stops dead in mid-clause, Pete has typed in bold face and then underlined the words: '**Xander: see file with your name**.'

Xander finds the file and realises it's one of the two that Mo had liberated from their base-level passwords. Xander makes himself a mug of coffee and settles down to read. It soon becomes apparent that this document is as much a letter to him as it is a recounting of events leading to Lucy's death.

If you are reading this before I have had a chance to explain it in person, I apologise. This would not have been my choice, but maybe my past has caught up with me sooner than I anticipated.

One of the reasons I never told you much about my time in Vietnam is that I'm not proud of what I did there. In short, I had a long-term lover there even though I was engaged to and later married your Nanna Kate.

The woman's name was Trang Minh but we called her Lucy. When I left Vietnam, I didn't know that Lucy was pregnant by me. She had a daughter that she didn't tell me about, her name is Linh and she is your aunt.

When Linh was just a few months old, Lucy was killed by an intruder in her bar. I was always led to believe the killer was an army deserter called Weighorst. I have recently learned this could not possibly have been the case.

307

It is to my eternal shame that I didn't investigate this crime when it happened, but now I want to make amends. I have recently spoken to Colonel, formerly Major, Tang, who knows who killed Lucy and why – although all he has told me was that the killer was a friend and ally.

However, according to Colonel Tang, this man had been compromised years earlier during an incident in an area of Saigon called Soul Alley.

As a result, he was recruited as an agent – a spy, if you like – for the USSR, which was financing the Vietcong and North Vietnamese Army. Lucy was apparently killed because she was going to expose this person to Tang, not realising that he was a double-agent.

Having been falsely accused of spying herself (while I was there), she effectively signed her own death warrant when she told Tang she was going to expose the spy.

Tang is long retired now so he has finally told me he knows for certain who killed Lucy. But I know his tricks and he may be looking to get some advantage by falsely accusing someone who wasn't culpable or in any way involved. Suffice it to say that I had two close friends in Vietnam and I believe one of them was Lucy's killer.

I am not going to name either of them until I'm sure. You know better than I in these times of internet trolls and the like, any accusations may as well be a guilty verdict.

I am writing this now because I think in investigating this crime, I may have kicked over a hornets' nest and maybe even put my life in danger. I believe the person responsible for Lucy's death is still working for the Russians, probably now as a sleeper.

I'll say no more at this stage except that I am calling my prime suspect 'Alden'. If I am right, the stakes are much higher than you could ever imagine. If I am wrong, at least

a good man won't suffer the consequences of a false
accusation that could destroy his reputation, his legacy and
what's left of his future.

Pete McAuslan

Mole Creek

Xander has just finished reading this when his phone vibrates.
It's Althea. He thinks about not answering, there's a text file that
he wants to read simply called, Linh, but takes it on what must
have been the last ring.

'Oh, thank God!' she says. 'You at the cottage?'

'Uh-huh,' he replies.

'Okay, you gotta get out now.'

'Why?'

'There are police officers on their way to arrest you.'

'Arrest me? What for?'

'They found your DNA on the jack that killed Johnny
Spangler.'

'They what!? That's impossible.'

'I know. I tried to tell them. But Danzig ...' Her voice tails
off, but then gathers renewed urgency. 'You need to get out of
there now.'

'Okay.'

'One other thing. The council dog pound was broken into last
night. Someone took Lorenzo's dogs.'

'Shit!'

'Yeah. He could be paying you a visit too. Just so you know,
Pete's gun is in the top drawer of the desk.'

'Who ...? How?'

'Never mind. Get it and use it if you need to. But right now
you need to get out of the cottage before my colleagues arrive.'

'Okay. On it.'

'And don't try to contact me. I'll try to fix it at this end then come to you when the coast is clear.' She hangs up before he can ask how long that is likely to take.

Xander hesitates before putting the laptop and USB drive in his bag and grabbing his hiking jacket, a groundsheet, some water, a couple of protein bars and Pete's binoculars. He goes out through the back door and runs across the narrow clearing to the edge of the pine forest. It's a commercial plantation so the trees stand in uniform rows, like an army ready to swoop down the hill and swamp the village below. The gaps between them make it easier to run deeper into their sheltering ranks. Xander finds a spot where he can see the cottage but is unlikely to be seen himself, and settles down to wait.

About ten minutes later, a police car cruises up the road from Mole Creek and turns up the track towards the cottage. Two uniformed cops get out and cautiously approach the house, their hands on the hilts of their undrawn weapons. Xander is still focusing the field glasses when one of them disappears inside the house. He reappears moments later, shaking his head. They go around to the side of the cottage and spend an inordinate amount of time examining the old Volvo, inside and out. Eventually they return to their vehicle and sit with both doors open, allowing the cooling evening breeze to dissipate whatever funk they have accumulated on their day's driving. After about forty-five minutes, as the first shadows of dusk stretch across the paddock, they close up and drive off.

Xander sits in the shaded solitude of his lair and waits. If they're smart, they'll come back and look for signs of life. He decides to chance it, raises his laptop's screen and reads the file called 'Linh'. It's a computer translation of a file probably written in Vietnamese. He reads and re-reads it. Some of the recent events in his life start to make sense. Not everything, not by a long chalk, but enough.

About an hour later a vehicle's headlights penetrate the misty gloom on the main road and the police car stops at the paddock gate. Xander surmises that they have been to the pub and, now refreshed and relaxed, they can't be bothered to negotiate the airlock gates, seeing the cottage sits in complete darkness. The car turns around and disappears along the road, back towards Mole Creek.

Sitting in the dark, tree branches rustling gently above him, cold rising through the groundsheet, Xander waits but the police car doesn't return. He has plenty of time to think about his predicament and knows he is in danger, but he's not sure from whom. He knows Althea has lied to him, but then she warned him about the cops. The question of how his DNA ended up on the jack that failed and killed Johnny Spanners can wait. He has the perfect alibi – he was sleeping with a cop – but only if she chooses to confirm his story. Meanwhile, both she and Donnie Carrick are pointing at Lorenzo. Was he seduced by the feeling that his grandfather's friend was so like Pete? Is that what Lorenzo wanted, so he could manipulate him? And what about Pete's note? Someone who was a good friend of Pete's is a sleeper mole for the Russians. Now Althea says Geoffrey knew Lorenzo was a spy. After another ten minutes of waiting, enveloped by darkness and doubt, Xander gathers up his kit, makes his way cautiously back to the cottage and re-enters through the back door.

Waiting for his eyes to adjust to the dark, he notices a triangle of white protruding from the jamb of the front door. He opens the door and it falls to the ground. In the half-light he can see it is a police business card. He picks it up and reads the message scrawled on the back in thin black ballpoint. Squinting at it, he reads: 'We think you might be in danger. Please call us as soon as you get this message.'

The guys sent to arrest him think he's so dumb that he'll invite them back to his home. Xander laughs and shakes his head just before a burly arm goes around his throat from behind and he feels something sharp, he's guessing the point of a knife, jab the skin on his neck, precisely on his carotid artery.

'Don't fucken try anything and we'll all be okay,' a familiar voice whispers in his ear. Then a dog licks his hand.

CHAPTER 38

Xander is glad that he's been exercising again, not because he's in any position to engage in hand-to-hand combat, but his muscles are loose enough to allow his hands to be tied behind his back and to a table leg as he sits on the floor.

In the gloom of the cottage's front room, he can make out Lorenzo's shape, but not his expression. The big man is also sitting on the floor, well out of sight of anyone passing on the road below, his back against the rear of the sofa. The dogs lie either side of him, blissfully content to be with their master again. He is holding a handgun.

'Give me one good reason I shouldn't shoot you,' he says.

'What for?' Xander asks.

'For telling the cops about my hide-out.'

'I didn't, that would be reason number one. But before you do anything, explain why you killed Pete.'

'I didn't fucking kill Pete,' Lorenzo says. 'He was the only friend I had in world.' The dogs stir at the anger in Lorenzo's voice. 'Only human friend,' he corrects himself.

'If you found that gun in the desk drawer, it was Pete's,' Xander says.

'Shit. I haven't felt the weight of one of these in years. You sure it was Pete's?'

'Althea told me I'd find it there. I'm guessing she maybe hoped I would shoot you with it if you turned up.'

'Your fuck-buddy.'

'My alibi.'

'For what?'

'Killing Johnny Spanners. I was with her at the time.'

'That's a shame.'

'Why?'

'If you'd done it, I couldn't have.'

'I didn't. Sorry.'

'Me neither,' says Lorenzo. 'Okay, convince me you didn't tell your cop girlfriend where my cave was and I'll let you go.'

'Well, I can tell you who did tell her.'

'Go on.'

'You,' says Xander.

'Me?'

'And me too, I suppose. Not directly, but you told Johnny that you had watched me along the trail until I was about an hour from the main road. He told Althea. I told her how long I had been walking. I guess they triangulated from that.'

'Fuck,' says Lorenzo. 'And you are sleeping with this girl?'

'Hey, as far as she's concerned, you're just a crazy Vietnam vet living illegally in a national park. A potential danger to yourself and passing hikers. Oh, and a spy.'

'A spy,' Lorenzo splutters. 'Who the fuck for?'

Xander's phone rings, loudly and unexpectedly, the light from its screen illuminating the looks of surprise on both their faces. Lorenzo takes it off the desk and shows the screen to Xander.

'Who is it?' Lorenzo asks.

'No idea,' Xander replies.

'Want to take it?'

'I think I maybe should.'

'Okay. No funny business.' Lorenzo swipes the answer button and presses 'speaker'.

'Xander?' a woman's voice says. 'It's Nicole. Nicole Swift.'

'Hi, Nicole. Good to hear from you again, and so soon.'

'Xander, is there something you're not telling me?'

Xander looks at Lorenzo, who shakes his head and puts his finger to his lips. 'Be careful' is the clear message.

'Not sure what you mean,' Xander says.

'You said you visited Donnie Carrick in Canberra.'

'I did,' he says. 'He was a friend of my grandad's in Vietnam.'

'And you weren't working on a story?'

'What story? He's a diplomat, that's all, and we didn't even talk about that stuff.'

'A diplomat for now,' she says. 'The word around the traps is that he's being considered for the top job at the Pentagon when he gets back to the States.'

'The what?'

'The current Secretary of Defence has got himself into some sort of sexting scandal and the Yanks are saying – off the record, of course – that your lunch buddy is in line to take over. He's a bit of a star over there. This guy has been there, done it all, and has a chestful of medals that would do a South American dictator proud.

'He gets around.'

'The rumour is that Canberra is just a staging post while he runs down the clock on the seven years he needs to be out of the military before he can take over at the Pentagon. That's the law there. And to make sure there's no chance of any controversy or scandal before he gets promoted, I guess.'

'That makes sense.'

'And you're telling me that you had lunch with the man who is going to be the most powerful civilian in the free world, after the president himself, and you didn't even know?'

'That's awkward. I had no idea. How did you hear about it?'

'When I asked around about him, all the Canberra Defence bigwigs were creaming themselves at the thought of that level of direct access to someone they know,' she says, adding, 'and like.'

'He said nothing to me,' Xander says. 'But then why would he?'

'You sure you're not holding out on me?'

'Nicole, I don't even have a paper to write for if I was. If I hear anything, you'll be my first call.'

'I better be,' she says. 'Bye.'

'You went to see Donnie?' Lorenzo says as he clicks off the call.

'Didn't you suggest it? Anyway, I found out Pete had been in Canberra. The reason why seemed pretty obvious.' Xander squirms. 'Now do you believe that I didn't give away the location of your cave?'

'Yeah ... and maybe the fucker who killed Johnny got something out of him too.'

'True,' Xander says. 'I don't suppose there's any chance you could untie me.'

'Oh, sorry, kid,' Lorenzo says. 'I forgot about that.'

He produces a knife of Crocodile Dundee proportions and slices through the bindings on Xander's wrists. They both stay sitting on the floor facing each other, Xander rubbing his hands.

'Okay, what did Donnie say when you met him?'

'Aaah, this is going to be awkward too,' Xander says. 'He was the one who said you were a spy and you got Johnny Weighorst to kill Lucy because she was going to expose you.'

'Fuck. I wish I hadn't untied you now.'

'It's okay. I know that's bullshit. I know who really killed Lucy and I think I know why Pete was killed too.'

'Okay, Mr Storyteller, do your thing.'

***

The story comes together in Xander's mind as he tells it, based on Pete's notes, Linh's message and his own research.

'Imagine an up-and-coming young army officer had been blackmailed and turned in Soul Alley, just as Althea said you had been,' he tells Lorenzo. 'Althea just took what happened to this officer and replaced his name with yours. That's why it all sounded plausible.

'But the guy who was turned, every time he did one more favour for the Russians, they had their claws in him deeper. Back then, the Russians were investing so much money and political capital in the Vietcong, they needed a reliable source of information. Who better to provide unbiased intel than someone on the other side?

'Then, when Vietnam is over, the officer returns to America and moves up through the ranks and then eventually into the diplomatic sphere, probably a sleeper as the Russians wouldn't want to risk exposing him until he'd gone as far as he was likely to go.'

'Secretary of Defence good enough for you?' Lorenzo says.

'Exactly,' Xander says. 'And let's not rule out the possibility that the Russians engineered the sexting scandal that has the current guy on the skids. But just when the Russians' prize asset was about to truly bear fruit, ascending to the highest echelons of the Pentagon – a juicy prize they wouldn't have dared dream about – Pete starts asking questions about Lucy's death, not realising that the man he was asking for help was her killer. Well, not until he figured out that he'd been lying to him.

'Carrick sensed Pete was suspicious and believed it was only a matter of time before he joined the dots. They may not even have known that he had tracked down Linh, his daughter, and that she was coming to Mole Creek to help her father piece together what had happened to Lucy. Whatever happened, she got here before they did. According to a note she put on the memory stick, she took Pete's laptop, planning to backup all his stuff and return it.'

'Why?' Lorenzo says. 'What's the rush?'

'She says Pete was distraught and maybe a bit drunk. He wouldn't tell her the name of the man who killed her mother – he gave her the cover name, Alden ...'

'The Quiet American ...' Lorenzo says. 'I looked it up.'

'Me too, but I didn't make the connection until I after met Carrick,' Xander says. 'That's what Pete used to call him. Anyway, according to Linh, Pete was very drunk and so ripped apart at being betrayed by someone he had loved and trusted, that he was talking about erasing all his notes. Deleting the whole thing. I guess he didn't know about Carrick's impending promotion. Linh wasn't having it. This is about her mother's killer, remember? She took the laptop away so she could copy all Pete's files for safe-keeping – from Pete, if no one else. After she was gone the Russian came here and killed Pete, making it look like suicide by sending a 'goodbye cruel world' note from his phone. When Linh went back to return Pete's laptop, he was dead and the police were already there. Meanwhile, the Russian set about tracking down and erasing every file that had anything about Carrick on it.'

'You do realise how nuts this all sounds, don't you?' Lorenzo says.

'It gets crazier, trust me. Two days before he killed Pete, the Russian broke into my flat in Sydney and took all my computer files. Then, when I got here a couple of days later and refused to believe Pete took his own life, he broke into my hotel room and deleted all Pete's backup files and bricked my computer. He probably thought that would be enough since there was no other evidence to implicate Carrick. He possibly didn't know Linh had made a copy of everything on a memory stick before she left Pete's laptop at the airport. Even if he did, he probably thought she'd keep for later. She'd be easy to track down when she was back in Vietnam.'

'What about you and Anthea?'

'Althea. I don't know. All the time she was telling me that

Danzig was trying to shut the investigation down, she was probably telling her boss that I was a crazy conspiracy theorist, just looking for an angle for another book. While I was visiting you, she concocted the story about how the Russian was called Alden and he was a hit man for a Sydney criminal. Bizarre.'

'Maybe she liked you and wanted to protect you without blowing her cover,' Lorenzo says.

'Maybe. You know, I wonder how involved she really is. She's made some pretty basic errors. Like lying about her police rank, and making up other stuff I could check with a phone call. And thinking I wouldn't find out about her and Dreevers.'

'Back up the bus, buddy,' Lorenzo says. 'You've gone way past my stop.'

'When Althea was a student she crippled a girl in a prank. Her tutor said it couldn't have been her as she was with him.'

'And now he owns her. What's his deal?'

'He's a judge called Geoffrey Dreevers. He told her he met you back in Vietnam. He was a radical anti-war campaigner back then. Says you were a spy and he was introduced to you by a Vietcong senior officer in Soul Alley.'

'Total bullshit. I never set foot in the place all the time I was there.'

'But now we have two people, both saying you were a spy.'

'And your point is?'

'My point is that it's Carrick and Dreevers who probably really are working for a foreign government. Look, I know it all sounds implausible. I'd have written all of this off as a set of crazy coincidences, except for two things. Colonel Tang died two days after I told Carrick he'd asked me to write a book about his life as a double-agent during the war.'

'Shit.'

'And all those deaths. Pete, Tang, Johnny Spanners, Rob the barman. The stakes would have to be huge to justify that level of mayhem. A shitload of money or some psycho revenge-killing spree. But then we find out that Carrick is in line to be Russia's mole in the top seat at the Pentagon.' Xander shakes his head, then a thought occurs. 'And that's why Althea warned me about the cops coming to arrest me.'

'Not with you, kid,' Lorenzo says.

'Because she wanted me to be around here. If I got arrested, I'd be safe in police custody.'

'If this is all true, she's probably on her way now,' Lorenzo says, rising slowly and moving in a crouch to the window. He peers out at the side of the frame. 'This is all coming to a head, kid, and you could use some sappernuity. These guys will not stop until every trace of what Carrick did back in the day has been erased.'

Lorenzo's dogs suddenly sit up, their ears like radar discs, all four pointed at the cottage's front door. Lorenzo crab-walks across slowly, picking up his crossbow from the floor. He loads a bolt on to the bow, leans with his back against the door and listens.

'You know I brought all Pete's backup files for you?' Lorenzo says.

Xander looks at Lorenzo as if he's gone mad.

'All those documents, the pictures, the proof – I hid them in King Solomon's Caves,' he says in a louder than normal voice.

'What?' Xander says. Lorenzo silences him with a finger to his lips.

'All the material that Pete gave me to pass on to you if anything happened to him, it's in a black plastic bag on the left, inside the inner door of the main cave.'

With his back against the door, Lorenzo raises the crossbow across his chest, ready for action. He gestures to Xander to take cover behind the sofa, but before he can move there is a deafening thud and the pressure inside the room is momentarily so elevated Xander thinks his eardrums are going to burst. A wave of hot air hits his face as he looks up to see the front door gone and a cloud of smoke, dirt and splinters has taken its place. The door is now on the floor with Lorenzo lying face-down under it. The big man shapes to heave himself up to his hands and knees but the Russian steps into the breach and fires two rounds from a suppressed gun through the timber door and into Lorenzo's back. Lorenzo slumps forward and lies motionless. Xander looks up for a possible escape route, but he's too dazed to propel himself in any helpful direction. The dogs are less hesitant, flashing past the Russian as they hurtle into the safety of the night.

'Don't get up,' the Russian says to Xander. 'We won't be here long and it could be prematurely fatal.'

CHAPTER 39

'By the way, full marks on your summary of the situation,' the Russian says as he sits on the edge of the desk, waving his gun like a bored choirmaster's baton. 'A couple of teeny errors here and there but otherwise spot-on.'

'You heard?'

'I bugged the cottage.'

'When?'

'Does it matter? It's what I do ... among other things.'

'Tell me, what's all this about?' Xander asks. The Russian loves to show off, he knows, and this is a chance to gain some time to think.

'As I said, you summarised the situation very accurately. Once a journalist, huh? I'm just tying up loose ends. Cleaning up.'

'If I can be a little critical, your cleaning up tends to be a bit messy.'

'You think so?' The Russian pouts, feigning hurt.

'Pete, Rob the barman, Johnny Spanners and now Lorenzo. Oh, and Colonel Tang. That was you, I suppose.'

'A colleague. Sorry about your book. I'm sure it would have been a bestseller.'

'That's a lot of dead bodies over an incident that occurred fifty years ago, and which would be hard to prove anyway.'

'Hard, but not impossible. And these days, you don't need proof to destroy careers. General Carrick's appointment will be scrutinised at the US Senate and any hint of scandal could sink him, especially if the internet gets hold of it.'

'So you have to quarantine him.'

'Your grandfather got it, of course. General Carrick remembers the look on his face the moment he realised he was talking to the man who had killed his lover. That's when Carrick called us and all this started.'

'You're saying this is all Pete's fault?'

'In a way. But mostly it's yours. If you had just accepted that your grandfather killed himself you would have spared –' he counts mentally '– five lives, including yours, six if you count your aunt. And I do.'

'Linh is dead?'

'Not yet. She's hard to track down.' The Russian thinks. 'Oh, and I don't suppose you could persuade your friend in the computer shop to get up here, could you? As a personal favour?'

'Mo is a misanthrope,' Xander says. 'He doesn't even do favours for people he likes.'

'I'll add him to my "to do" list.'

'This is turning into a bloodbath,' Xander says. 'So much for cleaning up.'

'You're right,' the Russian says. 'I'm thinking a small fire might be required. After I have retrieved the bullets from the bodies, of course. Burned bodies full of bullets. Such a rookie error.' He looks around at the doorway. 'And here she is, with perfect timing.'

Xander looks up and sees Althea standing in the doorway, bent under the weight of a jerrycan which, judging by the smell wafting through on the night breeze, is full of petrol.

'Leave that on the deck, Althea,' the Russian said. 'We won't need it right away and it's already stinking the place out.'

She returns from dropping off the jerrycan away from the door and he gestures to her to join them. She sits on the arm of the sofa behind which Xander is still crouched. She looks down, then looks away, tears forming.

'I am so sorry,' she says.

'Xander, come sit,' the Russian says, gesturing to an armchair. 'Althea, we were just talking about tying up loose ends. Xander thinks I make more messes than I clear up.'

'Sergei, I am in no mood for your shit,' she says as Xander sits in the chair. 'You killed Xander's grandad then you went around knocking off anyone he's been in contact with. You're like a fucking infection.'

'Althea, you said my name. That's not very clever, is it? Again, you're letting me down.'

'What do you mean? I've done everything you asked and more. A lot more,' she says, looking at Xander.

'I disagree. If you had been a little more convincing at the start, Xander here would have gone back to Sydney none the wiser.'

'Apart from wondering why you broke into his flat and stole his computer files. And do you know what you've done to the murder rate in Tasmania?'

'There were no murders. I have been very careful,' he says. 'Mr McAuslan, suicide; the mechanic, accident or possibly poor Lorenzo there, covering his tracks; the barman, hit-and-run. No one is connecting these deaths except you.'

'And if I hadn't been running interference inside the police force?'

'Can I just ask, what's the story with my DNA being found on the jack that killed Johnny Spanners?' Xander asks.

'A precaution – insurance, if you like, in case we needed to neutralise your credibility,' the Russian says. 'Oh, you mean how did we get it? Remember the lady with the shopping trolley in the station?'

Xander sags. Of course. Early morning light is casting long shadows through the open doorway. The dawn chorus is swelling into a cacophony of caws, shrieks and more tuneful whistles. In the midst of it all, Xander is sure he can hear the mournful yodelling of Lorenzo's dogs, desperate to see their master but too frightened to enter a house where doors suddenly and noisily erupt into rooms.

'Again, I'm so sorry,' Althea says to Xander.

'Just out of curiosity, Althea, how did you get into all this? I know about the girl you injured in the prank, and I know Geoffrey covered for you, but this?'

She looks at Xander in disbelief and anger. 'Do you really think I'm so weak, so easily manipulated? Yes, Geoffrey covered for me, but this has nothing to do with that. I'm really not that naïve.' She looks at the Russian.

'Carry on, this is fascinating,' he says.

'You aren't the only one whose grandfather served in Vietnam. Mine was a Vietnam vet too, except he came back seriously fucked up. He was an angry man who got angrier when he drank – which was most of the time. He mistreated my father and my dad grew into an angry drunk too. My dad beat my mother, and me too occasionally. University was my refuge and that's why I was so grateful to Geoffrey. If I'd been sent down after the accident ... I don't know what would have happened. I had a pretty promising career ahead of me, either in law or politics. But I chose the police first, just to be able to help protect women like my mother from men like my father and grandfather. I stayed with Geoffrey because I believed what he believed: the Vietnam War should never have happened. Australians should never have been there. When Geoffrey asked me to make sure you believed Pete's death was suicide, it was a no-brainer. A chance to get some payback for what the war did to my family.'

'Where is he now?' Xander asks. 'Your father?'

'In a pub in Hobart, I would think,' she says. 'Mum is safely on the mainland. And please don't think I'm a victim here. Geoffrey was asked by Sergei's people in Moscow to help cover up Pete's death and I chose to help him because I believe in the same things he does. It was supposed to be a small misdirection for the greater good. Neither of us thought Sergei here would start killing everyone who crossed his path.'

'Again, with my name,' the Russian says. 'Just in case you didn't get it the first time. Okay, enough of this chit-chat. Xander, I'm afraid it's time. I can't say it has been a pleasure, but it has been interesting.'

He raised his gun and points it at Xander.

'No, Sergei,' Althea says, standing between Xander and the gun. 'It's over. There's no way this won't be traced back to General Carrick. There's too much information floating around.' She points to Xander's laptop. 'Here. His aunt. Lorenzo's backup files. It's time to stop the killing and go. I'll make sure we keep a lid on this until you are off the island, at least.'

The Russian tilts his head as he thinks, but he doesn't lower the gun. He looks puzzled and disappointed. 'You know, I told Geoffrey it was a mistake to bring you in. Convenient, yes, with your police connection. But you are too raw. Too inexperienced. Not committed to the cause.'

'What cause?' Althea asks.

'See what I mean?' The Russian laughs.

'He means the restoration of the Russian Empire,' Xander says. 'Rebuild the USSR. Don't forget that President Putin was a senior agent in the KGB before the Berlin Wall came down. Called the break-up of the USSR the greatest geopolitical tragedy of the twentieth century.'

'Comrade Putin has a vision, that's for sure,' the Russian says. 'And the drive to make it a reality. But he is not alone. Oh, here's an amusing coincidence for you, Xander. The man who turned General Caddick was Vladimir's mentor when he was being trained at the KGB so, yes, he has taken a close, personal interest.'

'Are you fucking kidding me? That's what all this is about?' Althea says. 'You're talking ancient history. I wasn't even born.'

'I'm not kidding,' the Russian says. 'How can I convince you? Aaaah … I know.'

He fires twice. *Phutt, phutt.* Two small red spots appear in Althea's chest and start to spread through the cloth of her shirt. She looks down in shock rather than pain, and falls to her knees, then slumps face-down onto the floor. There's a gurgling sound for a few seconds, then it stops.

'What the fuck?' is all Xander can muster. He moves forward instinctively.

'Don't get up,' the Russian says. 'She's dead. Okay, a head shot would have been kinder, but the bullets, you know … very hard to dig out of skulls before the fire. And the holes in the bone. Too easy to spot.' He waves his gun in the general direction of Xander's knees. 'Now, we have some unfinished business. I'm afraid this will be slow and very painful, but we can shorten the time if you cooperate convincingly.'

'With what?'

The Russian removes the memory stick from Xander's laptop and holds it up. 'Let's start with who else knows about General Carrick?'

'You mean, apart from those already dead or on your hit list?' There's movement behind the Russian and Xander looks up to see a strangely familiar figure silhouetted in the doorway. He narrows his eyes and makes out a gangly man holding a golf club.

'Oh dear,' says the Russian. 'You're seriously not trying that trick again, are you? Fool me once, shame on –'

'What the faaaaaaack?' Ralphie yells, surveying the chaotic scene as he advances, golf club poised to strike.

The Russian whips round, gun raised, but that only serves to place his wrist in line with the imperfect arc of Ralphie's swing. There's a sickening crack as the carbon-fibre shaft meets skin and bone, followed by a clatter as the Russian's gun skids across the floor. He turns to retrieve it, but Ralphie is taking no chances and hits him again, this time on the side of one knee. The Russian drops like an Italian striker tackled in the penalty box and Ralphie hits him across the scapula and collar bone. He's aiming for the head, but suddenly stops, realising the person he thought he was attacking is, in fact, scrambling across the floor in the direction of Pete's gun.

The moment's hesitation is all the Russian needs. Kneeling on the floor beside Lorenzo's body, he sees the handle of the big man's hunting knife in a sheath strapped to his leg. As Ralphie stands over him, torn between finishing him off or pursuing Xander, the Russian flips over and lunges upwards, plunging the knife deep under Ralphie's too-prominent ribcage. Ralphie's expression is one of mild surprise but, with a knife having gone straight through his heart, he is dead before his golf club hits the ground. The Russian sprawls across the floor and retrieves his gun then gets to his feet, but finds himself looking down the barrel of Pete's gun, and with one knee threatening to give way any second.

'Don't fucking move,' Xander says.

'Or what?' the Russian mocks. 'You think you can shoot me before I shoot you. I think you told me yourself that you're not a gun person.' He chambers a round and raises the pistol, smiling at the indecision in Xander's eyes.

There's a sound behind him, more of a clunk than a pop, and the Russian looks down at his right bicep, from which a barbed crossbow bolt is protruding. His surprise is compounded when he loses his grip on his gun and it falls to the floor.

He makes a dive for the door, passing Lorenzo who is still prone, but trying to load another bolt. Xander fire's Pete's gun, almost surprising himself, but not coming close to hitting the Russian, who stays low until he reaches the doorway and rolls gymnastically out on to the deck. Xander ducks behind the sofa and trains the gun on the doorway, just in case the Russian comes back with another weapon. After a few seconds, he creeps over to the window where he's joined by Lorenzo, who has shrugged off the broken door. Xander raises the gun and aims as the Russian heads for some bushes by the fence, pursued by Lorenzo's dogs, who may not be sure if this is a game or a hunt. Lorenzo pushes down Xander's hand.

'Too far,' he says. 'You might hit one of the dogs.'

A few seconds later, they hear a car engine start and a crunch of spraying gravel as the Russian takes off, heading away from Mole Creek and Launceston, but towards King Solomon's Caves. Xander goes back inside and checks on Althea then Ralphie. There are no signs of life from either.

Lorenzo stretches and winces as he turns his back to Xander. 'Fuck, that hurt,' he says. It's immediately obvious that the bullets penetrated the door, but didn't get through Lorenzo's skin. Two flat metal discs sit just inside the first layer of fabric on Lorenzo's thick black waistcoat.

'Bullet-proof vest,' Lorenzo explains. 'I didn't know what to expect when I bailed you up. Certainly not this. That explosion winded me and the impact from the shots must have knocked me out.'

Xander walks Lorenzo out on to the deck and gets him some water. He dials triple-0 and tells them they need to send an ambulance to the cottage and police to the caves. When the operator hesitates, demanding more information, Xander says 'a police officer has been shot and killed'. That seems to do the trick.

'Are you going to be all right on your own till the ambos get here?' he asks Lorenzo.

'Leave it, son,' he says. 'Let the cops do their job.'

'It'll take them an hour to get here. It's only fifteen minutes to the tourist entrance to the caves. The slippery fucker will be long gone by the time the cops arrive,' Xander says. 'And he killed Pete.'

'I can't help you, mate,' Lorenzo says. 'My back is fucked. I'd be a burden and a distraction.' He reaches into his voluminous pockets and produces a black fabric case the size of a compact camera. 'Night-vision binoculars,' he says. 'You can't wear them, but they'll be handy for checking in the caves. And one other thing ...'

'Yeah?'

'There is no package of backup files. When the dogs sensed there was someone outside, I only said that in the hope they might piss off and go looking for them. Totally misread that one. But it means that if you do get there before he scarpers, you are going to find one very pissed-off Russian.'

There's movement off to the side and Xander sees, charging towards them, two very happy-looking dogs.

***

The caves haven't officially opened yet but it's clear from the broken padlock and discarded bolt cutters that the Russian had come equipped, which is no surprise. The neatly sheared crossbow bolt is evidence that they'd also been helpful in removing it, despite its barb. By the time Xander has found the inner door, which is sitting open, he is walking tentatively through pitch darkness. A flashlight would be handy, but it would also make him an easy target. There's every chance the Russian had another gun in his car. Xander thinks he hears a footstep ahead in the black perma-night but there are confusing water drips and the echoing gurgle of the distant stream that gave Mole Creek its name. The rivulet appears on the surface every so often before disappearing underground again.

Progress is slow. Xander uses the night-vision binoculars to make out the shapes of the stalactites and the concrete pathways between them, but otherwise has to feel his way, forcing him to pocket the gun to leave one hand free. At one point he thinks he sees the luminous face of a watch about 20 metres away, but it disappears. It occurs to him that perhaps he's not the hunter, but the quarry, and he stops to take stock. He listens. Water, both steady drips and in full flow. His heart thumping in his ears. His breath. No, two breaths. Then, for the second time in less than twenty-four hours, he feels the point of Lorenzo's knife in the side of his neck.

'Where is it?' the Russian hisses.

'The gun? In my pocket.'

'Not the gun, you idiot. The package of files?'

'Ah,' Xander says. 'There are no files. Lorenzo lied. He was trying to put you off the scent.'

'What?'

'He thought you might come here to look for it. Give us a chance to get away. He had no idea you would blow the door off.'

The Russian curses volubly in his native tongue. 'Okay, give me the gun.'

'That doesn't sound like such a good idea,' Xander says.

'Give me the fucking gun or I will cut your throat right now and take it,' the Russian says. 'I'm counting to three. One ... two ...'

Suddenly all the cave lights come on and the two men are momentarily blinded. Before their eyes have fully adjusted a door opens and a gaggle of schoolkids enters. In the midst of them Xander spots the Asian girl who accosted him on the bus. The Russian quickly lowers the knife out of sight and jabs it in the small of Xander's back. The kids troop past, mostly oblivious, chattering excitedly, but as the bus girl passes, Xander says, 'Hello, little girl. Nice to see you again,' in the sleaziest voice he can muster.

The girl looks up and screams: 'Aiyeeee! It's the pedo from the bus.'

She points at him and starts chanting, 'Pedo ... pedo!' and the other kids immediately join in. Xander senses the Russian moving away from him and looks around to see him sprinting into a side gallery. He thinks about letting him go, but there's a bunch of kids there and if the Russian took any of them hostage ... It doesn't bear thinking about.

Xander follows the Russian into the less well-lit passage, finding the gun in his pocket and gripping it tightly, but keeping it out of sight. Edging cautiously along every twist and turn, Xander rounds a corner and realises, as the Russian had seconds earlier, that it's a cul-de-sac. The Russian brandishes the knife and advances on Xander.

'Looks like you brought a knife to a gunfight,' Xander says, trying to pull the pistol out, but quickly realising the weapon has become trapped by the stretchy material in his hoodie pocket. The more he pulls, the more stuck it seems. The Russian senses his opportunity and charges. Xander steps backwards instinctively and slips, falling flat on his back. The Russian is right over him, lunging and he still can't get the gun out, but once again the instinct hard-wired into him over years of training takes over and he raises his feet and jams them into the on-rushing Russian's gut and pushes hard. In a dojo, the other fighter would fly over and beyond the man on the mat, probably flipping and landing on his back. The Russian flies upwards and over Xander, but stops in mid-air, his roar of aggression silenced. He wriggles convulsively for a few seconds then stops. Xander finally gets the gun out of his pocket and tentatively lowers his feet but the Russian, bizarrely, stays stuck to the ceiling.

Xander hears adult voices and sees the beams from flashlights approach. He carefully lays the gun on the floor, kneels down and raises his hands in surrender. Something drips on his face and he realises it's blood. He looks up and can see in the torchlights that Sergei, the Russian agent, man of a thousand voices, has been impaled on three stalactites, one having come through from the back of his neck and out of his mouth. There's a gut-churning sucking sound that could have emanated from a primeval swamp. Xander rolls aside as the stalactites release their prey and the Russian slides off the limestone spikes and slams on to the floor with a squelch. The first cop on the scene witnesses this too and promptly vomits. Xander shakes his head silently as he is handcuffed and led away, imagining what Pete would say about the calibre of modern cops. Xander is about to make a caustic comment, just to release some tension, when arms grip his elbows from behind, a cloth bag is pulled over his head and everything is darkness.

CHAPTER 40

The suite where Xander is kept for the next few days is comfortable and quiet. They are clearly in the countryside somewhere, he guesses in some kind of boutique hotel that, judging by the bucolic décor and framed prints of shooting parties and anglers, doubles as a fishing lodge or spa, or both. Right now, however, it's being used as a debrief centre by various law enforcement and secret service agencies. His bedroom, and the attached lounge room, are decorated in calming pastels and comforting chintz, which might calm and comfort guests who weren't brought here on the floor of an SUV with a bag over their head, as he was. Adding to his various feelings of confusion, irritation and ultimately amusement, Xander is told that no, he is not under arrest so, no, he doesn't need a lawyer but no, he can't leave.

He is treated well, with undertones of gratitude and apology, but questioned relentlessly. His first visitor is David Danzig.

'Xander, I want to apologise,' Danzig says.

'What for?' Xander asks, having decided from the moment the police commander walked through the door that he wasn't going to make this easy for him.

'For not listening to you about your grandad, for a start,' Danzig says, shifting uncomfortably in a dining chair he's taken from a small table in the bay-window space.

'Well, it is a start,' Xander says, his tone implying that's all it is. 'What about the gun? That was a bit of a clue.'

'What gun?' Danzig asks.

'The Russian's gun. The Ruger with the silencer …'

Danzig looks at him in obvious confusion.

'Oh. Oh, shit,' Xander says, getting it. 'Althea never gave it to you, did she?'

Danzig shakes his head.

'Man, she was a piece of work,' Xander says. 'I fell for it completely. Every time I thought I'd caught her out, she had an answer.'

'You and me both,' Danzig says. 'She was a fine officer until she wasn't. She'll be missed.'

'Presumably not after all this comes out,' Xander says.

There's a cough from a corner of the room and they both look up to where a youngish woman with short blonde hair in a smart suit has been sitting still and silent, so much so that she might as well have been absorbed by the wall.

'Someone will be along to speak with you about that,' she says, in a drawl that Xander immediately recognises was crafted in Boston or thereabouts in the USA.

The woman falls silent again.

'The current official angle is that she was shot in the line of duty, trying to protect you from a Sydney criminal out for revenge,' Danzig says.

'Well, that's almost true,' Xander replies. 'But what about the other stuff?'

'There is no uthah stuff,' comes the voice from the wall. Danzig's eyebrows say the rest.

'Can I ask who you are?' Xander asks the woman.

She says nothing.

'Aren't people going to want to know how a Russian hit man got himself stuck on stalactites in a tourist cave?' Xander asks.

'Only one other person saw that and he's being … um … counselled, as we speak.'

The vomiting cop, Xander thinks. He's not likely to be boasting to too many people about that.

'How's Lorenzo?' Xander asks.

'Lorenzo?'

'Gordon. My grandad's mate.'

'He's doing okay. He'll be out of hospital in a couple of days, then we have to decide where to send him.'

'What are the choices?'

'Right now, it's prison, a mental facility or an old folk's home.'

'The old bugger saved my life, don't forget,' Xander says.

Danzig winces at a thought that displeases him too. 'Okay, I gotta go,' he says. 'Don't worry. You'll be fine, but this is bigger than all of us.'

Soon after Danzig leaves, the questioning starts in earnest. First by ASIO, then the Federal Police, and even the Child Protection squad – due to the overheard if entirely empty allegation that he was a paedophile. Throughout all this, there is an ever-changing procession of smartly suited Americans sitting silently in the chair in the corner, whom he assumes are the CIA. When the suited watchers finally get round to questioning him, it's apparent they've been surveilling him since his lunch with Carrick, but then it was because they were conducting a positive vetting of the proposed new Defence Secretary.

The Americans start the whole process from the beginning again. The same silent observers who've sat in on every interrogation from day one take turns at cajoling, badgering, dissembling and threatening as they try to pick holes in Xander's story. At first, his inquisitors won't even discuss what has happened to the other players. But on the second day of the CIA's questioning, having been asked the same questions over and over, his recollection being challenged at every turn, it occurs to Xander that the authorities seem to be more concerned about covering up the fact that they had spies in their midst than investigating any crimes that may have been committed. Realising he has considerable leverage in that regard, Xander refuses to say another word until someone tells him the full story. After much discussion, conducted somewhere else in the hotel, the woman with the Boston drawl, who turns out to be the most senior of the CIA operatives, returns to the room.

'All I can tell you is that your summary of the events that you helpfully recited into the Russian's bugs was pretty accurate,' she says.

'That's what he said,' Xander replies. 'How did you hear it?'

'We had our own technology in play,' she says. 'We didn't send men into space just to invent non-stick frypans.'

'What's going to happen to Carrick?'

'Former General Carrick is currently undergoing a deep debrief,' she says.

'*Former* General?' Xander says. 'I thought you kept that rank for life.'

'Not if you have been spying for a foreign power.'

'Don't tell me, Carrick's done a deal where he gets witness protection in exchange for everything he knows about the Russian secret services, right?'

'He was their asset, now he's ours. He's already gone, flown out to Darwin for an initial debrief, then back to the USA on military flights. Once he's there he will announce his retirement due to ill health and disappear from sight forever.'

'Lucky him.'

'Can you think of a better punishment that won't draw international headlines and make our allies never trust us again?'

'Put him in a room for half an hour with Linh. Give him a chance to explain why he killed her mother.'

'Well, we know that. She was about to expose him as a spy. Unfortunately, she told the wrong person.'

'Major Tang. Another notch on Carrick's barrel,' Xander says.

'If they had a medal for covering your tracks, Carrick would have an extra ribbon on his uniform. If he still had a uniform.'

'How did Lucy know he was a spy?'

'Carrick told us she was worried that Tang still suspected her of spying, so she decided to expose the real spy. She set two traps. One for the man you call Lorenzo and the other for Carrick. It was a simple ruse – she told them each that she'd heard that one of the South Vietnamese leaders was going to be inspecting troops in different places. Whichever one the Vietcong attacked, she knew who her spy was. But when there was no troop inspection, Carrick realised he'd been set up and needed to silence her.'

'And Pete discovered this, when?'

'Only when he met Carrick. He told him he'd discovered that Weighorst couldn't have killed Lucy and finally after all these years of covering up, Carrick's mask slipped. They didn't discuss it any further at the time, but Pete went away to write down his suspicions and Carrick alerted his handlers in Moscow.' She pronounces 'Moscow' with the emphasis on 'cow'.

'Pete was a good cop,' Xander says. 'He'd have known Carrick was lying before he knew it himself.'

'Maybe so. But that's when the killing started. First your grandfather and then, when you refused to believe it was suicide, anyone who might ask too many questions.' She looks at Xander, her expression changing. She is no longer his confidante.

'I know you must be thinking this is going to be a great book. Maybe even a movie,' she says.

'A boy can dream.'

'And a dream is how it will have to stay. We need to put a lid on it.'

'I'm not sure you can do that. Even in your own country.'

'When I say "we", I mean you.'

'Why would I do that?'

'Hmm. All the killings? Including a known criminal against whom you were seeking revenge for an assault and a corrupt police officer who was your former lover. Oh dear. And you definitely killed a Russian national in King Solomon's Caves. There were witnesses.'

'Self-defence.'

'Sure, you might never be convicted, but it could take a lot of time and money to make certain that never happens and, by the way, they'll throw in the paedophile allegations – which will never fly, of course – but you'd better pray you don't go to jail on any of the other charges, even on remand, with even a hint of that on your charge sheet.'

Xander considers this. Suspected sex offenders tend not to fare well in prison, or outside, for that matter, as he knows better than most.

'You'll be compensated, of course,' she says. 'Not enough, but still a lot.'

'Okay,' Xander says. 'But I have a couple of conditions of my own.'

***

It turns out the Americans could not have been less interested in Lorenzo's fate. Parks and Wildlife are none too keen to let the fact that he'd been living illegally in a national park slide. And the Tasmanian Police are deeply annoyed by him liberating his dogs from their pound. But national security and international relations with a staunch ally trump these little local difficulties.

The American woman, who never did give Xander her name or reveal which agency she worked for, tells him that Geoffrey will spend several weeks being interrogated by joint Intelligence services in a 'black site' hideaway. Xander later discovers that he had been exchanged in a chain swap with the Russians for an Indonesian Muslim activist in Belarus, who was swapped for a dubiously convicted Australian alleged drug dealer on death row in Bali.

Xander's deal with the spooks of both Australia and America is elegant in its simplicity. He will sign a legally binding pledge not to tell the best and biggest story ever to fall into his lap, if Lorenzo doesn't have to spend another night in any kind of custody.

Xander also tells ASIO and the CIA they are free to spin the story any way they want, but they must either get an assurance from the Russians that Linh will be safe or, failing that, relocate her to Australia or wherever she wants to go. Eventually, a local coroner will record Pete's death as misadventure, while online conspiracy theories fester and grow, connecting Pete's death with Rob's, Johnny Spanner's, Althea's and the Russian's. All of the various narratives – including two true-crime podcasts – are fantastical and contain fragments of facts, but none are as outrageously unbelievable as the truth. Xander's determined and legally binding vow not to say anything about anything means that, not for the first time in his life, the facts don't get in the way of great stories.

With enough money in the bank to sustain them for a few years, Xander has persuaded Lorenzo to move into the cottage, along with his dogs, as caretaker cum roommate. Of course, because of the NDA, Xander can't write the book that would astonish the world. But he gets his agent to start pitching another yarn, about how a Vietnam veteran spent three years living undetected in a national park and became the celebrated 'Cave Man' of the Walls of Jerusalem. That's what Xander and Lorenzo are working on – a process that exhausts Lorenzo, but excites and inspires Xander.

Lorenzo is asleep, sitting almost but not quite upright on the sofa in the Mole Creek cottage. He said one of the great skills you acquire as a soldier is the ability to doze in whichever position you find yourself at any given time. As he does most nights, Xander gently pushes Lorenzo down onto his side, then covers him with a blanket.

Xander pours himself another nip of Laphroaig and nods contentedly. He misses Pete and he misses work, too. But, hey, he's safe and settled. Life could be a lot worse.

***

At precisely that time, about 15,000 kilometres, seven time zones and two seasons away, Vyacheslav Golovin is making his way to the upper floors of the Moskva Hotel, built on the site of the former Residences building opposite the Kremlin. This is the first time he has returned to the Russian capital since his tenure in Vietnam was cut short by 'a series of unfortunate occurrences' as the coded message from GRU headquarters had put it. Now he has to face the instigator of those occurrences – the allegedly retired former spymaster Zelimkhan Saforov.

Saforov lives in a three-bedroom apartment in the building which, from the outside, looks identical to the former Residences, the famed billet of artists, musicians, favoured politburo members, their senior staff and the occasional visiting foreign dignitary. Today, Golovin thinks, he'd be more likely to meet an oligarch or movie star than a government apparatchik in its opulently rebuilt and restyled interiors. In his mid-seventies, Saforov fits perfectly into this faux relic of the glories of days gone by. He survived the last of the post-Stalin purges and the collapse of the USSR and now lives well on oil and gas profits while his former connections keep him informed of dangers to his status and opportunities to enhance it.

His rooms in the Moskva would cost him, in one month, as much as Golovin's annual salary. He has no official position nor defined role in the Russian security services hierarchy, but he has power and influence, and the money those bring, as surely as spring showers draw worms from the earth. The door opens just before Golovin reaches Saforov's apartment, letting him know he has been observed from the moment he stepped out of the lift into the deeply carpeted hallway.

The unsmiling nod and wafted gesture to enter from the severe woman in the doorway – a housekeeper cum secretary cum whatever Saforov wishes, he assumes – is as much of a welcome as he expects or receives. Another gesture points him down a short hallway adorned with antique but not overly ornate furniture. A dark-oak, silk-cushioned armchair, a console bearing a polished silver samovar, and a naked bentwood hatstand, all speak to expensive simplicity. This is not a normal hotel suite.

Golovin enters and is immediately confronted by the sight of a huge mahogany desk, too large even for the generously proportioned room that it dominates. Behind it sits a large man wearing every one of his seventy-plus years in his liver-spotted scalp, exposed under wispy silver hair. His loose jowls suggest his doctors have at some point warned him that the good life he is living may be short as well as sweet. Golovin looks around for a chair, but Saforov raises a bony finger.

'Don't sit, Vyacheslav Petrovich Golovin,' Saforov says. 'This will not take long.'

'Comrade Saforov,' Golovin replies, noting the use of his full name as a signal that the old man knows more about him than he may be comfortable with.

'You should know that my brother's grief is turning to anger, Golovin,' Saforov says.

'With all due respect –'

Another bony finger halts him.

'Yes, I know I suggested young Sergei for the mission, but I feel that perhaps he was insufficiently briefed.'

And there it is, Golovin thinks. I am to blame for this monumental cock-up and there is no point in arguing. He shrugs apologetically and bows his head just enough to suggest regret, if not guilt.

'It is unfortunate that your nephew suffered great misfortune in this endeavour, Comrade Saforov,' Golovin says. 'But you should not take it personally.'

Saforov harrumphs in a combination of grunt and sigh. 'Not only was Sergei my brother's son, this project was one I myself launched fifty years ago when I was a young KGB agent in Saigon. Thus, you can see, I cannot fail to take this personally.'

Golovin nods again.

'All emotion aside, I consider this McAuslan person to be an enduring threat to the Republic,' Saforov continues. 'We don't know what he knows or how or when he may wish to share that knowledge with our enemies or, even worse, our allies.'

More nodding.

'I want your best man on it. I want it done quickly and untraceably and, should it involve a certain amount of suffering, that will, to some extent, serve to assuage my brother's grief.'

Safarov looks back at the papers on his desk and Golovin is dismissed with a flick of the wrist before he can say another word.

Later, having settled in the rear seat of his official Mercedes, Golovin leans forward to his driver.

'McAuslan it is,' he says, allowing a grim smile into the rear-view mirror. 'And Saforov wants my best man on the job.'

'Your best *man?*' the driver chuckles as she eases the limousine into the bustling late-afternoon traffic of Ulitsa Okhotnyy Ryad. 'I think we can do better than that.'

ACKNOWLEDGEMENTS

I want to thank Sandy McGregor for introducing me to the wild and wondrous world of sappers. To Fiona and Benjamin at Curtis Brown for not giving up on me. To Juliet and Diana at Echo and, especially, Abigail for believing in this book. To my testbed readers Stuart, Alan and Kieran for keeping me on my toes and to Sue for keeping my feet on the ground while encouraging me to reach for the stars.